SEMIOTEXT(E) NATIVE AGENTS SERIES

Published by Semiotext(e)
PO BOX 629, South Pasadena, CA 91031
www.semiotexte.com

Cover: Laure Prouvost, "From The Drawer, We Are Staring At You," 2017. Courtesy of the artist and Galerie Nathalie Obadia, Paris / Brussels.

Back Cover Photography: Hedi El Kholti
Design: Hedi El Kholti

ISBN: 978-1-63590-159-7
Distributed by The MIT Press, Cambridge, Mass. and London, England
Printed in the United States of America

The Letters of
Mina Harker

Dodie Bellamy

Introduction by Emily Gould

semiotext(e)

For Kevin Killian, always.

"I loved it when my tits or my cock or my asshole would destroy my own ego with their needs," writes Dodie Bellamy in "The Letters of Mina Harker." It's true that these body parts and many others assert themselves vehemently throughout the text, which is already a riot of warring impulses and contradictory or just chorusing voices. Most writing strives to unify impulses, to find harmony between the heart (or whatever) and the mind, the corporeal and the spiritual, the story and its narrator. Dodie begins this book by disassembling that expectation, mocking it as she discards it, bringing it up again and again only to find it eternally lacking. Formal contrivance can never compete for long with what's real and right in front of us. This book interrupts itself often to critique itself, or tell the story of its own creation, or take a break from itself to eat a snack, jerk off, begin again.

I have to admit, the first time I attempted to read this book circa 2012, I didn't "get it." I came to it because I was obsessed with diaries and had loved Dodie's then-latest book, which was a diary of an affair with a shitty buddhist teacher that she initially serialized as a blog. The central conceit of "Mina Harker"—that the minor character from Dracula has been transported to mid-80s San Francisco, in order to possess the body of Dodie Bellamy and correspond with her clique of queer poets, artists and theoreticians—seemed arbitrary to me, or worse, overdetermined: vampirism standing in for AIDS, yikes. I had entered the Dodieverse via a more straightforward strain of her writing. Reading "the buddhist," I was never wondering what Dodie meant. But in "Mina Harker," as the first-person voice trails off midsentence or shifts into italics, the reader is never exactly sure who is speaking. The fictive "Dodie" and "Mina" and the author Dodie document each others' existence in real time. The overall impression is of a huge box of tangled jewelry dumped out on the bed, some of it tarnished, some of it obviously fake, but with precious gems mixed in and not always readily apparent. At the time of my first reading, I didn't have the patience to sift. It had not yet occurred to me that the pile itself could be the treasure. "Bad metaphors are the only way we can approach the really important things, don't you agree?"

The first letter, dated July 3, 1986, is addressed "Dear Reader." In it, we meet Mina, who is desperate to set the record straight about Dracula, Jonathan Harker, and Van Helsing. We also meet Dodie, whose voice alternates sometimes interchangeably with Mina's. July 3rd was her wedding day. At first being married seems as much of a postmodern goof as any of the book's other antics, getting off on the conventional subversion of a gay man and a queer woman dressing up and promising "til death." 35 years later, this book is a document of one of the early years of one of the greatest and most artistically productive marriages of all time. Though Dodie describes and addresses several other love affairs in this book, Kevin Killian is the constant, the book's inciting presence and its reason for being. Their love is incandescent, funny and tragic and palpable in every sentence of the book. He is both larger-than-life sex god and droll observer, torrid bodice-ripper and quotidian meal-sharer. He and Dodie spend a lot of time watching rented videocassettes. He edits the book that he's in: "'Not another sex scene!' KK tosses my manuscript on the coffee table, "It would be nice if the reader could occasionally see me doing something besides coming." Moreso, even, than the transcendent sex scene that precedes it, this bit of dialogue is a portrait of ideal partnership.

Mina and Dodie write to Sam D'Alessandro both before and after his death from AIDS at age 31. Death is as omnipresent in this book as sex, intertwined with it exquisitely and painfully. Dodie wishes to be like Sam, in writing and in life: "I'd love to live in your writing, to fuck with abandon as if that were the easiest thing in the world to come by." After he dies, she writes to him as if he were still alive, memorializing by telling him about himself: "the Sam I knew was a typhoon of sex and hate, he loved the scars of others but flaunted his own beauty." She doesn't worry about boring him with her newsy dispatches from the world of corporeality, her love affairs and meals and outfits. This way of mourning could chafe or seem callous, but it's real. Mina/Dodie keeps a photo of Sam to stare at as she writes: "Your eyes will remain unreadable to me, will never "reveal"—but that's not the point, is it—the point is to look, not in horror not in pity or even in compassion, but to look as precisely as possible at the ever-wavering presence right in front of one—this is the closest beings as imperfect as we can come to love."

Dodie's descriptions of and evidence of graphomania make me jealous. She describes heading into a café for a caffeine and diary-writing "fix." She marries the ephemeral—the intrusive-thought horror movie fantasies, the embarrassing half-thought that flits through the body and mind during sex—with observations that reverberate with import. The sex scenes that KK called out for being too omnipresent in the book are revealed necessary, vibrant documents of moments that usually fade as fast as an orgasm. Since poets are fucking, language itself is a part of the sex act, and writing itself is also eroticized, ie, "my breasts are no longer breasts but titties *just the thought of keyboarding the word titties excites me SAY IT.*" Writing and sex are the same in this book. It feels radical, in our pleasure-starved and inspiration-stunted moment, to encourage or confess an appetite for either.

The Letters of

Mina Harker

July 3, 1986

Dear Reader,

KK says all horror novels begin with the locale and a description of the weather, "The Reader likes to feel situated." It's a cool clear San Francisco night, streetlights diffuse the vast panoply of the heavens but if you drive an hour north the stars are astonishing, the sky speckled like the black-suited shoulders of a guy with really bad dandruff, so many holes in the black your heart speeds for a moment *what if the black collapses* a misty glow flows along my recumbent silhouette, long white gown, long white neck, a livid face leans toward the bed, translucent claws lift my hem *immobile thighs, white, white* over my breasts floats Nosferatu's head, an exaggerated egg-shape, powdery with pointed ears, his lips stretch open pencil-thin, taut *I am so aroused my clit flicks like a tongue* so tender is his bite but I will never love him, he's too weird too intense *from my open throat dark rivulets curve* sucking sounds in stereo suck across the *suck* dim air of the Roxie Theater and *suck* dissolve in the audience's laughter *faces radiant with ridicule and popcorn* I shout, "That's *me* on the screen you ass-holes!" The laughter pauses then soars, fine grains of salt stinging the corners of its collective mouth. Who am I anyway? In *Dracula*, "Mina Harker" was this plain-Jane secretarial adjunct to the great European vampire killer, Dr. Van Helsing. I'm the one who gathered the notes, the journal entries, letters, ship logs, newsclippings, invoices, memoranda, asylum reports, telegrams— I transcribed them and ordered the morass so the Reader can move through it without getting lost *no hassle, no danger—i.e., a plot or an amusement park, Safari Land, Transylvania Land.* For my performance evaluation Van Helsing wrote, "Oh, Madam Mina, how can I say what I owe to you? This paper is as sunshine. It opens the gate to me. I am daze, I am dazzle, with so much light, and yet clouds roll in behind the light every time." After

Dracula corrupted Lucy Westenra I was next on his hit-list, but four brave Christian men destroyed 50 coffins filled with dirt to save my soul—but turn to the last page of Stoker PRESTO ABRACADABRA on the anniversary of Dracula's death my "saved" loins heave forth an offspring. A.k.a. "sequel." A big tease, a big mistake—for the past hundred years imitators have barged into my story and hacked out enough sequels to fill a library *bunglers with no credentials* they keep shackling me to the most insipid suitors macho types who stomp around with crucifixes and bad British accents their acting as wooden as their stakes: *these* men save my soul? Dodie's the latest intruder, getting it all wrong in her attempts to be civilized—forget about her forget about them—this is *The Letters of Mina Harker* THE AUTHORIZED VERSION if you want anything done right you have to do it yourself *sucking sounds suck up the silence my throat is a cunt* never will I perish in domesticity like a Jane Austen heroine—I dart across the moor fog condensing on my long plait of hair, my lives my deaths multiple as orgasms HARKEN THE WORDS OF MINA HARKER, FORTUNE COOKIES FROM BEYOND THE GRAVE.

The monstrous and the formless have as much right as anybody else.

Springs poking my butt, his arms and legs jutting in all my directions KK and I sit on the velvet sofa in front of a twelve-inch black and white TV, eating our first wedded meal, champagne and Kentucky Fried. He coos, "Don't you just love *Hill Street Blues*?" I look deep into his eyes, "Whatever." I'm happy as a hen, reminiscing *eleven o'clock last Thursday night, frantic meows at the foot of my bed were driving me crazy* he appeared on the landing with two cans of cat food. I was wrapped in chenille from neck to ankles, an irregular V of flesh splaying from cleavage to throat, I opened the door ... reaching for the can opener my gaze skimmed the bulge in his tight white pants, "Kidney in gravy is nice but how do you feel about Bits O' Beef or Kitty Stew?" The chenille was so hot so heavy—one tug at the tie and I became a shattering of V's, a Duchamp nude. I reach for an extra-crispy drumstick my wedding band gleaming *white gold for the moon* when he slipped it on my finger he whispered, "I'll follow you anywhere, like death follows life." I wipe my greasy mouth, wonder *now that we're in the happily ever after ...* Later that evening there's a power outage *carpe diem* on the dresser burn three brown candles, two in monolithic stands cut from red brick, the other borne on the arched back of a wrought iron beast with a bird's head *overdetermined archetypal but I'm not immune* the spaghetti straps of my leopard-skin chemise slide off my shoulders—KK's still in street clothes, he rubs the burnished silk across my hipbone, lowers his lashes, "Oohhh." I gobble the perfect air that touches his face. The shadow of a jade plant looms across the drapes and onto the ceiling, a tropical phantasm from the 40's, he says, "I've come to meet you in the jungle, jungle girl." I rub his ass the tarnished cotton glides easily over the firm muscle, I wedge my fingers beneath the waistband *tender ridge across his lower back* candlelight beats warily, as though nervous, along his thighs—I crack them apart and rub my nose against his soft-hard cock, nostrils itching with fabric softener and urine. Less than a year ago I stood in his hallway and wailed, "I love you" sob sob "I love you. Please let me spend the night." He said no *a mind like a ring sliding shut on some quick thing.* But now I have him, today was my wedding.

Clothesline binds her arms and feet, gaffers' tape her mouth; carpet burns sting her elbows. An hour ago she gave up struggling, lies on the living room floor still as a doorstop *intermittent rush of breath, heart, brain* she watches her captor, a knife-happy ex-con, slouch on the sofa, waiting. The phone rings, "Okay boss." He wraps an arm around her waist, lifts her to the sofa and wrestles a pillowcase over her head, she twists and grunts as he grabs tighter, locking his ankles around her slim calves, pressing

15

his jaw against her muslined cheek *he put a bag over her head* the pillowcase sucks against her nostrils and their bodies heave with the isolated gyrations of her fear *nipples erect* this man is a serpent he plunges his switchblade in her side, with each plunge she is more hole, more woman *outside the bag is God and cold steel, inside visions lunge forward in jerks and stops* but, Reader, where are you *inside the future outside the past* this letter is addressed to you but who/what are you, some kind of William Gibson plug-in to my virtuality? An audience distant and nameless as the billions of herbaceous plants in the Amazon *unimaginatively strange, potent* I never know which nut or berry will wind up on my kitchen table in San Francisco, tiny chunk in my Rain Forest Crunch *inside the bag the woman recites the rosary of privations: privation of light (terror of darkness), privation of others (terror of solitude), privation of language (terror of silence), privation of objects (terror of emptiness), privation of face (terror of Reader), privation of life (death)* my friend Sam D'Allesandro said it's all about putting yourself on the line: engagement: and Dr. Van Helsing agreed but I countered with *repression's more interesting.* KK's tongue is an oil rig drilling into my soul. Bad metaphors are the only way we can approach the really important things, don't you agree?

This book is the bag. So is my cunt.

Blue eyes angular skull lips thin as sin thick brown hair bent from brushing against his creamy shoulders *lucky hair* he's thirty-three, the age of all my suitors, so many suitors flickering past *Abraham Arthur Quincey Jonathan Renfield Jack* I grow ancient but the suitor, always replaced, doesn't change—except for KK—I've made him one of my kind. Last Friday I held his wrist to my lips and sucked *his blood was tasteless but I couldn't get enough of it, determined as I was to quench the unquenchable* he groaned with consent then I pricked my finger and squeezed a few precious drops on his outstretched tongue, "Yum." By Sunday I was bent over the toilet bowl heaving like Susan Sarandon in *The Hunger* though I could never look that gorgeous in a sweaty T shirt *maybe I should have worn a condom over my tongue* but too late now—alien cells have taken over my veins my vocal cords *neither red nor green like Christmas or motion I am the yellow light the spit, the flaw in Newton's machinery* we signed a pact on the back of a letter from Sam *forever implications* beneath our names two rapidly browning thumb prints, blood prints. No matter how light I set the xerox machine, on KK's copy Sam's typewriting showed through. Then we had sex on top of the letter (not on purpose, it was just there) I climbed on my hands and knees and he fucked me from behind which made me think: "bow wow" but I didn't say it even though it would have been fun because— have you noticed this—people who are about to come have a lousy sense of *humor* the air gushed from his lungs he dropped forward, I lay down on my stomach careful to keep him inside he nibbled my right shoulder and I wagged my ass like a tail. Sam's letter got crinkled but this he didn't witness; love is blind.

I eat my lunch by a fountain, water arching *I followed Grandma into the bathroom, watched her lean against the chipped porcelain sink and cringe as she stuffed bits of tissue paper in her ears, "Grandma can I have some Kleenex too?" She handed me a couple then turned toward the door bracing herself to re-enter my Grandpa's drunken rage, I followed her into the kitchen with wads of tissue arching out of my tiny ears* half of my lunch is good for Deficient Spleen Qi, the rest too green, too raw, with a bite of vinegar—if one combines the good and the bad does one get neutral—I almost typed "neural"—why does everything have to coil back to the mind—why can't I stick with the body. A bench away, clouds of smoke curl above the head of a Chinese man with a long gray beard—thumb and forefinger holding a cigarette to his lips, he sits erect, the still core of this continuous ghostly churning. I close my eyes *lapping waves, rushing water, darkness and favoring winds, someone's moving closer, Reader is that you?* When I open my eyes I'm looking down at my palm, upon its surface so many etchings that might be read as love, death, travel, I have this one line that curves to the left while KK's goes straight up and down—but it's all scrimshaw to me. Back at my office I phone him and make two jokes in one sentence, one joke about a night-mare, the other about sex—the two poles on either side of coziness, in the varied activities one can do in bed. Have you noticed how any activity can be classified into that which does and that which does not stain? My dear Reader, which do you prefer?

Dr. Van Helsing pokes a craggy finger at my manuscript, says, "You can always perk up your Readers' interest by asking them a question no matter how shallow, *can't you?*"

Remember: my kind can slip through keyholes, slide beneath doors. Alone in his pale blue bed KK lay beneath a blinding over-head light with his paperback, a man who dreamt books instead of Real Life. The first night we slept together was an "accident," our bodies fell between the sheets, rustling the cool air *two soft voices on a hard mattress* he said I made him feel too sexual *how could anybody feel too* … I leaned back and I leaned back *if I don't get an extra couple of inches quick* … beyond the plate glass euca-lyptus struggled toward a vast black broken by pinpricks. The next morning we pretended it never happened. I needed to take something with me to convince myself I'd been there, so I took his writing, I left his pale blue bed his nicotine-stained walls with a manuscript instead of a kiss:

> Once [he had written] I found a used sanitary napkin perkily
> sitting atop the wet crumpled paper towels in the men's room
> of the restaurant I worked in. The picture it presented, the
> triumphant incursion of the female principle into a Pharisaical

waste land, struck me forcibly: I took the bloody napkin home with me that night in the car, now and again glancing carefully down at it as though it were half alive or only unconscious. I had no immediate plans. The variations in color, and in scent, of the dried blood denoted a variety of sensual experience I felt excluded from.... Several nights later I parted the warm reddened cheeks of Sean's ass and inserted the mass into his rectum sidelong, using the bowl end of a teaspoon for leverage. He gave no sign that this intrusion was anything new in his life, giving off the impression, rather, that he welcomed its renewal. The language he spoke said as much. It hurt, but only a part of his body he was starting to believe belonged to somebody else entirely.

I thought *here's a man who knows the difference between sex and arousal.* My heart parted like those pages, that ass—*so what if he's gay* I had to steal that spoon for myself *the silver of his privileged birth shoving the old up my new* it's all about needing an edge to be up against—I seek a prose style precarious as crystal: words that crash against the Reader and shatter, bloody words that cost and cost *Dear Sam, Dear Sing.*

He said I was standing in his kitchen one day and his heart slid open like elevator doors. He let me in and after that nothing else mattered. Like Mina he has the soul of a secretary, this man who's read so many books Dr. Van Helsing calls him The Library of Congress.

I stop in at the Caffe Trieste to smoke cigarettes and write in my diary. To my left sit a young German couple *life force racing in paisley patterns beneath their translucent skin.* Gregory Corso's leaning against the jukebox, he catches my eye and staggers over. "It's been a long time," he says. When I reply, "No it hasn't," he sits down anyway, half an inch from just about every part of my body. I finger the tiles inlaid on the table, primary colors in abstract 50's swirls and dots—I've seen him with a small boy who was wearing a Superman cape, the two of them standing in front of City Lights, pants unzipped, big dick and little dick pissing in the street. He flashes his plane ticket to Boulder and tells me to remember: *poetry is the opposite of hypocrisy.* Then the German guy exclaims, "Well, the unknown is a known word." And when I leave a woman trails me down Vallejo yelling, "That was an isolated occurrence that was an isolated occurrence that was an isolated occurrence that was an isolated—" This goes on for half a block until I step on the 30 Stockton. Hypocrisy's not the problem, I think, it's allegory *the breeding ground of paranoia.* The act of reading *into*—how does one know when to stop? KK says that Dodie has the advantage because she's physical and I'm "only psychic." A naive assumption for a man who sustains his plots better than most men do sex, or even a conversation. The truth is: everyone is adopted. My true mother wore a turtleneck and a long braid down her back, drove a Karmann Ghia, drank Chianti in dark corners, fucked Gregory Corso *where I come from it is always dark and everybody is always in bed* Dodie keeps insisting I sit in chairs, have *opinions*—I can take a hint, but I make her pay for her demands—she's lying in her cotton nightie, eyes closed, mind blank *all the Readers are a million miles away, they might as well be stars* her breathing is shallow and regular, I stretch my long thin fingers around her heart, it feels heavy and obscene like a balloon full of water, I squeeze, tighter and tighter—a jolt hits her solar plexus *undefined fear* she rolls on her stomach, toes hanging off the edge, slips her hand down and plays with her clit, it's dry at first then warm, slippery as raw egg white *she rubbed her cunt juice behind her ears* parting the soft nest of verticals *when she went out on "dates"* she runs her thumb along the center groove I clamp her heart again—another jolt then *fear* then another jolt *like hiccups* jolt *fear* jolt *fear* jolt *fear* she sits up and throws her hands to her chest. *Nightly.* In figurative language the word is "anxiety" but that's so lukewarm—*if only Dr. Van Helsing could discover the secret to make the fear go away, something simple like a brain tumor wrapped around the optic nerve there's a 90% chance it's benign he operates saving her life but not her sight* the truth is: Dodie is much more constructed than I. She makes a clone of herself, Mina Harker. When Mina needs a steroid injection her right eye glows pure white—this is the only time you can tell them apart. Emotions, like everything else, are new to Mina, and they hit her with a violence; she hits whatever is nearby. She falls in love with Dodie's husband, KK. Mina and Dodie battle it out. Dodie goes up in a blaze with her computer, and I crawl in bed with him *the top sheet rises to the surface winds around our necks long and bunched and blue* I look down at Dodie's charred body, poor little fool, dead on her wedding day.

Yet all that was sick or hysterical about her behavior in day-to-day life could be turned into something valuable through the act of writing.

I Love KK, Mina Harker in the starring role of "I" a flurry of ostrich feathers, glitter pumps descend the winding marble staircase *comme de longs échos qui de loin se confondent dans une ténébreuse et profonde unité vaste comme la nuit et comme la clarté* we stood beneath a streetlight, his body from knees to lips sucking me in I pulled back and said, "Do you love me?" After a long pause he replied, "Yes, but with a tiny asterisk at the bottom of the page." I buried my face in his neck and delivered my critique: "I'm not sure this is a good *idea*." The night before I dreamt his tongue ejaculated covering my face with a thick creamy fluid, and my cheeks began to melt like wax. "I'm not sure this is a good *idea*." His tongue swelled to the size of John Holmes shoving the words back down my throat he tasted of cigarettes and whiskey I opened and I opened … he pulled back, whispered, "Take away the asterisk."

Light passed from my body into his eye.

Into your eye. I rub against your hands your brain your cunt or cock—this is me alone in my very private moment playing to the camera notice how I favor my right side. Dear Reader, I could fuck you better if I knew what you looked like—I imagine you at my kitchen table fumbling with a corkscrew, black leather jacket thrown over the back of your chair, vintage dress ripped under the armpits, nipples erect, your breasts move beneath the rayon print like fat ghosts, when you stand up and reach for the wine bottle your skirt catches in the crack of your ass, your face is striking with just the right touch of acne, your wavy hair needs washing. *Thanks to art, the soul is returned to that agitated zone between life and death* it's so lonely here, like in one of those dreams where you're walking down the street naked and strangers stare, offering you nothing—or where you're a flapper perched on the hood of a Model T like a silvery ornament, knees in midair legs spread *so* wide who do you think you are—Winged Victory? In the picture postcard I'm holding your stockings are the lightest gray barely discernible from the white inner thigh, your smile is provocative but with your clunky strapped shoes the ultimate effect is awkward. Moving closer to the lamp KK sticks his nose between your grainy legs insisting it's just the crotch of your panties. I huff, "Look at that slit in the center—can't you tell the difference between a woman who's been *shaved* and a piece of silk!" I can't bear the contradiction the hypothetical panties imply: to be simultaneously exposed and covered I mean the nasty part might as well have been *severed*. In *Re-Animator* a bloody though lively decapitated head goes down on a woman strapped to an autopsy table—but this must be confusing, obviously a severed head can't move around all by himself—this one maintains a psychic connection with his body (which wears a fake plastic head and carries the real head in a zippered bag so nobody will think anything *strange* is going on). So the body holds the head by the hair and guides it dangling veins esophagus and all along the screaming woman's torso, sort of like a plane on automatic pilot *a trail of blood from her left nipple to her pube* I laughed, though I empathized—her pale flesh quivers beneath the greenish light obscene not because it's naked but because it's too soft (the way a 50's pin-up is obscene in practical cotton briefs) as if something were rotting beneath that smooth unblemished expanse. *If only I knew what you looked like*—Dear Reader, you're twenty-two years old, you're a senior at Santa Cruz with a family in show business—I'll meet you in 1994 when this book is over, a boy twenty-two, so eager and dewy, raven hair tossed back into a ponytail, beetle-brown eyes, butterscotch skin as smooth as my chemise, you slouch on my living room couch in Doc Martens and a fringed suede jacket, a bead of sweat in the groove above your full upper lip, that goofy smirk *you're so cute it makes the enamel on my teeth go hard* the bottom button of your 501's is undone, a hole for the future to poke through *the tense air between us condensing with musk* I feel like a pervert just thinking about you, yet here I am—you greet me with aggressive cheek-cramping smiles then instantly flip to zombie-eyed autism *perverts are notoriously able to make the best of a limited situation while the neurotic is always demanding something more* I perch beside you on a stool getting drunk on cognac that tastes like soap everything about you so warm and untouched and me breathing ... why do you have to wear a T shirt *bare arm propped on the bar with just the right amount of muscle never a Mr. Atlas but strong enough to make me feel gorgeous* you utter the phrase *self-referential text.* Suddenly I am that gory decapitated thing lapping tongue, 20/20 vision ... I cross my legs beneath the counter my right knee brushing the dark peeling wood I feel a psychic connection stirring and this one isn't wearing any panties *the involuntary pleasure of the unseeable hole* it's difficult to sparkle in a body that's contemplating the Void—I'm as tense and gnarled as the gargoyles peeking from the armrests of my antique sofa. I need an Ann Landers of the soul, a mind sharp enough to slice the dark *psychic surgery* from across the room the Reader's X-ray eyes chase away the infection, blood bubbles from unbroken skin. *See me as I want to be seen and see me as I am. And don't lie.* C.U. OF MINA'S FACE, ALIVE.

Like mother, like daughter, the last time I died was in Corozol with gold trumpets sticking out my ears *with a bag over her head she's not so bad just sticky.*

Our marriage certificate, the embossed announcement, this year's journal, a Long Island newsclipping, letters from a handful of sex-crazed gossips (my writing community)—I lay the pieces out for you one by one but they refuse the easy linearity of my earlier manuscript. "All needless matters have been eliminated, so that a history almost at variance with the possibilities of later-day belief may stand forth as simple fact." *Oh, Madam Mina, good women tell all their lives, and by day and by hour and by minute, such things that angels can read; and we men who wish to know have in us something of angels' eyes.* I wrote *Dracula* nearly a century ago— you'd think by now narratives would spout from me like fountains, their meanings clear as water *black letters black paragraphs black pages, black gash across the naked torso of my desire* Reader, you're probably too young to remember Newlyweds, but in my childhood it was my favorite dessert, a jelly roll of devil's food cake and vanilla ice cream, a stripe of brown beside a stripe of white, spiraling together, neatly, serenely in a slice on a plate *you could eat it with a fork* I haven't seen it in stores for years—I have to make due with the chaotic fragmentation of Cookies 'n' Cream, the taste is similar but what a mess—it looks like a Newlywed roll that's been pushed through a paper shredder or tossed beneath the blades of a lawn mower *who's the jigsaw, who's the puzzle* fingers wrap around my neck, pull me towards his whiskered face my cells open like snowflakes and KK says, "I can only push my words so far like a knife through butter, then the butter stops and the knife is still useful, and the knife is so useful." *From my open throat dark rivulets curve; it's like whispering to oneself and listening at the same time* I lie back and he ravages me like the Amazon rain forest.

Love,
Mina

July 30, 1986

Dear Sam,

Stuck together in our bed the purpose is pagan … as far as that's possible for two people with college degrees … KK picks a long brown hair from my mouth and tickles my cheek with it *I am rubber you are glue* I wrap myself around his thigh and come *mascara smeared in charcoal arcs, hair gnarled, I must look like an Alice Cooper revival gasping and making those bulgy faces* I bury my eyes in his armpit it is moist but without scent, without that acrid mortal scent *my beautiful impostor my evolutionary vanguard, maybe some day nobody's shit will stink* the sheets are banded maroon emerald navy, long jagged layers like geological strata, I think *Pleistocene* but the white sailboats mean *sea*. Then KK went to work and I sat up in bed and read your letter, Gladys Knight and the Pips twirling in the background, coffee steam and cigarette smoke wafting. I laughed out loud when you asked, "Mina, do you hate me or just want to fuck me?" *He's leaving on the midnight train to Georgia* sang Gladys. Absently I slipped my hand under my nightshirt, my pubic hair was clumped from dried cum *to find a simpler place in time* I thought of the woman on PBS who'd been tortured in Chile—she was shown through a psychedelic camouflage effect, high contrast blobs of bright color moving across her face as she told of the electric shocks that convulsed her body on the floor, how a group of soldiers gathered round, and when the shocks finally stopped she heard a man say, "Keep going, I'm not finished yet," then she felt sperm spray on her *I got to go I got to go I got to go I got to go*. Do I hate you or do I just want to fuck you? It's lucky you asked me instead of Dodie—she wouldn't understand this line of reasoning, but it's my philosophy in a nutshell. On the next page you fantasize telling Nina Hagen you sucked off Andy Warhol then move on to "a debate over breakfast about a dim memory of my cock becoming exposed and about whether I or someone else was responsible." Van Helsing warned me that flirting is the only way you know how to communicate. I like to talk dirty too. But sometimes it's such a yawn since all the cards are stacked on my side—being female, anything I do is automatically twice as shocking as anything you do—even crossing the street if done with a certain *femme* finesse—in *Last Exit to Brooklyn* Tralala's stiletto heels step from the curb, her tits bounce up and down like broken headlights in a Looney Tune. Yesterday when I was jogging on a treadmill at the Y, my mind kept rerunning the gruesome description KK read to me of Oscar Wilde on the prison treadmill, his was more like StairMaster than this flat sheet of rubber I'm hopping up and down on, he climbed from dawn to dusk day in day out until his body and spirit fell apart *it was designed to grind wheat* this scrawny geeky business dweeb came up behind me, middle management is my guess, and craned his neck to see my time readout. Then he moved on to the woman on the next machine and the next, and so on until he had checked out all six of us. I lumbered along while the other gals in their wisps of bright spandex fluttered above the treadmills like beautiful butterflies. The business dweeb walked back and forth behind us snorting and looking at his watch. Then he cupped his hands into a megaphone and boomed, "Twenty minute limit on aerobic equipment!" I'd only been on for fifteen minutes, so God was on my side, I turned around, "Why don't you stop being so rude, asshole." "Watch your words," he whined. A trainer in a gray sweatshirt EMBARCADERO YMCA joined in, "Yes, watch your words, I won't have any *words* at the Y, if I hear any more *words* I'll have to ask you to leave." *I got to go I got to go I got to go.* You write, "My jeans have a 7 inch slice in the left rear thigh zone and someone kept reaching inside. I liked that."

You must have heard by now that we got married. Remember that time we went to the Uptown, nearly a year ago, when KK and I were still pretending nothing was going on—and I thought nobody suspected a thing—Jonathan didn't, my husband at the time. You sat in an armchair your lips pursed around the mouth of a Dos Equiis; I was trying to pull off hardcore with my Black Label straight up. From the jukebox Doris Day's tinny confession rang out: "My secret love's no secret anymore"—and my hand trembled, sloshing my drink. I yammered, "Sam I have a secret lover!" You answered, "I know," and nodded across the coffee table where he chatted with Sing, your gesture discreet as telepathy everybody Knowing or Not-Knowing according to whim. DON'T TELL ANYBODY are the three most erotic words in the English language, ask anyone at the Cafe Flore—in the 1986 remake Medea doesn't need a knife she just picks up the phone. I once saw a performance artist deliver the Gettysburg Address in Morse Code by squirting toothpaste on a sheet of plywood *minty dot dot, minty dash* and don't forget about sign language—the "L" looks like an "L," the "O" and "V" are similarly self-referential, but the "E" is the face of a sad little man the thumb drooping into a frown.

I leave a note on his pillow, lined yellow paper black ink, in my difficult handwriting: *My patent leather shoes shine upward I love you.*

KK gave me the first paperback edition of *Dracula*: 1947, when Literature was hardbound and everything else was SEX. On the cover I'm sleeping in a ruffled nightie, my long blonde hair spread across the deeply shaded pillow COMPLETE AND UNABRIDGED beside my head as if it were my dream. Penciled eyebrows and ruby lipstick cheapen my repose though the tiny flowers about my throat (garlic blossoms?) are innocent enough. The ugliest lamp sits on the nightstand coarse red swirls on frosted glass, red roses *red rhymes with dead* the Count glows with some inner illumination as he leans over the bed, left hand swishing his purple cape, the fingers of his right hand cramped open. Our first kiss felt like a pulp novel, me a married woman in wide-skirted polka dots and white pumps, and KK so butch in his new crew cut *I hardly recognized him* we were standing outside my apartment he took the cigarette from my hand threw it on the sidewalk and murmured, "There's more where that came from." He pushed me against the side of the building *he was drunk and wanted to have his way with me* cinder block scratched my back his rough sloppy kisses distended my lips like petals, his saliva tasted of Scotch and smoke—Jonathan could come home at any moment *his cock bleating against my belly* a woman in a bathrobe came flying down the front steps like a bat, yelling and shaking her arms: I was leaning against the doorbell and with each kiss the buzzer would blast, rattling her out of her dreams COMPLETE AND UNABRIDGED in the top left corner of *Dracula* a kangaroo leaps in front of a red sun and reads a book, marathon thighs parted, snout jaw dropped open—another volume pokes up and out of its belly-pouch *Pocket Book 452*. The night has a thousand eyes.

A diffuse Sunday afternoon, my attention flittered around a wedge of gouda and a jug of Californian burgundy ... suddenly a presence popped up beside me, a minor abundance of blond hair and a centerfold smile. "Hi, I'm Sam D'Allesandro." Though you're certainly droolable, we made light witty remarks about Joan Didion and travel—after half an hour of this I was ready to flee to the bathroom, but you clung on, "Mina, don't look now, but over there by the window, isn't that Armistead Maupin?" I snuck a peek. KK was handing him a copy of *Tales of the City* to autograph. "Yep." "Well, he doesn't look like the publicity photos." "Better or worse?" You rolled your eyes and leaned in closer. The room was crowded with famous gay men and I wondered *why's Sam hanging around me*. Your shoulders hunched ever so slightly. That was over a year ago but we've repeated this scene at party after party, literary event after event. "A lot of the time I'm more like a small fire," you write, "I just emit a lot of sparks that pass for writing, sex, behavior, etc." Without a plastic glass of wine in your hand I wouldn't recognize you.

I'm standing on the corner of 16th and Mission, the bus will not arrive. Last night KK and I sat in The Half Shell eating Happy Hour snacks, they were deep fried and chewy, and I yelled *who wants to be a rabbit's foot around somebody's neck!* He gulped his Scotch and water looking confused: "What's wrong with that?" then his face softened, "You know you mean more to me than *that*." I was tense as a cork in a bottle of champagne. "Why did you marry me?" I screamed. I'm standing on the corner and the bus won't come, after 40 minutes my legs are weak and I start to cry *thank god for dark glasses* tears dribble into my mouth as I make those funny sucking sounds. A woman in a lime green sundress is basking on the concrete stoop her arms back over her head, her face every inch of it covered with lipstick *greasy devil red sheen* I sit down at the other end of the stoop, at least 20 feet away, to prove we have different futures—between us a dumpster overflows—across the street a workman eating a sandwich stares at my repressed convulsions as if I were a TV. As I write this to you I sense these others—others at the far edge of utterance, marmoreal beings whose eyes hover like bats above my shoulders—they're reading every word, but existing as they do in another dimension, they're not quite getting what's going on *through eavesdropping the body becomes savage, universalized.* After we fucked Jack told me he'd picked up a guy the night before at the Stud—hearing you were there that same evening KK got inspired: "Maybe it was *Sam!*" I wish it had been, then we'd have a psychic connection—every time I'd walk into a room you'd freeze. The 22 Fillmore rolls up FINALLY its electrical antennae remind me of Martians, gliding along the overhead wires, a Martian shuttle receiving messages from the mother ship.

30

KK props his pillow against the wall and reads while I dream we're having sex on my parents' front porch *concrete and Chinese elms* I'm amazed at my erection long and hard and colorful, I've seen plenty but don't know how to use one. A blond man watches from the lawn, his eyes and nose are fuzzy but he's got your lips.

Two metal lawn chairs face one another, their plastic cushions indented by the weight of our bodies, the chairs tilt as we lean forward—KK lays his head on my breasts and rubs my ass *he's so dextrous* behind him a bush is loaded with flowers mottled green and white like poorly-tinted Easter eggs, I look up at the neighbors' windows thinking *this is better than a movie* his tongue is sweet with Tab and I want to kiss him 24 hours a day until my lips fall off. *How do I hammer the present into prose when the pre-pre-pre screeches toward me like a choo choo with stripped brakes* when KK proposed, my divorce from Jonathan Harker wasn't yet final (Jonathan is a dreamboat but he was stuck in the 19th Century) I pushed him away shouting, "Are you crazy, you're gay!" KK stroked my hair, "I want to marry you, don't be so technical." The next morning he went out while I stayed in his bed to ponder our future *"Should I" and "Shouldn't I" tottered on opposing shoulders like leaden epaulettes* finally in the shower my burden was lifted *I'd rather live in his world* I decided *than live without him in mine* when all the hot was gone I dried off, put on his blue plush bathrobe and wandered into the kitchen, linoleum chilling my squeaky feet—my vision followed the sunlight as it dappled across the floor and onto the kitchen table, where I spied Them, the xeroxes of his letters to Raymond Foye. I don't know what I was looking for but I couldn't stop looking. The paragraph about me began "My fractious and dangerous romance," and all the ugly things in the world came rushing into my unblinking eyes. I threw the letters in the trash, padded down the hall, crawled back into his bed and pined and pined—Sam you should have seen me, Garbo as Camille. Passing cars glinted through brocade curtains, skittered across the plaid blanket—out of the corner of my eye the mattress was full of mice, a portable Lionel Richie passed by the window his "wo wo wo" receding like Renaissance perspective *every tear on my cheek a vanishing point.* First the dial tone seven digital beeps click three rings finally Van Helsing's faint "Hello"—I blurted through the receiver "What does 'fractious' mean?" *He wrote I was neurotic as hell he wrote he'd rather sleep with my husband he wanted out.* Pillar of salt pillar of salt pillar of salt: the wise doctor deliberated then said, "That was *four* months ago and besides according to Ann Landers you shouldn't have been snooping."

INCLINED TO MAKE TROUBLE UNRULY IRRITABLE HAVING A PEEVISH NATURE. From FRACTION in the sense of breaking.

KK sat on the edge of his bed fixing his ripped zipper with a staple gun, then he pulled on his sutured pants and kissed me passionately. Naked beneath the brown blanket that smelled faintly mildewed, I didn't believe it. He said, "No brass bands or orchids but at least you have the pleasure of my company." *Why no orchids?* I thought fractiously, then I snivelled, "I'm sorry I was snooping." KK shook his head sucked hard on a cigarette I was afraid the fire would scorch his throat, his hand on my thigh read "trust me," he said *snooping's human nature, writing's not the truth it's black and white maybe pink on fancy stationery, its chiaroscuro a kind of exorcism.* A face like his thrift store clothes: worn but to the innovative never beyond mending. The scent of my cunt permeates his long yellowish nails. He waves his hand in an arc as if it were a guided tour, "This room has been wonderful for us this room has been *heaven*." A photo of Catherine Deneuve ripped from *Paris-Match* is pinned on the wall *black straps a bit of cleavage and then the jagged edge* scattered across every available inch are dirty clothes blue paper from the Chinese laundry books and manuscripts; in half a dozen cups and glasses liquids slowly evaporate; an overflowing ashtray says "Bruno's Restaurant." Goose bumps appear on his back like a thousand tiny Catholic miracles. In Florida I studied vegetative evolution, the greenhouse in my backyard was full of orchids, some were microscopic some spotted like leopards—beautiful but they gave me the creeps, stiff and waxy, extraterrestrial like Jane Bowles' sex life.

Our bodies are stationary the arms bend extend pick up things stick them in front of our eyes or in our mouths ... Saturday morning we evaluate the night before ... Sunday over TV dinners we rate Friday and Saturday ... late Sunday evening we lie in bed and evaluate Sunday afternoon *I'm afraid we'll grow flat as champagne or soda pop left to the mercy of unaccountable air* Monday I call him at work and we review the entire week then I throw the *I Ching* to see how the relationship is going ... in the middle of the night I wake him, fidgeting from side to side mumbling "you're just a ballerina"—he's flattered I find him so graceful—in my next dream he's dying of cancer and the doctors are about to give the injection. He hands me a snapshot, a letter, a reason to forget him—I wail as if rehearsing a Greek tragedy, and wake up. In other dreams a dog ate my hamster, my cat was flattened by a car, but this was the first time I mourned a man—I dragged myself from the bed, put on the sloppiest clothes in my closet, and shuffled to the bathroom distracted and sentimental *when inside is outside every organ is a messy eclipse, imagine a heart on a shirt sleeve, spastic red goo against the starched white surface ... it's all a matter of parallels and angles knowing when to drop the perpendicular—sometimes the tallest has to shrink—it's not my fault it's the vanishing point PLEASE DON'T LEAVE ME. A skeleton flies out of the screen into a room of gaping mouths (it's dark, the wire's invisible, we scream) he says let me enter you naked I want to ride you bareback I promise I won't come, Mina spreads her thighs in a puff of smoke electrical charges tingle our bottoms, molecules leap in and out of existence without warning, first I have no husband then I have another husband then he's dead in my dream, I read a poem about a horse, I don't know you then I know you:* "They would always grab me, take me in the corner and beat the shit out of me, and then fuck me against the bar in front of everyone. That always made me nervous." *It takes technique to jump a dimension and sometimes I feel so flat. I massage his neck his balls push a finger up his ass I spell out* LOVE *with my hands but how many get the effect?* I dreaded KK's party, my nightmare was still so vivid, but in the adult female obligations override moods I positioned myself in front of the TV with Sing cigarettes gave us something to do we made wisecracks about the 60's girl groups their wardrobes never the music I gravitated towards strangers HELLO EVERYBODY THIS IS MRS. NORMAN MAINE I refused to talk to my friends though they sat on the arms of my chair smiling and eager … why weren't *you* there Sam I would have clung to your together surface your disheveled interior I would have taken your hand though I never touch anybody first and said, "There are things on heaven and earth best left unseen by the eyes of mortal men" and you would have believed me.

I'm going to take a shower now, to wash away the hundred different sources of funk.

Love,
Mina

August 26, 1986

Dear Sing,

You are my best friend my confidante a staple of every Hollywood bio-pic, you listen to Mina you give advice, you're so good at it you should win an award *Best Supporting Actress* positioned beneath me like a cunt wet and ready to receive MY narrative drive. The rest of your life scatters on the cutting room floor *your affair with that black sheriff* too confusing *the girlfriend you want to tie up and beat* superfluous *your Orthodox Jewish boyfriend* edited out. Cute and perky you ease into the viewer's eyes but never compete with ME, you are the Ethel to my I Love Lucy, it's written in your contract that you remain fifteen pounds overweight.

When I step inside slamming my front door the wicker bell on the knob jingles and the world ends. I lie on my velvet sofa and you vibrate through the receiver neither inside nor out, explaining how KK lacks a "bottom line." I see it as a horizon, something the sun can rise and set against—In *Ladyhawke* Michelle Pfeiffer is a hawk by day and Rutger Hauer is a wolf by night and only at sunrise and sunset can they catch a glimpse of one another in human form, they strain their long transparent arms their fingers across an unfathomable dimension and just when they're about to touch, one gels like an orgasm into a wing or a paw and the human mouth opens emits screams of pain and frustration. Then after many trials day became night and night became day or was it when day was without night and night without day (regardless, the audience wasn't as stupid as the actors—we knew the writer meant eclipse) the ill-fated lovers scurried before an evil bishop and his unwilling gaze broke the curse forever. I felt such relief knowing they would finally get it on.

Sing: a name half nightingale half prison, the inmates at the jail where you work call you Miss Sing Sing—how did a nice girl from Stockton end up a criminal psychologist (outside my frame of reference) Sing, forget about those murderers and schizophrenics, listen to ME! One night KK crawls all over me his face glowing like a David Hamilton photograph, the next night with no apparent transition he switches plots, his birdlike nose lifts towards the ceiling smoke slowly rising from the thinnest of lips he shakes his head as if there were hair in his eyes speaks like an intellectual on a PBS talk show, "You see, physicality just isn't very important to me ..." OUR BED FEELS LIKE ANOTHER DIMENSION. Imagine sticking a hard little beak into a huge slathering jaw or vice versa. What impressed me the most was the way Pfeiffer and Hauer's human minds never retain any animal memories: even their suffering is tossed back and forth: never shared.

Sure we fuck, but only when he requests it—and when (I'm sure this comes as no surprise to you) I complain, he says, "Why can't you deal with spontaneity?" My fingers rise and open as if they had a life of their own. In this case there *is* a bottom line: he knows the rules of my kind: we can never gain entry without an invitation. (Even in this unsolicited letter I stand outside your window squawking like a noisy voyeur. The last time you asked me over I cried and yelled at your kitchen table, ran down the stairs even before we reached the cherry soup. Sorry. What I lack in charm I make up in sincerity, but when the technique is pastiche who wants sincere.)

So I gave him a bouquet of flowers (the transitory) and a fossil (the eternal) hoping that like night and day there would come that rare cosmic instant when there wasn't any difference. Sing, don't you think he's adorable, don't you think he's suave *Ethel, you gotta help me, we'll dress up in moustaches hats and overcoats, and Ricky will never recognize us* you are my perfect friend, my perfect device *an expositionary dream* Sing, stare back at us like the evil bishop, like Dr. Freud, set something free.

Love,
Mina

March 16, 1987

Dear Dr. Van Helsing,

Why's my skin so porous? I cut the tarot deck and Madame Artemis deals out my future in the shape of a cross. Her large graying head leans over the table then shoots up and into my face, "Your cards say 'baby.'" I lean back in my chair, "Baby?" She ponders a bit recharging her psychic intensity and smiles serenely, "Yes, a child a *human* child." *Whenever I hold a squirming little tidbit incisors swell instead of breasts … its tender young throat sweeter than white corn* I shriek *"No babies!"* "Yes, babies! And you're going to move too, *very soon*." Let's zip ahead a few months to my birthday—I hadn't moved and I wasn't pregnant—because of the ab crunches I learned at the Y my stomach was flatter than ever, so I poured myself into the pink prom dress I lifted from Marshall's and threw a party—February 14, one of the worst storms in San Francisco history, raging winds and rain rattled the windows, the palms on Dolores Street bent like stalks of limp asparagus, power lines were snapping, cars crashed on bridges—only a handful of brave souls made it to my party, I ran up to Sing and hugged her, fluffy and beneficent as the good witch of the East, "Did I ever tell you about my reading with Madame Artemis?" Her lips tightened like she was trying to lock her words inside her mouth, "No." "She told me I was going to get pregnant and move, but nothing's happened." She put her hand on my arm, "Don't listen to that Artie—she bragged to Cindy upstairs that she was going to get you out of this apartment so she could rent it herself." Lightning flashed and for an instant the night sparkled with silvery torrents, venetian blind shadows hurled across the living room wall, thick diagonal stripes like the vertebrae of a prehistoric beast *a thunderous growl exploded the darkness* Madame Artemis a quack? What relief! Sam, who'd been eavesdropping, stepped into the foreground and snickered, "Mina are you planning to have a baby?" I stomped my satin feet like Sylvia Plath did the night she met Ted Hughes, "Who? Me? No! NO BABIES!" Then you, Dr. Van Helsing, of all people, warned me not to underestimate my biological drives *an author on automatic pilot, motherhood bound ... she sits before a hand-painted antique mirror, pink and blue flowers frame a blonde organism that others seem to recognize ... who ... she drops her pen leans forward pores enlarge and open, eyes merge into a single greenish corona, all this mindless duplication I might as well be a xerox machine.*

Birth and Journey are so fucking Hallmarky. The birth-ee zigzags through Life's Passages, her Journey pre-ordained and colorful as a miniature golf course *first faltering steps, adolescence, Saturn's return, sloppy middle-aged boozy wifedom, score a hole in one for cronehood, and then on the other side of the last ridge the soul-ball disappears in a blaze of light* I once had a therapist who told me that writing a book is like having a baby, I stared at the stirrups of her red stretch pants with contempt. In Rosemary's Baby Part II, when the taller kids steal his Tonka truck and bob it above his head, jeering, Baby's pupils light up in beady red circles like the tips of twin cigarettes glowing in the dark ... groans of clenched-over boys, tongues drooping from their ornery mouths ... Baby steps over their collapsed bodies and into a hotel room, snatched from Patty Duke his real mother by an aging Tina Louise. Afterwards he doesn't remember. Satan battles God for world domination, but he doesn't remember, he just sits on the bed and lets Tina Louise steal the scene. Dr. Van Helsing, have you ever seen *Trog?* Trog, the lovable missing link, strapped in a laboratory recliner, transmitter sewn inside his belly, electrodes poking out of his shaggy head—scientists from around the world, lead by Joan Crawford, inject Trog with sodium pentathol and flash slides of dinosaur skeletons before his dazed apey eyes—a blue spiral twirls on his forehead as he relives the earth's fiery beginnings *animated dinosaur footage volcanoes explode red ground cracks open dinosaurs tumble* afterwards Trog knows the names of colored cardboard circles—blue—green—red! *No more terrorizing sleepy English villages* tears blur Joan's eyes. In the beginning of *It's Alive Part III: Island of the Alive* Michael Moriarty pleads to the judge, "He's just a baby." A cage with thick metal bars is wheeled into the courtroom, inside on hands and knees is a naked creature with a thick rather lumpy claymation body, the thick leather collar around his neck is attached to a thick chain, pinky-gray skin, big bulgy eyes, It's Alive snarls and the camera lingers on his fangs and claws, he wags his head with the same awkward arc of the monsters in the Sinbad movies of my childhood *soft spot* the prosecutor shouts, "This is an animal, a vicious animal, a perversion of everything that is human!" Michael Moriarty runs up to the judge's box and bangs the top, "That's a lie. Can't you see it's the baby that's afraid—the lights, the guns, it's afraid for its little life." That's his son in the cage. "They put a chain around his neck, they bring him in here, they got guns all around him and light—how would you feel if you were born into a world that wanted you dead! See he's crying. He's just a *baby!*" It's Alive sees the world with double vision, eats human flesh, communicates by telepathy, sucks up nuclear residue like megavitamins. He sneaks into a church, leaving behind a trail of blood and mangled Catholics as he scales the holy water basin to reach a painting of chubby cherubs frolicking midair, behind him stained glass cherubs glow in rich regal hues—if only It's Alive had wings, his squat deformed body too might be exalted *the line is so thin* Moriarty understands this because people treat him the freak's father as if he himself were the freak, even prostitutes shriek when he touches them. His acting is off-kilter and private, he stares past the rest of the characters as if he were in another dimension alone in another movie, singing little travel songs, his smiling face beaming—as his companions are ripped to shreds he scampers through the jungle fearless because he knows the monster loves him and that a monster's love is something you can count on *a love so strong it twirls your genes like a gyroscope* if I weren't already married, I'd snatch Michael Moriarty up quick. That night I dream I'm having his baby and someone mentions my upcoming abortion, this is the first I've heard about it, right-to-lifers swarm round shoving blood tests in my face and feminists grab me proclaiming, "It's your body!" and an abortionist tries to shuffle me into a cramped little room, but then I go to the toilet and notice I'm spotting and I'm so happy because now I don't have to make any decisions, I can just be me, Mina Harker *an artist in the age of mechanical reproduction* bumper sticker on the back of a van: my karma ran over my dogma.

I crouch on the base of my spine with a flashlight and mirror, peer inside *pinhead at the end of a tunnel* could this cervix *my* cervix really dilate to the size of a softball, push out a skull full of god knows what brains *first a softball, what next, the world?* I think of the recurring nightmares I had as a child, where elephants paraded down Columbia Avenue, shrinking to the size of mice, then expanding big as dinosaurs then shrinking and I woke up screaming. My cervix exudes a bead of moisture that looks like sweat *so timid and rosy* I remember the time in college when I visited these drug dealers whose country house made them top dogs in the hippie social register—I was the frumpy Phi Beta Kappa, a wannabe—I felt trapped in the TV series *Upstairs Downstairs* and I was the downstairs—marijuana only made matters worse, they sent me to the kitchen to pour some wine my legs lumbered in slow motion every nerve in my body exposed to their laid-back lordly stares eventually I receded through a door: taped to the refrigerator a black and white poster of Janis Joplin, microphone luscious as an ice cream cone against her mouth ... coleus overflowing macramé baskets, leafy purple and magenta where anyone would expect green ... jelly glasses full of herbs and teas of exotic origins ... mayonnaise jars brimming with macaroni ... adzuki and garbanzo in pickle jars ... gallon relish jars labeled "millet" or "wholewheat flour" in calligraphy with sketched posies … on the sink a shampoo bottle reading "Biodegradable Dishwashing Liquid" … but where was the wine … I poured a dark fluid from a wine bottle, I can't remember who was the first to spit his out and yell, "Are you crazy—this is *soy sauce!*" What happened to those little shaker bottles from Chinese restaurants? Drugged and heavy, I hung my head, hippie laughter pelting me like hail.

Smoky booth at Puerto Allegro, Sing licks salt from her lips and shouts over the three pudgy Mexican guitarists, "Babies?" She shakes her head and makes a face as sour as the lime juice in her margarita, "I'm more interested in women who kill their children." Her fork twirls in her refried beans like a flamenco dancer, her button eyes twinkle, "Mina have you ever heard of Munchausen's Syndrome by Proxy?" The indigent woman on the subway named her triplets Ronald Mick and Donald, after the famous hamburger clown, as if to squash the screaming multitudes into a single manageable entity *one life to live one nation under* my Sunday school teacher said *God is a hand His fingers the Trinity* and I thought: what happened to the other two fingers, did some horrible drug invade the womb like those armless babies in *Life* magazine *my one and only*. "Ronald, Mick and Donald?" Sing shakes her head and then a finger, "Those weird names are an early sign of Munchausen's Syndrome by Proxy." A woman uses her sick babies to gain sympathy—it starts with an accident, Baby Donald swallows a button and the woman falls in love with her doctor *a caring Cary Grant in a white coat* she has to keep those appointments coming, she poisons her babies slowly, drops them from dangerous heights, Mick and Donald wither and die off, the kind doctor puts his arm around the woman's distraught shoulders (in fantasy his arm = his dick) she jerks off on her hide-a-bed which Homicide has bugged, the mike screeches with heaving springs. As Death Mom comes "*Oh, doctor, yes, harder harder*" a detective smirks in the RotoRooter van parked across the street, he removes his headphones, "Jerry, you gotta hear this." Ronald in the crib beside her rips the plastic bag from his head and screams bloody murder. She winds up in the city jail and Sing does her psychological intake.

Sometimes I look at my cats, the look of love in their beady eyes as they bare their necks to my large hands, sometimes when KK's belly growls I lay my head there and listen *a language unlimited by syntax or meaning* Dr. Van Helsing is this how it feels to talk directly to God?

A doctor's waiting room in *Scanners*, a pregnant woman sits across from me in a smock with a Peter Pan collar, a field of wild-flowers shirrs across the yoke and billows about her global belly *Nature is a curtain that can be yanked back at any moment* she holds the bulbous mass her left hand stretching the length of Canada her right palm cupping Europe—the water cooler gurgles suddenly CUT TO MINA doubled over *my cranium tightens, psychic fingers squeeze my spongy brain I clench my abdomen SQUEEZE SQUEEZE* salty red trickles from my nostril and drips onto my lower lip THE WOMAN'S FETUS IS SCANNING MY BRAIN Reason Judgment Conscience Memory Feeling Imagination flood the charged air then whoosh into that ravenous unborn cerebrum *paragraphs quake themes jumble candid autobiographical vignettes tumble in the blood jet and crack, macaroni in a vat of Alphabet soup* you warned me about this in your last letter, "Do you know what can of worms you're opening? You think you're just going to *make literature* with impunity? Think again, sweetheart." You are my professor the *ne plus ultra* of abjection, you wouldn't go see *Godzilla 1985* but you read me Baudelaire instead, in French with perfectly intonated "r"s translating line by line, I recognized a few things *le ciel, jusque, autrefois, la douleur* Cronenberg's evil doctors are injecting pregnant women with a serum to create a race of extrasensory monsters that will rule the world—Dr. Van Helsing, I finally get what you've been hinting at: thoughts CAN kill.

Contractions every three minutes pain too deep to feel the obstetrician's scissors snipping away in your vagina pain too big to remember not even a *flashback*—when it takes over biology frightens me, when my mind shuts down and KK's touch hurls me through the dark towards my inevitable spastic conclusion—the Earth progresses through time the original fiery ball shrinking to blue then even tinier to a dead white speck *la grande mort* you do everything you can to make it a pleasant passage, darkened room warm water Windham Hill on the tapedeck, but still you birth a psychic misfit its brain burgeons beyond the cranial cage and conquers the world *every time he looks at me my nose bleeds* AT THE AGE OF FOUR KK read *Great Expectations* what kind of prenatal tranquilizer was *his* mother taking—he was born with a full grown tongue in an infant's body, when he tried to speak his tongue wriggled out of his throat like a tapeworm aroused at the scent of warm milk, vowels dull consonants murky, he pecked out stories on his parents' typewriter his little fingers hovering above the keyboard like mosquitoes, eventually a surgeon shaved his tongue to child-size, I wish I had the parings I'd keep them on my desk pickled in a jar *words leap from the mind across a vast amorphous chasm and are sucked onto the paper, no wonder they sometimes get scrambled along the way, a fly's body with a man's head, transitive love linked to the wrong direct object.*

My purpose was *vacuum cleaner* but in the glass case at the front of the Salvation Army a swarm of discarded Barbie dolls lay on their backs in even rows mostly naked an occasional silver lame outfit, a hundred permanently high heeled feet pointed directly at me *life is but a stage in the organization of matter* beside me stood a chubby little girl in Yves St. Laurent corduroy jeans, her excited finger punctuated the air: "I've got that Barbie and that

Barbie and that Barbie and oh look—Cher is pigeon-toed!" Then suddenly a silence her face lost its animation like a kaleidoscope deprived of light, she whispered "A horse" and it was, from the neck up—a horse head crowning the body of a sexy woman—a creature that could play both Liz Taylor and the filly in a low budget *National Velvet:* red lips on the end of an elongated snout—lavender eyelids scalloped like petals towards the brows—a mass of yellow Barbie hair pulled back appropriately into a pony tail, though her body was stockier than Barbie's, voluptuous with a corset imprinted on the plastic torso, corset and torso the same bronzy pink so that the corset erupted from the doll's flesh like an X-rated growth … who could stand the incongruity, God or was it Mattel had made a terrible mistake, pointed ears poking like horns out of her glamorous equestrian skull—I laid six dollars on the counter, "Oh Mommy that lady with the blonde hair is buying the horse-Barbie!" I tossed her in a paper bag beside a pair of golden apples as if she were a Sumerian fertility goddess or Persephone in the underworld *the simplest narrative is the history of gratified desire* she was mine but not of my body her molded flesh derived from the major crop of my home state—soybeans—she would be six inches tall forever, her cells fused into a glossy shield impenetrable to growth or decay *love doesn't need any opening but neither does the devil.* KK exclaimed, "Get rid of that disgusting doll it scares me!" *Reader he poisoned my mind against her* pulled out a paperback: page 66: a photograph of a glass case, the words at its base were bold DAN-GER DO NOT TOUCH! the exorcist stood before it corpulent and serious an expert from the Amityville Horror, and in the case nothing but a Raggedy Ann doll—devil worshippers made my plastic baby—stick an animal's head on Mae West's body the demon billows into your life rearranging the furniture making you talk crazy *whenever I turned my back to her something very big was watching … between my ears a ghostly whinny* we dropped her on a doorstep, her shapely tan body clattering against the concrete *strangers walked the streets with hands hungry for sin* we left her to a two-dimensional fate, a grainy snapshot on a milk carton *Missing Horse Barbie last seen …* we were on our way to Walgreens to buy condoms (bodily fluids trapped then tossed in the waste basket) *dangerous materials do not touch* what if I became pregnant with death—welts appear like purple continents across my arms my face, my lungs wheeze then stop. Dr. Van Helsing you are a man of science how could Love do this to me?

Aimless as monkeys we sat on folding chairs our senses dulled by cheap Chenin Blanc, mildly discussing Foucault, Blanchot, Judy Garland, Benjamin. Sunday afternoon. Another party at Small Press Traffic. As I fingered a few spines on the bookcase beside me, Sing smiled wryly and turned to KK, "Do you want Mina to have your baby?" Was this one of her experiments, a study of the effects of shock on the distracted subject? "No thanks!" KK barked, and we fought about it for days—not that I wanted to have a baby either but, unspoken, the possibility shimmered between us like the Dickens novel I'm always raving about but never get around to reading—or the horizon on one of the postcards Sam sends me, the Arizona/Hawaiian/Thailand sunset blooms orange and pink as if the world were a flower, fingerprints faintly dot the skyline like UFOs emerging from the fourth dimension *wish you were here.* KK said *having a baby now is an immoral act what with the human species bulleting towards extinction* and I thought what about *you—you erupted from practically nothing through the cracks in this pavement this bed.*

Gliding my palm along the length of his thigh I am piercing laughter a fire in the night, Dodie leans over her notebook, drives the muscles through systems of meaning as far from her grasp as mine.

Go to a painted sun, it gives you no heat, nor cherisheth you not.

Body Snatchers: the flowers her husband placed beside her bed are stunning, large waxy trumpets, white with deep red throats, she thinks of broken hymens as she pulls the covers over her shoulders and instantly falls asleep. The next morning when she wakes she is no longer some*one*, but some*thing*, her teeth cellulose, her smile complacently sculpted, like Lynn Redgrave's in the TV movie where she falls in love with Mariette Hartley, whenever Lynn speaks to Mariette she sounds so directory assistance, a voice half female half microchip *the-num-ber-you-have-reached-has-been ... dis-con-nect-ed*, KK exclaimed, "What's she on— valium—they should have called this show *The Stepford Lesbians!*" Half dead half alive the infective agent is ravenous for completion, it seeps into your flesh like a water into porous soil *why's my body full of holes* it seizes your nuclei, pumps out the "you" and sets up factories to manufacture itself *so full of holes, a fish net flung into a cold dark ocean.* "Dark is a state of mind," you write. "If it was just cock, for instance, for any of us, it'd be bad enough, but hardly an insuperable problem. Next time you panic ask God to enter." *But what if I get the wrong number* I stick toilet paper in my ears in case it's the devil talking, the devil whispers "m-IN-a."

Katharine, Sing and I sit around a battered wooden desk—on the window beside us Small Press Traffic is painted backwards in red. Customers mill among the shelves of books, Dion a young poet I've seen around barges through the door his eyes beaming contact and alarm, "Hi, how ya doing?" Gnarly shoulder-length hair, overblown pecs, a Neanderthal packed into a baby blue turtleneck, he heads for the New and Noted display, cracks open a thin paperback with huge callused hands, and reads *rational agency has no access to external reality.* Katharine lowers her voice and says she's been nauseous for days—recognition sparks across the thrift store desk as if the three women poised around it were neurons and the air a palpable synapse SING AND I HAVE BEEN

NAUSEOUS TOO! Dion turns the page *words draw in their horns and the physical world refuses to be ordered.* We each enumerate the reasons we can't possibly be pregnant, the main themes are *control* and *time* but fear is electric passing from womb to womb *what if our high school biology teachers were wrong and conception is random as lightning striking Striking STRIKING.* Dion turns the page *personalities do not develop they merely intensify* he looks up and catches my eye. "I hear you have a wolf," I say, "and you speak beast language to it like Michael McClure." He strokes his stubbled chin, "Yes—and his name is Leander, as in Hero and Leander." "And you're the hero?" He winks. I like it.

Who hasn't felt like a hybrid in times of stress.

Flaccid, KK's penis is endearing, so velvety and shy—but the trouble with babies (as my mother always said) is that they grow up—your bed inflates to the breaking point with thirty-three-year-old male desire panting and prodding *the thing inside burst through her belly, horror props, sausage links and ketchup* around my neck KK fastens a locket filled with a snip of his hair *to protect me from evil* I cross the street with my eyes closed, cars screech then cease to exist, the atom remains unsplit forever, cells multiply at a reasonable rate every death is from a natural cause LOVE LOVE LOVE LOVE LOVE LOVE LOVE LOVE LOVE remember when his nails were half an inch long, thick, hard, yellowed—he clipped them off for *me* parting my capillary pink flesh without a scratch *all it took was one "ouch"* claws retract, breathing softens. He extends his palm from the bathtub and says, "Sit on it," human form follows function, in Cocteau's *Orphée* gloved arms poke out of the walls holding candles, their flames trembling as Orpheus recedes down the endless corridor *I wish I could walk through mirrors* our entwined bodies tighten into a circle, a champagne bubble about to be swallowed by Marilyn Monroe *pushing the metaphor to the breaking point, in a word: orgasmic* when we fuck we are two great hands shaking *his cock a thumb* in an explosion of light the bearded creator in Blake's watercolor points from the heavens—mortal heads bow or stare up in awe and terror the way I do whenever I'm naked *a woman's hair is never thick enough to hide her thoughts* KK reaches for a condom, fumbles with its little blue capsule PRESS FIRMLY ON DOT AND PULL APART *town fathers pack data in time capsules burying them underground, schoolchildren dig them up, crack them open a hundred years later. Things.* KK can't open the condom, bends over and gives himself a handjob, I wrap my arms around his shoulders cooing reassurances and warmth *my inside is inside, his outside is obvious* I am eager for his ejaculation as I was for Emma Woodhouse or Elizabeth Bennet to marry. In my dream last night a spider cocooned me in her web and through the gossamer strands I could see the six-legged dead hanging in neat spherical bundles, then a swarm of arachnids fastened themselves to my cheeks my arms, sucking, and I cried out "Mommy why am I here?" "Storks birds bees," said the great mother, "little beings that don't know when to stop splitting, the unseeable swells until it's seen, you're my universe and Daddy was the Big Bang." *Metaphors mix because the mind is a cocktail* KK licks my ear and whispers *Tis the eye of childhood that fears a painted devil.* In *Eraserhead* the demon baby is just a goat fetus, dramatically lit— and *Frankenstein* was a product of post-partum depression *on my wedding band three diamonds flash like the tips of God's fingers* KK gasps in a New York accent, "I don't know where you leave off and I begin." He wipes the red stain from my lips, plasters holy wafers to my forehead *if only I could sprout wings* Herr Doktor turn to the last page of the last chapter, does my soul get saved, will it be safe to replicate my kind?

Love,
Mina

December 29, 1988

Dear Sam,

I hear you've been under the weather. Let me tell you a bedtime story. There is a wolf named Leander who's chained in the back-yard of a young poet named Dion. The first time Dodie met him Leander, always happy to make a new friend, jumped on her *his close-set icy stare his sawblade jaw* Dodie freaked and ran up the back steps, her tongue flapping like Little Red Riding Hood's cape. Leander raises his snout and bays at the moon—the neighbors listen in their down-covered beds in their little stuccoed houses. "Nothing but an overgrown German Shep-herd," they tell themselves, and fall asleep *beliefs flimsy as their pajamas* outside their levelor blinds he lopes, a killer with jaws so powerful he could eat a pit bull for breakfast. *To not be taken seriously, to be called a hyperactive family pet—don't you just hate when that happens, Sam?* One night Dion dreams Leander rapes his girlfriend, claws on her shoulders he pushes her down on the bed, Dion tries to stop him but of course fails since Leander *is* him or some Cubist fragment misplaced eyeballs and sharp mirrored edges *his instincts cry out for life and in his blind despair he ravenously devours anything everything.* My kind has always had a way with wolves as well as flies and bats, we beckon them with sonar brain waves and they with their funky smelling fur always obey. I will restrain myself from thinking the word K–LL.

She doesn't stop at the skin, the boundaries she experiences between herself and another though felt are not real. In most cases a person's energy field extends out from the physical body by a socially acceptable distance of two feet though experts say extensions of 20–30 feet are not uncommon.

I dream I move in with Dion, and Dr. Van Helsing is his room-mate *stench of lupine excretions the ground trembles with restless pacing* there are two beds in the room, Dion overflows his with his gnarled pectorals so I crawl in with Dr. Van Helsing—he and I are just sharing the same rectangle but I curl against him any-way, like Leander would, knowing that warmth is sometimes more important than desire. Dr. Van Helsing immediately gets up, says I'm too boring, and brings back a party—a fast worker. Rejected, I turn towards the other bed—Dion remains there still as death save for the onrush of air from flared nostrils and I think to myself too bad I chose Dr. Van Helsing, who has a cat so badly infested with fleas they swarm around it like a tornado. My legs are covered with bites which bloom into wild flowers.

KK says my glorious fleabites are stigmata like the paintings of Georgia O'Keeffe or the way bullets bloom in Raymond Chandler's chests.

Pale shoulders curling and unfurling KK grows smaller with each spasm I don't know how to hold this flesh that threatens to cover itself with red mucus … writhing, hyperventilating, brown strands sticking to forehead his contorted face manages to push out: "I love you" *as if he were bringing me a message from another world* it's awesome the way extreme pleasure looks like it hurts—when scientists stuck an electrode in a rat's brain creating a state of continuous arousal the tiny rodent died from exhaustion *la petite mort*. Flesh parts so easily for needles and knives, as if the bone and gel inside resent the skin want to merge with the world in a way the senses only dream of. Stoker said that all the suitors let their blood for Lucy, to save her soul. He lied, I'm the one who got the transfusions *my soul tottering before them like a spent gyro-scope* all those rational men coursing through *my* veins their white cells gobbled up shadows in orderly fashion, my blood was made pure my capillaries filled with light but now in the *nineteen* eighties when I look at the human pincushions around me I wouldn't want to be poked with these questionable fluids. Dion laughed when I said *no you can't go in there*—he swaggered in anyhow stood with his legs spread, arms folded across chest like a colossus surveying his kingdom, it was my bedroom: lace peeking from a drawer husband-stained sheets (this was the very first time I had him over to my apartment). When Dion barged into my secret place he stepped over: into my dreams my shady manipulations into a writing deformed and twisted as its content, into Mina Harker an insane RNA jumbling information to meet her own demented ends. Dracula knew you never cross a threshold uninvited—he survived centuries but he didn't race around like Dion does—it's hilarious the way these mortals see death as chaos when in fact the dead always follow the rules—only a mortal would use that extra key to sneak into his workplace on the weekend with a friend in a black leather jacket, the two of them strain under the weight of Dion's employer's xerox machine as they haul it to his car trunk—mortals are the ones who steal the wrong person's heart day by day—and day by day mercury vapors leak from the silver in their teeth, housewives have a higher rate of cancer than working women (beneath their kitchen sinks behind their spring-hinged cabinets carcinogens leak from tightly capped bottles *waxes polishes heavy-duty cleansers*), formaldehyde seeps from their 100% cotton sheets and embalms their skin as they lie sleeping, Salmonella incubates in sponges and cutting boards 8 chickens are gutted a minute it's inevitable the machine rips an occasional one apart feces spattering the 4th of July barbecue parasites in tap water sushi dried fruit carpaccio nitrate-laden salad bars 9,000 farm workers die a year from spraying pesticides on human food without wearing condoms EATING IN RESTAURANTS OR HAVING SEX IS TAKING YOUR LIFE INTO YOUR OWN HANDS or somebody else's.

Energy as an envelope something that surrounds her as she moves through life far afield or close to the skin permeable sensitive or tight and shieldlike a cloud enveloping her head or buzzing at her feet like electric shoes.

Around my upper arm the doctor fastened the wide band, then he pumped this little black balloon, and the band puffed and tightened. The building pressure cut off blood vessels to my brain soon I could think of nothing at all just this panic at the Unknown squeezing in on me—then the release more a fizzle than a climax—he ripped open the velcro shook his head, said my blood pressure is too *low*—all those oat-bran-eating executive types racing around, their frazzled cardiacs bursting—here I am on the other side with a heart so old and sluggish it doesn't want to pump the rotten ooze around. Sam, I'm too exhausted to even write this letter. I beckon Leander, and he my feral incubus comes to me in the night his long tongue dripping wolf saliva his fur so thick and coarse I could bury my fist there. Another dream: I'm at the neighbor's to pick up a litter of kittens, they frolic about me, fuzzy and white *a snowstorm of cute* then Leander rips through the screendoor clamping a tiny skull in his jaws of helter skelter. Dion pounds his head until he drops the cat, but as soon as he turns his heaving back Leander pounces on another, I squeal and slowly Dion turns. Like Joyce's god he is somewhat indifferent. But I'm frantic, can't be in eight places at once can't contain these innocents, these little feline Hummel figures who keep on frolicking, oblivious that a giant stalks among them with one thought in his brain—Leander, I can read it in your flared nostrils: BLOOD.

Desire walks into her life with gnarled hair and the blue eyes of a wolf. HOW DOES IT FEEL ABOUT HER? She tries to act noncommittal but finds herself unwinding like a spool, her coolness her awkward composure. Desire: It wills her to blush, shoots transgressions through her mind like poisoned arrows *the last thing she thinks of when she goes to sleep and the first when she awakens in the middle of the night in the morning, Its terrible secret splits her in two* she grows monstrous, infected, her head full of imaginary conversations that oscillate from shockingly aggressive to coy *the sacrificial eroticism of allowing herself to be known* Desire listens, Its whirlpool ears sucking in details *she cannot resist cannot withhold* she reveals things too early, slips in the vulnerable the unwise the embarrassing the scandalous. Desire storms into her bedroom, Its taut body emanating a dark cloud, the air so thick she needs a gas mask just to breathe—ghostly tentacles tease her cunt, fling her through the air—the walls bulge *energy ripples in all directions jarring your skin from the inside and from without, such unbearable pressure pounding such thinness, something flutters your ribcage it's not your heart, that's not sweat dripping down your back either it's psychic cockroaches the not you seeps through armpits breathes into eyeballs—when the magazine article says "the goal is to freely determine one's energy boundaries according to the appropriateness of the moment" somebody's laugh rattles in your throat.* I don't know, Sam, do you think I'm over-reacting?

Things were so much simpler when I was in college … Indiana University, the spring semester of my freshman year, the campus is shut down by student protests, as usual I'm lounging on the concrete bridge that leads to the Student Union's front steps. I love that massive building—a block long with towers, it looks like a moated castle, though the bridge arches over a mere trickle of a stream called the Jordan River, beside which runs a large meadow where hippie girls with bandannas tied halter-style around their breasts romp with large dogs trained to catch frisbies. Since I'm on acid my cigarette tastes sharp and crackles loudly—occasionally a fiery bit leaps through the air like a shooting star. It's so hot out each scorching exhalation singes my limp hair—I close my eyes: flaming pink webbed with red lace *the sun is a feverish placenta* I squint at the glaring outside: all these naked midriffs and torsos around me no classes it's great to be at the beach but where's the sand, why all this grass and concrete—oh yeah, I'm at college. I wish there were a real river to jump in, my cut-offs stick to squishy thighs and suddenly from out of nowhere a very deep thought enters my brain: my body is a sponge! Far out! On the bridge's wide ledge a dozen tanned students sit, hugging hello and saying things like "heavy, man" and "no shit," but I'm so alone, surrounded by this invisible wall—I could stick my hand through it easily as water and touch the others, but some arbitrary social convention constrains me. An incomprehensibly stupid situation. But then there's this blond guy sitting across from me: how can you describe a person's uniqueness: not just kind of but *very* cute, like you Sam but with longer hair, soft shoulder-length hair curling gently like a baby's, the sweetest mouth, eyes that beckon like they've seen a lot like they know something. "Everybody's ignoring me. I want some attention." Did I say that? There was a voice but did my lips move throw the thoughts into the open air or did the words just clamor around in my brain? The blond guy catches my eye. HE HEARD. I've really laid myself on the line this time what's someone so totally cool and beautiful going to think of *me*? Narrowing those drama eyes he rolls his tongue in his cheek as if what he's about to say is so earth shattering he has to warm up his mouth just to get the words out. Then he smiles oh god *that smile, I would follow it to hell and back* he's really pure it's like I already know him it's like we have this psychic connection I mean what are words anyway meaningless as time and distance. After the longest forever he replies, "You want some attention? Then ask for it. That's all you have to do—ask." Obediently I stand up on the ledge I'm so nervous I wanna die my knees shaking my heart isn't beating it's flip-flopping. My hands reach through a wide colorful aura *fingers tingling in this radiant thingness* I wave and yell out, "Attention! I want some attention—give me some attention!" Lo and behold a crowd gathers beneath me, applauding and cheering, I look over at my blond teacher on the opposite ledge and bow. He shrugs his shoulders. Wow—he knew all along how simple it is to move people from out-there to in-here, all the struggling and all the games people play, what a waste, when he tells me his name is Eric I say, "I knew it would be." After we play some pinball and watch the sun set I sneak him into my dorm room and we stay up all night talking. He turns me on to Nietzsche, who he studied in his comparative literature classes. I've never heard of comparative literature or Nietzsche before, but he and Eric are the most brilliant fascinating mystical men ever born. I'm hooked—that fall I switch my major from English to comp. lit., even though I still don't understand the difference, all magic being a form of imitation.

Orgasm does not have to originate or culminate genitally it can happen in any bodily position or location that is capable of gathering charge *the collection and spontaneous redistribution of energy in a pleasurable pulsatory manner* even a gulp of pizza or warm cat flesh can be orgasmic if you are willing to surrender to the extra energy you've built up.

I've been sick too, Sam—for months—my feline companions Blanche and Stanley have been a great comfort, lying beside me warm and purring throughout these months, these dark months when my mind's been too fuzzy to answer the phone. Though words fail I can relate to the direct communication of flesh against fur, timeless save for dinner and the occasional change of litter box *we're content I know they love me better than the radiator, will continue to do so even if I never get well* curled on my chest or stomach these two rumbling balls of coziness keep me from rising above my bloated aching body and flying through the ceiling. Still, I wouldn't want to be a mouse wriggling between their teeth— even these snooze puffs at the slightest whiff of rodent *change:* tails bloom like tropical plants pupils widen blue vision sweeps to black, crouched before their prey whiskers bristle claws outstretch and then that sexy little shake of ass right before they pounce. Who is predator who is prey—as the great Aretha sings, "Who's zooming who?" I've heard all the teeth arguments—my remarkably well-developed incisors—but I can no longer take into my body that which has been tortured then eviscerated while still alive— violence so sharp the hide is split before the stunned animal knows what's happening. I have grown tired of the taste of blood. Each night I come home to the same man the same bed, my microcosm content with chlorophyll, its parallel molecular structure. Marriage is definitely vegetarian. With each cellulose mouthful my eyes grow greener. To those keen bovine nostrils, imagine how thick the perfume of slaughter, eyes full of confusion and woe, the way I look when a stranger at work acts interested in me.

All anybody really wants is an autonomous existence in a non- alienating setting.

Dion's stepfather hit him between the eyes with a hammer, a kind of blue collar trepanning, a hole in the forehead to let the ordinary out and the wolf demon in. When he looks in the mirror he doesn't know which face will stare back at him, Leander's or Dion's. A person who claims to fuck until he's trembling on the edge of being/non-being, he tries to show me his poem *sex acts with another woman* but I resist, flickering on the threshold like the newly dead afraid to go that far inside. "I am MINA HARKER," I tell him in a huff, "Nobody has sex with anybody but me!" Dion sub- mitted his poem to *Sulfur* and *Sulfur* published it. Those eyes of his like Superman's or Poe's that bore through wood and flesh and glass. Someone the Dead can envy. But often I think to myself *I'm not supposed to know people like this not in the flesh* he belongs in a drive- in movie the kind that everybody but high school boys are ashamed to admit they like: Conan the college student gets caught cheating and outruns the campus police—when his roommate rips him off

Conan waits in a tree outside the cookie store where the guy works and every time he takes out the garbage Conan's muscles tighten, twitch—when Conan gets an F he pushes his professor against the wall—he chains his pet wolf in the backyard *125 howling pounds of metaphor* he dreams the wolf rapes his girlfriend. Leander shakes his foaming jaw and runs.

The first time I saw Scarlet he was at a party wearing a bath towel and shower cap. It wasn't a costume party as I remember it, but back in my undergraduate days we didn't haggle over distinctions, I mean if you get right down to it aren't all clothes costumes? Despite his exotic attire I didn't find him very interesting, never dreamed that within months we would be sharing a twin bed. Two bodies occupying the same space breathing the same air skin was enough to keep us separate—crashing at somebody's place was in the spirit of the times, I took home men like stray dogs— if I had an extra few feet of space and they needed it, why not. We slept in a glass porch which had been converted into a green-house and which by scooting over some of the pots and throwing a mattress on the floor was again converted into a bedroom. I only stayed there a few nights a week and when I did I would tumble in at three in the morning. Since Scarlet was a baker he got up at five a.m., so we only slept together a couple hours a night. Perhaps that's why I never got to know Scarlet very well. It was peaceful there, philodendron and ivy hanging from baskets above our heads and beyond them streetlights and stars—I never felt crowded surrounded by all that oxygen and night. In fact, I thought it was an ideal arrangement, that more people should follow our example—it was a perfect way to conserve beds, if a shortage of beds should ever arise.

Dion punches Leander in the jaw when he gets excited, when he's pouncing on his friends or chomping through the furniture as if it were made of balsa wood. How can Leander put up with this, how can he not fight back not rip that projectile arm right out of its socket? No animal should be chained in the backyard or made into shoes or have cosmetics dripped into its eye clamped open wide as the moon *but where are you going to go how are you going to support yourself in a world where all the others are either domesticated or in zoos* both you and I know his appetite the craving to swallow the whole world until the outside is inside and the inside is unconscious.

Intimacy that isn't satisfied by rubbing bodies together Desire is always bigger than her, poking Itself in, inviting her to dissolve … every detail of her life, her past is an offering to Desire … the voice on the radio speaks directly to her when it sings, "My love is stronger than the universe." Desire savors the subtleties of Its conquest, tosses a toothpick over Its shoulder. Nobody knows where It comes from.

Or why It leaves. Or why It returns.

Dion stood in a room strewn with rumpled clothes and said, "Good." I wonder if it *is* true, that you can never trust a person with a neat bedroom, meaning the only way to get to know a person is through stealing together for instance. Or sex. That's why the well-behaved are so lonely. I gag on the ordinary, on those novels Dodie's always reading: tiny fluctuations in the daily life of British spinsters, she wants to prove that lives far more boring than hers can make good Literature *trying to deny the need for a significant external* comparing herself to these spinsters Dodie's always ahead of the game. Whatever happened to that hippie coed who danced through life carefree as the young Leslie Caron, a girl who talks to puppets because she forgets to remember they're not real? I look back at her the way the dead watch the living *the way you watch me, Sam* slightly wavering with a deep sense of nostalgia mingled with incomprehension. The Fox the Beautiful Woman the Giant the Beau are her best friends she takes their little puppet hands in hers, sways and curtsies as they sing Hi Lili Hi Lili Hi Lo! Her love is clear as a glass of water—unpolluted—sparkling with those wonderful blues that Technicolor was famous for, blue as KK's eyes, he summons her back The Ingenue From Beyond The Grave. It's pitch black I lie beside him in that borderline region where sleep is sneaky as death, it waits to get you from behind *where does the wind go after it tickles the fine hairs on my forearm?* His arm's warm across my back, my breath falls into rhythm with his until he seems to be breathing me like an iron lung—I feel that helpless that surrendered. The first time I slept with KK I hardly knew him any better than I did Scarlet. One night after Dr. Van Helsing's writing workshop we went to a comedy cabaret at the Valencia Rose. When the comedian joked about LSD I glanced down at my hands—they turned jagged, multi-dimensional, moved like someone else's—what happened to the difference between word and hallucinogen *I became filled with mysterious heightenings* fire shot up and down my spine *local intensities* my heart raced vision blurred *alarming effluvia* I felt like I was shrinking, like one of those plaster camel heads that stuck out of the wall was going to bite me. I had to escape the crowded air and all that ionized laughter. KK and I rushed out front, the night full of concrete and salsa music—I was embarrassed to lose control in front of so casual an acquaintance. KK told me not to worry—he'd known lots of people who had episodes like this and I should just let him handle it. Part of me guessed he was lying but that part was vetoed, I turned myself over to him a malleable hyperventilating packet to do with what he would. He took me to his place, gave me a glass of milk then led me to his bed, "Let's lie down," the sheets were pale blue the walls yellow from cigarette smoke, he held me *his body was male with the expected protrusions but nevertheless felt safe* could this really be the weird guy who sat next to me in a bookstore and read those crazy poems I couldn't understand? Even though my spine was being electrocuted and I was seeing double I relaxed in his arms, all trust and wonderment *I was a kite and he was my string.* His chin resting against the top of my head he told me the story of the Mist … without shape itself the Mist embodied human forms and monsters, eating everybody in sight—when it took over an entire shopping center the people had to hide in the supermarket—when it took over that white haze that hovers above the frozen food cases the people huddled around the cash registers—the Mist became a giant fist and smashed a plate glass window, the Mist was inside me but even if it took all night KK was going to talk it out.

Who is Dion? The first time I laid eyes on him I saw a flurry in a Samsonite chair but didn't think much of it. How did he ever progress from that chair to my bedroom? A man who sleeps with a wolf *so flimsy is the border between desperation and love* Dion thinks he's safe because *he's* in control, the way these humans are always wanting to be their own creations, so resistant to revision. In that smelly bed of his with the ratty green blanket he's dreaming of people whose legs extend out of their shoulders and whose arms dangle down from their torsos, of beings who are part animal part human, a frog's head with his girlfriend's face standing on a pair of arms and hands instead of legs, Mengelian creatures like the naughty sketches he did in blue ballpoint in the back of his history book in junior high. Leander licks his master's dark furrowed brows, Dion jerks his hulky shoulders then sinks deeper into sleep peaceful as a William Blake lamb *bearing the fruit of night in his body* those hypnotic snores that luscious pink throat, jugular undulating like a woman who's just dying to have it.

Don't worry—we haven't slept together. Not yet …

Sweet dreams—
Mina

October 10, 1989

Dear Sing,

Dion confides how bored he is with his girlfriend, then casually asks, "How long have you and KK been married? ... That long, huh?" Suddenly his voice goes husky: "You and I should get together and have a little snack on the side." Like the subatomic meson a flurry of desire passes through me, it leaves a flash on a photographic plate for a few millionths of a second only to vanish out of material existence. "Dion, I think that would be disastrous." *A snack—not dinner or even Sunday brunch—an in-between a fat girl's nemesis greasy food products advertised on TV a nibble that can happen any old time* Dion and I are squatting on the wicker stools at El Toro's, he picks up his churro and starts mimicking fellatio on it—the more I slap his arm and squeal "Stop it!" the deeper he plunges the tubular pastry down his throat. I'm flushed frustrated charmed alarmed—people are staring, but what else is new? Against his baby blue T-shirt Dion's irises beam bluer than nature, on the smoke-stained walls hang an artist's first show *the colors gaudy, the figurative elements unintentionally stiff* I fiddle with my bendable straw; folding it back and forth is weirdly erotic, the accordion curve locks as I let go, clasp my hands together on the white formica table between us, without missing a beat in the conversation, "When I was a boxer I knew better than to slam anybody down on the mat," Dion leans forward covering my hands so softly *his palms the wings of a giant insect in a caveman tableau* then he pulls back clamps his coffee cup in a grip that could crush it.

SOMEBODY MIGHT GET IN TROUBLE.

We romped across San Francisco, a couple of large frisky dogs squirming and wrestling until his car shook up and down like a boat ... we pretended we were in a Wim Wenders film driving cross country our itinerary convoluted as our brains our destination Pleasure USA ... we sat on the concrete ledge at the top of Twin Peaks watching the changing light, a warm San Francisco sunset *weather rare as diamonds* from the Bay Bridge to the Golden Gate the city spread out before us glittering and gorgeous ... Dion in mussed hair and jeans, baby blue T-shirt boasting forearms dimpled from pumping iron *a body within inches of my fingers its heat rippling through the evening* arching his shoulders Dion commands, "Scratch my back." Baby blue air gels into a wall of muscle I rub my hand over it. "To the left ... now up a bit *harder.*" Blue cotton slides around his torso like bed sheets how can I stand it this craving to wrap my legs around his waist to swallow this savory morsel of junk food whole this corpus delectable that's ten years younger than Dodie. Dion jutted into my life like Carrie's arm jutted from the grave.

He kept lamenting "if only"—as if my marriage were a terminal disease. For days I had in fact been under the weather with stomach flu—but by the time we drove home the pallor in my cheeks bloomed to a blush my mouth swelled crimson I felt new as dew REVIVED *Dion my transfusion my 20th century succulence* I told him he was crazy if he thought I knew what I wanted.

The dark isn't really dark but flickering my parents and me at the drive-in, in our brand new '59 Fairlane, sitting through *another* Western, why don't we ever see anything interesting like Jerry Lewis—in the front seat my father pees in his popcorn container, I slouch in the back the warm hiss of urine drowning out the passions of the big screen, he dumps the gunk out on the gravel *a car is more than motion ... it can be a bed or a coffin or a room, any room* the second night when Dion backed into a spot on Twin Peaks I knew better than to wax cozy in my bucket seat—this time it wasn't the scenic vista but an elongated parking lot, our "view" concrete and a few shrubs. Fog formed a blowsy curtain across the windows. I said, "You're afraid I'm going to take these sex games of yours seriously and what would you do then?" He smiled as he leaned over and stuck his tongue in my mouth *it was thick with saliva like a dog's* imagine my feigned surprise! I was wearing a slinky silk blouse that really lived up to its adjective, Dion's hands roamed up and down my spine as if the knobs were Morse Code he couldn't quite make out *dot dot dash dot* suddenly in the middle of a deep-throated kiss he stopped, sat back, panted, stared straight ahead and murmured, "I've been wanting this for three years and it's every bit as good as I imagined." Sing, I try to maintain some semblance of control but how could I resist a man who made me feel like Jesus Christ on the cross, my ego destined to soar to heaven? *This really is going to happen clothes will be peeled away ripe flesh revealed body parts played like the greatest hits I dice my carrots to on K-FOG's Psychedelic Supper* I kept putting it off, that ultimate steamy moment when dreams materialize, when ardor eclipses the specific—in that leap across the unfathomable distance between two bodies a formula is set in motion—you can fill in the numbers, brackets, x's and y's with calculated abandon—kinky or vanilla you always end up on the other side of the equal sign with the same big Z for Zero. One Saturday afternoon my longing was so huge I felt like H.D. trapped in Emily Dickinson's body, I wanted to fuck endlessly and to be fucked *tossed across rituals I barely comprehend* I put on jogging shoes and ran to North Beach *I made my way by odor and feel and uninhibited touch, wheezing down California then Polk, over the hill on Pacific then through Chinatown the streets lined with amber ducks hanging from their feet as if a cartoon butcher had caught them midfall* but I couldn't shake off these jabs of arousal that had attached themselves to my groin like gnomes that cling to the wings of aircraft fiendishly tinkering with engines making the plane take a nosedive in the most far-fetched places, the Dead Sea, the Bermuda Triangle, Dion's arms …

Pushing his Ray Bans up the bridge of his nose Dion declared, "You can't get me in trouble because I *am* trouble."

The following week Dion and I park in the Marina as far from streetlights as we can get, sailboats clinking in the foreground, we shift beneath the frosty windshield *ghostly inhabitants, elusive and unbelievable as certain ideas* I roll down my window to let the boats in *an atonal Japanese interlude* Dion leans across me one hand squeezing my thigh the other rolling up the glass wall *the inside is us and forget the rest* he's trying to move things along to the Big Picture while I savor the details. Here in the dark I miss the fine lines under Dion's eyes that run to his ears, fissures in such a young face *something is coming apart* I'm having my period and Dion hasn't cleaned up from his day job—hauling around carcasses for eight hours his sweat is mingled with cattle ooze, his nails are caked with blood, he pushes his tongue down my throat as he pushes a finger up my vagina *all those discarded unsanitary world bits all that refrigerated death* he whispers, "I'd like to stick my biggest finger in there" *he's pointing in my direction* all I'm wearing is a camisole which might as well be nothing—with every zooming headlight I stiffen: COPS? Sing, how can I pass up the chance to fuck in a Camaro—it's so perfectly high school! But like high school it's damned near impossible—after numerous failed contortions I turn sideways and sit on top of that glove compartment or whatever you call that box thing between the bucket seats—Dion plunges into me his right hand clinging to the headrest for balance his left arm around my waist suspending me in a hot-blooded void *there's nothing solid for me to lean against or grab onto I can't adjust the cramp nagging my calf* head and shoulders bobbing around in open space a line of poetry sticks in my mind reasserting itself like a mantra with each thrust: Sylvia Plath: *something else hauls me through air* I imagine Dion imagining himself at work diving into one of those gleaming pink slabs his cock smearing white to fuchsia à la Francis Bacon *something else hauls me through air …*

KK wasn't hopeful. "You and Dion are two giant screens with different movies playing on each of you."

Afterwards I try to cuddle but Dion clings to his side of the car like a barnacle—I've heard of passion spent but once this guy shoots his load he's bankrupt—I guess I'm spoiled but I wish he'd curl around me like a shell. Instead he tells me about a TV show where one cell removed from a specimen's body could feel the effects of its home cells miles away. Waving a blood-stained finger back and forth Dion concludes: that's why people know each other so well after they make love, they leave specks of microscopic sentience behind. I snap back, "Don't start telling me that now you can read my soul." His cum in my cunt *sticky radar* while I'm washing the dishes will his emotions zap through me will I drop a plate—from now on when I'm happy will Dion smile to himself will he saunter to the bathroom whenever my bladder's too full?

Monday through Friday you ride your bicycle to jail and the iron gate slams behind you *a woman who knows the gut-rattling difference between inside and out* the first thing you do is check the "rubber rooms," the isolation cells for the wackos booked the night before *for their own protection, if they're too loud the other cons will beat them up, if they're nodding out anything could happen to their bodies* you peer through a rectangular slit in the door and say, "If you want to get out of here you have to talk to me." You determine who's psychotic, who's freaking on what drugs *people on crack sweat, people on speed don't* then you make your recommendations, you call this "separating the sheep from the goats." Sing, I wish I could sort through things as easily as you *if I don't calm down Dodie's threatening an exorcism, the pineal gland is a snake that pokes through my forehead making me eat psychiatrists' brains.*

I blame this all on Lilith one of those popular girls who wait in the wings ready to destroy Carrie's life or mine. KK and I entered the raised auditorium for James Schuyler's reading, Lilith spied us and quipped, "Here come THE MARRIED PEOPLE." *She might as well be calling us plotless* I, Mina Harker, the Famous and Feared, my trail of weeping jugulars spanning two continents, two centuries—can you imagine *me*, Sing, the joke of a popular coed! What did she want me to do, dump a bucket of blood on my head? When Dion came along, trouble on a silver platter, I had no alternative but to bite.

For three years our relationship was casual, hadn't even progressed to the point of those dreadful little hugs that people expect upon departure, stiff and mechanical with a light pat on the back optional graze of smiling cheeks occasionally the slightest peck of a kiss in the vicinity of (but not on) the lips, an embrace like a chastity belt. Someday I swear I'm going to latch onto one of these vacant fondlers and grind my groin into theirs. Imagine the look on Dodie's deeply pinkening face—her mouth an "O" straight out of Sylvia Plath as I proclaim to her, as the space alien with the bird face proclaimed to his shrieking hostage, "Horror is a luxury the desperate cannot afford." Then Dion dreamt his plane crashed—digging through the rubble he unearthed my unconscious body and carried it across the mesa, I was but a limp shell draped in his arms, torn skimpy gown draped across trembling breasts: only a dream but in the nuclear region of desire a quantum event *out of nothing a primordial something* Dion began to touch me, tentative pats on my arm or waist *was he testing me or trying to bring me back to life?* I warned him there are things on heaven and Earth that mortals shouldn't mess with but he didn't listen grabbed my kneecap instead of the stick shift. Once at the end of a joke he laid his sweaty head on my shoulder *punchline* his weight against me felt big, adoring, he said I was sexy said I'd look great in Ray Bans on the back of a motorcycle *thick engine between my thighs* said he had another dream where we made love and all the tensions between us dissolved.

How dare Lilith insinuate my marriage is boring—who does she think she's dealing with here? I prefer to think of KK and me as … "enigmatic." I can see some scholar in the 21st century huddled over our papers totally perplexed, he takes off his spectacles stares blankly at the shelves of dusty books, then he picks up his pen, like a space shuttle it slowly arches forward touches down on a yellow legal pad, he begins: *The Enigmatic Duo:* Chapter 1. Sing, I WANT TO SET THE RECORD STRAIGHT *RIGHT NOW!* As a lover the *mot juste* for KK is "graceful"—you've seen the swanlike flick of his chin as he smokes a cigarette *hands like water flowing over and into* when I admire this grace he shrugs his freckled shoulders and sighs, "They used to call me the Baryshnikov of love." So why am I creating Dion? BECAUSE THERE IS AN INVERSE RELATIONSHIP OF FOREST TO TREES! Repetition blurs details in a haze of privacy *anything even Patty Hearst locked in a closet begins to seem normal after awhile* on the California Street cable car a worker who rides it to the Embarcadero every weekday would never ooh and aah the way those horrible tourists do—if one more time I hear "Look, that's where they film *Hotel!*" there's going to be a polyester mess across the tracks—I just want to exist on the wooden bench my quiet interiority mingling with the fresh morning air *just a bunch of blue tubes inside a skin wrapper* it takes a stranger or an accident to bring the panoramic view back in focus.

My guest room was subtly lit like a museum case, Dion's arm a dead weight across my naked waist, "You're my anima," he whispered. I smiled and winced. Then I heard a suspicious jingling and scratching OH MY GOD KK'S KEY IN THE LOCK I hurled myself against the door and threw the bolt: "Just a minute!" Hopping around the floor on one foot Dion looked like a pagan performing some ritual, "Oh Great Pants God—Please Cover—My Bare Ass!" *I was trying to lead a life so trashy I'd be personally responsible for San Francisco's landfill crisis* KK seemed embarrassed and amused as if watching an X-rated episode of *I Love Lucy*. Later when the three of us sat in the living room discussing the weather the cat jumped on Dion's lap, with a sly smile KK remarked, "I see she's got a new boyfriend." *Oh, Ricky!* Dion won't leave the Cat Comment alone, "I could understand if the guy wanted to beat me up but this talk about the cat ... you guys are so decadent!" His boyish features grimace, I expect his irises to spin around like blue pinwheels. "I've never cheated on a girlfriend, never had sex with a married woman, never had sex with the wife of a good friend ..." I recognize his expression: my own a dozen years ago in a movie theater—I was so stoned on hash I couldn't tell if my body was moving or still—and *Satyricon* was freaking the shit out of me *gigantic tits and wacked-off limbs, hyena-faced spectators* in Dion's eyes I'm wicked, wicked as Salome, but not any old Salome—the only man who can do me justice is Beardsley, or maybe Oscar Wilde.

Dion's intensity was ultimately inaccessible to me. I hated him for that. I still do.

Sing, I've been caught before ... have you? When I was nine and my urine turned red the doctor prescribed a milky medicine that tasted of oranges and a weekly shot of penicillin. The nurse would pat my naked butt and ask, "Which side do you want it on, hon?" My cousin Pam lay on her stomach on my twin bed, her pants pulled down—I didn't have a needle but I did find a pencil and was preparing to jab the chosen cheek of Pam's ass when my mother walked into the room. Instantly she turned from housewife to Fury, wresting the pencil from my little fist and yelling, "Don't you *ever* do that again! Pam pull your pants up." I felt confused, hurt, "MOM I WAS JUST PLAYING!" She hadn't been exactly understanding either the previous summer when my night lamp caught on fire from the pajama top I'd thrown over it to attempt dim lighting—she found me in the 90° weather lying on my back on the floor beneath the smoking lamp wearing mittens, ear muffs, and my father's motorcycle goggles stuffed with cotton balls. "What the hell are you doing!" she shrieked. It had taken all day to reconstruct the sensory deprivation experiment I'd read about in *Science Digest* and she ruined it, I shoved the goggles under the bed. "Nothing, " I said, "I ain't doing nothing." "My mother thought I was crazy," I whine to KK, "and a pervert." He takes a drag from his cigarette, "Because you didn't have a hypodermic needle you used a pencil … ummm … sublimation … no wonder you became a writer." He's full of theory. Fifty percent of female serial murderers, he tells me, spell their first name with an "i" at the end. Dodie or Cindy is okay, but watch out for the treacherous Patti Judi Suzi Cheri or Mimi. KK adds, "Take my friend Teresa—all of a sudden she switched from signing herself "T-E-R-R-Y" to "T-E-R-R-*I*"—and she was a grown woman! I knew from then on that she'd become a menace." Looking back with the jaded eyes of an adult I see how my girlish exploration of Pam's ass isn't all that different from some of the sex kinks KK and I occasionally treat ourselves to—to this day, I'm sure if my mother walked in on us, she'd bellow, "Don't you *ever* do that again!"

With Dion, his girlfriend Tiki, and KK all jostling for elbow room I felt crowded out of my own bed; Dion turned impotent with guilt. I bitched, "If all you can think about is Tiki why don't you go home and fuck Tiki instead of me." That was the extent of my understanding *having been an Other since the day I was born, being the other woman was small potatoes to me* … Dion in his muddy backyard yelling through the cellular phone, "Well, maybe I'm just too young and inexperienced to have sex with someone as demanding and decadent as you—you and KK and your whole Anne Rice lifestyle!" His rage made objects and people abstract *souls hovered in the dark air under the moon* eventually he looked up and at his kitchen window stood Tiki in a vintage dress ripped under the armpits, nipples erect—taking in *everything*—a forbidden history and its confused future—his misbehaving cock. "Oh shit," he said, "can I hang up now?"

Real Life was sneaking up on him threatening to commit mutiny on the ship of his story it took some fancy navigating to switch tenses from the dangerous "I did" to the purely literary time frame of "If I were to … "

In build and character Dion was wolfman rather than the aristocratic Dracula of my young dreams—I've always preferred men with long bodies and soft asses—like KK or Dr. Van Helsing. Rubbing against Dion's acres of muscles his redwood thighs I felt like Jayne Mansfield in a leopard-skin jumpsuit. He was pushing thirty and leading a sedentary life *I had to taste him quickly before he went stale* all of him: unshaven jaw broken nose scars chipped yellowing teeth *skin you would never mistake for candy* armpits reeking of musk and meanness. His views on poetry were tedious and naive he thought Chopin was a great composer decorated his apartment in a style that I could only call "boys dorm" cooked jambalaya with a prepackaged seasoning mix—but when he lay down on my back I felt so hollow, his arms looming on either side *pterodactyl wingspan* his colossal heart pounding my rib cage like a drum. I like a lover with lips that talk as well as kiss—hours of Dion's arousal pale before his off-hand remark: "Last night you looked so good I got a hard-on just crossing the street with you." We were on our way to a Cambodian restaurant—I ordered green curry, traded him a shrimp for a cashew, impatient to get the business of public eating over with—predator that I am I have an instinctual need to keep moving, at work I take as many trips to the bathroom as possible, rinsing my hands in the antiseptic white sink I gaze at my reflection on the wall, framed in a simple rectangle it moves like a painting, I try to imagine what he finds attractive in the creature before me: tattered grave clothes spattered with mildew and mud fluorescent skin of the undead chapped lips oozing blood *no temperature whatsoever, like a piece of paper* ... who else could he be seeing ... blonde hair ... green eyes ... a woman who crumbles with his touch into pure sensation? A rush of fear swells through my chest: "You made me hard crossing the street" his testimonial superimposed onto my perceived image *an impossible contradiction, an unwelcome drug* the mirror glares in the afternoon sun *who am I to believe: the government scientists with their cover-ups their whitewashes—or the slimy thing thumping down my hallway, whenever I turn my head I catch a glint of fangs or extraterrestrial steel.*

His cock curled back on itself, a finger beckoning.

The funky sheets have been supplanted by freshly laundered cotton—a team of forensic experts would find no traces of hair skin blood NO INCRIMINATING MOLECULAR FLAKES. Sing, how did it feel last week when you crashed on the futon where half of the X rated action took place? Were your dreams shot through with flashes of heat and confusion the way a psychic clenching the dead boy's shirt glimpses his killer's face? Were your nights restless as mine—waking then waking then waking again, lips parched cheek pressed against a vanishing chest—Dion's—I can't hold the dream just its afterimage no limbs no head, a wide-angled close-up of torso: a panorama of beige skin, smooth, oily polished with unnatural highlights like airbrushed aluminum: as I move my eyes the frame ripples with muscle, strata upon strata of muscle a Grand Canyon of tortured flesh stretching above the sun drenched horizon—the camera backs up to reveal long skinny stick legs and arms poking out at awkward angles, a huge upturned screaming mouth by Salvador Dali.

SING, ARMAGEDDON—NOT GOD—WILL COME IN THE FORM OF A KISS.

A perfect Saturday night, pizza and a slasher video *a small mushroom, a large sausage* KK recognizes the slasher's M.O. from the true crime books you and he barter back and forth *Fatal Vision, Fatal Dosage, Blood and Money, Bad Blood, Poisoned Blood, Bitter Blood* during the credits he gets that faraway look I know so well, blue eyes boring through the flittering screen to the delicate web of intelligence that holds his world together, absently he picks up his Tab takes a swig and sets it down beside the 50's panther lamp. "Do you know the three things all sociopaths have in common?" A shake of my slouched head from the other end of the couch. "Well, as children they all wet the bed, tortured small animals, and lit fires. Mina, if you ever meet anybody who did *all* those three things they are *not normal*—STAY AWAY! Ask Sing if you don't believe me." A few days later while Dion and I were driving down Haight Street he started talking about vengeance in the 7th grade, to get even with a girl who framed him he filled a balloon with urine, climbed on top of a roof ... she was drenched and screaming when I "innocently" asked, "Did you used to wet the bed?" "Didn't everybody?" STRIKE ONE. "Did you light fires?" "Yeah, I lit kleenex boxes and put them on the dining room table." STRIKE TWO. "But you never tortured small animals?" "Yeah, I hung snakes from a fence—upside down—so they'd bake in the sun." STRIKE THREE—LET ME OUT! "I'd rub them with suntan lotion, it kept them alive longer, kept their skins soft." I thought I was going out for a cup of coffee and here I was living the second reel of *Frenzy the 13th, Part II* ... my mind reversed itself rooting out all the "quirky" anecdotes Dion had entertained me with the past few months: how he stuffed dog shit in his enemy's mailbox—slammed his coworker enemy down on con-crete—"lucky nothing broke"—trashed his neighbor enemy's house—poured sugar in his roommate's gas tank—slammed his fist through his landlord's window and smeared the blood over his face like war paint as he raced home—the list of Dion's enemies swelled irrationally, out of control like anything exposed to radiation in the 50's—would he stop making dates and just break into my apartment whenever he wanted to see me, make me his moll like Stephanie Zimbalist—poor Stephanie, a *Movie of the Week* lawyer who falls head over heels for an imprisoned client with X-ray blue eyes—Alec Baldwin—she hides a gun in the court bathroom and they drive off together in a baby blue van pretending she's his hostage—end of romance, beginning of hell. She winds up in a cheap hotel her hair dyed cheap blonde, broke, desperate, not even liking her beer-guzzling con very much. I began searching for a reason to storm away from Dion, shouting that "it" was over.

His cock curled back on itself like a question mark—I should have guessed I'd never know what he wanted. I wanted his heart on a silver platter I wanted to have some kind of effect on him.

It's no accident that I Mina Harker am a vampire rather than a serial killer: Dodie's never going to run into me in a dark alley or mall parking lot, about me the neighbors the former classmates the coworkers will never say, "She seemed so normal kind of quiet volunteered to man the barbecue no one would have sus-pected anything she did her job kept to herself." Beside a nightstand *Fatal Vision* might be titillating but I don't want a maniac messing up *my* bed *the tip of his cock spurts* TERROR KK says the sociopath always knows who suspects him and goes after her first FATAL FATAL FATAL Dion my demented little darling, so sickeningly sweet but inside his tightly packed cells hides a gene that spells M-U-R-D-E-R: KK the crime buff who lives next door is the only one who can read the clues, the dead bodies that litter our neighborhood like candy wrappers—*The Bad Seed*—I'm moving to *Woodstock* Nation where shaggy headed promoters call their financial disaster a huge success because success is about Something Money Can't Buy: Meaning. And the meaning of Woodstock is: "being afraid to walk down the street at night isn't living." The aerial camera tracks over an amorphous mass of stoned hippies THERE ARE NO STREETS IN WOODSTOCK I feel so safe, the guy from Ten Years After squinting and frenetically pouting "I'm Going Home"—I want to go home too, back to the era of the fake fur coat I wore in college an ancient *faux*—it wasn't the fuzzy gray stripes I paid $2 for, but the satin label in the lining its brand name embroidered in red script: "Mutation" with a heart instead of a dot over the "i": a label I could flash before my friends, casually cooing like a drag queen, "How do you like my Mutation?" A coat that flies me to a streetless world where consequences don't happen: pre-Hiroshima pre-pyramids pre-overdose pre-Patty McCormack pre-fig leaf pre-toxic over-load *can you dig it the New York State Freeway is closed man* a world where people pick up each other's garbage and civilizations don't sink beneath heaps of non-biodegradable artifacts *where plastics are awesome and it's diamonds that mean forever.*

Sing, we both know there's more to being normal than not having hallucinations.

All you wanted was a place to crash for a night but Fate inserts you into *my* story—you are the innocent who stumbles onto the scene of a murder only to find herself chief suspect *her finger-prints all over the gun a white haired man across the road sees her running away when the squad car siren comes blaring up the street.* You sit alone in my living room—writing—it's very quiet and from time to time you stare out the bay windows … in the dis-tance you see a giant crane and towering beyond, Twin Peaks …

Dion and I appear beside you a couple of iridescent ghosts half on the floor half on the couch unzipping each other's pants in slow motion ... you lean closer to examine the last decadent flowering of Dion's flat stomach *his navel protrudes, his gut so full of funk it's ramming against the umbilicus ready to erupt* I was a fool to materialize for Dion *a handful of moans and peristalsis, a highway of secretions* I should have heeded Ann Landers *never sleep with friends or married men or any of one's own characters* I should have stayed offstage pushing around commas. "MINA I'M A *VERY* PRIVATE PERSON!" warns Dion. Sing, please don't show him this letter *lips skinned back jaw clenched he shakes his lupine head and growls* what if he trashes my apartment pisses on me what if my teeth turn up in Daly City my wallet in Sacramento? *Her body was shredded like paper the insides pushed through some holes in her shirt blue and greasy and jumbled.* Sing, you left your fingerprints all over me—the whole world knows you've got no alibi—whenever you tell me about your job, all those clinically depressed felons, I find myself losing my sophisticated cool *poor Youth poor disfigured Desire.* "A therapist can learn a lot from the crime scene—what was done to the body, how it was positioned, how long it was kept." *I can't concentrate can't map the larger pattern of conflicts and contradictions* a man murdered his common-law wife and fucked her dead body *I can't concentrate can't reconsider* then he cut deep gashes in her flesh, stuck rifle shells in the gashes *absent centers reciprocal relations* he carried the body around in his car trunk forever then he threw it on the front lawn of an attorney where he got caught trying to blow it up *the more I hear the more I fester* you lean towards me as if to hurl your words into my gaping mouth, "Now this guy you can tell is big trouble. You know what I'd like—a beer, a really dark draught beer." *The Moors Murderers are starting to sound like just plain folk* horror swells my moments both waking and sleeping *I have to switch on the night lamp to get up the nerve to get up and pee* I don't know whose horror I'm feeling—that of your deadened clients or my own.

How ludicrous to presume our sex demons or even our partners will allow us to maintain any composure—they'll fight you prick and claw until your sassy aspirations expire in smoke until you forget who you are until you're nothing a question mark with legs pumping inanely like a full frame porn shot of two anonymous pink asses connected by a piston of cock—in the dark we become these asses or Chuckie the Killer Doll blurred between animate and inanimate our mechanical body parts possessed by Santeria, we each are Ella the monkey who loves too much murdering our quadruplegic desires, insane twin gynecologists, all of us, devising jagged instruments to gouge out alien genitalia—GIVE THE BIG THINGS IN LIFE A BREAK—sex shouldn't be shouted over a Scotch and soda but whispered with a scarfed head—I don't want to be tasteless as those dead who come back, not to haunt us, but to boast of death, as if they had any say in the matter as if the living should be awed by their windy ephemera *pale blue in the fore-ground swirling a muffled woooo woooo.*

One of the attributes of sociopaths is phosphorescence … match-like, quick, they make connections that flash brilliantly through the night, drawing the unsuspecting into a warp of reality. Typically they invent wild torturous pasts to gain sympathy from women *their fantasies gather strength over their heads, insidious haloes black as dried blood, glittering with the thunder of snapping bones.* Dion told me that men from the neighborhood bar gave him quarters to go buy ice cream so they could get his mother alone—KK doesn't believe it but I swallowed his fable hook line and sinker, felt pity for burly little Dion standing outside his mother's bedroom window licking his Rocky Road to the rhythm of creaking springs *knee-deep in a lime green fog populated by see-through ghosts skimpy as the kleenexes that scorched the dining room table* with such a gastronomic beginning no wonder he performed sex acts on a Mexican pastry. KK scoffed, "That's not anybody's childhood—that's the plot of *Marnie!*" "What's *Marnie?*" "*Marnie* by Alfred Hitchcock!" Against the screen of my mind shadowy figures arise … blonde girl … scantily clad mother … a strange threatening man, a sailor maybe … the three of them having an emotional scene near a stairway. KK continued, "That's why she became a kleptomaniac and stole the money from Sean Connery's safe. And look at Tippi—she spells her name with an "i" at the end!" A few days later on *Santa Barbara* Dr. Scott Clark confesses to Heather that every Tuesday his mother would give him a quarter to get a soda after school. And what was she doing all those afternoons at home? You guessed it—turning tricks to pay for his Christmas presents. When Scott found out he threw those tainted toys down the cellar stairs. I know how it feels, Scott *I know how it feels to find out.* Damn that Dion! I am Mina Harker Queen of the Undead, not some gullible bimbo! I'm turning State's Evidence, Public Enemy Number One in Dion's screwy cosmology *who cares if it's true or merely a dream spiraling into the darkness, a piece of cheap dinnerware covered with jewels.*

NOT A SOUL! Dion tossed me around the bed like a rag doll, pleading PLEASE DON'T TELL—favor escalated to warning DON'T TELL escalated to vow PROMISE YOU WON'T—TELL—which in realistic terms meant I only blabbed to C. and A., and with A. I didn't mention his name. How could Dion demand such a sacrifice of me—I'm an artiste *secrets rattle around in my cunt like bones* that night you crashed at my apartment I was in agony, hoping you wouldn't notice the bedlam vibes, trying to pull off composed and low key when I was dying to burst out, "Sing, you wouldn't believe what's been happening!" You are my best friend my confidante *I can't reveal any details his forehead his nose his eyes his lips were all quite distinctive in a way that I found attractive.*

Maybe it *is* true the body's full of memory *last night's quarrel is buried in my left shoulder a lifetime of love and anger lies hidden in this galaxy of cells* but I don't have a Rolfer on call to unlock the sensation *of all that smoothness Dion crouching over me on all fours his chest gliding the length of my back* by the next morning his touch is already dissolving like a ghost—it's imperative I translate this mute soup of physical undulations hissing atomic whirls into a syntax the mind can comprehend *all that smoothness Dion crouching over me on all fours his chest gliding the length of my back* the delicate chiaroscuro of aging bodies and young gestures *I couldn't roll over, his arched physique is a giant mouth I feel completely swallowed in him I say, "I'm completely swallowed by you."*

Love,
Mina

January 6, 1990

Dear Dr. Van Helsing,

Submission being a form of ecstasy … I am doing exactly what I *can* do: lying on my back flanneled in apricot gingham … feverish … beaded flesh so hot the word "furnace" emerges but there is no furnace *a bundle of chemical reactions* no need for fantasy with the physical world itself so bright and gauzy, blue radio on dresser olive Boy Scout shirt in closet, the foam mattress is *so* supportive … I sit up knees raised *pressure on heels ass and back* I lie back down eyes closed *pressure diffuses* harmony of traffic and birds outside the window … I breathe slowly let the nausea move through me in waves … circular cat purring gently to my left so intimate my knowledge of this alien species a marvel of sublimation … two drives seeking an object ….

In his recurring nightmare KK runs into a movie star on the street … he always asks for her autograph and she always agrees … she's his best friend … then the moment of horror when he searches for a pen that never appears five o'clock shadow pricking my right shoulder comfortable weight of his leg across mine I ask him questions— but typing and answering the phones have left him too exhausted to speak, something that never happens to the characters in his novel *promiscuous teenagers and mistaken identity* you've got to keep the narrative moving—Dion stood outside the bedroom window of a woman he adored content to watch her form stirring behind the curtains *a heightened sense of night the air brisk a perfect phase of the moon, when the extreme thingness of things makes them seem unreal* for a moment he felt he had stepped out of his life and into a work of art.

Like Sebastian in *Suddenly Last Summer* I need to write my yearly poem, to condense the buzzing swarm inside my head into a lapidary nugget *apples and oranges* the thoughts won't separate and regroup into something I can hand around *isn't she talented breathtaking witty au courant deep* I know I ought to seize my life by the throat and get on with it but the pink sheet crumbles like a pink sheet and the cat's purr vibrates my ribcage *object to object* a rise in temperature a change in blood sugar can distort the construct almost beyond recognition … all the nagging physical stuff that spells out *flu* or *fatigue*, all the internal stress and giddiness for which there is no vocabulary, it's as if no one who spoke ever got sick.

Floorboards creak in the apartment next door … the comforter puffs me up immense with down, KK cuddling and nuzzling like a child who has just met Mother Goose … his body so warm and open his eyes closed, breathing slow *the luxury of taking someone for granted* I babble for the two of us explaining the days before panty-hose, those awful girdles that came down practically to your knees, garters pressing into your flesh—in gym class they made you wear these hideous legless blue jumpsuits that snapped up the front and all the girls had keyhole-shaped indentations on their thighs it was gross and I was so embarrassed they made you line up naked for the showers with just these little hand towels, you had to choose to cover the top or the bottom, they weren't big enough for both, most of the girls chose the top, breasts being somehow worse than pubic hair which curls so far away from one's head—flat—disappearable beneath clothes … it is the rhythm of my words not the content that matters, KK is falling asleep but I don't feel ignored *every object in a dream is a piece of the dreamer* it's as if the words exist outside the two of us like a radio or the room itself. In his dream we relive Jules Dassin's *Dream of Passion* he is the imprisoned murderess Ellen Burstyn and I am the great actress Melina Mercouri badgering him with questions about a past he doesn't want to remember … Virginia Woolf driving though Richmond and thinking "nothing makes a whole unless I am writing."

Dishes go sour in the sink … who could … do … anything …
clothes all over the bedroom floor convoluted as a brain … fever
burns through to a simplicity I need but rarely have touched …
nighttime along the Marina sailboats delicate as wind chimes, the
bay mostly black an occasional iridescent sheen, Dion asked,
"What are those two towers over there?" His embarrassment when
I said "the Golden Gate Bridge" after all he's the native *born and
raised* and then there's you, Dr. Van Helsing, lulling yourself to
sleep by reciting your list of fears *no one loves me I'm all alone I'll
never get published in a good place die poor in the streets of some horrible disease* the process takes 45 minutes to an hour but works
every time *unconscious in your jungle sheets your dreams as frail as
your hands.* "Of course," you say, "this litany is the opposite of
Zen" but I wonder—given free rein the mind that overgrown
sentence rushes towards its inevitable pause, sinks into a comma,
the second "m" like an extra chromosome makes all the difference
coma comma coma comma sutra last night I tricked the cat into
biting its own tail and giggled "uroboros."

My mind's as twisted and rambling as a shaggy dog story … I
remember reading *East of Eden* in KK's bed … his books, in his bed,
what could have been sexier … but where is the punch line … KK
shifts, places my hand between his thighs the flesh is tender and lazy
the way I like it. Even after three and a half years of marriage I rarely
go there without an invitation, he has a big surprise: a hard-on *how
could this happen, he was falling asleep and I haven't done* anything …
desire implies a future I can't imagine: maybe if I was just tired but
the nausea … I rub its heart-shaped tip … he says, "I just wanted to
let you know." I roll into his body, flannel nightshirt bunched
about my waist, make my voice low and husky like a black and
white movie star: "Tank you, dahling, for zee standing ovation."

Love,
Mina

November 5, 1990

Dear Quincey,

I like your face … relentlessly pleasant and smiling a face devoid of dark corners. The first time ever I saw your face was in Norma's kitchen—I was feeling awkward and you were standing near the guacamole—whenever I looked in your direction you'd catch my eye and wouldn't let go *a missile dying for a target* I squeezed in next to you grabbed a tortilla chip and murmured, "Save me—that woman over there keeps trying to talk to me about Madame Blavatsky." I motioned towards the toaster oven, where a tall lean chestnut-haired woman hovered: Lucy. She was wearing a wool sheath, heels, a beige cashmere sweater, pearls *she looked like a First Lady* you just smiled and drank your Beck's. Then Lucy appeared at your side and whined, "Quincey, I need to go home now." I zoomed in on your left hands—and sure enough you had matching gold rings—thick and gaudy—like cigar bands that had won the lottery.

We wandered to opposite ends of the hall—as you idled by the stairs with your coat on, I stood in line for the bathroom—your eyes like ferocious beasts snared me and no matter how much I feigned interest in the ceiling or the doorknob they wouldn't let go. I stepped forward and said, "You make too much eye contact." You locked your arms and pouted, "Then I'll stare at the floor" and I was amazed how sexy you looked—all tiger like the long-legged women on MTV languishing in their negligees and anger. Your eyes are the devil's playthings their pupils glowing violet, the room threatening to dissolve.

We've met before, you and I—and when you read *Dracula* it will all come back to you. It's been a century since you poured your heart out to me and I still haven't recovered. Have you? The occasion is lovingly recounted in Dr. Seward's diary:

Van Helsing was evidently torturing his mind about something, so I waited for an instant, and he spoke:—

"What are we to do now? Where are we to turn for help? We must have another transfusion of blood, and that soon, or that poor girl's life won't be worth an hour's purchase. You are exhausted already; I am exhausted too. What are we to do for some one who will open his veins for her?"

"What's the matter with me, anyhow?"

The voice came from the sofa across the room, and its tones brought relief and joy to my heart, for they were those of Quincey Morris. Van Helsing strode forward, and took his hand, looking him straight in the eyes as he said:—

"A brave man's blood is the best thing on this earth when a woman is in trouble. You're a man and no mistake. Well, the devil may work against us for all he's worth, but God sends us men when we want them."

Quincey, DID YOU REALLY THINK YOU COULD GET TO KNOW DODIE WITHOUT HAVING TO DEAL WITH ME? She can tolerate ambivalence but I *Mina Harker Queen of the Dictaphone and Typewriter* always want to know what's what. Call me Mia— Sigourney—Catherine Deneuve—Fay Wray—I am the heroine of every horror movie—fearlessly I turn in the direction of your words/telekinetic activities and demand: WHO ARE YOU AND WHAT DO YOU WANT FROM ME?

He fails every test I throw his way yet, crazily, I keep coming back for more.

Beside me on the couch a young man called "Quincey" sat folded and morose *is this any way to show a girl a good time?* When the words HELP ME etched themselves across his forehead in reverse he simply sighed, "It's been a rough year." His soft blue eyes stared at the polished oak floor, with that HELP ME throbbing his forehead he looked like the lead in an Excedrin commercial, Excedrin *Plus*. A demon was inside his cranium scribbling her way out—I saw her last week in *Prom Night, Part II*—it was prom queen Mary Lou *burned to a crisp on the biggest day of her life* she came back from the grave *her dreams her young soul up in smoke* she came back. The jewels in her tiara were the source of her power—she possessed teenagers and computers, seduced all the wrong men, with a single evil glare she crushed a row of lockers accordion-style. I saw her scratch the same backwards HELP ME on a blackboard. Mary Lou (hidden on the other side of the board) was really writing forwards, but we the viewers reversed her words like a mirror. When a schoolgirl leaned towards the blackboard caressing the H with a manicured fore-finger Mary Lou's dead arms poked through the slate and jerked her inside—the board's chalky surface churned to a tur-bulent pool of black liquid as large block letters swirled around her screaming face. The young man sighed, "It's been a rough year." END OF TRANSMISSION. He sank down deeper into the cushions as if the year were a whirlpool drowning him in real time. Before this brooding man this vat of alphabet soup I had to grab onto something solid—my own elbows or the arm of the couch.

God sends us men when we want them. Quincey Morris—in *Dracula* you stomp around London and Transylvania with Stoker's motley gang of Victorian Eurotrash—but you stand out from them, a little apart from them—so American, so squeaky clean. Perched in front of my MacPlus my fingers itch for your "goshes" and "gee-whizes," your throat so pink beneath your button-down collar, all that unripe ruby potential—your inno-cence makes you exotic *firm and lean on the palate though not as exuberant as some* a fresh berry character I'd gulp down rather than savor—as a connoisseur I'm interested in your potential *a spiciness that could develop complexity with a few years of cellaring.*

He doesn't even have the patience to finish a novel—how's he going to deal with *me*, my line-up of selves as long and gilded as the Great Books of the Western World.

Reading this letter you will say *how dare she be so bold with a man she barely knows*—but I bet you won't show it to your wife. My epistolary urges are simultaneously high tech and primitive. Your letters are tame, your black scratches hand drawn in perfectly even rows—virtually marginless—no sides for the Great White Whatever to creep in, you keep to well-mannered topics, the nicknames of your relatives, an in-depth critique of Franz Wedekind (the claustrophobia of live personalities bungling lines from another world). *Shy yet persistent aromas of creamy lemon and apricot ... faintly grassy flavors that betray the region of origin ... a touch of light oak.* I can be elusive too. In one letter I made Dion sound so hot that Sing sputtered, "I can't imagine *him* that sexual." Glancing around the bedroom, I replied, "If it suits your writing, you can make a vacuum cleaner sexual." We were on the phone so she didn't realize I was seated on the floor beside my Hoover with the broken bag. Safety pins kept the dust from flying in my face.

Small of the Back, 1 pat = just passing by, 2 pats mean "Is anybody alive in there?" while 3 is a definite, "Hello, honey." What are you who do you want from me?

In the Ethiopian restaurant, did you know it was my thigh you were rubbing your leg against or did you think it was the table? I realize that touch is not an idea, but do you think this is a good one? A person can never tell what hocus-pocus an idle burnish will release. Look at Aladdin—take it from me—his survival was pure blind luck. Quincey, for all you know I Mina Harker who possess Dodie could in turn be possessed by Mary Lou who might be a marionette manipulated by Freddy Krueger ... WHO ...

that isn't blood on the front of my nightgown it's juice from the pomegranate I was eating during *Nightmare on Elm Street, Part 3*. All the special effects made me kind of messy—a mute boy, his arms and legs bound to the bedstead with tongues, the mattress dissolves to a rectangular pit over the fires of Hell—those tongues writhing around his wrists and ankles like fat snakes *even in his dreams the poor thing can't scream out his despair* my breast bloomed crimson in sympathy, like your breast, Quincey, bloomed for me in *Dracula*, page 408. If you had to save my soul all over again would you still impale yourself on the blade of a wild Gypsy? Dying on the manly shoulder of my betrothed you gazed up at me with your pragmatic blue eyes and feebly exclaimed, "See! the snow is not more stainless than her forehead! The curse has passed away!" I hate to break this to you, but with my libidinal atmospherics as of late, Love, I fear you may have perished in vain.

Yours,
Mina

February 7, 1991

Dear Sam,

Quincey is absent, absent as you. He's been in Barcelona for twelve days with his wife. Hieroglyphs litter my computer screen, I look back over my shoulder: a messy bed, a bed devoid of Quincey, of me, of both our bodies. I swivel in my office chair to better study these vanished others those two naked forms on the bed rolling about from pillow to pillow, silent and in slow motion like some corny film, gauze filter over the lens, shiny moments glinting in little star bursts. Twelve days is an eternity. My own ass is as good as anything, I suppose, to remember him by ... tender, burning from the inside out *in this coffee-scented morning an invasion incongruous as Magritte's locomotive* ... our last night together I wrote my love all over him: purple bruises with a flourish of red filaments, how's he going to hide that from his wife when he takes off his pants in Barcelona?

Writing has always been more sexual than sex, the sustained arousal of never quite getting it right.

A bit of post-orgasmic conversation returns to me:

> Me: And he lived to tell about it.
> Quincey: Who would he tell?
> Me: He tells the sunset.

I imagine Quincey flying all the way to Spain to try to forget me in the Mediterranean sunset—it's so Marguerite Duras. I underline a passage from *Blue Eyes, Black Hair*: "She looks at him. It's inevitable. He's alone and attractive and worn out with being alone. As alone and attractive as anyone on the point of death."

A married man who drinks by himself and sleeps on the couch. I tell myself I'm better off outside his life, his tortured take on the mundane.

He mailed me a postcard from Berkeley the day he left. His thoughts are elegant and black—a large passage is written over a smear of white-out—with the tip of a butter knife I scrape it away. A corroded message slowly emerges—I can't make out every word but the subject matter is Freud on cryptography, how it reveals the inner man. Quincey knew I'd excavate his secret, so well has he trained me in the labyrinthine pleasures of the *hidden pulling away from the toll booth Quincey says softly but firmly "I thought you were going to abuse me." I know this is a code but for what? Tentatively I pat his thigh, fumble with a shirt button … yes? … no? … then the waistband his zipper parts as easily as his lips and I bow my head to the inevitable … over the Golden Gate Bridge, down the endless expanse of Lombard Street … Quincey won't let me see where I'm going, my cheek brushing denim my mouth full of cock. From the waist up he's a model citizen of the road, observing the speed limit, smiling at fellow motorists at stoplights as he murmurs "Oh wow" or "This is great."*

My lover has lips as round and swollen as life preservers, but they don't make me feel very safe.

Slits of world peek through levelor blinds—Quincey's out there, maneuvering his way through a foreign tongue. The distance is inconceivable: thousands of miles, a handspan in an atlas. Is Spain any farther from San Francisco than Berkeley? Hours pass, days pass, but not my appetite, its impenitent accrual … I burnish my favorite moments like worry stones, superimpose them on the daily, try to survive their unavoidable dilution. Does Quincey flicker through these words like a summoned ghost—or am I driving him even farther away with my insomniac urge to reinvent him *no wife, willing to slay dragons, etc.* no wonder I'm always surprised when he's through the door—suddenly—actually—rubbing his erection against me, all pleasure, or apologizing with tears in his eyes. The head of his penis is unbelievably soft, velvet without the nape.

He is flying far above me in the ink-colored sky UNREACHABLE. Days Without Someone. I should have asked him for something—something funky of his, to wear. One unseasonably warm afternoon he left a sweater here—I hardly knew him but I pulled it over my naked breasts—the sleeves hanging to the tips of my fingers were his hands holding me down, the rough brown wool his chest, his back *sheathed in his molecules I felt positively amniotic* ... after I came I wiped the collar between my legs. And the magic worked—we were lovers in a couple of weeks. When I told him my ritual he wore the sweater to work the next day, idiotically smiling to himself, my secretions a necklace about his fine German throat.

His Lou Reed cassette, a prison novel by Albertine Sarrazin, a magazine from San Diego: Quincey clings to the things he loaned me *these fragments I have shored against my ruins.* High-strung and schmaltzy I play "Classic Film Scores for Bette Davis," a CD he bought in admiration of my intelligence and drama, the large gestures with which I snub him at parties. If he lit two cigarettes in his mouth at once, he knows I wouldn't laugh ... graciously I take what he offers, suck the moist tip with a broad jerky movement *let's not ask for the moon* Quincey points out the constellations, the brown stars in my iris, Venus, Orion. "You look good." He said it whenever we got together. Sometimes he added a flourish of adverb, "You look really good." But sitting here at the keyboard in a flannel bathrobe without Quincey to look at me, do I look like anything at all? Sam, can you see me? In the vast black Beam Me Up Scotty, how's my reception?

There's not an inch of me he hasn't licked—some residue of him must linger, an astral impression radiating from my body pink smeared with yellow trailing off into the atmosphere *his skin smells of soap, his hair like cherries* in public he blankly wavers beside the Mrs.—how do I pull off casual with this man who just that morning stuck his tongue up my ass, I strain to look past those pale eyes instead of burrowing. As he steps past me his body fractures into a galaxy of adorable touchables, and now, oh, Sam, all those pieces are in Barcelona with Lucy.

Quincey says we're Paolo and Francesca, a damnation so beautiful it made Dante weep. I'll never understand the ease he can come to … then walk away from … such pleasure. I've always been either not there or too eager. My writing like grave worms moves in on Quincey destroying his last grasp on corporeality. I sense his spirit yearning for something to embody: the stiff daguerreotypes of my memory, a brace clamped to his neck for these unreasonable exposures: Quincey ravishing my armpit, his penis probing my mouth my ear my ass my cunt and then my thighs my breasts anything that can be clenched, Quincey brushing a lock of my hair across his lower lip, holding my hand through his colorful glove. I'm growing antsy with this script of the remembered, nothing but theme and variation—I want to defile him, rearrange his history as easily as my hairdo. Quincey is a red brick wall. Before him a man in a brown suit is upside down in midair, having fallen from Quincey's window—the artist has drawn the man's scream very clumsily so that his mouth looks like Howdy Doody's, giving an unintentional comic air to the impending squash. Quincey as the red brick wall is impassive through all this.

The writing won't let me be—I have to keep pen and paper beside my bed—it sneaks up on me in the middle of the night. Then leaves. The world encroaches, Nina Simone on the jukebox, two glasses of red wine on a table the size of a crossword puzzle. Dion sits facing me, with blue eyes, black hair. As he leans forward his chest seems to swallow the table, he says, "The only thing I have under my wings are shadows." Occasionally his large hand wanders across a bit of my body: a stray I could easily fuck with affection, then walk away from. Quincey is off drinking sangria with his wife *there is nothing in our situation to remain faithful to.* Quincey grows tiny, crushed with immensity, like the end of *The Incredible Shrinking Man* when the infinitesimal merges with the infinite and we know we're not watching any ordinary Hollywood schlock but a slice of Deep Meaning. Still, he won't be eradicated—as I make coffee Quincey's still wearing his denim jacket he lifts up the back of my nightgown pulls me to him biting my lips his cold hands cupping my ass—this memory inflicts a pang of arousal, a cramp in the groin, painful.

Late at night the phone turns tensile, surreal, an implement aliens use in their sex experiments: his wife just a room away, Quincey begins to masturbate through the receiver *"I'm going to tighten my hand around your throat so you can't move and then I'm going to stick my ... "* Across the bay I self-consciously whisper, "I'd like that." He's amazed at the volumes of cum sprayed across his belly, scoops some up with a finger and eats it. He's so kinky, yet sweet, with a cleanness about him like a Cranach ... beneath his dewy skin that fine chiselled bone straining ... he asks me to squeeze his nipples, hovers above me a bright ecstatic angel eyes closed biting his lower lip, he quietly throws his head back then slowly brings it down chin to chest then back up again: this cum shot is precise, yet flattened and blurred like a color xerox of a collage; as I type it a frenetic neighbor stomps above my head. Sex, no matter how fondly recalled, comes across so generic. Only the spurts of conversation between gasps and undulations remain with me, the way he calls me "Babe" when he's excited—nursing my neck or shoulder he reaches up and sighs, "Anything you want, Babe," and I feel cheap in a way I want to go on forever.

We lingered in the shadow of the coastal highway, the salty breeze cooling my exposed cunt. "Suck my cock," yelled a man we couldn't see, exiling us to the beach ... small birds scuttled along the wet sand as if animated by Disney ... the onrushing waves left soap suds at our feet. Quincey reached under my black silk overcoat, under my skirt, his forefinger twirling pubic curls—the shore was scattered with city dwellers their features surprisingly distinct beneath the full moon—before their eager nocturnal eyes I felt like a potboiler, the kind of book read by people who shop at Walgreen's *let's fly into the sun let's fly anywhere these beachcombers can't see.* Last night falling asleep I looked into the shutter of a camera, a giant mechanical iris spiraled closed, blocking out the light, blocking out Quincey. Maybe I should call it quits maybe I should wipe my dirty fingers across this page, have his bastard baby.

His eyes are the color of my coffee cup he has two hands tendons form deep ridges on the top of his feet: a minefield of camouflage: if his wife sees through my writing I may never see him again. His name's not Quincey, he's not in Spain really: encoded in my language Quincey remains disembodied as he is from my life. His corpse walks in Barcelona—it is beet red beneath a peeling nose and baseball cap *desire that giant burrowing nematode sneaks up and grabs me* rattling my chest, Quincey's wormy laugh. He fucked me sideways while I fucked his mouth with my right hand, he sucked so hard I thought the flesh was going to fall away like over-cooked chicken—he said he was coming at both ends one long vibrating tunnel ... what's inside ... what's out ... the hair on his ass grates against my tongue ... when I lick him there I'm leaving more than saliva behind: sibilants ... fricatives

... a layer of soul ... I removed the belt from my robe and tied his wrists to the bedstead—do whatever you want with me, he said, make it hurt *he wanted to be pliable, pliable as absence ...* beyond a few entries in my diary, the gush of a schoolgirl, I never could write about Quincey *I was silenced before the undefinable thingness of his lips, his hands, his cock, all the insistent anatomical components ... then he left and the words rushed in like vultures, picking away, redefining.*

I am aching. I am alone. If only I could give a bourgeois patina of meaning to this. Something French: "Pleasure is the creation of the mind, the body can't do anything without it." I'm lying on my stomach and Quincey is fucking me from behind—it feels pretty good, though I don't take his efforts seriously—I wriggle my bladder into the optimal position, patiently anticipating My Turn—then abruptly the flesh of my vagina crystallizes *the unsuspected is inevitable there is no stopping* and when it does happen I raise up on my arms and cry out. This is an ideal state of discourse—unmediated, with a totally receptive audience. Quincey, how could you throw me into this solitary confinement? Here on the inside we call it the "hole." I'm distressed by this lack of feedback. This silence. I jump out a window *wheeling around for one second which is long and good, a century* my foot breaks with the impact so I crawl on knees and elbows, dragging this useless lump to the highway *I am oozing mud, thorns scratch me at random from bushes—another century goes by, I can't recognize anything*—then I hear the air brakes, the slam of a door, boot-sized footprints—"Monsieur Le Truckdriver," I plead, "I'm a prisoner of love, the dark side of someone's double life. Please, will you sneak me to Paris!"

Eagerly he licks his cum from my mouth: I want to bring the reader this close to writing. Into a barely imaginable future I try to project this erotic reader, an incubus complete with organs that function and hands to hold my pages. This image isn't any more satisfying than if I were to tape an obscene message for my phone machine *sorry I'm not home right now but I'm hot for your …* it just isn't the same as having a body on the other end of the line, the bona fide heavy breathing.

Quincey, where are you? Wrap your phone cord around your cock. Remember me.

When he was aroused, Quincey turned monosyllabic, which really did it for me. I'd be chattering away and all he'd say was, "Yeah," his voice low and raspy, urgent as a wet tongue in my ear. Passion did a quick dissolve and I waxed silent as Quincey filled the frame, became the frame: his body, his emanations. "Yeah."

"Dear William Gibson:
   Right now I'm reading *Blue Eyes, Black Hair.* I'm afraid that Marguerite Duras is going to destroy my style—I find myself wanting to do all this frou-frou shit that I don't like even when she does it. I've been working on this prose thing about longing and absence, what it's like to experience a person who is not there. Sitting here at my MacPlus, I wonder about my main character—is he a sort of entity haunting the screen—*where* does he exist? Since I've so recently read *Mona Lisa Overdrive*, I'm reminded of cyberspace, how cyberspace is your metaphor for desire and longing, the way we spend most of our time away from the loved/coveted person, and are frustrated by our unrealistic wish to have them with us instantly on demand. In cyberspace we can relive heightened emotional/sexual states otherwise lost to us just by their being transitory—at the end of *Mona Lisa Overdrive*, Angie becomes not a physical bride, but a bride to her lover's imagination. I'm hesitant about responding to your writing because you must have responses to your writing up the wazoo."

The present tense just won't stick to him—narrative has thrust him finally, irretrievably IN THE PAST. The tendons there are so pronounced his feet look webbed—I used to run my fingers in the fissures that extend from toes to ankle, daydreaming of roads carved between mountains, of running away. He said that entering me was going home—but what's home, Quincey—the couch in the living room, where you spend the night, depressed, after your friends leave? When he looked at his house through my eyes, he claimed his things look interesting. From the little I saw of them, his things were simple, mostly secondhand, suggesting a lower socio-economic status than his own. One night while I sucked his toes and he sucked mine, we somehow managed to fuck at the same time, a sort of elongated 69 pivoting on his cock. I turned my head and smiled at him, said, "This is very Kama Sutra." "You're right," he answered, "But what would they call it … something like 'turkey clawing under bright moon.'" And then he fell out of me.

Quincey's flown into the sun and my heart is in a window display in North Beach—a valentine of dried roses and grass, it looks like a wreath you'd see on a pet's grave.

Before I'd ever touched him I wanted Quincey dearly—just the thought of him would get me wet. Once I had his body I was no longer moved by the idea, but by the thing itself. Next to him everything else feels bland and disconnected *maybe it's all been a dream, a very small and savage dream* his eye contact hypnotized me, leaning so close his breath flushed my cheek, peering *into* me, he learned every dot in my iris—he used them to navigate his way to my soul. He stole it. And then he went to Barcelona, carelessly tossing it back at me.

All I can imagine saying upon his return is, "I don't know, Quincey, you feel so alien."

Duras: "A swell surged up to the wall of the house but fell back at his feet as if to avoid him; it was fringed with white and alive, like writing." Alive, yes, but at whose expense? I ache for the innocents like you Sam who try to befriend me. Bloodthirsty and iridescent, writing sucks the marrow from the unsuspecting then sits back picking its teeth with a rib. Poor Quincey never had a chance *do what you want with me, he said*—now he totters along the shore, his tortured features barely recognizable: a body pink and bloated from fermenting gasses—his pale eyes plead—but the damage has already been done. I've seen enough movies to not touch him—the slightest pressure of my hand would upset the delicate biochemical balance. A heap of dust or something more gooey collapsing at my feet, not even a shell would I be left with.

A shifting, a readiness—fear—my body is a mold waiting for plastique. Late this evening Quincey will return.

My mind is clear, clear as the night we parked in Marin overlooking the bay. There in the front seat of his car Quincey first made me come. He marvelled, the witness to a miracle—or, a child with a toy that finally works. I teased, "Quincey, it's a normal body function." The Golden Gate Bridge filled the windshield, gold and gleaming. "The tower of Camelot," he said. Craning his neck up at the heavens—boyish—he pointed out Orion, only visible in the Northern Hemisphere, only in winter. We huddled together, our clothes still undone, watching the crescent moon blink through wisps of clouds, and I thought to myself this is happiness. The last time I kissed him he was in a doorway, leaving. I stood on my toes to get closer and breathed, "I'll immortalize you." There's something Faustian about this story. I can invoke his name, his personality, but my loving descriptions of his body are bloodless, as though I were parroting another author. I remember his penis was friendly—just like him. But that's it. If I touch him again will it merely feel awkward ... or good as a first time?

In just a few hours he'll be near enough to know ...

Writing versus life—is the one flight, the other hot pursuit? I don't remember. I once was a nerdy high school girl with nothing much else to do than lie on her twin bed filling a spiral notebook with poems of isolation and black curtains a vulnerability so coddled it grew sentient. If this were a modernist novel, in the end I suppose I'd choose Life. The phone rings after midnight. A man's voice on the line, urgent and impossible. He doesn't identify himself, implores, "Can I come over I need to see you. Right now!" Without missing a beat I chirp back, "Well, Babe—what are you waiting for?"

Love,
Mina

October 22, 1991

Dear Dion,

At Stephen's housewarming Quincey and I pushed our secret
affair to the limit by having a fight in the window seat, two
"virtual strangers" making faces at one another and whispering
angrily. The effect was definitely Dada—we were a flurry of
angles that kept shifting planes, me a woman wailing (under her
breath) that her heart had been decimated, him using that god-
awful word "ambivalent," whenever his wife would peek around
the corner we'd freeze—his German lips pursed, me fiddling with
a slice of cheese and a Triscuit. When I spied you in the doorway
my face lit up like a jack-o-lantern—I snatched up this unex-
pected visitation, this opportunity to dismiss Quincey as a piece
of fluff in the glittering social phenomenon known as Mina
Harker. I swaggered into the kitchen and said something seduc-
tively snotty to you. As I leaned against the sink full of crushed
ice you leaned your leg against mine cooing that letters were
made for flirtation *the camera was off kilter I felt so Dr. Caligari*
then you shifted the angle of your hip fusing our bodies from
knee to waist *we were practically superimposed* I nervously took a
sip of Johnnie Walker and really started getting into your ideas
*maybe, I thought, maybe I was wrong, maybe Chopin is a great com-
poser* until Quincey appeared beside the refrigerator, glaring. I
grabbed your arm and we exited to the back porch. Did I make
a fool of myself thrashing about like that? The air was cool, the
rails of Californian wood held me up, as I stood beside you
drinking and smoking, entirely and artlessly myself—it was sort
of like being on drugs.

But that was ages ago. Another lifetime. I sit here at the computer my hips spreading across the chair full and funky in a
cotton nightgown, a couple of striped socks dangle from ankles,

the left foot is beige and yellow, the right foot beige and pink, my hair a messy French twist thrown together with a pair of chop sticks. It's been six months since I fucked anyone but my husband. Stereo headphones press Leonard Cohen into my brain *she said I'm tired of the war I want the kind of work I had before a wedding dress or something white to wear upon my swollen appetite*—I am blesséd, the Joan of Arc of monogamy, translucent beams of sunlight stream through the Nottingham lace curtain, glint off the edges of my sword, glow softly along my deeply mysterious cheekbones *in the fields among the sheep dead saints come to me whispering the evils of self-representation lalala lala la* I don't know how long I can stand such peace. Sprawled at the end of the couch with his shirt off KK muses, "I've enjoyed being your lover lately." I snap back, "What do you mean by this 'lately?' What was wrong with it before?" The framed poster rattles on the wall behind me—don't worry, it isn't another earthquake just some heavy-footed neighbor climbing the stairs.

It's been six months since I broke up with Quincey. At least now I always know which basket my eggs are in … fucking KK and then Quincey and then KK, and so often, two such different men, I felt like a cross-eyed hooker mouthing the same endearments to both—one liked me active the other passive I became the Yin Yang symbol a drunken circle the white paisley threatening to devour the black or vice versa it was all so confusing who liked it hard who liked it soft who was bigger who was smaller I felt like Goldilocks grabbed his balls and squeezed all the while groaning out those dirty words he's always asking for—KK's voice rose an octave as he scuttled to safety, "Mina, did you learn that from Quincey … is he into pain?" Oops.

Dion, the past year has convinced me that in bed I could get into *anything*. This is why, as a character, I'm so universal.

Barefoot in T-shirt yeasty armpits sleep-encrusted eyes and jeans I heat up minestrone in an old pot. Axl Rose blasts outside my kitchen window—I'm trying to construct my opening paragraph but my attention is divided as the time I had sex with you on the floor while watching *One Flew Over the Cuckoo's Nest.* I want to pitch that god damned radio in a hydrotherapy tank fry the bastard who cranked up the volume. Last weekend I threw open the window and climbed into KK's side of the bed ... *his hands should be patented* ... I screamed out, my lungs quivering all over the mattress, the page. Then I heard the brat next door ask, "Daddy, what's that?" "Nothing, come on inside." Perhaps you were right when you wrote, "She's more of an exhibitionist than a narcissist." I'm pushing 40 and I've just learned how to keep my whites white, folding my wash I'm prim and proud as a femme in a daytime TV commercial my panties so bright I need sunglasses to look at them *it was deep into his fiery heart he took the dust of Joan of Arc and then she clearly understood if he was fire oh she must be wood.* QUINCEY SAID HE COULD NEVER MARRY ME BECAUSE MY BLUE COLLAR BACKGROUND WAS ALSO HIS *beyond that, the lean sentences, barely long enough to hold the verbs still* in his youth Quincey worked in a paper mill—the thought of a life with me brought back Bosch-like visions of pushing around pulp with a pitch fork beside his alcoholic father ... sweaty ... twisted ... ineffectual ... during sex he wanted me to be pushy but ... "If I were free and you were free," he told me, "I still wouldn't marry you." Dion, I offered him my fabled nectar that ruby burst of divinity that mortals have sold their souls for—and was Quincey Morris grateful? Not on your life—he plummeted me with the mundane, flailed me with tales of his weasel-eyed wife *her* medication *her* hand-knit sweaters *her* suspicions *her* sexual indifference *her* American Express card *her* New Age pretensions *her* hysteria *her* rich warring parents *her* food preferences *her* awkward kissing techniques *my* blue collar background *it isn't ink that forms this dot-matrixed missive but my bruises.*

If I only could see these major experiences as meditative opportunities rather than crises or traumas, we'd all move on a lot quicker.

When I returned from the bathroom KK was lying on his back his shirt unbuttoned and crumpled around his shoulders his pants unzipped exposing an erect penis languishing to the left. By the way he ran his hand through his brown mane of hair I could tell that more than his clothes were undone. The pink lampshade made his flesh so rosy against the muted green of his shirt he looked like a sex angel, like the cover of a gay novel instead of my husband. I crossed my wrists in front of his face and said, "Tie me up buttercup," and I felt like Paula, the trampy young heroine of his first book—not his wife *sanctioned by 2,000 years of patriarchy and KK's insurance* afterwards he said I was so full of life so vivid *a beautiful tropical bird in a death frame* an ancient woman rides the bus her puffy white hair topped with a glitter-gold tiara studded with blue rhinestones, she keeps fussing with her hair, yanking the lot of it, a cheap wig, back and forth, when I squint it looks like her skull is made of elastic, on her feet white disco pumps with soles one inch thick, she opens a gold filigree lipstick case raises its mirror to her cat's eye glasses then pulls on elbow length black lace gloves *I can't get enough of her* she begins talking about opera. Every time you open your eyes environmental bits and pieces find you, stick to your fingers like angry birds squawking for a context *the burden of Modern Art weighs so heavy on my shoulders* I rush from one nodding head to another gather bits of data like a lint brush leaving behind bits of the last nodding head's life, images jar and jumble, become something *other* lie on their backs with their skirts hiked high, Melanie Griffith vacuuming her boss' apartment in bra and garter belt *no purpose but to be nasty* flipping through the channels I land on a woman in a hospital bed, in her persistent vegetative state she doesn't look anything like her graduation photo (mascara-globbed lashes hair swept back from her cheeks

102

like wings)—until her watery-eyed father mentions a pronoun I think I'm watching a young boy as she rolls her close-cropped head about incessantly chomping her front teeth up and down over her lower lip like a distracted Bugs Bunny *something's very male* his penis twitching against my ass *galvanized*. "It's been days," he says, "I'm overdue like a library book."

A process of freezing boundaries in the emptiness of the mind … plot is black cover stock onto which I paste whatever sparkles.

Other women I'd seen there were turning tricks but I was having an affair. Quincey paid $30 for an hour and a half in the hot tub and two Calistogas—it was his wife's money, so why not? We walked down a hallway under neon track lighting the pale blue glow adding an avant garde twist to an old story. Quincey locked the door as I sat on the double bed, really a muslin-covered slab of foam on a platform—sometimes we didn't even get wet, and when we did it was just an afterthought. Our love chamber was stark with concrete and chlorine—the only light wavered from the bottom of the whirring tiled pool, eerie and steamy like the mouth of a volcano. After our fight at Stephen's I fucked him only twice—Dion, here we are—in the midst of the penultimate moment—Quincey and I are going at it with the intensity of people in the movies, he should have ripped my clothes off, instead he put on my slip—black with a lace bodice—he looked so luxurious black silk night clinging to the creamy skin of his torso, Elizabeth Taylor, *Cat on a Hot Tin Roof*, I tied my braided leather belt around his wrists and turned up the jacuzzi to muffle the slaps. Even though I was giving him this special true extra-marital treat he was absent, lost to me, his pleasure incongruous and insubstantial like the hologram of Liz in Michael Jackson's video of "Leave Me Alone." When we repeated the above a week later at my place, I sat up lit a cigarette and murmured, "I'm having an anxiety attack." *Desired ends were no longer attainable: this was it: our final telesis* THAT WHICH WAS IS OVER.

When I untied his wrists the braided leather left an impression exactly like an inch wide tire track. I exclaimed, "You look like you've been run over by a Tonka truck!"

Quincey would come in my arms and then start weeping—he made me feel like his salvation *the flames they followed Joan of Arc as she came riding though the dark*—and I am salvation, Dion, I really am, salvation personified, I am the new voice America's been waiting for—first there was Lenny Bruce then there was me then Christian Slater in *Pump Up the Volume* the pirate radio DJ stands on a jeep as the FCC closes in. He squints at the crowd with his Jack Nicholson eyes and shouts through the microphone: "High school is hell, but suffering teens everywhere, the point is to Get Through It." *A most satisfying escape from the baggage of subtlety.* Rebel DJ wears glasses and hunches over when he walks: this means he's a sensitive intellectual *right up my alley* I could teach that Christian a thing or two rolling about on his parents' lawn his shirt finally off moles spattering his back like the Milky Way such a perfectly imperfect body get rid of that little tramp you're with drive your stake through my heart I won't complain *he saw me wince he saw me cry he saw the glory in my eye.* The point is: there is nothing to get through—high school is an existential condition—*my* hormones have been raging for centuries the point is: how can two people fuck like demons then keep it casual.

Out of context out of mind.

Hair as blond as Quincey's, though not the same eyes—these are bluer and rounder—like the world. Let's call him Rendezvous. He's sitting across from me in the Mexican restaurant, antlers and stuffed birds hang with Christmas glitter above our chatting heads. Why just push my chile relleno across the plate, why not push him a bit: "Do you know why I wanted to know you, it's because I dreamt about you, I had these *very intense* dreams about you." Does this line sound familiar? I stole it from you. Rendezvous says he's flattered to be part of my unconscious, rather than the typical line women use on him: "you've got such big blue eyes." Blue eyes trail me *dreamlike, the sea, the sky; needles* the last four men I've slept with have had them (including you) a statistic that says more about the demographics of San Francisco intelligentsia than my desire *they call her the Aryan mistress—naked together their skin is so white you need sunglasses just to look at it.* I continue, "Rendezvous, you don't seem like the kind of guy who'd be lacking in interested women." "Oh, quite the opposite." The opposite of what? I can tell from his tone he isn't talking *drought* but he isn't bragging either—as always Rendezvous is understated. Across the room, a drunken woman shouts, "Olé!" It's been six months—still, how did I, Mina Harker, end up with a textbook heterosexual, a man in a million, sexually secure, in charge *where are the interesting little wormholes for me to poke my fingers into?* After a few more sips of *cerveza* he comments, "There's something very male about you." He says this casually, as if observing my shoe size. Fidgeting there in my black lace bra and panties I feel like one of those cross-dressing married men Dear Abby's always featuring, who get run over by a car and at the hospital their secret is found out. *Get this guy in the Fredericks of Hollywood!* I wipe the cheese from my chin, "Male about me?" This is where I tell him that getting to know a person feels like crucifixion. He puts down his fork peers sincerely through his glasses and replies, "No one's ever put it to me quite like that before." DODIE ARE YOU OUT THERE? THIS IS MINA SPEAKING. DAMN IT, GIRL, YOU'VE GOT TO DO BETTER BY ME THAN THIS!

With my weapons I was a woman and if I was to die I would not die as an insect in the jaws of the spider monster. Rendezvous is teaching my Hanuman book this fall. He has me where he wants me—on his Freshman Lit syllabus sandwiched between Aeschylus and Ibsen *Mina Harker an assignment, a literature machine* how can I proceed? I NEED AN OBJECT OF ILLICIT SEXUAL FASCINATION! Will you be that for me again, Dion, a little erotic trinket, the latest charm dangling from my bracelet? To be realistic, it would have to be a necklace to hold all of my charms, one of those flapper necklaces that descends to the navel. I've been at this a long time.

When Rendezvous asked if I had a marriage of convenience I snooted back, "No, we have lots of sex just like NORMAL PEOPLE do!"

Dismemberment, however, has this advantage *we get to see all the parts.*

In college I was pals with a gay man named Ted. This was in Southern Indiana and Ku Klux were performing their hooded hijinx in the next town. Since Ted was black we decided to play Interracial Couple. After midnight, arms locked we staggered down the jasmine-scented streets in bell bottoms drunk and high. We had our moments of glory: on Kirkwood a boonie in overalls stared hostilely, and outside the Bluebird a guy hollered something rude from a pick-up truck. Laughing our asses off we yelped, "Honey, if you only knew!" Then we stopped beneath a streetlight to make out *my tongue slithering down to meet his tonsils* sometimes we'd forget we were pretending and then things would get tense. Eventually Ted fell in love with a law student and moved to Indianapolis. Ted suggested we check out a drag show at The Golden Door, the acts were imported from Chicago, supposedly the best in the Midwest. I was hesitant, intimidated even—never having been to a drag bar before I was afraid I'd lose my edges there, get trapped in some Isherwood *Cabaret* time-warp, my fingernails green my gender so bent children would snicker and throw rocks at me. A couple of frail old-timers sang in thin off-key altos, but Sasha D'Or, flashing her boas and cleavage lip-synched through a smashing Donna Summer. When she leaped on stage a dozen lesbians ran up and stuffed dollar bills into Sasha's black lace panties *there was something very male about her* it was all great fun—I marveled to Ted how these queens were so much better at being women than I would ever be *femininity as a conditioned response* all young women should come and see this, I argued, as a sort of rite of passage, then some consciousnesses would really start getting raised *love to love you baby* I stumbled to the restroom through the hooting continuum of men and women and wooden chairs—there was only one stall, so I squeezed in line with the herd of drunk, bawdy, apparently females. I admired myself in the mirror: flushed but acceptable in jeans and a see-through blouse spattered with a jungle print *I was a walking Wild Kingdom monkeys mastodons exotic birds*—the chubby dyke in front of me turned around, poked her finger at the sheer menagerie which gamboled across my breasts, and whispered, "I like your elephants!"

The image a fountain spilling forth … words.

Dion, I miss you, miss your callused hands like claws pawing my cunt, my cunt weeps just thinking of you *hot salty honey* your long skinny cock curling back on itself like a question mark *let me be your answer, let me put my lips around that cock and suck it until my throat caves in* WHAT AM I SAYING? I'm sorry, Dion, to objectify you, your hands your cock your name *what's private what's public* I CAN'T STOP MYSELF *is there anything out there that isn't sexual* I'm a prisoner of jouissance *and then you pressed your thigh against mine and I thought of pistons churning, my intestines were slippery longing in their formlessness to consume an unusual external and yes I have a cunt and yes it was involved in all of this,* "Dion" *I murmured my lips of cool copper beckoning* HELP ME TURN IT OFF *I bang my metaphorical fists against the door of meaning* tell Tiki to pay no attention, stretch out your arms and yawn *Oh, that's just Mina being Mina, poor thing, trapped in the midst of her literary conventions.* You are the dressmaker's dummy I project my fantasies on—the robins and mice and I rush in with ribbons and satin and *voila!* you stand there radiant with a twinkle in your eye. You should have been at the *OutWrite* party last March—the gala event was held in a vacant mansion—a gilt elevator rattled and art nouveau banisters snaked to the second floor. As I tunneled aimlessly through the maze of empty rooms I thought of *Mysteries of Udolpho*: anybody with this much money who would choose red flocked wallpaper had to be demonic. In the grand ballroom an apparition, the seamstress son of a Wisconsin welder, with this glorious tutu flouncing from his waist, ruffle upon ruffle of stiff sequined netting in violet, red, gold and green, the top layer an inspiration of camouflage-patterned cotton, colliding blobs of khaki and brown—scary when neofascist youths parade it on Haight Street—but on a tutu it gives the effect of lush tropical plumage peeking through the bush. I ran up to the dressmaker and gushed, "Do you make those for women too?" He undid the drawstring, stepped out of it and handed it over! I slipped the tutu over my party dress, the dressmaker threw his arms in the air and exclaimed, "There, you're officially a fairy!" And I was—in every sense of the word—transcending gender, transcending species *Tinkerbell à la mode.*

I just committed a forbidden act in a public restroom. Afterwards, for the first time in two weeks, when I looked in the mirror I felt attractive.

I was spending the summer in Sarasota with my friend Darryl who was groundskeeper at the Selby Botanical Gardens—orchids grew from banyan trees in my backyard. Tourists paid $2 a head to come in and look at them. I expected to stumble upon a pretzel-legged Siddhartha, the bright waxy petals floating above his head announcing Paradise. Instead, I stumbled down the road to the only "hip" bar in the city. At twenty-three my hair hung to my waist and no amount of feigned sophistication would eradicate the freckles from my nose—bouncers saw me as moving prey—after the usual hassle over my expired student ID *why don't you get a driver's license little girl* I draped myself on a stool like a seductive alien fauna, drinking wine and writing in my diary. A man with a burr haircut pointed to my notebook and said, "I never expected to find someone like you in a place like this." *Every time you open your eyes environmental bits and pieces find you* I don't remember his name, but later that night we had sex on the front steps of a stucco church—they were stubby little steps, no more than three inches high, so it was relatively easy to lie down on them. I loved the erotics of the landscape— the salty gulf breeze, his cum gleaming beneath the streetlight, palm tree shadows skittering across the tan on my normally pale Northern flesh *I was a sea shell he'd found on one of his walks, he glued me to his cock an incredible feat of visual condensation* the next morning I waited for the bus in a denim jumper exhausted, headachy, gloating over how perfectly the church step escapade fit in with my project of leading The Most Decadent Life Ever Lived By a Girl From Indiana—the only time women in Indiana had sex outdoors was when they went camping—and that was in a tent—I had really done it this time. An old woman sitting beside me on the wooden bench struck up a conversation. When it came up that I was just visiting for the summer, the woman said, "Did your parents let you come?" What an insult! Here I was trying to be Christine Keeler and she was treating me like a high school girl! *A self-image an object-image and an affect.* To make matters worse, when we finally got around to doing it in the guy's bed the sex was dull. He went in the living room to sulk among his piles of junk. I put on his boxer shorts and told my woes to his roommate, who'd been having psychic piano-playing experiences ever since he'd taken an overdose of mescaline in Canada. As the roommate and I fucked I could hear the other guy kicking a hubcap across the living room floor, and then I came—the first time ever, with a man—the musician had a more varied palette, let me rub myself against his thigh until I went as crazy as he. Afterwards we broke into that same church and there in the stuccoed dark he played some incredible channeled music on the pipe organ—a scene straight out of *Phantom of the Opera* only better because it was orchestrated by the Beyond.

Waking this morning I could barely move my head *against my ear a rumbling like a motor* my cat Blanche was sleeping on my hair *gray blur in the periphery* straining under the weight of that feline slumber I dreamt I was a statue coming to life … images approached me unbuttoning their meaning like a lover his shirt *Quincey swore he loved me but in the end he was nothing but a myclonic jerk* I decided to blow off the day in North Beach, on Powell a young woman in greasy hair and jeans was seated on the sidewalk munching a powdered donut, when a pigeon approached she burst into a rage and yelled, "What the fuck do you want you little bastard!" And then I turned the corner and bumped into a Chinese funeral—brass band in dark uniforms with gold piping, marching up Vallejo, behind it a small white car with a distraught man maybe thirty sitting behind a poster-sized photo of an old woman, framed in a splash of red and yellow flowers topped with a white plastic dove. Behind that a white hearse then black limousine then half a block of compact cars *environmental bits* and so here I am finishing your letter in the Caffe Puccini, my blouse patterned with vivid yet somehow subdued pears and apples *hang there like fruit O my soul til the tree die* before me on the tiny round table sit a foamy cappuccino and a Swiss cheese sandwich on pale crusty bread with mayonnaise. I feel like Isak Dinesen, who ate only white food. The woman at the next table is maybe fifty, she has long frizzy yellow hair and is decked out in black stiletto-heeled boots a leopardskin velour miniskirt and black stockings with jungle vines climbing her thighs *two hundred million eggs for a single mortal being* what more can I say? Wish you were here.

Love,
Mina

February 14, 1992

Dear Sing,

When I met Quincey he seemed so helpless, a blind noun fumbling about for a seeing-eye verb. For six months he carried my photograph and letters in his pocket a frayed lump over his breast that he switched from jacket to jacket *to hide them* his fingers were long and thin, pale as axolotls, with squat filed nails— immaculately clean—if I were Brian De Palma I'd cast those hands as artists or murderers *perfect for leaping octaves on the piano or curling like deranged tendrils around my neck.* Now that he's dumped me I feel smeared, erased—when people turn in my direction they stare right through me, thinking of rain. It was great seeing you at Norma's cocktail party—in a desert of polite conversation you were a big juicy cactus—leaning against the stove in tight black jeans and T-shirt you sipped California wine and threw your head back banter and laughter bubbling from your bright mobile lips. Two years ago I met Quincey in this same kitchen *his eyes like ferocious beasts snared me.* "Sing," I said, "let's go out and have a smoke." Even though I no longer smoke. A bare bulb cast a harsh pool of light around us *overexposed* you feared bugs but there weren't any as we crouched in the cold on the back steps. I couldn't think … of what to say to you, just wanted to drink my cabernet and size up your lopsided hairdo, the tilt of your chin as you took a leisurely drag from your cigarette. You laughed and said, "So, Mina, what mischief have you been up to?" Well, Sing, since you asked …

Ours was an affair fueled by wealth and insanity—both of them Lucy's. I still don't know how much she's worth or what's really wrong with her. Lucy took a lot of "medicine," the scary kind that makes the air feel thick as water, that kept her from "hurting herself." Its side effects were noted as lack: of sex drive of personality … her eery silence as she sat stiff-backed, her round mouth open—the first time Dion saw her he tapped my shoulder and whispered, "The chick with the eyes, what's she on?" She moved so slowly. But she certainly got invited to enough parties—perhaps because of her stern Irish beauty—but maybe because she was psychic *she's not weird she's zoning in on the vibes.* She held workshops on automatic finger painting. My mouth was full of sourdough and brie when she appeared at my side and asked in a little girl's voice if I "read" pictures—still chewing I stared down at her face—it was a riot of lines and circles—like a late Kandinsky. "What's reading a picture?" "It's seeing the true reality behind the representation. When I first started dating Quincey he showed me a snapshot of his mother, a pretty blonde toasting the camera with a champagne glass. But I saw through the festive image, intuited that she was going through a lot at the time." "Oh really." Whenever Quincey speaks of his mother the pain in his voice is palpable … my eyes become his eyes as I watch her rock and chainsmoke for hours on end *she stares past the real presence of leaves and earth and beasts and weathers into an almost sexless luminousness a tube in her throat so she can breathe* after she died he didn't get out of bed for two months. Don't you think it's best to keep one's delusions where they belong: private … or on paper?

So what if we both were married, my desire was clean and sharp, cutting through all the practicality crap—he was a radiant compassionate animal hung with ribbons and flowers.

The top of the Art Institute auditorium is hot and airless—as if Hell has risen to float above our heads. Quincey and I watch a film adaptation of Bataille's *Dead Man.* As *Edward falls back and is dead, emptiness swells up in her. A long sigh sweeps her and lifts her so that she's like an angel. Her naked breasts go all pointy, and they're like a church you might dream of.* An art student with hideous glasses leads an orgy in a roadhouse—she's naked and throws herself from table to table like a petulant child—the Marie I imagined from the book was coarse, yes, but far more graceful *Ken Russell directs Audrey Hepburn* she'd never obliterate her pretty gamine eyes with those glasses the frames so thick and dark, rectangular as movie screens. Bolted to the concrete in a wooden folding chair I slouch beside Quincey, my arms wrapped around my torso like rope—this is our first secret meeting. He shoves his cup of popcorn between his legs, grins mildly and whispers, "Want some?" It pokes out like a hardon but I reach my hand *inside—yummy hermaphoditic snack* our hands touch and a spark leaps from finger to finger. Quincey says our movie date is an example of living a narrative. Dodie interrupts, "Quincey, you live a *Life*. You *tell* a Narrative." His instant historicalization is beyond her ... until you lend KK *Precious Victims* ... when the dead baby's mother swore she felt the blow that knocked her out her alibi cracked—experts testified: A PERSON NEVER FEELS THE BLOW THAT KNOCKS HER OUT there is always a delay from the moment of impact to the brain's registering of it *where did my now go?* The present like death is always after the fact, glimmering in Oz. The present is a short story, a disease spread from character to person ... not knowing where their feet are at any given moment how does anybody ever make it across a room? Dodie's hand, is it inside or outside the popcorn box? And Quincey's cock ... *her brain is so shifty whispering its incessant gossip* the future hits her head on—we could be unconscious before she gets to the end of this sentence we'd never even know it.

Standing beside that corpse, she's not aware, she's beyond—but she's ecstatic too. The dead man is the narrative that blows through Marie—she sticks her fingers up her slit, sniffs the cunt-smell because of him, because of it.

Quincey belongs to Lucy. She doles out plenty for his upkeep. And then I come along and vandalize her property spray-painting its delicate complexion with my cunt LOS MINAS. Lucy hates me—Priestess of the Primal that I am I can respect that—but—give me a break Quincey acted out of his own volition and he'd been volitating long before he met me. He was so duplicitous his face blurred like an unfocused viewgraph: the bottle of whiskey he kept hidden as a teen, he'd sneak it out of the car trunk on icy midwestern nights the driveway slippery and sparkling as his dreams … the woman he picked up at that convention in D.C., she bruised his nipples so badly he had to hide his chest from Lucy for a week … the occasional guy he'd suck off. One of Lucy's medicines was a sleeping potion—without it, she complained, the bed shook and rumbled—to appease the bed she'd prop her pillow against the wall and frantically sketch figures of winged lions. Once when Quincey's friends were over she got up, walked into the living room and urinated on the carpet. The potion made the night her coffin *nothing* could wake Lucy—with her first snore her husband crept out of the house into her worst nightmare. One of his jaunts began on Halloween and ended in a concussion—as Lucy lies in the next room Quincey drinks himself into a frenzy. I imagine him surrounded by bags of undistributed candy—what's your favorite kind Sing—Mary Janes? M&Ms? Quincey stares at the heap of Hershey's kisses their foil wrappers glittering like the future if he sits on the tacky beige loveseat a minute longer he's going to die he bolts out the front door and into the dark *more than his leash has snapped* aimlessly he races down the streets of Berkeley GO BOY GO! danger is what he craves he can smell it in the air then he runs through a pile of wet leaves OOPS forehead hits gutter *he had so much pent-up energy he was about to explode and explode he did week after week inside me.*

I wanted what I've wanted with every lover, to eclipse all their others, I wanted to be the center of Quincey's universe … and of KK's universe, to go beyond fiery to SOLAR. After Quincey's first kiss I had a talk with KK. "Mina, whatever makes you happy." He tossed off these words with a shrug, tilting his birdlike profile, "I'm not the jealous type." To me an incomprehensible stance. Your black sheriff is married too—I can understand you handling that better than me, but you told me you *like* it. You even go shopping with him and his daughter—at Costco! "It's harder to have casual sex with women, they're always wanting to get involved." You grimace at the word "involved" as if it were a blasphemy. How come you never feed me any details about the women *thrusting these cocks in my face like crucifixes.* "What impressed me most was his size." "His size?" "He's fat." "His penis is fat?" "No, *he's* fat. Fat is under-rated," you pat the T-shirt stretched tightly across your breasts, "except on me of course." He drives you home, you say "thanks for fucking me so well" and dash into your apartment, satisfied—I wish I were more like you, Sing, my needs my desires clean and precise as etch-a sketch. The following week you go to an action film, snuggled beside the sheriff with "his big fucking arm" around you for once you feel tiny, "I've never had a daddy before." You're letting your hair grow out, you paint your toenails. "Afterwards in his car I gave him the longest blowjob. I liked that." Quite a few have visited my boudoir and I've been green-eyed with every one of them. How many? A multiple of all my fingers and toes. But compared to gay men I've known, compared to KK, I'm practically a virgin. Maybe there's a critical number of lovers—hundreds—thousands—I haven't yet reached and when I do sex will become a simple exchange—like shaking hands—rather than this peristaltic anomaly this big thing that gulps my spirit naked and kicking into its bottomless maw. Anything's possible.

My doctor says, "No more red wine ... too many tannins to irritate the bladder." So I drink half a bottle of grassy sauvignon blanc thinking of urine. I turn off the computer and dial Los Angeles. "Hello, Mark, it's Mina. I'm living in an erotic fantasy."

On Mondays Quincey came over at eleven, after his therapy, and we'd fuck for ninety minutes then he'd drive me to work. He'd also come over on whatever night Lucy was teaching her psychic finger painting workshop. If KK was out we'd fuck for a couple of hours then drive to Vesuvios or the Hotel Utah and drink and talk, then we'd make out in the car and he'd drive me home and we'd make out some more. If KK was home we'd go to the hot tubs and fuck for an hour, dip in the water and go for pizza with goat cheese and sun-dried tomatoes. Or get cappuccinos first then go to the hot tub then to a bar *the Wells Fargo instant teller on Columbus Avenue gave off a golden paradisal glow, spitting out endless stacks of twenties from Lucy's account* sometimes he'd wait for her snore and drive over around midnight—the hot tubs were closed by then so we'd find a secluded spot and fuck in the car— this worked best in the winter because the windows would fog up. On rare occasions he'd tell Lucy he was stressed and needed the night alone—those weeks were great, getting to fuck three times instead of two. Then he switched his work schedule so he had Fridays off—he'd get up early and come over around nine— and three times a week became the norm. Once I cooked for him—we chatted about our day over plates of spaghetti *prosaic enough for prime time TV* but eating the food ate up most of the evening we could only manage a quickie before KK returned. Nix on dinner. And we had one whole afternoon together—it was one of those nonreligious holidays that nobody understands. For hours we fucked to the Cowboy Junkies then lunched on Polk Street (spanikopita and iced tea) bought a pair of sunglasses for his trip to Barcelona held hands on the cable car kissed passionately at the escalator to his subway stop *I was desperately in love with him though love be melodrama* our hours of sunlight were stolen and few—how silly of us to believe that injections of experimental serum could immunize us from deadly solar rays the vials always get snatched or switched or broken the formula goes to the grave with the demented scientist, the colleague of

Darwin and Huxley. How foolish of us to overlook one simple ruthless variable—chemical reactions degenerate or your body builds up tolerance one day when rosy-footed dawn steps over the threshold your blood boils your tan bubbles you fall to the ground sizzling and convulsing *a charred slab of bacon in a Victorian suit.*

Quincey grew to like that beige loveseat, crouched on it naked at three a.m. jerking off over the phone with me *damp spot on the cushion.* Lucy should have been grateful: talking to me was so much … fun … he was hanging around the house more often.

The high school girl at the next table smokes a cigarette and I watch *carmine half moons stain the filter as if her lips are leaking* her clawed hand delicate and dangerous clenches a Marlboro *rhinestones pasted on the nails* she flicks the ash with awkward taps *Hitchcock close-up of her forefinger* flick flick flick *the camera just loves her to death* she flicks it so much I get dizzy watching … she takes a quick squinting puff forcing the smoke out of the corner of her mouth with a little huff then flick flick. Forbidden to smoke at home Quincey smoked Gauloises with me. "Nicotine lowers your vibrations," insisted Lucy, "and then I'm afraid of you." With each sharp drag he smiled, baring his teeth as he tried to hold it in his lungs, like someone smoking grass. Quincey stumbles home in the middle of the night reeking of Scotch, cunt and French smoke—how could Lucy not suspect? To be on the safe side he took a lot of showers—whenever he kissed me he smelled like soap, pungent American middle class. Squeaky clean.

In my dream Lucy stalks me through a labyrinth of hedges. She's wearing a red gown with a bustier bodice, her red crepe skirt billows wildly in the rain, her long wavy hair is dyed to match her dress *black stripe of roots down the center of her scalp black asphalt to hell* I speed up but when I peek back over my shoulder she's right behind me, a décolletage wound moving through the night, she puts a curse on me: "Si ça continue," her dark eyes glow like coals, "je te tue!" The next morning I wake up with a sticky red blotch spreading beneath my hips *so much for super-plus tampons* then when I'm getting dressed for work my sock drawer falls out of the dresser crashing down on my left foot. I pick it up and limp down the hallway to the bathroom. When I flush the toilet it overflows spewing forth a noxious soup of piss and shit and blood then I step on a sliver of glass (with the good foot) and as I hobble towards the medicine cabinet a computer voice booms from my phone machine threatening disconnection. Who wouldn't think: LUCY ... my therapist listens then nudges, "You feel guilty writing about her." I snap back, "Never." But, Sing, who knows—maybe this letter is a matter of Life and Death—with each word I type Lucy's curse deepens:

> *When Lucy pulls you down below*
> *Your death will be gory and slow;*
> *You'll see her coming and everyone will know.*

Lucy put the MEAN in Mina.

If I were Joan Crawford I would have bumped her off long ago, then lived out a tortured but extravagant nemesis on her money. I'd parade around in severe black and white gowns incredible gowns with satin wings trailing behind my butt, stunned workmen would erect a grand curved staircase for my descents, which would be unfaltering *nothing but high heeled clicks on the sound track* I'd hold my head high as I pulled on black shoulder-length gloves a huge glittering bracelet on my wrist *now I can die happy* I know it's gaudy but who cares: I've studied the Gumps catalogue: diamond-studded bumblebees and bears with emerald eyes, *gaudy* is an adjective that sticks only to the poor. But although we're filthy rich Quincey and I can never be happy. We glimpse Lucy's eyes at the window, hear her curse in our dreams *gory and slow.*

I know—I'd better show more compassion or the reader won't think I'm a good person, but, Sing, I'm not a person—if I ever was this story ended that—I am I I am she I am Mina Harker a sexy construct a trope a simulated force of nature Dodie's embarrassment a vortex of urges swirling around a void: all I see is my character: a woman in a bath an empty bath but she's oblivious, masturbating under a jet of water ... another female incompetent at being female in a culture where the feminine ... is muted ... Sing, what I need from you is the permission to behave excessively, will you grant me that much?

When we didn't have any place else to screw he'd drive over in Lucy's Jaguar with its cushy bucket seats that folded ALL THE WAY DOWN. His own car was old and cramped, punctuated with dents and scrapes, painted flat white with gray and rust-colored patches. It looked like something spit out of a body shop in *Beyond Thunderdome.* Imagine this wreck rumbling down the manicured streets of Berkeley. Quincey's collar is blue as his denim shirt but you can't tell it by looking at him. Artists of all classes dress down that's part of the job. He comes into focus: a certain hesitancy in speaking, a tendency to listen *so* politely, his constant enigmatic smile—he nods approvingly at everything you say, voices gentle encouragement and queries during the pauses: this is the awkward formality of someone who's passing. He's better at it than I. After my reading at Forrest Books one of the radical bourgeoisie tapped my elbow and exclaimed, "You don't look like the kind of person who'd be smart." Quincey once said that sex with middle class women felt like taking a vacation. As opposed to the awesome familiarity of fucking me *his politeness collapsing into cries for mercy.* Then he went with Lucy to Barcelona for a couple of weeks and things were never the same between us *such unbelievable noise the living make* he said that if Lucy found out about us she'd punish him *for a long time*. I wonder if he was looking forward to that. He certainly liked it in bed. I'd never spanked a man before—it was against every sexual inclination I ever remember having—but he demanded it insistent as a cranky child. I obeyed. And this obedience was arousing in turn—I was as submissive in my dominance as he was dominant in his submission. We bickered over who got to be on the bottom. My palm stings as his ass blooms bruises and his cock hardens. He barks "More!" but he doesn't need to—the more I do it the more I want to—after a couple of months I even do it in my dreams. His taut quivering ass reminds me of my childhood, when I found a skinned rabbit in the basement sink its muscles gleaming rose-gray *its beauty scared the shit out of me I darted up the stairs*. I'm lucky that beauty can't blind a person ... otherwise I would have been smitten a hundred times over: when Quincey was excited warmth radiated from his translucent skin ... the film stock turned ultraviolet and he glowed. He was too ethereal for decadence—it passed right through him *Bruno Ganz as Wim Wenders' angel*.

He was still fucking Lucy a couple of times a week "to keep up appearances"—adding in the time he spent with me we arrive at a subtotal of four or five times a week—plus he jerked off every day, often twice—or more—still he claimed to be constantly horny. Orgasms were to him what hamburgers are to McDonalds. I started feeling like a drop in the bucket, a McNugget in the bucket. I was endlessly willing ... with both Quincey and KK. It isn't easy to be bigger than life on a daily basis *to maintain my human materialization I needed to enlarge my hidden tank of methane gas or somebody was going to see the real me* I'd wake up in the morning and vow I was going to think about something else—anything—but SEX. By nightfall I'd be a miserable failure *cunt for brains* life didn't flow along it pulsed, huge and pink and veiny and globbed with mucus. Occasionally I'd bump into the rest of the world all those gray vague others and one of them would ask me, "What have you been up to?" My face would flush my jaw drop open, "Up to? Oh—nothing in particular."

At her husband's dinner party the slutty wife named Zandalee fucks Nicolas Cage in the next room—on top of a washing machine. A few scenes later she fucks him in a confessional. Nicolas Cage rolls his eyes up at the ceiling, "Thank you God." KK and I roll our eyes up at the ceiling too and I grab the remote, begin flipping through the channels. Not much is happening— Joan Rivers plugs her personal line of imitation Faberge egg jewelry, "Just like the one Edgar gave me." When we return to Cinemax a wide-eyed Zandalee is wandering through the streets of Mardi Gras. When she stops she mumbles, "I don't know why I do these things." KK shouts at the screen, "Because you're living in a trashy movie."

The night is a minefield of eros we were desperate nomads hulking through it once we bumped into a proofreader friend of Lucy's— literally—in City Lights Books. Quincey squeaked, "Oh—Ben! Excuse me." Ben peered at us through his glasses *round as binoculars* he wasn't a proofreader after all but an FBI goon from the McCarthy era and Quincey's politics were as red as his face he stammered on about how we were just checking out their selection of "Mary Butts—you know the forgotten poet she's very mystical." We browsed around until Ben left, then Quincey rushed through the theft detectors and onto the sidewalk his footwork was film noir you've seen it dozens of times when the crook leaves the scene of the heist he sticks his hands in the pockets of his wide-lapeled jacket and saunters like crazy until he turns a corner then ZOOM he's history. I trailed a couple of steps behind to his multi-colored car. He snapped "WHY ARE THERE SO

GODDAMNED MANY STREETLIGHTS DON'T TOUCH ME SOMEBODY MIGHT BE WATCHING" as he drove like somebody driven to an industrial part of town … only when we were lost in warehouses did he lean over the stick shift and kiss me fondling my breast filling my mouth with saliva *door handle in my back every joint in my body collides with the glove compartment* GIVE ME A NORMAL LIFE OR AT LEAST SOME ELBOW ROOM I peek out the window—the fuzz of factory behind Quincey's head sharpens to foreground—stuck in the middle of a concrete lot the factory is so out-in-the-open—wide open—a fighter bomber's dream target huge squat and loaded with gleaming tubes and glass its corners curved as a woman—fidgeting in my cramped plastic seat I felt like one of its products, stuffed into a carton shrink-wrapped and plopped into Quincey's arms *the future stretched out before me a conveyer belt to the unknown.*

Love was so much easier when I was your age, Sing. You meet a German psychologist in the Caffe Trieste, you take him home. His favorite movie was *Last Tango in Paris* (butter for lubricant) he edited a communist newspaper in Munich—or used to—I was never quite sure of his tenses. It was an accident that he sat at my table *an accident with an accent* he was gorgeous and on his way to South America to observe the proletariat. I lived in the Mission, Folsom at 24th: taquerias panaterias Day of the Dead skeletons welfare recipients funk music blaring from cars Elvis wall-clocks children bouncing around. I licked the cappuccino foam from my lips, savoring his coffee-colored eyes and mountain-climber's thighs, "What's your rush? My flat is in the barrio it has tons of atmosphere I mean the people there are really oppressed and there's plenty of room—if you don't mind … uh … sharing a bed." For a couple of weeks we gorged ourselves on thick hand-made tortillas and sex. He'd do anything to make me come, then complain about it afterwards: "My—what do you call it?—is raw." That's realism for you. I chainsmoked and he emptied my ashtrays *the controlled motions of his long feral body* I thought to myself he's too handsome for me. The English he studied in *Schule* came out as adamant abstractions, garbled and bent as if his intelligence were underwater *a world where the streets connected at "right angels."* He was a poem that took itself too seriously ... his face stern with pleasure as he sat in my room listening to Kraftwerk's *Autobahn* over and over. We were both twenty-nine. I didn't ask for much: *want* was a concept elusive to me.

Quincey wasn't born with his flat face any more than Mount Rushmore is the countenance of Nature. His nose and jutting chin have eroded over years of talking Lucy down. "Get rid of those tulips," she screams, "They're trying to kill me!" Her eyes begin to flick mechanically up and down, focused on the wall behind his head—this "headlighting" is always a sign of impending disaster—she throws her hands over her ears and whispers, "The mice in the attic are stomping like elephants." The evening ends with her crouching in the closet or racing barefoot down College Avenue or passing out at the dinner table facedown in her mashed potatioes ... dutifully Quincey phones the in-laws then shows up at the hospital clenching a bunch of roses ... his smiles are prim his questions patient as his soul beats about outside the window with the humming birds. He'd call me after midnight crying, "Lucy can't kiss her pubic hair is like brillo pads she threw a knife in the kitchen floor." My life became a pastiche of the wrong novel: *Jane Eyre*. And Lucy like all "madwomen" is misrepresented here—maybe she can hire a ghostwriter to do a sequel from *her* perspective—Dodie's busy how about Jean Rhys? Or some struggling Lacanian: *Quincey was her fantasized phallus, attributing to her a shape, a clearly defined, erect form in order to combat the threat of her formlessness, her totalizing, oceanic presence.* I've felt pathological myself—but something has always kept me from going over the edge: finances: no trust fund no private doctors I see myself sprawled on the sidewalk begging, 300 pounds with paper bags over my feet, and I get normal real quick. *When he finally penetrates her with his stake his heart is revealed to be hollow.*

Once a cheater always a cheater. In *The Creeping Flesh* the Victorian scientist discovers the source of Evil: black hairy corpuscles that gobble human corpuscles transforming the host into a violent dancing lunatic—when the scientist injects his beautiful prim daughter she dons a fiery Toulouse-Lautrec dress and hits the street her little fox eyes darting from side to side she stumbles upon an inn full of prostitutes gulps down a couple of whiskies and begins to hop around in circles with her arms swaying above her head—her lowcut breasts bulge and bounce around frantic as her rapidly-devoured corpuscles, they're so squishy and white and dewy all the men want to touch them a sailor grabs a handful and squeezes hard, the scientist's daughter breaks a bottle on a rough-hewn table and gleefully slashes his throat, the crowd yells "Get her!" Those little fox eyes dart side to side as she runs out into the street she doesn't know what she's doing but like Quincey she can never stop.

Quincey's skin was white as phagocytes.

I'm sure he's repented plenty, just like Jimmy Swaggart. I remember him beating off *knuckles and wedding band in a choppy smear like a video on fast forward.* He looks a lot like the serial killer in Argento's *Terror at the Opera.* Even after the ravens gouged his eye out I thought, "That killer is really cute."

I flush the toilet and step into the hall Quincey is leaning in the bedroom doorway all smiles his hips are cocked his thumbs hooked into belt loops *superimposed on his crooked anatomy is a pink grid with a digital readout lining up the coordinates of LUST* he grabs me and rubs his erection against my belly. Lucy's across the bay at her psychiatrist's I've never seen their bedroom before— the covers are tucked in so tight they'd squish your toes the bottom sheet is taut as a trampoline a *bed that cries out for efficiency* as we kiss I peer over Quincey's shoulder, the top of the dresser is cluttered with quart-sized pharmaceutical jugs of Thorazine, chloral hydrate, Nembutal, and Deprol, as well as a crystal decanter of booze; there's something weird about the bookcase *he's biting my lower lip* basic Scandinavian blond *cupping my ass in his hands* it's not the wood it's the books: all their spines are white or black or neutral … six rows of gradient vertical slats like a gray scale. "Quincey, where do all the colored books live?" "They're in the study. They scatter her vibrations." As he pulls me down on the mattress I make a quick scan: Lucy's Rothko prints … Lucy's bathing suit draped over the closet door … Lucy's Russel Wright nightstands *just like my parents' bedroom nothing belongs to the husband … a space both sacred and tainted … where the unthinkable gets thought on a regular basis … a bed that fills me with revulsion* Quincey bounces me across it like a dime then opens the nightstand drawer and takes out a condom, size extra-large, the kind that inevitably has a photo of a black man on the box … my cunt is already wet so he plunges inside *zip zap* he comes then rolls off me, his condom drooping like a tiny ski cap, "Lucy will be back soon—we'll take care of you later." Quincey folds his hands under his head the pale hair of his armpits gnarling like cauliflower. I pout and stare at the foot of the bed. Lucy slowly materializes, floating and wobbling about like a marionette, her mouth is so round I think of a gargoyle blowing bubbles. I feel sorry for her. *Lucy, is this what you put up with?* then I blink and she disappears *ce n'est rien* just the sun flickering through eucalyptus leaves … twenty minutes pass tick tock tick *no time to take care of me* tock tick … I perch on the edge of the bed and wrestle with my panty hose … an inspired look crosses Quincey's face his blue eyes turn toward me …

lazily … like they're about to melt and drip onto his naked shoulders, "I've been developing a plan—in case Lucy comes back early." This was his plan: he would throw on a bathrobe and greet her at the door and make some excuse to take her into the backyard. Then I would hurriedly dress and go out the front door and ring the bell then he'd answer it and act like I was making a surprise visit and then after the three of us chatted for a bit he'd offer me a ride home *a Playboy version of "I Love Lucy." "Hi Honey!" "Ricky what are you doing in a bathrobe at three in the afternoon?" "Oh, Lucy, you're so funny! Let's go out and look at my jalapeno plants—we'll pick one and I'll make a nice Spanish omelette!" He grabs Lucy's arm and scurries her through the kitchen to the backyard. The doorbell rings. Ricky darts back inside, "Ethel—what a surprise!" "I was just passing by …" Ethel is not her usual model of bovine composure but avoids Lucy's gaze, her metallic gold blouse is buttoned wrong—without a hole the top button droops above the rest pale and unblinking* as I rebutton my metallic gold blouse I turn and stare at Quincey all the muscles in my face straining to make my expression of disgust so poignant that a verbal response would be redundant.

Wouldn't a real psychic know her husband was fucking another woman in her own bed wouldn't disruptive adulterous carnal vibrations cling to the sheets like lint?

I suppose I wasn't being very realistic. Quincey was Lucy's dark fantasy, a projection she couldn't control in her drugged state, he'd materialize on his own and fly around the Bay Area wreaking orgasms. When she began to suspect us her rage set off an ancient alchemical reaction her powers grew enormous *over my life she's cast a shadow as tall as a building* lighting strobes the Victorian night CRACK she summons Quincey back into the mildewed convolutions of her psyche.

We're more than kind of drunk, perched on red leather stools sharing a Glenfiddich straight up *bitter perfume with a sweet after-bite* I scoot the shot glass toward Quincey across the dark wood, all the nicks and scratches glisten with shellac—I'm cozy, massage Quincey's calf with a nyloned toe, my rubber neck rolling around, Quincey scoots the glass back, says that if Lucy finds out about us he'll never be able to talk to me again NEVER not even to say good-bye—the image is that of Quincey as this will-less protoplasmic doll with Lucy the big Momma-God looming over tugging away at his strings. I falter—he's not an invalid or a schoolboy, not inca-pacitated in any way, he's a grown man with a body to die for drinking a Scotch SING, I JUST DON'T BUY IT my mood turns easily as the page of a book I start pushing to define the situation but we're committed to different dictionaries, mine is standard and his is so full of Funk he can't find his Wagnall's—I pull out the forbidden "C" words, hurl them at him *child coward con-servative* Quincey's face flushes red as the cover of Webster's Ninth—we're out of there and in the front seat of his car screaming at one another then Quincey's slamming his door and huffing away down the street *Claudette Colbert where are you when I need you.* Not a soul in sight. I'm shivering. Around me freeway on-ramps curl like a surrogate mother's arms ... not a living soul. I walk around the corner back to the tavern. *I come to a stop, rest at the wall. I open my coat, stick fingers up my slit. I listen, frozen with fear, sniffing at the unwashed-cunt smell on my fingers.* The door is locked I peer through the window *moist ghosts on the cold glass* inside the bartender is setting a chair upside down on a table. When he hears me banging he rolls his eyes ... Quincey pulls up alongside the taxi, "Get in." "No way!" "God damnit, get in!" "Don't you ever," I growl, "call me *fuck face* again ..." The yellow cab recedes down Fourth Street, a bright dot, a yellow point on the vacant stretch of concrete.

Reality penetrates her. The living narrative must die.

The highway is empty at three a.m. as Quincey swerves home across the Bay Bridge. In the distance orange flames light up the road like a god's torch—Quincey drives—past the wreck in—slow—motion—the curled charred driver has amalgamated with the steering wheel, the skeleton in a body of vermilion fire. The soundtrack is dead silent. Alone beneath the streetlights and the vast black stratosphere Quincey stares at this out-of-control *thing* roaring a few feet from his windshield and he thinks, "This has to end." And there was nothing I could do about it—I mean, who can argue with a vision? He expelled me like a wad of phlegm and raced back to Lucy. But something went wrong—the corpus is gone but he left behind this ectoplasmic dolor. His expression is obscured by words—my words—scrawled across his face. Eventually some underpaid janitor will come along and slosh them with toxic chemicals scrub them away *day by day his features dissolve along with my caring this letter holds the last of him—here, Sing, I mail him to you. Rip him up or bury him in pendaflex just don't tell me.*

A century ago I sprang full blown from Bram Stoker's skull. In a way I am he, it's encoded in our names:

BRAM STOKER
MINA HARKER

ten letters each, five of them in common: M-A-K-E-R. Mina Harker the fact gatherer the transcriber of tapes the puller together of manuscripts. Quincey and Lucy have always lacked that kind of initiative … they live out their lives in the legend of *Dracula* never questioning our lot as modular units. In novel, play, film, our roles and partners shift with the awkward grace of a line dance. But beneath the screenwriter's thumb I squirm … as the credits scroll by I stuff popcorn in my mouth to distract my racing heart: am I single? betrothed? married to Jonathan?

who runs the insane asylum? does he live? do I die? Sometimes Lucy is my best friend sometimes my sister sometimes my husband is my father, I don't even look for Quincey he's forgotten so often, and in a couple of radical versions MINA DOESN'T EXIST EITHER. For some reason Lucy is *always* there—hissing and panting in sexy grave clothes she gets to be the (non)living embodiment of sexual abandon and danger while I'm the secretarial ingenue *my collar is so high my head looks detached tottering on a column of tatted lace and brocade* in one cult classic we switch—it's Mina who succumbs to Dracula's bite in the first half hour *I was stunning, I should have won an award—but what did the director do—he buried me in a sewer!* I was shelved save for a few poorly lit frames of fangs and shredded gown, while Lucy hammed up my part, the leading waif whose soul all those Victorian hunks fight for. Bitch. IF THE PLOT DIDN'T KILL ME THE UNCERTAINTY WOULD HAVE THAT'S WHY I KICKED DODIE OUT OF THE DRIVER'S SEAT. I WANTED TO INCITE A RIOT IN WRITING—the character storms the page, Literature assaults the reader without the interference of the writer—in my remake Lucy loses—sure she's married to Quincey but his heart belongs to Mina they fuck like demons and Quincey's sexual ecstasy binds him to her FOREVER. Lucy snaps flies in Dr. Seward's asylum. I think this is an exciting conclusion, don't you? But those two wouldn't let things be—oh no—randominity made them uppity *the text remains pliant, flickering, and subject to instant evanishment, leaving nothing in its wake, no order, no dimly-starred words, simply silence and stupor, a restoration of chaos and old night* RIGHT NOW I FEEL SO small ... human almost, slouched in my desk chair in flannel bathrobe and white crew socks ... Sing, I'm shrinking ... soon I'll be nothing but a comma ... a period ... then I'll merge with the margin a vast white cryogenic crypt *fast frozen* I wait for the ideal reader to stumble upon me with a cure for every terminal disease and the technology to regenerate my body from a single icy cell.

Quincey—5'10" tall, size 9 shoe, lives on a street named after a tree—a man so normal he could be anybody. He was perfect for a romantic like me: a blank screen with a big cock. *Her expression alters as she remembers how he used to kill her with his vagueness.* I was just another lonely woman from beyond the grave—until I exchanged body fluids with him. I never went on a date in high school—twenty years later I finally made it to the prom: wherever we went whirling lights danced giddily over rented tuxedos, organza, and toilet paper carnations *he made her beautiful and she made him extraordinary: honor roll, sports hero, chic James Dean ambiance: she slaughters anyone who gets in his way.* Each murder is the representation of the victim's darkest cravings—the fat science teacher's chest is scooped out and heaped with ice cream, goo and tiny flags *human banana split* the vain guidance counselor is strapped beneath a hair dryer that leaks battery acid (Mina in beautician's smock cracks her gum) the obnoxious jock's football turns midair into a bulbous drill that nails him to the goal post *character upon character squirms in a plot with no exit— this is the erotics of writing.* I pushed Quincey over the threshold hissing *get out of here go back to your boring life, your boring wife, your boring beautiful trophy wife.*

The only way to get rid of a sexual haunting is to sacrifice a soul.

My toe is tentative as I poke it in the scalding water, the porcelain is chalky with age, calves and ass ease into the claw-footed tub *short and deep and cornerless as my breath* I curl my fingers over the curved brim feel like a Disney mouse bobbing around in a tea cup *the cartoon character never really gets cooked* my submerged mousy legs waver through the misty tisane of lavender bath salts—to my right a bookcase is crammed with towels, on its top trinkets are scattered dinosaur the size of my thumb wooden carp three polished stones probably agates (a gift from Tina Darragh) a taper of rolled beeswax casts a faint amber glow, there is no toilet in my bathroom and I like this singularity of purpose *steam on the mirror resembles a row of priests holding candles* deeper I sink in the tub my pubic hair flickering like anemones knees poke above the surface I spread them apart the pink V of inner thigh suggesting any number of female possibilities ... on the other side of the sweating wall neighbors bang and shout ... "You're gone all the time!" ..."I've got to figure out what I'm doing" ..."I'VE HAD IT!" ... invisible solids thump the floor like an insistent memory *my heels are black my dress as red as blood* I'm about to enter the gallery where Quincey works ... I haven't seen him for months not since the night we broke up *a scarlet dress on a scarlet woman, wardrobe is destiny* the gallery's plate glass window is covered with hefty bags—Lynne Tillman stands beside me. She's visiting from New York—what happens next thrusts her into a plot she doesn't belong in—yet she loves every minute of it. We find a gap between bags and peer through: the darkened room is packed with people in folding chairs their upturned faces illuminated by the thin focused glow of a slide projector ... when we step inside my pupils slowly widen filtering details from the dark—on the screen books and chairs hang like paintings from the walls of another gallery. Then beyond the beam of dust motes and colors I see him. It's him. That's him sitting behind a desk an eerie tableau flattened by the dimness *inaccessible* the shifting lights across his stationary figure give him a pre-cinematic appeal a nineteenth century spectacle of illusion *phanorama pleorama*—he's been going through a lot. *Pores flare open beneath the steaming washcloth I squeeze my eyes shut I want to scorch my face until the flesh melts away the same with my words I want to be that pure* when the lights came on for intermission I stared at him as if he were a picture tube instead of a person. I was that hungry for information. He was slightly soft focus and impoverished like a peasant in a 40's horror flick, he'd grown a beard, his blond hair had darkened not exactly to brown but was drained of color an undefinable neutral like his shirt, his hair was chopped in irregular tufts it wasn't its ugliness that was disturbing but its lack of rationale *a telekinetic attack by an evil pair of scissors*—beneath his eyes drooped bags so dark and puffy that for a second I thought they were stage make-up instead of flesh, crowsfeet radiated out towards his temples HE GLARED BACK AT ME *my words dissolve and the letters crawl away* then he turned stiffly towards Lucy who was sitting across the room in a folding chair. Not a word was spoken but like one of her hounds from hell he'd been given his instructions. He stood up and said in a monotone, "I have to leave." He ambled towards his wife … brittle … like his veins had been sucked dry and stuffed with sawdust … Lucy was no longer the distracted dreamlike creature of a few months ago, as she willed Quincey toward her, her pale complexion blazed rosy her lips were full and red and slightly protruding she swiveled her head towards the door and I swear I saw a glint of extended incisor. Before I knew it they were gone.

An absurd termination to my violent exertions. Lynne gapes, "Mina what did you do to that man?" "I'll tell you later."

The steaming lavender bath has softened my muscles to mush … sea wool drooling white foam across my breasts *I am a savory mouthful seasoned with lemon and tabasco* Beethoven oozes from a tape player on the salt-and-pepper rug its electrical cord winding down the wall an umbilicus to danger *there are so many Others camping out in Dodie's body, who knows what they are: Freudian figments fragments archetypal squatters characters waiting for their big break, what if one of them what if LUCY takes control—moodiness metathesizes to crazy she snaps grabs the tape player and hurls it in the tub SZZZZZZZZZZZZZZ Dodie and I light up the room like a Christmas tree … blink … blink* KK followed me outside I leaned against a brick wall it was scratchy and cold through my scarlet dress, metallic threads glittered beneath the streetlight, I lit up a cigarette sucking in the sharp poisonous smoke and exhaling rage—virgin rage. But wait—there's Quincey's car—I'd recognize that amorous hunk of junk anywhere. KK urged me to scrawl a message in lipstick across the windshield, "How about something simple like, "HEY BABE—CALL ME!" I took a drag of my cigarette absently watching a Volkswagen rumble down the Berkeley street it left a smell of gasoline in its wake. "Walking out on me was the greatest gift that man ever gave me," I declared. "It adds a nice touch of melodrama to my plot, all that primal infusing his repression it's kind of admirable." KK probed, "Wouldn't you ever think of making that up?" "Uh-uh, I'm not that imaginative." "Then are you living a narrative?" "Of course not," I snooted grinding the butt beneath my shoe, my black pointed toe swiveled like an arrow gone haywire, "I don't know what the hell that means—living a narrative—I'd never do something just to write about it. Like do you think I'd go out and get my heart broken just to write about it?" My approach is more in the mode of John Cage—you manipulate whatever fate throws your way. That's why I hardly ever haul myself down to Tower Video—you fret through row upon row of colorful boxes for the perfect 90 minutes of inspiration—and nine times out of ten it's a big fizzle. Take that movie about Claus and Sunny von Bulow you'd think it would be a natural for this story *when his drugged wife falls into a mysterious coma his wide-eyed mistress betrays him* but there wasn't an image I could use in the whole damned thing. Flipping through the channels and landing on a tempting tidbit of schlock is more consistently useful—I mean, do you think I paid to see *Prom Night Part III*? I often wonder how people wrote before remote control.

Spoonfuls of fluid oozing from his eyes and cock and little pink mouth whenever I was lost in the desert I would lick the dew from his armpits and I was lost many a time ... Quincey was so watery that when it rained I was afraid his physical manifestation would break apart in a million droplets and spatter the windshield ...

many a time … *tennis shoes silent against the concrete Quincey undulates over the sidewalk his pale translucent skin shimmering along the edges, I reach out for him half expecting my hand to slip right through* only during sex did he feel real COCK—BALLS—FUCK—SLURP *I came in spasms that cramped my subjectivity* but afterwards I could never quite believe it happened … until I caught Lucy's bladder infection. *Quincey floats past me, adrift on the page, staring into bare, heartless immensities* he's just a bumbling malcontent who found his cock in the wrong neighborhood—I took advantage of him, made him pull it out during Lucy's stupor—with a wild roaming expression I stood in my bedroom window pale tits bulging like eyeballs out of my lowcut Victorian gown, I hissed and scratched at the casement, intoned COME TO ME and the jerk raced zombie-like across the Bay Bridge. I never dreamed that Lucy's magic would be more powerful than mine. Okay, I admit it, sometimes it's hard not to admire her drive, her triumph *I was just this B movie queen while she was so Big Budget, her fabulous designer gowns, those lush Berkeley locations, her FX done the old way—in camera—she zooms toward me on a little platform on wheels that's yanked by invisible strings.* I'd catch myself, mostly in those fuzzy moments between waking and sleeping, rooting for *her.* I *am* a feminist, but sometimes I wonder—was Lucy starting to burrow into my brain, to bend me to her will? If I'd kept Quincey just a while longer, would she have summoned me to their bed? She thrusts my dark presence before her to ward off Quincey's naughty prick *wand of the undead,* "You and your cunting girlfriend!" Chaos grips the room, the bed violently jumps about, Lucy's body is pulled up and slapped down as if by an outside force, she rolls the whites of her eyes, spits green bile, utters a savage snarl. Pharmaceutical bottles and furniture whiz through the air. Lucy's head turns round full circle, she knocks Quincey to the floor with one punch, stabs her cunt with a crucifix. In a deep gutteral voice she screams, "The sow is mine! Lick me!" The skin of her midriff bursts open and popcorn comes spewing out ... explosions and crackles fill the soundtrack *freeing me from the silences of the interior life.*

Oh, Sing, I wish I were more like you. KK says I should be glad my genre is horror instead of true crime—Quincey and/or Lucy would have returned to the gallery with a gun and blasted me away.

Pink venetian blinds add a rosy glow to the Mapplethorpe, Isermann, Haring, Pettibon, Shaw ... Vija Celmins' little "Saturn" ... KK and I are spending the weekend in L.A. with Mark and Dennis the four of us sprawl across their living room wilting from the Santa Anas ... an occasional shuffle or sigh ... suddenly Dennis sits up so excited I can see a light bulb blinking above his head he points to the VCR and pipes, "Want to see Michael Jackson's hair catch on fire?" Nods of approval all around. Afterwards Dennis pulls open the sofabed, says the sheets are fine—Nayland's the only one to have slept in them *not exactly Best Western but Nayland has always struck me as having a firm grasp on personal hygiene* KK and I climb onto the rickety mattress and say goodnight. On the wall behind me Mike Kelley's fetus gazes down broad-stroked and dreamy—if this were Wim Wenders' film he'd enter my belly eager to experience movement and progression *the sausage Sartre calls Life* but this sketched bit of potential looks content on the wall static and impenetrable as an avant garde poem. To my right twin strips of glass on either side of the front door allow the outside to peek in ... the ceiling fixture feels so bright—a dome swirled with cactus, cowboys, bucking broncos, rope. Is something scratching at the door? A long rectangular strip of woman is staring in at me, about her pale ancient face white hair gnarls like a snowball from hell. I nudge KK but when I turn back to the window a white cat has taken her place. Lucy's familiar. It opens its round mouth and hisses, "Si ça continue, je te tue!" *My psyche was war-torn England and Quincey's cock an American GI stationed there: how could we help but fuck like rabbits* ... the narrative doesn't care about Quincey's response or lack thereof. *Everything* that happens to me is Poetic Justice *ditto everything that doesn't* as I sit on KK's lap his semen dripping out of me and onto his thigh, he purrs, "Sizzzzzzzzzzz! I'm singed by your hot molten effluvia of lust." *The triumph of matter* he warned me that I'd never settle for playing second fiddle *illuminating points in the dark waste* the psychic surgeon pulls out chicken liver instead of a tumor and Quincey vowed he loved me over and over and over and over. Mike Kelley's opening at Rosamund Felsen Gallery—forty years ago Marilyn's famous calendar nudes were shot in this same studio, now it's hung with portraits of rag dolls a wall of them, human-sized black and white they loom above the actual dolls which lie on the floor in miniature coffins *representation has killed them* in one corner white-haired and tall as a legend John Baldessari stands in a bright blue shirt chatting with a couple of academic types ... in another Mike Kelley's long graying hair is pulled back in a ponytail, his arm is being pumped by a corpulent man in a plaid leisure suit. There is a tiny door on each coffin over the face *an abyss that divides the axis of vision from the axis of things* a woman in camouflage stretch pants lifts one of the doors and peers in at the stuffed cotton expression then up at the canvas *without imaginative interiority a face is a nothingness* a guard rushes up and grabs her by the shoulder DON'T TOUCH THE COFFINS over and over and over *her breasts round hollows for themselves in the sky-green water, her fingers sift the pale water and drop it from her as a lark drops notes backwards into the sky ... the lady lies against the lipping water, supine and indolent, a pomegranate, a passion-flower, a silver-flamed lily, lapped, slapped, lulled by the ripples which stir under her faintly moving hands. I too create corpses.* Quincey's cock was large and pink and well-proportioned, reasonably thick and straight no oddball lumps curves or bulging veins it worked whenever he wanted it to OVER *I can't put it all together I need a body bag to hold the parts ... naked cunt naked ass wet cunt-and-ass odor free her heart* as we lie together our limbs tangled as tumbleweed KK chimed that he could feel love running back and forth between us like a gossip *and so the body melts like a glimmer of light in the abstraction of words* I stick this page up my slit it's black and white and re(a)d all over.

Happy Valentine's Day—
Mina

October 31, 1992

Dear Sam,

Last summer in Vancouver I walked into an art opening and
there he was, sitting on the window ledge. His chic glasses convinced me he was an intellectual, though he was glamorous
enough to be a movie star, his shirt black, his hair wild and gray.
Beside him perched a petite woman dressed in dark arty clothes,
with a shoulder-length perm and a perky nose. I whispered to
Lisa Robertson, "She looks like a poodle," and Lisa snapped
back, "Yes, she's his poodle he takes her in to be *clipped!*" The
girlfriend is a performance poet who does one-woman shows
"with lots of cleavage." Whenever she turned her head her
boyfriend would try to catch my eye. I was wearing the same red
dress that figured so prominently in my Quincey story—right
now it's wadded in a pillowcase on the closet floor, slated for the
dry cleaners. I wandered into another room and stood with Lisa
by a table heaped with lychee nuts and grapes. Mr. Glamour
Puss appeared in the doorway. Then at the table. He grabbed a
couple of grapes and stood there a few feet away and stared at
me as Lisa filled in his details. "He hangs out with a crowd that
get married a lot and when they get divorced they never speak
again to the people they used to be married to." *Her lumpy
cranium flails beneath the full moon as she rips the transgressor
limb from limb spattering the cornstalks with blood.* Then he left.
A few minutes later I looked up and there were those eyes again
roving like beacons above the grapes, then they went away only
to return again and again and maybe even again—like in every
other movie on TV tonight: a bare rectangle of earth begins to
undulate then a splayed hand pops out *the grave is no longer a
grave* he never said a word to me. I watched him closely, acting
like I didn't notice. Both of you and I, Sam, are fuck*ees* positioning torso and appendages in sexy diagonals and waiting for

the big thrust. It enters our nethers as a tube of funk and muscle and sprays out our rubious mouths as gossip.

A thousand bedrooms couldn't solve my problems.

Sunday night KK urged me to sit on his face: "You can be a stack of records and my tongue will be the spindle that plays them!" This image gave him a sense of power though I was the one who could bear down and smother him … *tottering on the brink* … when he came he said "I'm open" then he gasped "Christ, everything's rushing in!" I thought *no it isn't it's just me the world as always is out there beyond your reach.* I kissed his forehead his brains whirling beneath my lips *a self-contained cosmos like the homunculi* in Bride of Frankenstein *a ballerina beneath a bell jar a lascivious king with a squeaky voice* I lay in his arms breathing our bodies soft as warm butter *I have no need for genitals with all these … cells.*

Happy Halloween! This is the day when the ordinary grows enormous oozing slime around the edges when aliens roam the streets with too many legs and eyeballs or not enough when physiology swells within you rendering the flesh flimsy as tissue paper there is no stopping its inevitable implosion … glistening like rubies if rubies could rot it sucks you into another dimension rattling the walls corroding your moral fiber … tiny bits multiply to zillions with a group consciousness bent upon destruction pins poke out of the face of something that forgets it is dead … species meld—a man with the head of a pumpkin or a woman with a vampire's heart … the radio announcer assaults you with the tackiest Dracula accent: "Imagine if the creepiest costume around is you in a bathing suit! […creepy music…] The last thing you vant is to be scared of the way you look!"

In this topsy-turvy world the Dead roam the streets while the Living study them in an underground mine ... a scientist feeds dead soldiers to his pet Dead, Bub, who bolted to cinderblock lumbers about in the small circle his chains will allow. His clothes are shredded his decaying flesh hangs from his bones like pink lace. Through the miracle of operant conditioning no longer is Bub an uncontrollable cannibal like the others, he listens to Beethoven through walkman headphones reads *Salem's Lot*. The scientist hands him a razor, Bub slowly lifts it to his face and shaves off part of his cheek. The scientist concludes Bub has MEMORY. And when Bub feels his Dead spirit rising and roars his Deadly roar, the scientist throws him the leg of a colonel which he gnaws like a pit bull. It's not the flesh he craves but the faint scent of life that still clings to the colonel's leg. A mortal-like expression spreads across Bub's bloody face *maybe he flashes on his chubby childhood in the Midwest a mysterious impression of I WAS or maybe it's just another autonomic contortion* he reaches out his arm as if to grab something. Then he pauses, looks at his crumbling hand. Confusion. He lets it drop. The Dead, of all people, know the incredible pull of Life.

Black marker on the zen bakery's bathroom wall: GENDER IS THE NIGHT.

I'd been in one of those sex-free zones where a girl gets spiritual after a while ... then one night a petite orgasm shook me awake, legs closed as my eyes I squeezed out that last spasm of pleasure ... I'm at my Grandmother's house, cleaning out a dresser full of old clothes ... when I find a package of nylon stockings all I can think of is rushing home bolting the door ditto the chain lock drawing the blinds and there in the utmost privacy of my bedroom—alone—I marvel at my new legs, taut and slinky, strung from a white garter belt the garters etching steer-head shaped indentations in my flesh *metallic Georgia O'Keeffe* and then I came *dreams are the arena that eros has carved out of the night* Sam, why would one dream about nylons when one could have anybody *Val Kilmer as Jim Morrison, Tawny Kitaen the med student on the shuttle bus who looks like Kiefer Sutherland Uma Thurman my funny uncle or you, Sam D'Allesandro* ... no lover no narrative ... just the incredible pull of lingerie.

Dion's letter made her want to fuck him ... for a few minutes. Life is so elusive the ghostly trails left behind a moving hand on acid, whereas Writing is the hand.

It's a drag to be stuck between worlds, to bicker for possession of a bag of bones ... half the time I'm on the page with the other greats *Anna Karenina Catherine Morland* the rest of the time I'm riding around in Dodie's body like a taxi. Dodie KK and I are cramped together on a thick slab of foam—it's after midnight and the woman downstairs is washing her dishes, clanks fill the lightwell and waft in through the open window—why we always end up bordering these Joan Crawford compulsive types I'll never know—as Dodie rolls over to kiss KK the soapy neighbor shouts to her companion "I don't love him *that* much"—sex is in the air KK smells it oozing from Dodie's pores, tonight she's flat on her stomach legs as open as the window his right hand between them doing the old in and out *"I get the idea you've been a bad girl"* in all honesty she answers *"Yes, I've been very bad"* WACK his cock grazing the cheeks of her ass *"Now don't you flinch you deserve everything you get"* WACK *is that our brains buzzing or is it hot water rushing through the pipes and into the night?* While KK and Dodie play out the story of the big O, I go to the movies—the hot stuffy theater is packed as a jar of raspberry jam a thousand seeds suspended in dark cinematic goo, my vagina the rubescent core—craning my neck around the highly perfumed head in front of me I can barely see the screen—a faceless man is definitely seated to my left and another (when needed) to my right, they order me to sit absolutely still while they hike my skirt and spread my legs, cold metal from the chair arms indenting my outer thighs—conveniently I'm not wearing panties—Mr. Left slides his hand sticky-slow across my belly and over my cunt *what's flickering me or the movie* Mr. Right materializes to unbutton my white silk blouse his fumbling anxious hands would rip cheaper fabric I bite my lower lip stare straight ahead, still as the Dead are supposed to be, I can hardly breathe *stainless steel and crystal percussion* on the screen Demi Moore gives up her own life for the doomed baby's which so impresses God he cancels Armageddon *my body begins to quake: Apocalypse now* Dodie and I clench our thighs together in perfect synchronization as if we were a couple of heavy-headressed glamor girls *Ziegfeld Busby Berkeley and don't forget those languorous rows of long-legged kicking Rockettes.*

... I'm a little person out there in the dark ...

This is the first letter I've been able to write in months. I've been overwhelmed with pain and details *I wanted to fuck—as long as he was bad news it didn't matter who* Life was Life I couldn't differentiate fore from ground *I would have settled for a rendezvous in a greasy diner* I had wants enough to fill a novel *I wanted to find that place where violence and beauty mingle* Life had lost its shifting images the pretty patterns I wrote nothing *I wanted to roar through the streets at four a.m.* The middle of the horror is always the best, when narrative is squelched by an overriding paranormal vision. The forest recluse begs for his life and the camera closes in on his terror-stricken face—we the audience close in on him too at the other end of the lens, we are the marijuana growers the government has turned into festering monsters by spraying our crops with an untested powder, we are the Toxic Zombies about to throttle the recluse's pleas with a machete or our own truth.

Despite their intrinsic lack of direction the Dead are constantly shooting out tentacles in hopes of a progression. *I was the indifferent shore and he was the surf* KK sails his hand along the crotch of her panties tries to slide a finger under the elastic but she says *no I like what you're doing* she likes having a cotton cunt the cells knit together in this new stretchy way, no hole, a glowing white border the Dead cling to she likes having seed pearls and lace instead of pubic hair he quickens his hand and she comes of course she comes *I am a vortex panting beyond his reach a red flare on the wrong side of the highway.*

Life is like marriage: who could stand the constancy if you didn't take it for granted. Sex and Death: you and I write about them as if our lives depended on it.

It's Saturday afternoon which means Dodie's on her weekly quest for the Perfect Used Garment. She's about to enter Buffalo Exchange on Polk Street when a schizophrenic approaches us—I recognize him by his overall dusty patina and by the tense inwardness of his gaze. Mud clings to his frayed cuffs—in his hooded sweatshirt and full beard he looks like a woodsman in a fairy tale. But wait there's something about him that's closer to home—very familiar—it's the way he walks, that lock-kneed lumbering—he's the scientist's pet Dead, Bub! "Hi, Bub, it's Mina!" Both arms are extended downward *stiff as cocks* sticking out about six inches on either side of his hips—he's rapidly tapping the fingers of his left hand against his thumb, the way you or I might make a hand puppet speak—suddenly he stops in front of the retro-70's window display and stares at his jabbering bits of anatomy as if nothing else existed—the fingers must be telling him something really important. Then his right hand comes into focus—in it is clenched the latest *Poetry Flash* with John Ashbery's picture on the cover. One night at the Cafe Babar I was sitting next to this real big mouth, a Poet who apparently was some kind of construction worker, and he kept bragging about strippers—he bellowed to his companion that other people try to rip you off but god damn! strippers always pay immediately—IN CASH. I stared at my red wine in an attempt to feign deafness—though I was itching to ask him, "What *are* the construction needs of strippers?" This guy made it sound like he was building things for them day and night. *Tossed like a stone into an immense pond of language ... chatter-waves surround me ringing in ever-widening circles from my heart to the horizon.* I hate geography.

In a tank of estrogen-based blood serum the scientist stores the exploded hookers' body parts. Slamming the lid he promises, "I'll take care of you girls later." When their evil pimp Zorro comes looking for them the parts pop up out of the tank like gooey popcorn—and have they changed! They've joined forces coalescing into Dali hybrids: random fusings of mouths hands legs high-heeled feet eyeballs lots and lots of tits they strain across the laboratory floor and pounce upon Zorro. As they drag him back to their tank the pimp yells out, "I own you girls!" I am not the same woman Quincey fell in love with—my tits sway behind my head one leg sticks out of my belly the other replaced by a manicured forearm my eyeballs are missing *a fleshy vagueness above my open waxy mouth* I pounce on Quincey drag him screaming back into my estrogen-based writing.

Halloween is a vacation from those dreadful plot points. I'll forget about Quincey, I promise.

It's debatable whether the Dead can drive cars. They lurch about in the uniforms of all classes and professions. They like to eat brains. If one of them bites you, you'll become Dead yourself. If you chop them in two their guts will squiggle out of both halves of their body, thick bloody worms, and the top half will crawl toward you snapping its

145

decomposing jaw. Decapitated, a Dead head will fall to the ground and stand on its neck as if the neck has rooted itself, the head will then flail about in circles, shouting at you violently in a big-tongued way. Some Dead can be killed by electrocution, others by a bullet in the cranium. The Dead are always ravenous, even when their digestive organs have been shot away by a flame-thrower.

A record-breaking heat wave hit Vancouver the week I arrived … I am standing in Stan Persky's kitchen my cotton nightgown clinging to my sweaty chest as if it were Kathleen Turner's blouse, the one she spilled the cherry soda on in *Body Heat*. KK and Stan are at a writing conference—I thought I was alone—so what's this heavy metal music in the back yard blaring so loud it woke me up? Barefoot, groggy and fumbling with the thin blue ribbon on the front of my gown I peek through the window … a young man absently throws rock after rock at a maple tree. Stan's street hustler friend turned gardener. He's attractive in a caveman sort of way: blond hair shagging wildly to his shoulders, tattoos, tanned muscles leap-frogging across his naked chest and arms *he looks so … anatomical* his jerky regular movements tremble with eros … everything about him is impending like a pit bull bound to break his leash. I feel like Lady Chatterley, afraid to take a bath in this house where he has all the keys, where he's trimming the hedges of Japanese yew, he looks up at me with piercing eyes then he reaches for a huge machete and begins to sharpen it *my neck's a feeble tube of breath and jugulars*. Because the body I dwell in happens to be female there is no place for this scene to go *gender is the night* so once again I opt for clothing over narrative—I hurriedly dress and begin to wait. But, what I would have given to possess (for just half an hour) a gay male body with a fistful of cash. Sam, how I'd love to live in your writing, to fuck with abandon as if that were the easiest thing in the world to come by—I want a selfish fuck, anonymous, alienated, a fuck devoid of the daily—I want to fuck like Caligula like a god on top of a mountain or in a dark mildewed alley garbage oozing from my knees like body fluids—I want to be voided to have my cunt turned inside out by the void, to fling myself like you so violently into Life that neither of us would ever survive.

Trick or treat—
Mina

November 17, 1992

Dear Sing,

It was Matt Dillon's fault … his cocky smile his raven hair, those eyes … I hadn't spoken to Dion in months, not since the night he stood me up—I sat fuming in the Cafe Picaro *an hour and a half of weak bitter coffee and my boring wrist watch* finally Dion rushed to my table, sweating, his cheeks full of corpuscles. "Well, it's about time!" He said he'd been busy beating up a former roommate who'd skipped out on the phone bill *Mina, that was the only time I could catch him! I thought you'd be a little more* UNDERSTANDING*!* But I wasn't, and he was (once again) history. Then I saw *Drugstore Cowboy* … Matt Dillon in twenty-foot close-up made me yearn for Dion … drunk, I called him from a pay phone and wailed, "I godda see you!" Dion yelled through the receiver some bullshit about betrayal, then: "How about tomorrow night?" So we started seeing each other again—just as friends—and we were very "just," our interactions friendly but empty as the bobbing head of the hula maiden in the the back window of his car—occasionally he still came on to me but halfheartedly: some people shake hands, Dion comes on. I couldn't understand what I'd seen in him. Then he mentioned he was moving to Louisiana in a couple of weeks. *An aura of imminent departure crimson and gold ghosts flared from his groin—a Southern carrot forever out of reach to my erotic donkey* BITE NOW *…* we were sipping rotgut red wine when I let it "slip" that his leaving was sexy. Dion grinned and licked a bead of red from his lower lip, "You mean we could have an affair, no strings attached?" I didn't reply to this but things were settled, it was just a matter of working out details. We went back to his apartment and sat in folding chairs in the middle of the packing mess … James Dean poster beside the bookcase, 3-D cigarette poking out of a hole drilled in the wall above James' left ear … irregular clumps of fur made the avocado shag carpet look like camouflage, like a war zone ... a cheap portable tape player warbled Lulu's "To Sir With Love"—ELEVEN TIMES *how can I thank someone who has taken me from crayons to perfume ... it isn't easy but I'll try* Dion's chair creaked as he leaned toward me his blue eyes watery and earnest, his thighs and balls splotched with poison oak from pissing in the woods, he took my hand in his and waxed on about communication and people teaching and giving to one another while Lulu belted out his favorite song *a man who taught me right from wrong and weak from strong ... that's a lot to learn.* It was kind of cute.

"Okay," I teased, "I'll lie down with you but I won't take my clothes off." A dirty foam mat tossed on the floor, no sheets, we rolled around on it agreeing to be "platonic"—while Dion took off both our shirts. No drapes on windows, wolf eyes peering through the naked glass—my favorite earrings fell, like my good sense, off my ears and into his bed. I unhooked my bra and Dion flung it across the room. Sing, it was great fun to smear myself all over this body I'd been so resistant to *never quite permeating the barrier between self and arousal* a passion distant and surprising as the soaked crotch of the panties crumpled about my ankles. He laughed as he ground his poison oak splotched thighs against mine *holes for his meanness to seep out* I wouldn't let him penetrate me, but he was satisfied—he didn't want to fuck me, he just wanted to talk me into it. At home I itched like crazy, kept checking my thin dry skin for eruptions. None appeared.

If every time I scratched I slapped his face instead he'd be black and blue, but then he's always black and blue, his raven hair, those eyes. Then he gave me his story, asked me to critique it. It's about V.D. Listen:

Well before Shari was diagnosed with The Disease with which Jack had inflicted her, there seemed something mysterious he tasted in her kiss. Something morbid yet familiar. He had recognized the taste and smell of his own blood in her saliva—warm, sour, sweet, resuscitating, uncanny. It was as though his nose were bleeding each time he kissed her, and he liked that, liked the resurgence he imagined it gave him.

Imagine 30 pages of this ... handwritten on hot pink paper ... Sisyphus oh Syphilis ... this is how I would do it:

> Shari's kiss tasted like a broken nose—his nose—and why not Jack had given her The Disease and what a kiss it was: sweet sour uncanny like Frankenstein's lightning bolt it zapped him back to life *finger-licking good.*

It still has problems ... but ... I showed Dion's manuscript to Dennis, who's studied handwriting analysis. He examined the cramped slanting scrawl and announced, "Extroverted ... passionate ... nutty ... but he won't shoot you." I asked Dennis how he'd do it:

> Jack cut himself shaving. Luckily the nick was right next to his mouth, so he licked it. It, his blood, tasted like Shari. More specifically, their kisses—that weird soup of him, her. Ever since he'd accidentally passed on the virus she'd had much more ... content, whatever.

Dion calls me on Tuesday as I feed the cats: "I have to come over—RIGHT NOW!" I rinse animal byproducts from a spoon and then he appears in my doorway with the off kilter intensity of a psychosomatic illness. His left hand is wrapped in a wad of old T shirt. He pushes past me and begins rummaging in my freezer. *Where's your ice—look at my hand* (I did—it was huge and puffy a five pound blister). *Ice!—I think I broke it!* "I don't have any ice." *Well, this will have to do.* He sits at my kitchen table, unwraps his wounded paw and tenderly rubs it with a package of

Lean Cuisine frozen entree. I can't help but smirk—the contrasty photograph on the package of choppy substance is red and tan as his flesh ... *Less Than 300 Calories*. Every summer since high school Dion's bussed tables at the Bohemian Grove: male movie stars and politicians down gourmet food in an idyllic wine country bower: one of them is Ronald Reagan *rapid cut from Reagan's toothy popcorn smile to the towel draped over the busboy's pumped-up forearm to a medium shot of excited Secret Service men to a close-up of a finger cramped on a trigger*. Dion slides the TV dinner across the back of his broken hand, "*THE PRESIDENT OF THE UNITED STATES WAS SITTING RIGHT THERE IN FRONT OF ME AND WHAT WAS HE DOING? HE WAS MAKING RACIST AND SEXIST JOKES!*" The cheerful efficient staff of busboys had to get up every morning at the crack of dawn, and, being young wild boys, they slept one hour in twenty-four. Tensions ran high. *One thick fragrant night the stars above his head were so big Dion was afraid the heavens were going to collapse ...* I imagine the scene brimming with swollen purple grapes, bees and hummingbirds ... Reagan with a crown of laurel tilted jauntily over one eye. Dion ordered his coke-snorting cabin mates to turn off the Def Leppard—he was going to go crazy if he didn't get some sleep. The one he wanted to kill was Mickey the supervisor who gave him demerits for sneaking a glass of orange juice. As I hand Dion another TV dinner we move to the present, or at least its vicinity: he went to sign up for this summer's tour of duty and found out he'd been black balled! The orange juice scandal had come back to haunt him—Dion waited for Mickey outside the hotel where he worked, threw the snitch against a wall in an alley and BAM! BAM! BAM! he headed straight for the guy's skull ... and then he came over to my place for the frozen Lean Cuisine *who can resist a man with a wounded limb it's so Lord Byron*. I yawn, "I'm late for my yoga class, you'd better drive me." When I get into his car there are spatters of blood across the window on my side. Dion rolls his eyes and says he has no idea where they came from.

I imagine you reading this letter and shaking your head, "Mina—Mina—*Mina*." You warned me about him—I haven't forgotten, it was in the Art Institute cafeteria. You were wearing a Fifth Column T-shirt and small rectangular wire rims. My camp shirt was an unbecoming egg yolk yellow. You said he was a textbook case. "Stalking is always a bad sign—Mina, keep away from Dion." Students danced in the hallways before hand-held video cameras—intuitively they know that time is plastic, easily bent by the most awkward of hacks. If I were to script my own 60's art film, I'd have *you* make love with Dion. *Glumly I look into the mirror I am so distraught I expect it to crack then Sing's fine bone structure superimposes over my moon of a face her expression like mine belongs to Liv Ullmann.* You're trained to handle his type. Not me.

As Dr. Van Helsing always says *once you let the camel into the tent it takes over the fire.*

Flattery was a toy he couldn't get enough of, like a Nintendo junkie he was going to play it until he was champ. Polishing off a bag of cookies he'd brag *I told Shelly she had the most incredible hair vermillion angel floss and then I told Deana that her big brown eyes looked like big warm honey combs they made me buzz and Cheryl had such sexy legs they made me tremble and Megan's skin was like ... I couldn't think of anything so I said "porcelain"... you should have seen her—just like the rest of them—every one of them—she turned to putty right there in my hands!* After he came he made a point of staying inside them as long as possible because this made them think he was sincere. At dinner when Dion started in on how sensuous my lips were I told him to cut the crap—I wasn't in the mood. He peeked under the table at my new tennis shoes smiled slyly and ground the sole of his boot into the white canvas. Gulping down a mouthful of carne asada he laughed *I just had to do that ...* and then something clicked something within me tentative and tinged with repulsion: desire: I'd been smudged.

I may not have liked what he did but he made me feel alive, over-burdened with random meaning.

Sitting before my mirror you twist your bangs into a pony tail that pokes straight out of the top of your head like a geyser then you smear on lipstick a very red red at odds with the cranberry of your jacket ... witnessing these details is so much more pre-cious than conversation—when Southern belle Marlene Dietrich conspires with her black maid in her dressing room we see the true Marlene (as opposed to the banana-curled wimp the men lap up) the maid moans they'll never get out of the jam they're in but Marlene looks shifty, inspired—with a retractable brush you dust your face with powder to hide the flush of your excitable cheeks *make-up ad in a recent magazine: Good girls go to heaven but naughty girls go everywhere.* At dinner Kathe B.'s red/black lip-stick smeared across her cheek ... as if talking and eating at the same time had pushed her mouth into overdrive. This made me like her. Whenever I see a person who is a mess affection jabs my heart ... the hefty office worker clenching her folding umbrella at the bus stop a run in her nylon diving beneath the hem of her skirt, a shapeless blend of ramie and polyester, her jaw tense: a woman swallowed by the dark night of the xerox machine. Out-side the Pacific Heights grocery store where they sell a dozen brands of capers a black man sits begging, cross-legged on the sidewalk braided hair peeking beneath his baseball cap ... wire rims ... a pigeon lands on his knee and he pets it ... shy crooked smile. Rush of lipstick and perfume, a white couple approaches, sweaters tied round the shoulders of their crisply-pressed week-end wear, their hair slightly crunchy from hairspray *so perfectly groomed the sidewalk turns into a runway.* The model-man tosses a quarter beyond the reach of the beggar so that he has to leap up to catch it. The model-woman laughs she's sexy she's understated and her boyfriend throws another quarter farther from the reach of the street person who leaps up even higher ... like a dog ... *I want to smudge those spotless oxfords splash something putrid on that Polo-by-Ralph-Lauren shirt body fluids ammonia rotting muck from the natural world paranormal effluvia. Volatile molecules are released into the air when cells are broken by crushing, chopping or heating.* Rubbing his hand along my back Dion asked if I could feel his scars and callouses ... *No* I lied ... *only tenderness* ... his arms and thighs clamped my body like a vice, my spine cracking in his chiropractic embrace.

Our next date was the following Friday. I was drained from working and in the throes of PMS, but given a nurturing environment, I could have made the transition to a nice unencumbered fuck *daisies come to mind rather than heavy-headed roses or the operatic odoriferous freesia.* I was the first to arrive at the coffee house so I took a seat in the back, beside the condiment table. Within minutes a dusty man was standing there shoveling sugar—a spoonful at a time—out of the burnt orange Fiestaware bowl and into a heap on the table—it looked like an ant hill made of white sand or a pale crystalline breast. His hand shook as he lit a cigarette and turned towards me puffing away, enveloped in smoke, chimneys of it ... *how did he produce these clouds of exhaust—was it technique or biochemistry?* And while we're asking questions: what about my welling anxiety—how much of it was circumstantial, how much hormonal? *Why's he glaring at* me ... I had to pee so bad it hurt, but couldn't deal with squeezing by Mr. Magic Dragon to get to the bathroom ... so I fidgeted with the *SF Weekly* "not noticing" his mumbling *rrr rrrr rrrrr bitch rrrr rrrrr rrrr cunt rrrrrrr* ... finally Dion walked through the door. Glancing over at the four-alarm condiment table he quickly surmised this was not an appropriate backdrop for our emotional drama, "Let's go get a drink." My vulnerability and derangement were increasing and the sun kept setting and setting and setting: I knew it was a bad time of the month for alcohol: I said, "Fine."

When you switch the channels the shows don't die, they fly into the ozone layer.

Remember the time you and KK and Sam and I went to the Uptown? Back then it was an artist/sleaze bar: creative types played pool with bikers while listening to jazz and oldies on the jukebox. The walls were lined with neo-expressionist paintings *dogs with large jagged teeth doing humanoid things, women with canine expressions.* All of us who went there felt hip and wild. Eventually the artists moved on. The sleaze remained. In its post-trendy phase the Uptown was Dion's favorite haunt: they had Lulu on the jukebox. As we passed through the cracked swinging doors a handful of low-rent men horsed around at the bar. A couple of stools down from them sat a heavy-set woman, very drunk in stretch pants and a plaid smock. Grimy tennis shoes dangling miles above the floor she chainsmoked and flirted, mostly with a bearded man in paint-spattered jeans and a T-shirt that said *Coors.* Sing, the words I heard come out of that woman's mouth were as dirty as her shoes. I stopped listening when I got a better look at her huge bulbous stomach. I nudged Dion, "That drunk woman's pregnant!" *Pregnant*: his gal was so blasé about it: she looked as if at any moment she would squat down squeeze out her load and jump right back on her stool and slur, "Why don't you buy a girl a drink, Babe." *Presence and absence make up everything: language, skin, bodies.* On the soaps when a heroine switches from white wine to mineral water the viewer immediately knows last month's one night of illicit passion has caught up with her—she may have been reckless then but now that she's *in a family way* she obeys the Surgeon General's warnings to the letter. I stared at the bawdy pregnant woman, quite overcome, I thought of Chaucer the Wife of Bath I thought of space aliens controlling my TV dials in the Outer Limits. "Come on, Mina," Dion pulled me to one of the broken down couches beside the jukebox and went off in search of drinks and quarters. On the next couch in a disheveled business suit slouched a man, his head drooping to one side, drooling. Totally zonked out. Occasionally he'd sense an agitation in another part of the bar and he'd jerk to life, shoot up out of his seat kicking stiffly and flailing his long arms in the general direction of the commotion. Then he'd sink back into the cushions, drooling and semi-conscious. Sing, I know what you're thinking, *not* another *weirdo*—I couldn't agree with you more *too many weirdos spoil the plot*—and in the service of narrative economy I left out the sex maniac at the Cafe Babar *insect eyes, salt-and-pepper hair* as far as this story goes I never went there and neither did Dion. But the zombie man on the next couch was real, I guessed he was flipping out on a potent drug. He seemed very strong. The pregnant woman sauntered over and started doing a dance in front of him ... wrists locked over her head, rolling her hips, her belly swayed like a giant eye-ball about to pop its socket *how can I thank someone who has taken me from crayons* ... Dion appeared grinning behind two juice glasses full of wine. The next thing I remember the man had disappeared and the pregnant woman was hysterical—he'd taken her bag. A few minutes later the man returned and said, yes he had her bag and that he would take her to it. Then she left with him and was I feeling disoriented! Just like Eileen Myles did in India: Eileen locked herself in a hotel room for a few days and read the most American book she could find ... *I* went to the bathroom, sat on the toilet merging with the unbroken mass of graffiti vining the walls *meaning painted upon meaning cryptic and decipherable* sex with Dion ... that's what I was supposed to be doing, not that I wanted to—but how could the other night exist without it? When I returned Dion had moved to a booth by the window and gotten me another drink ... then he let the bomb drop: he was leaving a week early. I'd set aside the rest of the month to screw his brains out and he was leaving early? HE DIDN'T WANT TO FUCK ME HE JUST WANTED TO TALK ME INTO IT! Then he brought up my lost earrings, how I'd left them back at his place—but—no—I didn't go anywhere with him! When he dropped me off I slammed the door of his Camaro and snarled and that's the last time I saw him. Ever.

Sex was never Dion's main source of arousal. When Dennis tires of his narrative he excites himself by murdering an unsuspecting character. I want to be one of those people whose problems are so big social scientists write books about them.

I forgot the punch line: when Dion and I were at the Uptown he told me how he often went there alone to observe the regulars. "I wonder if a lot of guys slip drugs into their dates' cocktails … I bet that guy over there—the one in the leather jacket—does it." Then he pointed to my half-empty glass and said, "Drink your wine." I felt unusually high for a glass and a half of burgundy—drunk even—and Dion kept giving me these deep-eyed looks like he knew something. By the time I got home I felt so queasy I threw up—the vomit was caustic, burning my throat. I rinsed out my mouth and walked down the hall to the bedroom where KK was tangled in the floral sheets, gently snoring. I lay down beside him and tottered across the night on a tightrope strung between paranoia and poison—time turned Baudelarian the clock ticking on, twisted and abject *wave upon wave of nausea … my blood feels carbonated how could I have so many veins how to untangle them … desert winds flush upward through my torso and into my dizzy head where brain cells pop open spewing volatile molecules … soup …*

I entered the Aqua Disco party and stood awkwardly beneath a pâpier-maché shark. In a loft high above Mission Street a hundred or so costumed revelers danced and drank. A mermaid shuffled past me—a young babe with a turquoise check tablecloth saronged about her waist, starfish painted across her naked breasts, her long blonde hair swept up into a high "I Dream of Jeannie" ponytail. She frightened me. I looked around for a friend, for an anchor to cling to. Leaning in the bedroom doorway was a woman in a platinum bubble wig, slinky polyester knit evening gown slit thigh-high, glitter pink toenails—could it really be Sing! I waved excitedly and you rushed toward me, your breasts jiggling like captive trout, your platform shoes clattering against the wooden floor, "Shit, you recognized me." "What happened to your T-shirt and jeans?" You cocked your hip and took a drag from your foot-long cigarette holder, "My cons should see me now—there's this schizophrenic who's always getting locked up, and there's me with my T-shirt and jeans, and he tells me, 'You'd think with the money you make you could dress better than that.'" You grabbed my arm, "Mina I'm gonna get you drunk," and pulled me to a bar where a cute guy in a sailor suit scooped up blue koolaid vodka punch from a fish tank—I flashed back to college, to a group of hippies dancing like ghosts in the dark along the Jordan River—they'd filled a plastic garbage can full of acid-laced koolaid which they handed out to anyone who happened to be passing by. Right after the last paper cup had been gulped *bottoms up* I arrived, the sad-faced outsider to their sparking psychedelic group mind. "Here, Mina." I stared at the sloshing blue cocktail you held out to me, "No, thanks, I think I'll have a beer."

The "Do" of Dodie and the "in" of Mina: Do in: Dion. THIS IS THE END OF THE SOMETHING-TO-WRITE-HOME-ABOUT LIFESTYLE— FROM NOW ON THE PLOT HAPPENS IN THE PAST. OR IN FANTASY. I am writing this for the Hunchback of Notre Dame, for King Kong, for every fat girl ridiculed walking home from school, for Dodie Bellamy for Dion for the armless-legless-woman who's not in the Lisette Model circus shot ... announced in the sign behind the Human Skeleton her thick generous torso is propped up somewhere beyond the right-hand border of the frame ... we have to wait for Lisette's student to actually *see* her ... this paragraph is for every person Diane Arbus photographed *(the paradoxical fragility and tenacity of life, of love)* it doesn't matter if Arbus really had sex with her subjects, not with the lens she used—I may not have fucked Dion that unfortunate Friday night but I'm fucking him now, I'm fucking every geek in that sleazy bar even the drunken fetus and, Sing, I'm fucking you, may I?

In her world view and in the world of her fiction, evil is both real and hard to spot. It does not advertise itself with elaborate dinner jackets, sinister moustachios, and wicked repartee.

Dion was gone but I couldn't get rid of him we were Siamese twins, physical removal the least of separations *birth be not proud* ... Dion as a locus for multiple shifting perceptions which continue *in absentia*—six months pass and I don't hear a word from him ... imagine an Eisenstein montage of calendar pages flying through the air like angry birds, my fretful angelic face intercut with a baby carriage rocking down a staircase—he takes the South, victorious as Marlene Dietrich ... jasmine flowers call out his name in the night, gasp "you're great" in mint julep accents ... he makes it so easy for repressed types to feel wild: he fucks them standing up and suddenly they're cats on a hot tin roof—where the hell is Dion why doesn't he write or at least place a personal ad in a magazine I'd be sure to read *I am currently incarcerated in prison and have been in solitary confinement since June. I would like to correspond with readers of* Vegetarian Times, *P.O. Box 4000, Chaingang, GA*—I'd send money orders for cigarettes and candy.

I keep getting off track ... Dion come back to me, help me squeeze out some bit of enthusiasm like the last dribble of sperm from a spent penis or that last teeny clitoral spasm ... stay inside me long enough for Sing to believe I'm sincere.

Styrofoam plates of greasy noodles and vegetables ... you and I sat in the Art Institute cafeteria discussing wardrobes in women's novels, Dion. "Keep away from him." I was suspicious of your vast knowledge of psychoanalytic theory, your enthusiastic adjectives. "Fantastic!" "Marvelous!" From your bag you pulled out a battle-scarred xerox—fluorescent yellow slashed through the text, a trail of red ink along the edges, words, exclamation points, stars. "Mina, listen to this: 'Emotionally and sexually unfulfilled, the female psychopath seeks revenge on society, particularly the heterosexual nuclear family, because of her lack, her symbolic castration.'" You laughed and popped a steaming cherry tomato in your mouth. Tomato bits spackled your lips like gore *all she wanted was love.* L-O-V-E. The "V" becomes a vice, the "L" a boomerang ... the "O" is a noose ... and the "E" with all those arms that cling and cling ... I want to be a hero the scent of blood carving deep spirals into my cheeks ... a dagger pokes out from between my words and pierces the reader's throat a mysterious light appears on the face of my writhing victim: the page is a mirror reflecting bright cinematic lights (I am behind it with my raspy hyperventilated snicker) as the reader is forced to witness his/her own death. Afterwards from the strange shape of the puncture wound the police suspect Satanism. *A watched plot never boils.* Surrounded by those smiling spoiled others who take physicality for granted, who have never had their senses break down like an appliance past its warranty, the Wolfman begs Fraulein Frankenstein for her father's diary *the Secrets of Life and Death*, it's not power he wants but a way out—you see, he can never die because the full moon feeds his life force *the most gynecological of monsters* he's got to learn how to use the dead scientist's dusty fire-bombed machines with their neon tubes and dials that point to DANGER he has to thrust the generator in reverse to drain off his furry energy, all those volatile molecules ... SIGNING UP FOR CABLE TV IS LIKE CONVERTING TO A NEW RELIGION ... people keep dying and going to the Other World—initially they cling to their earthbound personalities then there is a commercial and in the next scene they have a distant, suspiciously serene look on their faces ... the young Diane Keaton is hurled by scoliosis into the dark haze of singles bars—teacher of the deaf by day she returns to her roach-ridden apartment and obsesses on a glass mobile (etched with pornographic drawings it gently whirls and clinks above her bed) she points to it and sighs, "That's me" then she wanders like a womb through the sin-studded night she'll sleep with anyone as long as he doesn't love her, the foot-long curve of scar along her lower back connecting day and night ... a ridge or a crack ... *disease is a catalyst, it makes nice people sin* ... this morning the crazy woman who yells on Divisadero Street had a screwdriver which she used to hold a bus stop hostage, she brandished the screwdriver at tense sleepy commuters and jabbed it North West East South, shouting hysterically, "San Bruno is *that* way." I prayed she wouldn't stab anybody. Especially me. Behind her a woman was crossing the street in a suit that was so red she glowed. When a car skidded to a halt just missing her the almost-accident-victim joked to her companion, "At least the blood would have matched my outfit." Strip of white blouse against her crimson jacket she looked like a kotex on two legs ... or a piece of performance art ... to represent the cunt two women stand side by side pretending to be flowers unfurling as a red-clad woman moves back and forth between them: MENSTRUATION: I turn to Dion and declare, "I'm never having sex again!"

Love,
Mina

January 8, 1993

Dear Sing,

You tell me about the show at Cinematheque, "An Evening of Films Dealing with Women's Sexuality," you expected it to be a bust *distressed found footage, oceanic Anais Nin banalities, yet another contrasty SM scenario, "Pierced nipples, big yawn."* But then a woman spread her legs pushing her skirt down between them *Mina she was so hot* the camera so lovingly trained on her, the sentimental overdubbing, verisimilitude did a quick dissolve and the screen became her body sensuous and super-eight—as I sit on the bedroom floor in a slinky pink dressing gown your soft syllables gliding off the receiver, the phone becomes my body *I feel utterly … grainy.* I pull back my pink brocade collar to reveal a pale neck that smells of coffee lavender and funk. A pulse as elusive as you. Hint of freckled shoulder softened daily with calendula and honey. I want to live in a cheap hotel with cigarette burns in my clothing.

Girlfriend, there's something I've been keeping from you, a tidbit that even my therapist doesn't know: it's about the night Quincey and I broke up. I said *put your pants on and get the hell out of here* he lingered in the hallway his long arms reaching out for me, I shuddered and yelled DON'T TOUCH ME! and pushed him out the door. Literally. There were tears in his eyes. Scenes can be so deceiving: if the reader had entered this one just a few minutes earlier she'd see that it was me, in fact, who was being dumped. I knew he'd be back *oh my soul NO* I couldn't go through it again, had to do something quick—before he had his key in the ignition I was on the phone with his wife, "Hello, Lucy, this is Mina. How're you doing? I just wanted you to know that Quincey and I have been having sex several times a week for the past six months …" Lucy screeched through the receiver, "Thanks for fucking up my life."

Kiss and tell: because of my big mouth KK treated me like a criminal (Mina, that poor woman, how could you!) but, Sing, I couldn't help myself anymore than my cat could for massacring that bird in the living room last week *orgy of down and feathers beneath the bay windows, rotting avian corpse under the couch. I am the dark lyrics of a dark era the eros of the oral.* I felt guilty and misunderstood as Conceptual Artist Lesley Ann Warren. Lesley Ann made her New York name creating metal sculptures with guillotine arms in sharp serpentine arcs that snap down trapping observers' body parts. For a change of pace she puts an ad in the personals *Call Apology and confess your sins* she even records a male friend on the answering machine to mimic a priest. "I'll splice together the best confessions and lock unsuspecting audience members in a metallic latticework confessional where they'll have to rate the sins on a ten-point scale!" Lesley Ann theorizes that the piece is about linking humanity. Nobody but me seems to buy this. Then a psychopath named Claude starts calling and the other characters blame Lesley Ann for his murders. I'm worried for her—I've seen enough HBO to predict Claude will soon come after *her.* She's a very complex unconventional woman: she smokes cigarette after cigarette as if she's wrestling them. Lesley Ann traps Claude in the confessional and sets the whole contraption on fire. Then she repents and cancels her show even though it would have made her a world-renowned artist. Shame on you, Lesley Ann, for TAKING ADVANTAGE OF PEOPLE THROUGH ART!

Quincey impaled my heart with his cock and that type of thing changes a person night and day flip flop you feel so close to death you have to steal a gulp of life wherever you can get it. He left a gaping hole in my chest that only his eradication could fill. And Lucy, I hoped, would finish him off.

Sing, *I* haven't learned my lesson—quick—before we lose momentum—pretend I'm Lesley Ann's clergy machine tell me something about *you* something mushy and true.

Love,
Mina

June 3, 1993

Dear Dr. Van Helsing,

You asked Dodie how it feels to live in a woman's body, asked Dodie to mail you a list *5–10 observations of aspects.* Point number one: as she walks down Market Street her pubic bone itches a sharp jabbing itch a pinching it's maddening but unlike the men I've seen absently clawing their crotches she endures hers. Any analysis of this would be feminism and as you well know, Dr. Van Helsing, I'm too *post* for that I'm so full of posts straight men sometimes mistake me for a fence. Why bother *Dodie* about these corporeal verities? She's just passing through, a breeze animating a few molecules, while I Mina Harker am here for the duration. When Dodie isn't in the mood she whines to KK, "Sorry, but I just can't deal with physicality right now." See what we're up against?

Rendezvous slams your letter down on my kitchen table and exclaims, "Male voyeurism! Don't answer him." On the edge of Mina's mouse pad there sits a piece of "candy" made of blown glass she flicks it with her finger making it twirl: NO COMMENT.

Point number two: the morning rush hour train glides to a halt … through the windows humans newspapers briefcases the occasional quality paperback are packed in there like ice cream, a carton of hot stuffy ice cream … to me a singular one on the platform with air around me so much air I can stretch my arms in any direction *entry* seems an impossibility … when the doors slide apart a half dozen frazzled commuters charge out and I slip in *a woman with red lips and these cloying yellow walls* within moments any spare cranny of emptiness is completely swallowed by bodies I grab onto a vertical rail a couple inches beneath a man's hand a rough hand attached to a metal watchband attached to a muscular bare arm attached to the sleeve of a T-shirt *blueblack vein a fuse* mahogany hair sweeps down his forearm like birds in migration *their group consciousness tugging* ... my back is turned to the owner casually I glide my head to the left, sunglasses appear in the periphery then flash of face too quick to register as image *a face I want to float behind me forever whispering commands and biting my neck* his fist slips down the rail or mine up and our hands brush: warmth ripples from forefinger to elbow *I'll take this man's arm his faceless face home with me tonight any necessary personality I can easily supply I've got plenty stashed away in the embossed stripes of my damask sheets: narrative lines: his blueblack vein a fuse igniting desire.* Dodie notes this all in a journal lined with cork—a tribute to the greatest of prose stylists—but cork is confusing *brittle yet elastic whorled as a slice of desiccated brain* in Proust's case I was so naive assuming that cork kept the clamorous outside at bay: KK swears it was to keep his sex kinks in *he got off on torturing rats* how would he answer your letter? *Shoulder-length black hair kind of messy, thick-rimmed glasses dorky-chic, white letters on black jersey chest* Dodie dreams of the day she'll boot me and this new narrative business to the moon (*NEVER*) she wants to churn out novels that get reviewed wants to take these pages and pages of *veins arms T-shirts cunts* and ascribe them to *imaginary* constructed characters she can control a circus acrobat an environmental attorney riding a subway in New Jersey. *Dodie, didn't you learn anything from Mary Shelley—a monster stitched together from stolen body parts hobbling and drooling and crashing through walls—do you really want to substitute that braindead* THING *for the graceful cohesive eyewitness Mina Harker?*

THE FEMALE BODY IS NOT A BARREL OF MONKEYS.

Folding one sock inside the other Rendezvous beams, "You don't see me doing my laundry with anyone else but you!" I bite my lower lip, fire back: "Rendezvous, you'd better watch out for these declarations." *Sartorial monogamy* his girlfriend gets his tongue Mina gets his speeches *his cute clumsy hands on my pink Victoria's Secret French-cut briefs* I slap him, "Stick to your own pile. I'll fold my own."

Long ago I learned never to trust a mortal *their tunnel-visioned interpretations devouring the dead their endless revisions* … from Aeschylus to Christa Wolf … how dare you teach Dodie that the text is my body! It's taken me five years to ram it into her star-struck skull THE TEXT IS NOT MY BODY as if emotions weren't visceral as if I Mina Harker the debutante of the (un)dead could be concrete in such a flat way, page number typed in my upper right corner WHERE ARE MY ARMS MY LEGS WHY CAN'T I MOVE ABOUT—THE TEXT IS NOT A BODY it's a coffin … or a space alien's cranium … to study that ever elusive creature *the human being* the intergalactic lifeform projects a Victorian mirage and peoples it with actors in period costumes … for decades the characters wander through this desperate Shangri-la still young though never alive … conscious of their own illusion they play canasta listless and bored … the alien holds all the cards … then a young man exhibits "hope" and the mansion dissolves into a giant pal-pitating cerebrum surrounded by trees THE TEXT is my nimble-footed footprints as I race from thought to thought.

It is absurd to dissect a poet's brain to find the cause of his sonnets; his cortex undeniably had to exhibit specific brain-wave patterns to produce a sonnet, but they have evaporated and been carried to a realm hidden by time.

Imagine fucking the TEXT … when Sam tried it with a porn magazine the glossy contortions of ass and torso became crinkled and globbed with his ecstatic goo men from previous pages stuck together bled through, a wash of encounters and positions, top-fucking-amalgamated-rough-cock-sucking-pierce-nippled-naked-leather-bound-bottom-boy many-limbed as Shiva. Sam was always one step ahead of his time … now that the pathetic is the hot thing in art he could display his matted inspiration in the Arts Commission Gallery *What Was Once Perfect Is No Longer.* It would be hard for me to mess up a magazine. I suppose I'd have to sit on it. I thumb through the new Victoria's Secret catalogue in search of my favorite model, Frederique—my cunt has lips but no tongue it clenches dilates and drools but will never speak *who needs words when Frederique has those tits* I imagine her classy jaw chiseled between my thighs—KK says Frederique doesn't have a brain in her head—but who needs brains with that ash blonde widow's peak rosebud navel that beigy-pink mouth with its mysterious smirk *my cunt gulps down her image whole.*

LIMBO DELAYED

So, Dr. Van Helsing, how many points have I plotted thus far on this graph of physiology? You can never predict what will happen when the body moves from dimension to dimension—sometimes it merges sometimes it shatters sometimes it dons overdetermined eye make-up and mimics Liza Minnelli. People breathe into petri dishes—time ticks, cultures spring up—an artist displays them in a show in Chicago and I read about them in a xerox Liz Kotz mails from New York *the last frontier where the me meets the non-me insensate and uncontrollable creeping across brown jelly* Dodie believes one should desire only appropriate objects *beings in available bodies who toss their reciprocity around like a fiery ball* but Dr. Van Helsing, don't you think it's more interesting when they don't want you back when loving you would never cross their minds—or better yet—the thought of your love makes them laugh on the street THERE ARE PLENTY OF SKELETONS THESE LETTERS DON'T DISCUSS in the next booth a couple of retirees sip martinis … amid a ricochet of blue wall blue shirt blue eyes a stuffed marlin arcs above Rendezvous' head he swallows a mouthful of pancake and pokes his fork in the air like a cue stick: "Van Helsing wants you to push into alignment that which is out of line—typical male gaze—don't answer him!"

Dear Dr. Van Helsing: Imagine you're a balloon full of water—*obviously you're not a metaphor but Dr. Van Helsing set aside your penis and hairy epidermis DO IT FOR MINA step inside HER contextual skin*—imagine you're a balloon full of water and instead of latex your edge is made of tissue, taut and easily punctured, webbed with a tangle of charged nerve endings *the slightest breeze makes them prickle* imagine the unrelievable pressure an inside that wants to disrupt and slosh all over the sidewalk you cup your breasts in a futile attempt to hold it all together *unconscionably bulbous, fecund* the rosy tips ache as if invisible fingers were pinching them ... imagine how exposed you feel how terrified of collision—of implosion—the lines of tension originate behind the eyeballs and zig through your brain like the kinks in the Bride of Frankenstein's hair people gape as you pass them swishing bloated as a cow's udder *titty-pink and squinting* imagine pulling panty hose over this mass.

Standing before me was an anatomical materiality with its arm outstretched I walked along the curb, conscious of its chemical composition, its capacity for brute action. It asked me for money and when I ignored it, it muttered *you fucking bitch* but even before it spoke I saw those words floating in a thought bubble above its skull.

Prepare for the vision of the inward eye.

Rendezvous twisting the wheel on the freeway off-ramp: "Americans have to have it coming out of their mouths before they realize they're eating shit!" Just a stick shift between us yet his body seems remote, suspended *this isn't the first time I've had glaucoma in the relationship department* I slap his thigh—to illustrate a point *a by-stander not knowing the techniques* I wonder what it's like to live in Rendezvous's body does it feel androgynous—or testosterone-crazed? Does he play with his cock dreaming of that time I kissed him *lips as wooden as the Trojan horse.* You warned me about him, you said, "Mina, if you stick your fingers in jam things are bound to get sticky."

IDLE MALE BODY—I LAY MODEL BED

It takes more than two eyes to take it all in ... I'm strolling past the B of A parking garage when at block's end I see this guy approaching *lanky dark-haired WM* every few feet he pauses and slams a vinyl raincoat against the wall *concrete corridor, splash of dayglo yellow* I speed up, stare straight ahead at the buses on Mission Street while in the periphery I monitor his movements, scanning for any verb projecting that intrusive preposition *towards* he gives the garage a good flail *shiny yellow whoosh truncated by a crackling thud then him growling,* "Hey babe, need some dick? I'll give you some dick." *Hormonal signals go racing down your neurons to focus your eyes, prick up your ears, jerk your back muscles upright, and swivel your head in alarm* I know he doesn't want to *give* me anything. I imagine accosting some unsuspecting dude walking home from work in his London Fog *I whack my linen jacket against the wall and snarl, "Need some pussy?"* never could I attain my desired response *this woman's a creep I'd better cross to the other side.* That's why I stick to Literature for my effects HEY RENDEZVOUS, NEED SOME PUSSY? I'LL GIVE YOU SOME PUSSY.

If only I cared more ... but when Quincey left me my caring left too, it flapped after him and was lost in the night sky between San Francisco and Berkeley. As I bend over to unjam the xerox

170

machine my breast falls out of my bra. Reaching inside my blouse I flash to the woman last Saturday on Joe Bob's Drive-in Theater her tits were large as world globes *spinning in the classroom they invite you to plunk your finger down on an unknown continent* lasciviously she lifted them and on the underside of each emerged an animated head its rotund stretched-flesh face scrunched and beady-eyed as the man in the moon's. Things have never progressed that far with me.

On my way to the Taoist restaurant my pants were the wrong color the wrong size cutting into my crotch like an inept lover—so I bought a new pair. At the top of the red carpeted stairs is a makeshift temple—through plate glass windows I peered into a room filled with bouquets and sticks of incense ... Asian faces all male hanging from the walls in gold frames ... apples and persimmons and powdery cakes arranged in mounds beside an altar *a god with a sweet tooth, like Mina during* PMS I disappeared through a swinging door *Ladies* locked myself in a toilet stall and CHANGED then I stuffed the old clothes in the bottom of a trash can *I want to wipe out that face that stares back at me in the mirror a face that's witnessed too many stories with bangs that look like they've been run over by a lawnmower.* In the dining room I eat my Lo Han rice plate vaguely watching a young hippie couple—she in a blue floral ankle-length dress, brown hair pulled back into a bun, no make-up, big nose—he with curls the color of milky coffee, tie-dyed T-shirt, glasses, faded jeans—beside them a canvas Sierra Club bag. They're chatting—very politely—with a parental-looking couple as the young woman reaches under the table and rests her hand on the boyfriend's thigh ... then she begins to creep her fingers up his leg like the eentsy-beentsy spider ... when she gets to the crotch she looks over and frowns at my nosiness—so I chase a wild mushroom across my plate with a chopstick. The next time I sneak a peek he's covered his lap with a napkin. Dr. Van Helsing there are so many crotches in the world and I have so many fingers ... how could I end up empty handed?

MALE BODY LIED—DEADLY MOBILE—I YODEL BEDLAM

Ninety-eight percent of the atoms in your body were not there a year ago. The skeleton was not there three months ago. A new skin every month a new stomach lining every four days a new liver every six weeks. Even within the brain, whose cells are not replaced once they die, the content of carbon, nitrogen, oxygen, and so on is totally different today from a year ago. There is never a definitive edition but zillions of editions, each time you greet a living being you never know which one you're reading THE TEXT IS WHOSE BODY?

(NO)body

I've been corresponding with a fan in D.C. "I adore you beyond belief," he wrote out of the blue, "your sentences are like truffles, white chocolate, raspberry, a dream of the Caspian Sea." So, of course, I answered. After a few letters he asked for my picture. A ghostly lover is fine by me *eros scurrying like a mouse beneath a bedspread* but this lure I couldn't bear this twist from the Personals *MWF* I felt my hair grow puffy, wanted to put on spandex. When I refused he wrote back, "Then how about a DNA sample?" My body felt generous I was having my period *a surplus flux of genetic debris* I coated a finger and smeared a watery red arc inside a greeting card *cunt blood on white cover stock* beneath it I carefully printed in black ink "DNA" then I stuck on a stamp and the relationship was history *I was giving him more than he asked for and I hardly recognized myself in it ... purged in the fires of the Book of Life I felt utterly bewitching my flaming hair crinkling like seaweed my logo-glossed lips spewing opinions* the point is to fibrillate the sophisticated facade *you're not as cool as you thought you were, worm.* In Argento's *La Setta* devil worshippers insert hooks all around the edges of a woman's face oversized fishing hooks attached to lengths of strong cord *the measure of aesthetic distance* the devil worshippers tug on the cords stretching up the skin beneath each hook like an ant hill then the woman's features rip off in one fine wobbling piece *pink silk spattered with lymph and blood* the red dripping head that remains droops from the woman's neck ambiguous and precise as a plate from *Gray's Anatomy* the lovingly-rendered muscles striped with shock. As I write this I pinch my cheeks pulling cones of flesh away from my skull. It hurts. I think *these are hooks of rejection … compliments pass right through them like air.*

ALL LETTERS TO MINA ARE LOVE LETTERS *struck by Zeus and raped by Apollo … it's all so sticky …* a woman could go crazy trying to wrestle *sensation* from these obdurate words: the acidic flush of my infected bladder versus the blunt jab between my shoulder-blades versus the shy insistence of my bruised calf *that tender inner portion just beneath the knee* where the woman whacked me with a bright blue umbrella I was pushing my way out of the sub-way train as she was entering I tripped on something that's what I thought then this pain in my leg and her yelling, "That's what you get for …" but the doors closed and I never found out— what I got this—for—the motion of the tibia punishes the flesh a soreness that advances and recedes with each step *people were rushing in I didn't even see her coming* SO MANY POINTS OF PAIN I sit here tapping away at the alphabet while beneath my skirt my black satin slip my olive tights my practical cotton briefs beneath the spongy mush of my belly I burn with a discomfort the word "urgency" doesn't begin to approach. Dr. Van Helsing, does it show?

This doesn't mean I'm undifferentiated magma.

Are not the thoughts of men and women in the agony of death often turned toward the practical, painful, obscure, internal, intestinal aspect, towards that 'seamy side' of death which is, as it happens, the side that death actually presents to them and forces them to feel, a side which far more closely resembles a crushing burden, a difficulty in breathing, a destroying thirst, than the abstract idea to which we are accustomed to give the name of Death?

MILE LEAD BODY—DIE BODY ALL ME

Science is relearning what the NOSE KNOWS: typhoid smells like baking bread, German measles like stale beer, yellow fever like a butcher shop, smallpox like sweating geese. The gallbladder is rancid, the heart scorched, the spleen is fragrant and sweet, the large intestine or lung is rotten. The man on the bus stinks of shit *a disturbance in identity, system, order* has he rolled in it or are these his insides seeping into the mass transit atmosphere, mingling with the gasoline and tired perfume. I cover my nose and squint my eyes *the body dissolves in language salt on a slug* the skin talks, and says I'VE HAD ENOUGH *I want X but I do not intend to do it/I want X but I am not doing it/I do X (in fantasy) but I do not (actually) do it/I want X but I do not want to want it* lying on my stomach hipbones press into the mattress gas moving through the left side of my gut *a prickly ball* garlic for supper hormones for days KK beside me long and hot as a blistered frankfurter and then there's the genitals, Dr. Van Helsing *I would like to eat this I would like to spit this out* after his paper at the post-structuralist conference Rendezvous moaned he felt like a condom with a Happy Face *hisssssssssssssssssssssssss.*

From the balcony of Josie's Juice Joint I scan the crowd below *papier-mâché iguana plaster stork* a gay man reads the word "titties" out loud and laughs; others are silently eating coffee cake I take a bite *cinnamon crunchies and gooey pink fruit marbleized in a moist buttery crumb my mouth is in love* I remember sitting beside my mother and her friends at the kitchen table, they discuss their husbands and operations, I am drinking milk from a cobalt-blue aluminum glass *my brother and I have scraped away the paint around the rim with our teeth* now they're on their pregnancies the heroic feats of pain and near-catastrophe from which issued all the neighborhood children, my mother philosophizes *Thank God you don't remember pain* the other women nod then proceed to detail the hours of unendurable torment they endured delivering Joey and Pat, Bridget and Dodie my mother slaps my arm *stop scraping that rim you're gonna die of lead poisoning* I put down my fork my latest lipstick *Grecian Goddess Gold* staining the prongs *orangy metallic gleam* a woman beneath me exclaims, "I've already told you more than I know!" Absently I browse through my Victoria's Secret catalogue … the term *form fitting* has been replaced with body conscious as in *eyelet embroidery decorates Frederique's body conscious tee* or *the bodyshaper bike short creates a perfect silhouette under the season's body conscious knits.* Clothing conscious of the body? Extended proximity with human flesh has caused it to mutate an awareness … cupping the breasts the bra comes to desire the milky orbs … or to punish them … curved wires press into my torso and stretch toward a hot pink binding across the middle of my back—lacy elastics indent my shoulders bearing a weight that feels simultaneously like self and non-self … if words replace the body and clothes replace the mind … then … *stretch lace offers a splendid shape, offers more noticeable décolletage, offers firm support with a front closure.*

Love,
Mina

August 22, 1993

Dear David,

Up to now Dodie's been signing the letters you've received, I've been guiding her hand by remote via a transmitter embedded in the base of my skull—or I've tried to. *"Direct input," Harvey Keitel intones in* Saturn 8. *"Brain to brain." Farrah Fawcett gasps.* Robots are such a struggle, developing wills of their own, sucking up the dregs of their creator's subconscious, smashing the space shuttle with lean articulated steel, so now I'm writing to you directly—you, David, are my sticky core the tar baby my narrative bits glom onto—or at least try to *no one is more elusive than a fan* your postcard is propped against my copystand … unsigned … no zip code … you gave your sleep tips: *"How about like extreme doses of lactic acid, counting sheep, reciting the tetragrammaton backwards, making peace with reality, waving the crucifix, hurling all your china at the wall, yogic postures, imagining yourself dead in the 23rd century."* Your first letter was so sweet, you wrote my words were like truffles *white chocolate, raspberry.* Six months later all I get is sleep tips? The postcard's a thesis, on the front a distraught woman stands beside the Transamerica Pyramid comparing the landmark to the picture she's holding *real* Egyptian pyramids, the caption reads SAN FRANCISCO ANOTHER ILLUSION SHATTERED on the left edge of the card you've pasted an inch-square photo of a mannequin in a scholar's robe *Mina Harker is studied and dissected beneath David's cool abstracted gaze* dream on Love you won't gain control that easily.

I'm willing to chop off my nose to spite my face.

Where did you ever come from? Your postmarks say Washington D.C., but that's no answer. When you were a boy did you squat in the backyard learning to crow *ur ur urur* did you play Statue …

crisp scent of freshly mown grass neighborhood kids in shorts and T-shirts twirl with their arms outstretched, when the leader yells freeze you stumble to a halt and hold whatever position you "happen" to land in, then the leader pushes the button on your shoulder and you act out the statue your pose suggests *the revelation of subjectivity as an accident, as an intersection of extra-subjec*tive *circumstance … bear, soldier, scholar* I always managed to throw myself into graceful swanlike relief, "Mina you're cheating—you can't be a ballerina every time!" *my characteristic distrust of spontaneity* if I left things up to Dodie I'd be grubbing the lawn like a worm. How often does a guy get his favorite heroine to write him back—it's as likely as a sign from a merciful God … *"If you can't handle me as a fan, fuck you and the space-ship you rode in on!!"* Molested by a compliment. David, you don't answer Dodie's letters but you ask for more MINA *my writing is a speculum you press your lens against, my cervix round and puffy as a pair of tightly pursed lips a bead of mucus exudes from the center glue for wayward sperm* Dodie snaps her knees together GET HIM OUT OF HERE! She stands between us like a Victorian chaperone—though you're pretty prim yourself: in your "decadent" novel men and women hurl their bodies together and then the quick dissolve.

There is a bathroom to the left of my desk—whenever I'm dazed I stare at the Argento poster pinned above the porcelain tank, amid a crimson rectangle floats the horizontal profile of a woman, her visible eye is closed, her striated rosy lips relaxed *sleeping beauty* her nose points upward to white serif type TWO EVIL EYES the back of her head dissolves into an almond-shaped pair as large as my fists *vertical black slits in a yellow field edged with bursts of vermillion—cat eyes*—bowed skeletal fingers clamp on the gold chain of a pocket watch, the time is 11:30—white helvetica bold on either side "WHEN I WAKE YOU… YOU'LL BE DEAD." I liked the image better before I saw the movie, before I found out what it "meant" *if you die when under hypnosis you can't enter the land of the dead—the Others will possess your body—you'll end up a zombie that wails "WAKE ME!"* The cat eyes are another story. To the right of the toilet a drainpipe is painted the same red as the poster, an artery in the belly of the beast *like something out of a dream, a pipe dream—is that blood being pumped out of the wall and into the floor? Or vice versa? Is my bathroom a mortuary?*

And if I swallow anything evil put your finger down my throat.

So what if you're out of reach, 3,000 miles away, I'm not a materialist—I see a man with dark hair designer glasses hunter green socks, a fortyish writer with a wife and child, a sketchy youth spanning South America and Europe, a businessman who grows wealthy framing art *fragments dense with narrative possibility* you eat cookies chocolate Tandoori drink darjeeling jog *suggestively displayed but not definitely arranged* you think me the daughter of Genet Burroughs Almodovar—well think again. Look outside my bedroom window you'll see my three faces spray-painted across red brick—the left Mina's yellow happy face is sandwiched between a mint green WORLD CAUSE her black dot eyes and crescent mouth are bleeding she has a cute red button nose *I've never disputed the existence of objective reality* the middle Mina is more literal, humanoid eyes nose lips arched yellow brows, two gold medallions—TITS—beam south of her throat—the Mina to her right is a Picasso baboon, swollen red eyes crooked wrought-iron lashes black slashes for tears frenetic curlicue nose, her face funnels down to four little humps: teeth or truncated fingers beneath her chin wriggling *Hi, David.*

After six years of marriage I still wake to a love note stuck on the TV screen: three-by-five yellow Post-It: *Sorry about last night. Don't ever leave me. p.s. Don't forget to tape the show—it's* Inner Sanctum *with Tanya Roberts—on Cinemax.* That evening we press the PLAY button and enter another marriage *cheating husband, crippled wife* she dreams her lips have melted together and fused *a taut wall of putty* from her wheelchair she watches her husband fuck Nurse Tanya BAM *squeak* BAM *squeak* Tanya's garter belt is antiseptic white to match the mini-skirted uniform crumpled on the floor BAM *squeak* with each giddy thrust the wife's putty maw roughens and blisters BAM *squeak* her eyes bulge with tears her flat bubbly face grunts as the camera pans over her breasts *beneath her gown they wriggle pale and urgent as hungry piglets* there's nothing wrong with her legs beyond some muddled hysterical fear. Last week's movies were just as miserable—*Freud* and *The Tingler* back to back I could hardly tell them apart *if something scares the shit out of you, sign up for therapy or scream because if you don't release it a hysterical symptom/multi-limbed monster will arise out of the base of your spine and crush you* hysteria is more common than tinglers because memories are easier to repress than screams—when mad scientist Vincent Price tries to frighten himself to death with LSD the tingler zaps up his spine his eyes bug his hands clench the edge of a table *I mustn't scream I mustn't scream it will ruin my experiment* then he shrieks bloody murder and the tingler shrinks back to microscopic potential—Price's only recourse is the deaf mute silent-movie-theater owner who already faints at the sight of blood *the coupling of remembrance and reciprocal persecutions* and tonight James Woods shoved a videotape into the VCR-cunt in his abdomen *talk about a visceral response* DAVID do I ever give you one? *Fingers paralyzed above the keyboard terrible knowledge shocks your buttocks* TZSSSSSSSZZZZZ *you should have known that desk chair was electrified.*

Noisy demons crouch beneath pink matter yelping SHIT FUCK PISS FUCK SHIT SHIT FUCK PISS SHIT FUCK there's an ear inside me armed with a knife it won't stop listening. These are my symptoms, what are yours? Tarzan yodels from the Brazilian pizza place *probably the Samoan boys playing pinball* cats sleep at the foot of the bed a pair of overlapping fur circles *jungle geometry* when KK opens the door he's made up his mind, "Mina is heartless I don't want her in our bed" *DAVID CAN YOU IMAGINE THE …* Dodie's face goes blank but that doesn't stop him—no—he continues: **any love or kindness is Dodie seeping in** MINA TAKES FOR HER OWN PLEASURE SHE HAS NEVER DONE ANYTHING NICE FOR ANYBODY! Dodie's vocal chords remain suspiciously limp so I take possession, muse, "What about sex—Mina gives a lot through sex." "Besides sex." I purse Dodie's lips, roll her eyeballs to the ceiling to give the impression of thinking: "Mina tells funny stories to entertain people." "Even a heartless person can tell funny stories." Dodie's hands flatten against his chest, her lips collapsing to grimace, "Mina's stories aren't heartless, they're warm and human in the tradition of Thurber." KK, that sly dog, latches onto Thurber, turns the conversation around to rabbits and then Jack Spicer. I untie Dodie's bathrobe spread her legs glide my hand across her snatch *moist putty … I am the puppeteer* I squeeze her labia open and closed like a mouth, "Mina says hello." Then I pull him down, circle her legs around his waist, rhythmically clench and rub her sex against him like a child humping the arm of a couch.

My vocabulary did this to me.

A presence arrives erratically in the mail its name is David it sends me its novel *a long-haired American seeks God and fortune among drug-dealing Eurotrash* whenever he walks into their rooms women in knock-you-dead shoes fondle his rod, ravenously fuck him anyplace they can lean their tushes against *as long as you're up Menschkin it's a pity to waste it* incredible shoes: red with short blue heels studded with scores of tiny rhinestones, black cardboard bows glued to sides—white polka-dotted purple open-toes—stack-heeled paisley, straps twining in helixes up her thighs—white cowboy boots—sequined scarlet vamps with silver buckles yellow bows and sharp heels wrapped in foil—red alligator boots—razor-heeled snakeskin, midnight blue bows straps painted in zebra stripes *"I picked one up and held it in my hand like a tiny animal"* what other kinks lie beneath his 100% USDA butch surface *a box full of snapshots that reek of Deborah Harry and absence* David I suspect I'm too stodgy for you—I type this with ratty terrycloth on my feet, colorless from dust and wear *a humdrum Scheherazade* how can I entice you to come night after night … what if I invent a new persona—Lilith *she strips off her outer gear, throws open her chemise and shows her person and all the rondure of her hips—a construction so tantalizing even gay men have wet dreams about her* Lilith will be anything you want *the dimples on her ass are deep enough to cup the head of your dong* tell me what really turns you on and I'll turn you and she'll turn you, believe me you'll turn.

"As far as your skin collapsing and having your entrails pour out like sludge, I'd say it's a twenty-to-one longshot."

I smear my dejecta on paper, a messy ambiguous space where pathology meets pleasure—let me smear Lilith, her Balinese hair ornaments her strutting vocabulary—I peeked inside her closet once, it was divided as Clark Kent's *corporate drag colliding with skimpy nocturnals* I've seen her purse her lips like red bouquets toss off sexual predilections with the ease of naming her favorite flowers *cockscomb, virgin's bower, night-blooming cereus, vanilla, winter cherry.* Tuesday at the Thai cafe she ogles the toys from Sunday's SM party, "I didn't know what half of them were for—but did I find out!" Languidly she points to her lace stockings and announces, "I think I'm turning into a lace queen." Her lips sear with chili peppers and innuendo, "Though I plan to get more butch as I grow older." Ladling out seconds of lemon grass soup she muses, "After all, you can't be a cream puff forever!" Demure sip of water from a plastic glass—she peers over the rim with bedroom eyes—then sets it down and tilts her chin at a jaunty angle, "No, you can't be a cream puff forever!"

You write me a poem, you want to perform magic, you turn to Mina's primal simultaneity. *"I had to gain some kind of access just because of all the faulty rhymes the chinks in consciousness letting up for just a moment he fell through into some twisted little pigeonhole. It's two a.m. and I'm wearing pale blue underwear as I write this."* David isn't it spooky down there in that pigeonhole? I bet you never twist that little pigeonhole with the lights off, I haven't met a man yet who enjoys doing it in the dark *"but I want to see what you look like"* PSHAW what you really want—all of you—is a visual anchor to tug you back from those godawful spasms, those cataclysmic lacunae *you pretend your cock is a lighthouse, cry out not for pleasure but for rescue—chicken shits* my life's work is clinging to borders, like the sweat that beads the kitchen window on icy winter mornings *through the misty glass the twin golden domes of St. Joseph's church gleam in the first rays of sunrise* standing before this vision barefooted in a ripped flannel robe I grind coffee and remember of my color photography class back in Chicago *not even a crack under the door to ground me among the living … the darkroom is a sweltering closet with sinks full of water I'm supposed to hold at an exact temperature somewhere above 100° but the thermometer always wavers and my slides end up mottled with weird FX … in this absolute blackness the same tubing is used for both the hydrogen and the oxygen if we don't clear the tubes between agitations, the instructor warns us, the whole contraption will blow up … my wet trembling hands grope for tanks and dials.*

Dennis and I emerge from the parking garage, walk to INTERNATIONAL ARRIVALS, wait in the airless florescence for Earl's flight from Amsterdam. A short woman in a shawl descends the gently-sloping ramp, her roundness and advanced age announcing a cozy Old Worldness ... slowly she places—one—foot—directly—in—front—of—the—other, still she falters and grabs the rail. An eager triad *man woman girl* watch on, their faces rapt with her progress they reach out their arms spread their fingers *suction cups pulling her closer* "MOMMA!" When she finally steps off the ramp they run over the yellow line of NO ENTRY clamp onto her cabbage-scented body squirming and groaning—we stand beside this gyrating clump of three generations *lips pucker shoulders are squeezed waists encircled cheeks rubbed* their weeping escalates to wails, salty tears streaming down their faces *MOMMA! MOMMA!* Dennis is caught up in them too, he blurts out, "Can you imagine feeling *that much?*" I think of the night Quincey left me the door slammed and I ceased to be a woman or any abstraction for that *matter* I was a body that ate and shit and sniveled and resonated with pain *basso profundo* KK held me in his arms to keep me from vibrating off the edge of the bed—I think of those four or five days each month when the decision to keep Dodie alive is gruelingly weighed *the Mina Harker slouched before this terminal is no accident* Earl rushes towards us, hickeys blotching his neck, rope burns on wrists *he checked out every sex club on Dennis' map* black leather bag bouncing against his thigh *he spent his vacation in a coffin.* "Great," he exclaims, "It was great!"

Lacking contact with flesh, pearls in bank vaults grow brittle and dull ... Erica Jong could make a poem out of this. Lilith makes a living. "My glands are miraculous," she's been known to say, "I'm the best pearl reviver in town." When the tellers have all gone home to their lackluster lives Lilith arrives at the vault and strips, then a guard enters and drapes her flawless physique with string after string of pearls cold jolt of beads against her sternum *she gasps* but soon her bustling biochemistry warms them to weightless *nursemaid to mineral deposits* fat white orbs float about her neck soaking up oil and perspiration *paid to be nude and to exude—finally a job that doesn't conflict with her principles* Lilith grows drowsy, lets her eyes slip shut as the pearls' sheen swells translucent in the thin green air.

Your first letter was an entry, an infection: *"I close my eyes and cross my hands, touch the keyboard, reach for you across electricity, some kind of villain braille, some kind of synapse created for just this moment"* that night I started making love with men I'd never seen … I've had these dreams for months now, precise masculine features that refuse to gel into memory their touch is always tender *sacred is the love between character and fan* one of the men was an artist and one as I held him turned into a baby *David I never asked for this, never asked to be picked up by your smooth successful hands* the groomed half-moons of your nails pinch my laser prints *can you feel my phantom pain?* I'm trapped inside a prison sentence *who said words can't hurt you* the ascenders and descenders are the bars of my cage, unknowable eyes keep peering through *strangers with hats in their laps* they expect me to entertain them—glistening with saliva I stretch and flex my text, my syntax sliding across the sentence like a pin-up girl across striated satin *the naked truth* mane of golden locks thrown back, reversed C of silken shoulder arched spine and buttock *narrative twists* limbs leaping like a Deco faun, leg thrown back arm thrown forward, Marilyn Monroe is in the *throes* her body a diagonal gash on the wavy draped backdrop *she knows it's a frame-up* her hand juts into the top righthand corner, splayed fingers poke and scratch *if only she were strong enough to pull herself up and out of the page.*

> And this with eyebrows all his passion writeth;
> And that with eyeballs all his passion readeth.

I wanted to have the sex that KK writes about in his books I crawl into a strange bed in a strange room—the comforter is light as air, the bed is on wheels—whenever either of us shifts we roll across the hardwood floor *a collision course to romance* KK sticks his tongue in my mouth and I wonder if this constant shifting of ground had anything to do with his prose style I open my eyes to the wall above the closet door it angles upward like a German Expressionist cityscape or a funhouse room I moan *my perpendiculars are shattered* KK yanks me back to *reality* points out we're in an attic room—with a slanted ceiling *I hate it when passion crashes into architecture* then I start to get into it, pretend I'm in a rocket, muscular expenditure hurling me through the galaxy *creak creak Jupiter here I COME, the only word I know is oh ohhh ohhhhhh ohhhhhhhhhhh ohhhhhhhhhhhhhhhhh.*

There's metaphor on one side and literality on the other and I'm stuck between them *two mountainous silicone tits crashing against one another.*

Lutz leaves a message on my phone machine *meet me at the Best Western, 9th and Harrison—Saturday between two and four.* When Sing and I arrive, Lutz in gold sunglasses is stretched out on a plastic chaise lounge beside a swimming pool littered with algae and leaves. Her husband is across the parking lot in a station wagon and Sing jokes *that's a good place for a husband.* Lutz smirks and points to a row of identical turquoise doors, "Go on up to room 202 it's open." We climb the concrete stairs, enter a coordinated cube of beige salmon teal, pastel cityscape above bed of blond veneer *a space where the most elementary distinctions are constituted but also threaten to break down* a muffled voice from the bathroom draws us in *eerie flicker across white and blue tiled walls* we pass the shower and face the toilet: seated upon it is a video monitor and inside the tube is a person, a looped tape of William Kennedy Smith on the witness stand: "I uh did have my penis" grimace "I uh did have my penis" grimace "I uh did have my penis" grimace "I uh did have my penis" grimace "I uh …"

Professor Brian O'Blivion all over again the scent of lysol overlays his well-scrubbed charm … I think of operating rooms, of rubber-gloved specialists inserting video cameras up women's vaginas *blobby pink hot spot—not rape but technical difficulties, lubricate the nozzle* a few months later Leslie and Cecilia will fill this same space with flowers stick a label on the phone *Beverly Hilton* and film "Joe Orton" partying with "Peggy" (his agent, played by KK) when a fuse blows they hide the lights and camera before they find the motel manager *we were blow-drying our hair while watching TV* … yesterday they used me as an extra *"Joe" wins the Viewers' Choice Award* in hippie gown and stained-glass earrings I sat beside Rendezvous in the Art Institute auditorium (the site of my first date with Quincey *remember* we ate popcorn in folding chairs while the screen was orgy orgy orgy) this time I do whatever Cecilia directs me to do—for three hours *smile applaud hoot* first in color then in pixel vision *instamatic flashes bubble like champagne the year is 1967* I'm still the audience but like you David finally *inside.*

In ankle-strapped pumps of plum velvet Lilith handles filth manipulates waste buries placentas and burns the cauls of newborn babies for good luck she makes partial objects useful, puts them back into circulation, "I'm working toward a world where kitsch can masturbate itself."

It's futile to try to rush to work … the ten-foot-wide sidewalk is packed with ambling bodies shoulder-to-shoulder "*running* late" what a joke I feel like a rebel corpuscle in a sluggish bloodstream I bump into a woman holding a cardboard sign **Cancer colostomy patient** PLEASE HELP *specificity makes her dense, the Venus of Willendorf in a ski cap* the light's turned green I try to evaporate her with a broader category *homeless* but she doesn't waver, looms on the curb before me wretchedly intestinal shoving her magic-markered plea in my face Cancer I unzip my coin purse and shake out all my change *"God–bless–you"* I can't remember if I dropped it into a cup or a palm so hypnotic was her voice, extremely low, without any inflection *"God–bless–you"* like a dictaphone at the slowest speed *"God–bless–you"* this repeated reference to the deity at the expense of all other conversation made me wonder if she wasn't really the dupe of some religious cult, dropped off on this corner out of a smokey-windowed van to gather funds for its campaign to zombie-ize the woebegone *an entire fantastic world, made of bits and pieces, opens up beyond the limit, as soon as the line is crossed* her cardboard sign gave a narrative to one of these incomprehensible bodies that line the streets with their arms outstretched, when you ignore them they yell after you *have a nice day* my quarters and dimes were buying a story: hospitalized heroine bravely beats every odd in *God Bless You* (ABC) an Emmy-winning role for Mare Winningham *the line between them and us way too crossable* a block later I saw a man eating a chewy substance *disheveled in wheelchair, can for spare change in lap* as I hurried past him I noticed a glob of white in his pink and brown "food" then FLASH I knew it was a lunchcake, the kind I hated as a child—Snowballs—rubbery marshmallow and coconut skin *capillary pink* stretched across a half dome of creme-filled chocolate *a dessert that looks like rotting meat or ski tragedy* then I went to work and on my way home I saw two men crossing the street at right angles to one another, their cheeks lips eyebrows were swollen and spackled with liver-colored welts and crusty scabs but each seemed nonchalant *ears walk armed with a knife bird-headed bellies open* recently KK was on Howard Street when a man emerged from the shadows with an arrow sticking out the side of his head, he staggered then collapsed at KK's feet— apparently dead—a group of people gathered round and a woman began to scream *KK said it was like being in a movie* the next day's paper reported that it wasn't an arrow but a child's toy which he thrust into his brain with a tremendous force—just last week, the article continued, another man hung himself from a street sign at

10th and Harrison *his last willful act producing the desired visual result: body, metal, halogen and the ensuing chemical narration.*

The interruption of things that "exist" in a theatrically conceived time and space. SAN FRANCISCO ANOTHER ILLUSION SHATTERED.

Knockers hard as grapefruit she swears they're *real* a nude Lilith lies on a chaise lounge upsidedown, her curly platinum mane dangling off the bottom edge and merging with the white ground—perpendicular to her washboard tummy her unfathomably shapely legs are raised and crossed at the knees *squeezing shut her little pigeonhole* she smells like jasmine, her calves V out like a pair of shears poised for action *whether they snap down or spring apart all depends on you David* the stiletto heels of her maribou slippers point to the stars ... white phone to match her white hair Lilith smiles into the receiver, "Operator give me a wrong number." *Fanning out her decadence like a peacock.*

My own bedroom is so cramped my shins are awash with bruises *dark sallow islands beneath a forest of faint hair* I feel like Agnes Moorehead in *The Twilight Zone* the episode where she's tortured by toy spaceships and tiny bullets sting her ankles, then the camera zooms in to reveal that the miniatures are in fact fullsized U.S. aircraft and for the past half hour we've been sympathizing with the monster instead of ourselves *it's always a matter of dimension* on one bedroom wall hangs a Harry Jacobus pastel *a hysterical attack of pigment inside the pallid matt, the black metal frame, as if a box of Crayolas has exploded* I bought it because I couldn't *see* anything in it then a demonic Gerber baby appeared to KK, and Brett Reichman pointed out a man spewing blobby blood-stained vomit *thanks a lot guys!* then one Sunday afternoon as KK sat in bed reading a biography of Oscar Wilde he looked up and gasped—Wilde's volcanic face was starring back at him! *the Gerber baby is his eye, the vomiting man's ass the tip of his nose* as Mark sleeps on the couch on the other side of the wall we begin to make love, our movements subtle and controlled I lick my palm and encircle KK's cock it's heavy for its size like a perfect eggplant a Japanese variety from the Farmers' Market long and purple warmed in the sun I pull on it my fist is full and slippery I squeeze down *I want to know how it feels to grow desire this dense* I stroke and pull harder and faster if I pull hard enough maybe I can pull out an answer, "Dodie," KK whispers to Dodie, "are you trying to drive me nuts?" On the other side of the wall Mark groans faintly, the rickety wooden frame creaks, fingers clamp into my shoulder KK's mouth opens wide wider *behind twin curves of teeth morphemes line up to burst forth* "sshhh" he snaps down on a pillow, quivers in my arms silent as the great silence of matter silent as Al Pacino's sex life in prison—so adept became he at mute climaxes that when he's released he's incapable of expelling even the tiniest sigh his face strained and miserable like someone with the dry heaves *knobby eyes* then he gets a job slinging hash and falls in love with waitress Michelle Pfeiffer—her beautiful misshapen lips demand, "Let me hear you!" Pacino's bellow quakes the sofabed *deeply twisted deeply conventional* KK spits out the pillow, his smile angular and elfish, the Gerber-baby-vomiting-man-Oscar-Wilde a vivid constellation behind his head.

Voice spit tears shit a cry—the refusal to emit seems like a crime. *Cry to show I love you* the man says to the woman, the inquisitor says to the sorceress—and somewhere Freud must say to the hysteric. KK says to me my cunt is so different from time to time we should be like the Eskimos with their dozens of names for snow.

OUT OF WORK MOTHER NEEDS WOUNDED VET WILLING PLEASE.

Designer glasses pale blue underwear hair on chest dark but turning gray—David that's not much to base a fantasy on—lock

189

me in a room like Colette, I'll fill you out if you'll be my Willy. "He once was a playboy," I'll write, "but now he's matted with a marriage framed with a business he wears Laura Biagiotti glasses eats Tandoori takes in a quarter million a year." He tunes in an oldies station *Jim Morrison's apocalyptic croon: there is danger in the ancient gallery* he knocks back Advil pens a thriller hangs Flaubert and Brian Jones above his desk *flattened behind plexiglass the specimen is still alive, twitching* pale as the moon he shifts in his briefs, the Psychedelic Furs buzz through headphones—it's 2 a.m.—he reaches for a ballpoint and spiral notebook, scrawls his fears to a woman he's never met, *"Words are bubbles, a thousand colors, floating beautiful, but you can't pop them, they're tougher than glass, you can't see the face inside them, you might as easily look inside a star…"*

Born with a flashcube in her mouth—Lilith is photogenic as all get-out—still, the camera never does her justice, never quite captures her vivacity her air-brushed animation as she slithers from cel to cel in fuck-me pumps and see-through bodysuits teddies camisoles—or nothing but her long beigy skin *sometimes less is more* a carefully-placed animal or pumpkin sets the scene, when it's time for tennis she ties a sweater around her neck *is forecourt anything like foreplay* her torpedo tits defy gravity, shoot nipple bullets at the sky and your gaping mouth. *And always, everywhere in the hysterical sagas, there is the feminine character to whom Freud gives the role of homosexual object; the character with whom the hysteric "identifies." The feminine Other, solidly in place, a reference point without which transgression, whether real or fictive, in actions or focused on the body, cannot be carried out. For Dora—Mrs. K.; for Katharina—cousin Francisca, whom her father slept with; for Rosalie—the "aunt," mistreated by the "uncle" (the mother, the father); for Elisabeth—the dead sister, before whom she stands frozen; for Lucy—the two little girls who, above all, must not be kissed; for Emmy—her sick daughter, who hugs her "until she smothers"; for Mina—Lilith, whose beaver she studies through an Agfa lupe. Everywhere, the other woman. "Thus," writes Lacan, "the hysteric experiences herself in hommages which are addressed to another woman, and offers the woman in whom she adores her own mystery to the man whose role she is taking, without fully being able to enjoy it. Seeking endlessly for what it is to be a woman, she cannot help but betray her desire."*

"Every image is frozen image; a living popsicle." Well, lick this: a naked woman is sawed in half through the waist … closeup on cross-section of torso *chopped meat in a casement* something's wrong with the realism here *no bloody pool no ooze* the slab she's sprawled upon is stark as her alabaster skin, her pubic triangle is perfectly groomed—a photographer, Harvey Keitel, rushes in and releases the murder weapon a giant pendulum, the Homicide dick yells, "Why'd you do that?" *for a stronger image* the pendulum swipes into the slab grinding to a halt. Cut to an editor looking at the proofs *great stuff but you've got to vary your repertoire—something intense as true crime but something else* so the photographer hooks up a foot pedal to his camera and strangles his girlfriend's black cat in front of a cubist painting CLICK CLICK CLICK CLICK CLICK CLICK CLICK *cat screeches fill the soundtrack* when the girlfriend discovers her missing pet tortured on the cover of his book the photographer fixes his Two Evil Eyes on her *chop chop with a hatchet* he buries her in a wall … then it's raining cats and dogs as he works out an alibi—he attaches a lifesize glossy of his girlfriend's face to the pillowy lump huddled in the carseat beside him *poor disembodied babe I know how it feels to love a man stranger than Poe* he ties a scarf under the figure's "chin" and drives past the elderly couple who live next door— through the rain-spattered windshield the neighbors see her "arm" mechanically waving good bye *a string attached to a gauzy sleeve where am I in this tacky female assemblage* the neighbors smile and wave back *a smattering of adjectives like cheap jewelry*

accessorizes my abstraction, green-eyed white gal with crooked smile and then I'm theirs to do with what they will David you're right about Dodie she's too concrete for you she juts into your line of vision like the Art Deco clock tower that faces my computer ... as I key this I stare through plate glass at a red rectangle foregrounded with a white *DRINK COCA COLA* beneath it twelve red cubes form a clock face against the flat cream of the tower, red hands point to two adjoining cubes *ten to nine* behind the tower the sky's an unbroken periwinkle more cibachrome than real, invisible air currents flap the American flag atop an adjacent office building, sometimes a bird.

It's there a stain in the atmosphere—walking down the sidewalk you are overpowered by the stench of urine *invisibles have been set into circulation they're going to get you.*

David, I'm dying to break a heart *a throbbing bagatelle to elide the ellipsis in my marriage/novel:* I asked KK to have a three-way with me and Quincey ... a triangle squared is a pyramid, ancient mystical symbol, New Age trinket with miraculous powers ... KK's razor blades would never dull, my wilting houseplants would bloom before my eyes in Disney stop-motion, my computer would never crash *three-way threesome third sex our three irresolvable bodies strapped together* **whose** cock **whose** cunt **who's** *writing* **whose**—never happened—sirens interrupt a reading at Forest Books—a man has been murdered at 16th and Mission *the poet stops mid-sentence* peering over the police barricade she sees a pile of "fecal matter" and perhaps a small pool of blood *her stolen thunder* Quincey's killing my plot with his absence WHAT IS THERE LEFT FOR ME TO DO *donate my brain to science? Download it into a computer?* Technicians will place clones of my brain into a number of different robots programmed to communicate with one another, so that while each brain lives a separate afterlife, I, the omniscient narrator, know them all. *If only I could break loose* *from this page* I'd possess you in front of an audience, David, speak through your human body *your bespectacled face would twist with my wisdom* we'd dole out the answer to every problem LOVE the hall is packed with clean-cut types *$50 a head* they press crystal balls to their throats, strain to decipher our intergalactic brogue *if only I could break loose* after zazen a bald-headed monk relaxes on the sofa sipping tea with Dr. Van Helsing (beneath the starched blue layers of his ceremonial robe celibacy stirs like a hungry snake—a year later in Los Angeles Kathy Acker will tell Mark there is *absolutely nothing* this monk won't do in bed) he brushes crumbs from his chest, leans forward for the last macaroon, says to no one in particular *there is truth in anything if you view it with a soft brain* head buried under the down comforter I collapse into a trance *womb voices blow through dictating evanescence—Aeolian harpies—a child with the face of Virginia Woolf dissolves into a belly with a bird's head—to know not the thought but its effect black hole sucking you in making its content your content sweet coronary compression the heart spasms shoots out roots to tap this edge this delicate balance* ... when I come to nothing translates—I turn on an Italian horror film—Barbara Steele knows how to handle an unfaithful heterosexual: slash him with a straight razor *slash slash slash slash slash slash slash slash* the focused reaction on Barbara's wide elegant face is zeal *slash slash slash slash* the blood of Quincey flows down the camera lens a thick red waterfall *slash slash* Barbara rolls him up in an Oriental rug and pulls his gurgling body down the long staircase THUMP THUMP THUD THUMP blood drips over the edge—cut to the foyer—a slowly-widening crimson puddle *drip drip*.

It is the intoxicating power of vulgarity that breaks her out of the deadening, self-sufficient, unchanging reality of *things*.

A dozen naked women relax in and around a steaming pool of midnight blue—Osento Baths—Lilith flounces her tits above the water level *feminist movement* her pale aureoles are small but puffy, suggesting readiness or PMS—surveying the room she slowly licks her lips, "There's a lot of cuties here tonight." *Breathy Japanese flute ripples through invisible speakers* she flashes me her perfect teeth, winks, "I like your red pubic hair." She rhapsodizes about the women at her Adult Children of Alcoholics meetings *"so many of them are absolutely gorgeous"* I imagine a hybrid of Bloomsbury and Nastassja Kinski in *Cat People*—a circle of exotic languorous creatures flexing on Samsonite chairs, sleek gleaming panthers in velvet collars and drop-waisted gowns, they pick up dainty cucumber sandwiches with enameled claws, nibble one another's childhood abuse. Lilith's nipples bobble above Jacuzzi waves *hard and pink as eraser tips, handy for her endless revisions* she shifts into her *MSG of friendliness* mode, "Mina, tell me the truth—did you fuck Quincey so you'd have something to write about?" I swish my back against the jetstream, wish I had that much control, wish I could flip on my subject matter as easily as my TV. I never know when it will happen the most benign of circumstances sprouts wings, swoops down, and starts pecking at my thrashing limbs my screaming face *muck spatters my rumpled French twist* only then do I switch on the computer raise my trembling hands to the keyboard *Dear David ...*

Dear David, my legs are crossed at the ankle, twisting my little pigeonhole shut. The cursor blinks in the middle of the word "thumb" as I eat a slice of phosphorescent yellow watermelon, dripping juice on the keys. My fingers stick to D and V *I always knew it would come to this Mina fused to the word-machine* like the man who talks to his right hand outside Harvest Natural Foods *thumb pressed to ear, middle fingers clenched, pinkie angled like a mouthpiece in front of his chatting lips* as I step off the curb he grumbles "Hold on a moment," puts down his "receiver" and stares up at me, "Yes?" I shrug, "I'm s-sorry"—he rolls his eyes then leans back against his sleeping bag and continues his conversation with whomever it is at the other end of his fist—I can tell he's dishing me—he waves a cigarette in his free hand for emphasis. The following week he's writing in a composition book its cardboard cover speckled black and white like insect droppings—"Yes?"—carefully he draws each letter in blue ballpoint cramming the lines together in humps and valleys across the page, the text is a frothy mass, an undulating blue wave of signs *his perpendiculars have been shattered* some days it's not about English at all—he yells through the receiver in an unearthly tongue sputtering with fricatives—or he slouches on the concrete, silent, his eyes cast down, gently holding his hand to his cheek as if to say, "Oh my."

You've heard of body language? Well, Lilith's very outspoken. When she emerges from the bedroom her forties hostess gown has been exchanged for a black leather miniskirt *her lips glossy and pink as hallucinogenic strawberries* she yanks the chopsticks from her bun and declares, "Let the dancing begin." Standing in the doorway with her perfect posture cocked at the hips and her hair cascading over her long forearms she looks like a sexual Alice in Wonderland, a girl who can convolute to the shape of anyone's desire *female body parts stroll about looking for action, if they don't get any they attack burn shred* Lilith straddles your cock in a black diaphanous gown, "Let the sacrifice begin." She throws her head back then looms down ejecting snake after snake from her bloated silicone lips—the writhing snarl hisses and nips and hisses and nips and nips your ecstatic face and throat *you look like my Harry Jacobus by the time she's through* … Lilith shimmies her shoulders, "I do these *things* … to hurt people and I know I should feel guilty about them. But I don't. In fact I never had any feelings at all until my mid-twenties." *Cream puff dentata.* On the eleventh night of the seventh moon Lilith steals the soul of a married man, only two things repel her, true love and a jagged dagger in the heart—she steps towards me in blue platform shoes with silver buckles, reaches for my earlobe, strokes an amber teardrop. The moon turns black, she swells into a fifty-foot gargoyle flailing webbed wings, flinging her head from side to side, squawking *a mechanical awkward effect, Japanese horror circa 1959* I leap out of the margins and plunge my jagged dagger into her reptilian heart PUFF she explodes into a sludgy puddle at my feet *three gallons of marsh gas and a crust of bread.*

You say writing is the opposite of dying, but David you've never been at the other end of the prod, you've never been WRITTEN *one husband one book one fan* my saga is winding to THE END how'd you like to be wrapped up this way *bound and distributed by printmen in coveralls* Dodie moves on to another project and Mina imagines herself undead in the 23rd century *hope has left me but I still know fear: nothing new will ever happen to me!* faceless readers flock in to pick over the carcass, I dream I'm being fucked in a park with a dildo, surrounded by a vast expanse of green bordered with shrubs and maples *getting away safely means finding the right distance* people in the midst of picnics and volleyball freeze then somebody presses the buttons on their shoulders and slowly they turn toward me *I am the dumb fuck at the center of their gaze* a lubricated tool pistons my snatch raw— it won't quit 'til I come—and I never will *not exactly a writer's block, more like cabin fever* Dodie framed me DAVID it's growing cold the margins come rumbling in EEEK! there's a telephone growing out of the end of my arm *so few gentlemen callers lately* static voices decree: FEAR ALONE DOES NOT KNOW THE GODS you're my biggest fan the trueblue reanimator—if I squint I can see you out there, alone, on the other coast of this vast country, jerking off beneath the stars, lurid pink shadows trail your zigging fist *the paraphernalia of existence whooshes away* DAVID I'd lend you a hand but I can't reach that far YET—give me another chance, Love, rip out that dreaded last page THE END *the gods are very vain, they want to be loved too, and hopeless people do not love them* DAVID your ear is large as a radar disk HEAR ME keep rereading my letters *the unrequitedness of life in general made specific through a love story* imagine I'm one of those wide-hipped women who sit sideways at the front of the bus *born to breed* a couple of grubby kids grab at her ruddy complexion her cheap cotton dress stuffed with arms that encircle and bazooms so softly huge you want to drown your head in them and drool *the tit of the iceberg* imagine I'm the child of the first atomic family conceived on a test site ten miles underground concrete walls BOOM the roof beams come caving in imagine me the perfect baby happily gurgling at momma's breast then the nurse takes me away and my parents burst into flame *the Oedipal complex up in smoke* the heat from their raging bodies melts my plastic carousel imagine me the first human nuclear power plant I'll char anybody who gets in my way *crusty black horsie ash pumping round and round* imagine me walking into the living room, KK's jeans are unzipped he grabs me, crouches down and pokes his dick between my thighs *fortunately I'm not wearing panties* but DAVID he can't keep it up forever imagine me needing you as I do—imagine a whole showcase of designer glasses lined up to magnify ME *bigger than big, brightly brilliant, sparking significance and funk* David imagine me!

Love,
Mina

January 28, 1994

Dear Sam,

You know Mina doesn't like to be kept waiting. I've been writing
and writing all these letters but not knowing where to mail them.
I was sitting around my apartment when suddenly I remembered
the time we dropped acid *how could I have forgotten* whenever we
went to touch an object, a ball a toaster a piece of paper the toast,
our hands reached through a wide colorful aura fingers tingling
in this radiant thingness then I realized I haven't taken LSD since
1980, years before I met you, so our "trip" never happened except
maybe in my dreams. On Market Street I saw this guy who
looked like you, blond hair pillow lips Klimt T-shirt, he was
shading his eyes with one hand like the look-out in a child's game
*I can't see you but in the dust that coats my desk I know you're there,
in the fog that breathes against the window* it's been five years since
you died, and I've been writing and writing all these letters—but
not knowing where to mail them. So how's Eternity? In story
after story you seek a perfect cellular wipeout, but it's a wipeout
with borders: the serious fuck *let me be that border Sam, rub your
nothingness against me* confronted with the dead mortals are so
unimaginative cowering crossing bowing screaming *fleeing
fainting, every participle points to respect or terror* I can't imagine
you'd want either, not the Sam I knew, a man who liked to be
slapped around before it was chic *slip the garlic from your cunt and
think of Mother England* Mina is sending you a letter her tongue
shoots out of the mailbox and burrows down your throat a
French kiss FROM BEYOND THE GRAVE. I was absent from your
death as I was absent from your life *a relationship of parties and
letters* we only got together alone, once it *happened back in '85 to
a couple of ghosts she still ate meat and he ate … lots of drugs … or
was it '86?* The buzzer rings and there you are—blond—boyish—
your pouty lips lending consistency to a face otherwise erratic as

the weather *they're still pouting—Mina's mouth flattens against their puffy resistance, so much saliva* SAM: cocky and interesting in a captivating way as you heat up the room with a careless sexual nature that slightly threatens and promises nothing, your 50's suit jacket droops from your shoulders like a smirk. "Sam I'm famished! How 'bout McDonalds?" We pile into your jumbo sedan and float down Bartlett Street—three blocks later you make the Illegal Left Turn *falsetto siren funnelling towards us, red light pulsing in your rearview mirror like a big zit* the air is thick with grilled steak and coriander, cholos with greased-back hair jingle change in the pockets of Ben Davis work pants *monkey logo on every ass* a lowrider cruises by, its tremendous bass throbbing my chest like a heart then receding, the cop leans over your window his tooled-leather belt sagging with violent paraphernalia, you flash him a California-boy smile, "Hi officer!" *SAM: strong and incredibly adaptable in every sexual situation, seizing just the cream of what's offered* the cop chortles and flirts right back, dashing off your ticket with a wink—you are his captive a babbling slab of cunt he lords over with his twelve-inch club. Your pouty lips, "Shit." Who knows where I left you—for me the night ended like all nights—in KK's bed he was still so new a big Hershey's kiss I wanted to suck on nonstop—you were the interruption the foil wrapper I crumpled and carelessly tossed off no wonder you bitched about it *Sam the golden boy the bright sparkle in the eye of every party.* And now you're dead, dead of AIDS, age 31.

Perspective gave us the artificial feeling we could get away from things.

"The cemetery," you wrote, "is full of cats, plastic flowers, and pictures of the dead leaning in gilt frames against crumbling and ornate Christs. Those who live here often leave letters for the dead. You can see the little envelopes with the name written formally across the front, gripped by a masonry hand or held between stems in a bunch of roses." It's lonely writing to the dead—words and words and words. And then your silence. At least it's not a rejection, I have that consolation. *Your eyes cloud over and you stare off into nothing ... glazed berry lips locked shut* it was on Valencia Street that I first saw you, the same block where Roberto and Bryan got into the fistfight maybe the same night, I was having trouble with my outfit a plaid disaster no amount of attitude could camouflage. When you appeared before me my mouth dropped open *the kind of guy who steals the foreground from every background.* Now that I'm married and you're dead I have all the time in the world for you but the question is *what world.*

Standing room only at Anti-Matter, the man sitting on the floor in front of me keeps leaning against my knees, I have to accidentally kick him four times before he wriggles forward a few inches ... an evening of "auditions"—art school coed in black corset lip-syncing to Marilyn, macho painter dressed in drag— the usual—then onto a folding chair plops The Godfather he's a chubby woman in a royal blue mini-skirt that splays out like a bell, when she spreads her clapper-legs ripples of cotton swaddle her thighs, Don Corleone clenches her pink fists APPLAUSE then we herd over to the Uptown ... I'm on my first Scotch and soda and leaning against the juke box when the MC sashays in, cigarette glowing between her long flashy fingers, black velvet gown plunging beneath an expensive leather jacket cleavage to die for *everything Mina should be but isn't* she takes a drag from her cigarette purses her pencil-thin lips and throws her head back for a languorous Dietrich-esque exhalation brittle blonde perm triangulating out around her jaw it's impossible to tell how old she is with her make-up so thick—as if it had declared war on her face and won *somewhere between thirty and fifty.* She sits on a broken couch with her legs crossed—pantyhose poke out about a mile long, striped with tiny black leaves *mythological* leaves *as if a spurned Aphrodite has turned her limbs to ivy* my gaze slides off her spiked heel and trails the vining nylon over ankle ... calf ... knee ... her taut cone of thigh—but wait there's more—mesh leaves stretch to the size of thumb prints over the full curve of her ass *no panties* O botany! She catches my eye and stretches her lips horizontally *the animal loneliness of the flesh* TOWARDS Dodie turns our head away *this book is nearly over, Dodie's given up on research but* MINA'S NOT I should have nudged and squirmed until she either screamed or walked over and said something, something simple like, "You're incredible." Dodie's tucked in my wildness like a transvestite's genitals *it's time for a haunting I can feel it in my bones* Sam why don't you join me inside her—with your sexy etherics maybe we'd get a little action going *Dodie relaxes on the futon sofa* faint scent of cat urine *she's just hung Brett's drawing a demonic pixie floating in a wash of red—the frame is perfectly tacky, gold-sprayed wood* her legs are open *suddenly the pixie goes long and stretchy like the opening credits of a panoramic movie on TV* a screaming vortex opens at her feet *a windy whooshing sound a poof of white smoke rushing up from her knees she sucks in her breath and lets it out with a little "humph"* and here you are Sam swirling through her tissue with Mina—you can lounge in her left breast, I'll take the right—they're get-away-from-it-all cozy like those egg-shaped chairs that were the rage in the 60's.

Stability galloped off bright and watery as a Kandinsky horse ... her smile ... Sing said the Mistress of Ceremonies was an actress with lots of small parts in Hollywood movies, somebody else said she was from New York, Randy said she invited him to come home with her but he didn't go because she and her husband are "too weird." Randy's one of the new breed of arty transvestites, he's currently dating four men plus a lesbian who's having a sex change—he helped her get her gig on *Geraldo.* Too weird for Randy? I look over at the couch blue smoke curls like fingers above her chiseled cheeks *come to me*. Randy nibbles the corner of his lip, juts his chin forward, "I'm into normal things these days." "What's normal?" Flipping the ponytail on top of his head, "You know—like one person at a time."

You shuffled on stage wrapped in white gauze every inch of you *the real Sam was buried inside, a talented mummy* then came the dramatic unwinding, your bound mass flapping across the floor like a trout as an assistant reeled in yard upon yard of gauze, and out of the rubble of bandages you sprang up hurling plastic skeletons at the audience, I tucked one in the cleavage of my camisole *worm on the rose*. I clench my hand and the three-inch skeleton curls forward from the hip, sits up in my cupped palm, its coffin *wedding band for a tombstone* my desk is scattered with parts: your books and photos, that ridiculous stuffed monkey—SX, who latched onto me at your memorial service *thin little monkey voice, "Help me"* beside the pulpit heap of monkeys on the floor *"Help me"* the dozens of chimps apes gorillas baboons you rescued from thrift stores and dumpsters, a mission mangled as the Civil War, no toy was too grungy for you *"Help me"* dusty vomit-encrusted *things* I could only imagine held at arm's length between the tips of finger and thumb *an autonomic squinting of face* SX was the handsomest primate of the bunch, sewn from brown socks, spotless, big red heel for a mouth *one of your minions* SX slumps jauntily atop my dot matrix printer and its "dust cover" the floral pillowcase Grandma gave me when she switched to satin *sleek surface to protect her perm* roses daisies mums, stems hacked off *purple red pink red purple red* orangy sap of blue and yellow what-nots splatters across a choppy green field *purple red* who decapitated all these flowers? SX did it, sprawling across the carnage so cock-sure of his speckled brown body his pouty snout, eyebrows flapping across his forehead like a bat. Do I love him? When I was six my bed was a mountain of frogs and bears my grandmother made me. I burrowed through horsey elephant zebra octopus bumble bee dog unicorn lion ape, humping their squishy bodies between my legs, humping myself to sleep *I know SX wants to fuck me.* Grandma sold dolls in the winter *stuffed with old nylons* threw apron parties in the spring— across the living room ceiling my father strung lines of rope, Grandma stood on a chair to hang the aprons and I stood beside her holding a muslin sack lumpy with clothespins, I snapped each little wooden jaw open and closed before I handed it to her, my cheek grazing the hem of her dress *powdery cloud of talcum and vanilla it's hard to believe this is me, Mina, capable of love so unquestioning so fierce* the rope sagged with the weight of all the aprons, row upon row of dirndled cotton fluttering above our heads like colorful fairies.

Her face is no longer as pale as the rest of her body, as though reanimated by his gaze. The left hand supports the chin while the right hand moves toward a more immediate personally dangerous touch. This hand will expose the disquieting genitals will cut the body into fragments. I want to deconstitute myself.

At your memorial my brain went fuzzy with all the data being transmitted—like you graduated from Santa Cruz like you failed at modeling like you had this dense web of friends who all seemed to be in love with you like you went through a punk phase *black hair ghost face* like you were the pride of the local 4-H *color xerox in the hallway of a small Sam holding Blue Ribbon vegetables.* Your father was handsome and statuesque with full pouty lips *your spitting image graying, calmer* when I met him I almost blurted out, "But Sam said he was adopted!" Your father told me he had this one monkey you'd coveted, near the end he wanted to give it to you but didn't because "it would have con- fused Sam." Dementia? The Sam I knew was sketchy, his biography random as a case study in a self-help book—the travel agent from Chico could just as easily have been a secret agent from Davis *obsessions and insecurities were all we bothered about* the Sam I knew was a typhoon of sex and hate, he loved the scars of others but flaunted his own beauty, terrified of the certainty of its betrayal *color xerox of Sam nude, contrasty pink organ prominent as the logo of a world's fair* the letters you wrote me were so dirty they were awesome *beyond transgression beyond personal, a kiss of grace* no wonder everybody wanted you I'd fuck you to get closer to that mouth ... your place after the service ... I'm sitting in the bay window in the brown recliner your father bought for your illness ... the world I view is at waist level like a child's packed with incredibly tall nervous cheerful people maneuvering plastic dinnerware as they mill from conversation to conversation—I feel your arms around me Sam *soft as stuffed monkeys* electricity sparked in your every interaction or there was no interaction—like the postcard you sent me of that motel, ballpoint arrow pointing to a bungalow, you scrawled, "I fucked him here." *A gap a cut an ungraspable point behind Tiki-patterned curtains* you wanted to die famous *a big before and a big after* your death a media extravaganza like Carol Wayne's TONIGHT SHOW REGULAR DROWNS IN ACAPULCO *a million color xeroxes on teenage bedroom walls a nowhere* "we loved him live now we love him dead, here it's all the same, only better."

I'm already posthumously afraid of myself. You'd been sick with "a cold" for a month when I bumped into you at a reading—your face looked drawn, coarsened, I muttered to KK, "Sam's not aging well." This was the last time I ever saw you. Now a fig tree is planted over your ashes. Your boyfriend made jam out of the fruit. That's you in a mouthful, sweet and kind of seedy—a thick line gashes through your memory.

"If the Nazis came and said you had to give up either your children or your husband, what would you do?" A heated discussion ensued among the members of my mother's bunko club. The shaking of dice. The only one to keep the husband was my mother. I stood in the doorway, shocked *Grandma would've hid me under her apron.* By the time I was nine Grandma had me embroidering pillowcases fringing afghans stitching together squares for her patchwork quilt crocheting lace on hankies *the thread so fine it slices into my fingers* my mother grumbled, "You sit around the house like an old lady—why don't you go outside and blow the stink off of you, make some friends!" *A gigantic child hamstrung by her strength a prehistoric Garbo unaware that she is a Garbo* the scent of cat litter as I write makes me feel so animal I stare into the bathroom, Grandma's embroidered runner hangs from pushpins like a flag over the window, red mercerized flowers reflect the blood-drenched Argento poster, sunlight striates yellowed linen. Her wind-up Timex encircles my wrist her cameo ring my finger *apricot oval relief* her great aunt's crystal vase catches my pens her heart-shaped necklace coils in a glass box on a doily she crocheted *droopy pineapple* on top of the box sits a photo of Grandma's father framed in tin, Mr. Whitton. White mustache round glasses. You can't see the hole in his throat, the cancer that tunneled through skin and windpipe *unsealed the body is insatiable* beneath a tree beside a lake he rose shakily from a lawnchair inch-wide blackened canker drawing in all eyes. I turn to the photo that hangs to the left of my computer *turn-of-the-century sepia* two young women in floor-length dresses stand beside of an elderly woman seated in a rocker *choker-collars* the house is humble, a single wreath of gingerbread beneath the beamed roof, a wooden sidewalk bisects the overgrown yard, in the right half a hand-painted FOR SALE sign. These women preceded Grandma and then me—that's all I know—in the foreground a slat is missing from the picket fence. I rub against these images with abandon but never release *the subject is isolated in a pool of light and then there's the immediate drop-off into darkness* I crack open a pomegranate, fruit-blood sprays across the keyboard, tightly packed seeds glistening like souls *acidic sweet with an afterbite of raw garlic from lunch.* When I was nine I read about Carbon 14 dating *skeletons as old as God could be measured* I pondered the invention of fire that burst of rare drama in the stillness of prehistoric life *picture this*: museum tableau of shaggy-headed Neanderthals, a chubby blonde child transfixed on the other side of the glass, bearskin-clad father mother and baby frozen around a campfire blank eyes staring into another world, above their heads dragonflies as long as my dachshund Leo hang from wires *fossilized wingspan bone-words the sprinkle of sesame seeds over motionless bodies.*

Never the Big Picture. Parts.

Mocha Harrar and tenax assault my nostrils ... neurotic tremble in the periphery ... love rushes through me like MDA but when I turn my head you vaporize SAM COME BACK TO ME!!!!!!!! Things haven't changed much between us—even alive you wavered on the edges of my thick world *desire is never enough* I need details to hold you in focus *the sharper the better* loving little stakes to pound into your palms. I dial Jono, "Sam's mummy performance—were you there?" *I'll pin you down* according to Jono, *he* was the mummy. In the middle of your reading he jumped up out of the audience and bombarded you with negative thoughts, "What if the next time you answer the phone a wire short circuits and sends a deadly wave shooting through your brain what if the next time you take a shower glass comes out instead of water what if your penis falls off or your fingers grow inside your hands or your skin shrinks"—you yelled *shut up shut up shut up shut up* as you cocooned him in tape "what if you wake up and everyone else in the world's dead" *shut up shut up* then you read a poem about overcoming adversity NO ONE WAS UNWOUND *shut up—I still like my version better—Ingrid Bergman never said "Play it again Sam" either* Jono doesn't remember the plastic skeletons but my junk drawer proved their existence—rummaging through batteries and broken earrings I found two—they hang from my copystand side by side *Mina and Sam do the old soft shoe* their heads are turned to the left but their eyes—all four of them—stare forward *perspective gave us an artificial feeling* their flat pelvises look like intestines, vertebrae clench their necks like chokers, flat-white flat bones, embossed teardrops of ribs. Jono works with HIV-positive inmates at San Quentin. I hang up the phone, moan to KK, "I'm such a fluff."

The next morning when I switch on the computer I start to cry. You can never turn it into just words *when is a bullet hole a bullet hole and when is it a textile* I abandon my machine to the fireworks of its screensaver, crawl back in bed with KK who sits up against a pillow casting about for a plot to his next story. Above his head a lime green Barbara Steele stands beside the words "Young Torless" looking perplexed. I lift up my head from his thigh, "How about the time you got a blow job from that pet monkey?" He sticks out his tongue, the very idea has put a bad taste in his mouth, "*You* write about that." "Then how about the priest with the rosary beads up his ass?" He scrunches his face, "Everybody does that these days."

The clank of dishes awakens me—SX is moving about the apartment again reciting your best lines. *SX: He stares at my fear and indecision like a grocery list. He's going shopping in there.* The garbage bag rustles, a book drops to the carpet with a muffled thud. *SX: The tongue's on the wall and I think I've been swallowed.* SX dreams he's plastic like your skeletons, dreams he maintains his form in a landfill forever. As my captive he grants all my wishes—but only half-way—at the worst possible moment my Porsche my pockets full of twenties my love affair with Quincey all turn to shit. SX rattles my bedroom door, "Everyone looks at you, wondering whether they too might melt one day. Let me in."

Now which of the two is supposed to be nerdy … both look like GQ models—I'm at the Castro Theater watching the latest version of Leopold and Loeb—when the closing credits begin to roll Brett leans over and exclaims, "I slept with the guy who murdered Loeb—I didn't recognize him until he stepped out of the shower with that bloody razor!" KK smirks, "Sam picked up that guy from the Patti Smith Group and I had that affair with that Hitchcock star *remember* in the elevator at the MLA and Felice Picano had sex with JOE ORTON—but Mina you've never slept with *anyone* famous!" I elbow his ribs, "I want to be the famous one that others have sex with—like when I read with Richard Hell." White plastic tables and chairs scattered beneath a stage, booze oasis in the back, row of creaky wooden stools along one side: Cleveland. Richard perches beside me in the dimness an outline of a man *not sex in the gross physical sense but foreplay's libidinal flux in the public arena* it's hard to tell what look he's giving me behind those Ray Bans *dark glasses in a dark room* shadowy figures hulk through haze, banter emanating from their blurred shadowy lips *as if words were ambient instead of directional* Richard's a very atmospheric guy, talking out of the side of his mouth he huffs and grimaces baring large interesting teeth, throws his head forward hair the color of faded asphalt falling in his face, slaps his knee, flings his hair back and takes another drag off his filterless cigarette. His heart-shaped lips shout into my cocked head, "Readings—isn't the purpose to get laid?" To prove his point, throughout the evening babes sidle up rubbing his back patting his thigh with tiny seamless hands. I snoot, "Get *laid?* Obviously you've never read in San Francisco." Then I remember how Kathy Acker met that zen monk: "He kind of jumped on me after my reading and these days I'm very jumpable." Who knows—maybe I *have* been limiting my options maybe I should focus less on writing more on wardrobe—though whenever I put on anything with cleavage I feel like a bad actress *she sucks in her tummy and teeters across the movie set, halogen lamps turn the bed into an operating table* in the midst of the murky clutter of patio chairs I zone in on a gaze it's relaxed yet focused intently on me—the guy is leaning back against a white plastic back, his arms resting on white plastic arms *isosceles V of open thighs* he slouches down thrusting the apex towards me I avert my eyes then peek back STILL STARING avert peek back *occulted beneath black denim his cock is vigilant* STILL STARING *a Bermuda triangle of desire* STILL STARING dark hair dark-rimmed glasses short dark beard. On stage a woman recites poetry coordinated to karate punches APPLAUSE peek STILL STARING *oh shit* it's my turn ... I fiddle with the mike slip on my glasses stagelights bounce off the lenses bright as the tunnel of death and hot too I begin *In this topsy-turvy world we are all suspect from the beginning* glare from the page eclipses the audience *a boozey morass shuffling and coughing, the occasional flare of a match* my black patent shoes point to the edge of the stage—in the very front chair The Guy sharpens, his eyes are raised like a supplicant's *privy to the black crotch of my black satin opaque hose* it's like he's the only person in the room for me *talk about a cinematic experience* APPLAUSE I weave through the dense enthusiastic crowd ... while the bartender empties a tiny bottle of wine into a goblet men close in around me saying those banal post-reading things people say, I've said them myself *that was great I really liked that* still I have to pay for my drink ... back at the stools Richard's with another bimbo—this one has long wavy raven hair and an arm around his shoulder, she giggles and hurls herself against his valentine mouth, I murmur, "I get talk about my perspectives—you get a kiss." Richard blows a puff of smoke above our heads, "After what you read a thousand people want to kiss you." I roll my eyes over to the pit of chairs The Guy is STILL STARING he shudders then tenses *a coagulation of nerve* stands up takes a deep breath—pauses—steps forward towards the stage then he turns *oh shit* he's angling back towards me *familiar as a fantasy* dark hair dark-rimmed glasses *the fan I've been writing to* in D.C.—*but with a face* he has a nice face, not particularly handsome but good enough. "Hi." "Hi." He alights on the stool to my left, "I enjoyed your reading." "Thanks." *Arms and thighs parted, his torso an open corridor* when I ask his name he laughs to himself *a noisy tremor he sucks back in* I think it was "Chris," neither of us says a single interesting thing but I'm stuck on that shudder and then that laugh that *private* laugh, tender gestures cryptic as the *I Ching.* "Nice talking to you." Then he walks away *I'm just another abandoned site in a red dress its legs and feet dangling beyond the head's perceptions as it watches the narrative trailing off into the dark* THE PURPOSE OF READINGS IS TO GET LAID maybe I should have flirted should have worn that look where my eyes turn to green neon flashing FUCK ME FUCK ME maybe I could have brought "Chris" back to my room at the Holiday Inn *two double beds and a long diaphanous gown* I could have unpeeled that gown *white gauze flowing from my shoulders like ectoplasm* could have nibbled those inward-curling lips bounced his midwestern frame from bed to bed *his balls whirling like a slot machine that always comes up cherries* the problem with marriage is you never think about getting laid—but then I'm such a hog—an affair is my smallest unit of desire *if marriage is a sentence, an affair is a word, it may not go anywhere but at least it* means—*getting laid is a mere jab of punctuation dot dot dot a tremor that wasn't meant for me but I held it anyway dot dot the body.*

HE WALKED AWAY FROM ME by the time I realized he was a figure to be developed I was on a plane to Indiana *as I compose this letter his features decompose it's been months, fragrant gasses bubble between the lines* Mom's kitchen table plastic-coated oak, she's in my father's chair, wall phone hanging above her head like an idea, she leans forward, "Men," frowns knowingly, "they think with their peters." *His pupils were perfectly round black and shiny like buttons I want to push them want to see not the me of the mirror but a brightly-plumed Mina with energy enough to fill a room I want to jump from the frying pan into the fire.* "I always told you, 'If a boy starts breathing hard, go home.'" *Form follows fantasy ... his receding back my desire* a month later a letter arrives from Amy, the organizer of the Cleveland reading, "There is a very odd local poet named Chris, who was there the night you read, and has glasses, but no beard. (And very little hair.) He likes to talk in puns and riddles, and his poems are semantic jokes. Could this be the man?" Half My Guy and half some balding other—like the creature in *The Fly*—a simple man a simple beast get scrambled in the teleportation terminal, that's memory *a naked monkey trails me from state to state, socky lips reeling, "I wanted to be challenged but not in pain. Help me."* I write back, "Semantic jokes ...?"

SX: It's as if I'm some escaped idea that accidentally fell out of someone. Someone who has voice, has visibility, has embodiment. It's as if I fell out of someone's head and was forgotten and left behind.

Imagine a 30-foot-long, two-legged cross between a crocodile and a mountain lion. Add a huge skull and the predatory behavior of a shark. The Minasaurus. A thousand men want to kiss her.

When you were too sick for your reading at Small Press Traffic we all read parts of your work. I dreamt I unearthed a rock video you starred in—my picture tube gasped when you danced onscreen, muscular, bare-chested, tanned skin gleaming with oil, platinum hair glowing like cumuli *a man more beautiful than any mortal an Adonis. Over Sam's mythic succulence flash of racing ruby veins, flash of neon skeleton, flash veins flash skeleton flash veins, in sync to Patti Smith's buttery croak, three bare-breasted vampiras are her back-up singers oooohh ooooohhh.* Then I thought of your inevitable emaciation—so thin you would soon disappear beneath the buzzing of the room's silence *pleasure and sorrow leaking from your sockets* you zip your pink jacket, your bones light as balsa, a good gust from the Bay lifts you above the tinkering sailboats above Mount Tam, your pink jacket arcing across the sky like a sunrise. I burst into tears shaking the bed in extravagant spasms. KK awakened and took me in his arms, "You okay?" When I told him my dream he said, "You know what Adonis is, Mina?" "What?" "An anagram for NO AIDS."

SX sprawls across my printer on his stomach with his ass facing me *big red lips in a creamy circle, the same as his snout* his ass-lips growl, "I want to be that queasy feeling in the pit of your stomach. The subject of your lifetime novel, the hard-on, the sexual anxiety, the neurotic obsession, the vertigo and salmonella and impetigo of a lifetime. Like some kind of dirt under your fingernails that's driving you crazy and will NEVER come out." My fingers wriggle across the keyboard like grave worms as his soft cottony body disintegrates to bytes, he is now in another dimension bone dry and expansive as Grandma and Sam *ring around the rosy pocket full of posy ashes ashes all fall down* when SX smells sex he will destroy the world.

Purple bat stamped on envelope from D.C. phone bill blue-inked missing child Thrifty Junior's two-day sale on Q-tips zine from Toronto I lock the mailbox and trudge up the two and a half flights, when I get to the top Blanche darts into my neighbor's open apartment he's lying on a tan couch surrounded by faux Deco frames and vases, "Excuse me—my cat." He stands up, "Come on in." An attractive man in his early thirties, small features, lightish hair, a fine beige powder covers the lesions on his face *a visual ditto for what I've already heard* the talk of getting on disability outside my front door, his cough as he climbs the stairs a wheeze and a rattle deep in the lungs sometimes a gurgle *spasms trail me through thin wooden walls, irreducible, obscene* AHHHHH-HHH AAAHHHHHHHHH behind me on the toilet it sounds like he's jerking off then there's a fart *atonal bellow* then OHHHHHHHH OHHHHHHHHHH *maybe not sex at all but a really good shit* a cough rises up the stairs pauses on the landing opens and closes the door the cough joggles through the living room the hallway the kitchen then into the bathroom where it switches to AUGHHHH-HHHH OHHHHHHHHHHHHH *pleasure or pain* AUGHHHHHHHHH *his body made airborne, scraping my ears with raw emissions* Blanche skitters into his bedroom, striped tail twitching, "Bad cat!" I follow her … the room is lined with mirrors, so many mirrors … long strips lean against three of the walls, three irregular pieces are obtusely angled along the bay window—the only furniture in the room is a double mattress positioned on the floor dead center *the Real in every reflection* I look over my shoulder at his eyes *hazel sex organs* he coughs and reaches for a cigarette I turn back to the multiple mattresses *endlessly receding … uneditable … a porn flick a docu-drama* OHHHHHHHHHH in three shiny dimensions and six directions HIV etches itself upon his body Blanche streaks across the mirrors like a wink *thousand-faceted insect eye, single mountain eye through which the sky eternally threads itself.*

In *Over Her Dead Body* Elisabeth Bronfen writes, "The pain the courage of the dying Sam is subordinated to notions of artistic ability and aesthetic effect. This is a form of violence which stages the absence of violence, a move that allows the writer and the reader to ignore the painful battle of a dying Sam. It allows a blindness toward the real by privileging the beautiful play of forms, lines, colors. Sam is denied his individual meaning, a possibility of signifying other than in relation to Mina. His death appears as a condition and pretext for a meaning that lies elsewhere and allows the writer and reader a stable position before the death of the other and thereby implicitly his or her own death."

The whole matrix shifts and we shift with it. Marina Tsvetaeva as a young woman: "In the life of a Symbolist everything is symbol. *Non*-symbols don't exist." Then on her 48th birthday, the year before her suicide: "My difficulty (in writing poems—and perhaps other people's difficulty in understanding them) is in the impossibility of my goal, for example, of using words to express a moan: ah—ah—ah. To express a sound using words, using meanings. So that the only thing left in the ears would be ah—ah—ah. Why have such goals?"

I turn off the alarm and raise the shades, the elegance of English lace punctured by the gravel below, I pull the curtains aside and snoop at the body shop's parking lot—beyond the chainlink fence a butterfly-shaped puddle flings out cirri the color of iron ore *a configuration I recognize from* Tuesday Night Terrors *portal to another dimension* last night terror came to Minna Street as local art students filmed another god-awful picture from dusk to dawn—out of the pool in a fountain of fog shot the actors: statuesque woman in leather bikini, short red-haired punk in rubber bodysuit, Asian dude jerking in a wheelchair, glam-rocker in black velvet hat and cape who lights a cigarette each time a scene begins *spotlights on giant tripods define them* the punk in the rubber bodysuit was particularly vile hissing "You're the shit in my toilet" into a boom mike the size of an overfed house cat, camera rolling toward him along a railroad track contraption—I wished it would roll right over him—after midnight the neighbors started to complain, a squad car pulled up and emitted the word "disperse" but, undaunted, caterers spread out a banquet on a picnic table *the slaying happened around 5:00 a.m.* I peeked behind the windowshade the glowing strip along its edge spreading in a cold V across my naked shoulder and breast—in a bluish pool of light the corpse was lying on his back spreadeagle *then the immediate drop-off into darkness* he held his breath as a crew of a dozen huddled around, a photographer crouched over his chest snapping close-ups of his dead face, the blood was behind them in two translucent jugs, squarish with molded handles, like containers for anti-freeze, I released the shade and turned to KK, "They just murdered somebody." "Oh." Snore. I scratched my nose and snuggled against him my chilled flesh melting to dreams.

All skeletons should be plastic.

Memories moisten and rust *so many molecules leaking meaning* Sam dissolves from man to character, a mate for Mina *they rendezvous in Morocco over sweet umbrellaed drinks* it's easy to fall in love with the dead *tattered rectangles fingered in wallets, hung on walls* I stole an 8 x 10 glossy from your publisher *your flesh gelled in silver, scaled gray, a gradation of parts* you're sitting on the floor of a boxcar leaning against the open door, railroad tracks extend from your right shoulder, scarred whitewashed wall supports your left, your expression is serious, butch *characters grow stronger and longer than mortals they grow machine guns for arms and wipe out their originals* naked chest tight faded button-front jeans, accordioned denim pulling across a serious bulge in the crotch, on either side like frames or arrows your hands rest on your hip *cut off at the knuckles* if this picture were the world ships navigating south along the dangerous undulations of your fly would plop off the edge, masts of massive sails snapping as they tumble into the dark Unknown.

In the back of a kitchen cabinet I find a baggie stuffed with refrigerator magnets, I brush off the dust and pull out a handful of felt letters sprinkled with sequins and glitter, Grandma sent them on special occasions instead of cards HAPPY EASTER HAPPY ANNIVERSARY—my refrigerator is already overloaded, lop-sided heart I LOVE KEVIN lop-sided heart stretches across the freezer while gold-dimpled strawberries and pastel birds float about the main compartment—I stick the letters on the side of my file cabinet—lots of "Y"s no "C"s "F"s "B"s or "L"s only one "I" they must spell out *something* a message from Grandma—I shift the random jumble around the blue metal to form a couplet:

SANITY PARADED HEAVY PURPOSE
HONEY DIARY NAP

a treatise on life and death, the illusion/parade of our earthly pretensions followed by Grandma's sweet dream from the daily. A "nap"—maybe she's coming back! *I have a lavender clown Grandma that you can enter* a real cozy possession *we'll sleep together every night and during the day you can cuddle beside Sam's monkey on my desk, never again will inspiration fail me* I bump the first line of Grandma's couplet with my chair pink and blue letters sail to the ground SANITY collapsing to ANT. A week later the evil ghost Catherine possesses a hi-tech gym's electrical system and blows up the neon sign out front STAR BODY HEALTH SPA fizzling to D EA TH SPA cut to a dozen soapy women in a shower *steamy lens loving many inches* doors lock—the shower head turns molten—tiles fly off the walls shredding balloon boobs skeletal waists *others are repelled by beauty in such an agonized state* but the camera doesn't flinch as it lingers over these agitated figures rippling with blood, these flushed faces swelling to screams.

ADONIS = NO AIDS.

By addressing you and others like you these letters circumvent the anonymous reader *eyes swinging and glinting in the dark, ghostly eyes I barely believe in* but who's more ghostly than a dead man? Last night I talked to an old friend of yours, Ed, who told me about the Sam he knew, the Sam who compartmentalized his life, who never let different parts meet, who gave each person a different set of "facts." We were all your projections and you were ours: startling, psychedelic, like the opening credits of a James Bond picture *words and guns glide across the sinuous leotards of showgirls, even in silhouette you recognize their 60's coifs.* Were you a middle class guy from Chico or were you Sam the glamorous Sam the mysterious *you told Benjamin you were Joe D'Allesandro's son* bursting with plots you never stopped narrating. As the illness progressed the "real" biography emerged like a skull tracing its bony landmarks beneath the cheeks—your real name was RICHARD ANDERSON a name as exotic as crew socks—or was it Rumpelstiltskin? If I stand before a mirror and say it quickly five times will you appear *Richard Anderson Richard Anderson Richard Anderson* will you appear behind me a hook flaring from the end of your arm *Richard Anderson* a hive of angry bees swarming your torso *prickly yes but with honey in your veins Richard Anderson* the night before you died you told Ed about the people living in the hills and valleys of your brown blanket *SX: a lover can be a best friend, a piece of furniture, or an eternity* I should have asked him what you looked like.

The ground of the tiny cemetery is soft from melted snow, I sink slightly with each step into the grave of Jean Stafford Jackson Pollock Ad Reinhardt Lee Krasner Stuart Davis Elaine DeKooning A.J. Liebling *so many celebrities chiseled in marble it's like wandering through a Stone Age autograph book* Frank O'Hara's tombstone is embedded in the earth an unbroken horizontal of dried grass and slab *grace to be born and live as variously as possible* a fan has left a plastic snowshaker of New York City, as I shake it KK kneels and kisses O'Hara's name it's cold and mossy, he stands, "Your turn." "No way." So he presses his grave-stained lips against mine, "For genius." You're next Sam but I'll never find that fig tree, your ashes—I pick up *Zombie Pit* kiss your silvery face a slick pressure that smells of ink, blur of magenta *one of us is bleeding into the other: SX: take the death as a lover and sleep with it and eat it and purge it and suck it back in quick.* Even when I was with

Dèath I recognized him by his absence, our interactions stark and disconnected a languid black and white. The night of the power outage we kneel on a vinyl sofa and stare into the courtyard of his building: silhouetted figures flicker behind curtains lights float down hallways flash of polished wood and knob, velvety gleam of moonbeams along drainpipes *Death presses his hand over my arched throat, a caress?* I'm wearing a brambled coral necklace a vintage dress, navy and white, the sheer fabric slides over my slip and crumples as Death lays his head in my lap *brimstone searing down all the way to my cunt* I loved it when my tits or my cock or my asshole would destroy my own ego with their needs.

Variegated blond or brown Death's hair shifted hue with the emotional climate like a mood ring *eyes reflect images and thus capture stray souls* his were glacier blue and came in a hundred settings *the Marquise cut ... his teeth in my shoulder his bare ass glowing like uranium in the night.*

Death and I sit on his bed discussing language and desire *a disturbance of limits, nothing more* he tells me about his notebook, each partner gets a page listing name date place and acts performed "in chains with great weights hanging from tits" 700 partners/pages shifting across time like minimalist music subtle yet baroque *Sex for Airports.* "Still the body refuses," moans Death, "to give up its meaning." "Yeah, like you can't translate it." He brushes his thumb across my cheek his bluish-brown veins tracing an arborescent pattern on his forearm, almost imperceptibly at first then growing stronger like the scent of espresso as one approaches a cafe there arises between us a tantalizing blend of tenderness and passion. "Hyperbolic ideals." "Radically uninhabitable positions." I scoot half a foot closer *his skin white as dry ice.* "Representations stumble and falter before the real." "I know what you mean, want another beer?" Returning from the kitchen with a Dos Equis Death sits down hip to hip slides his hand tentatively across my back, "Is this okay?" I lean into his palm, "Uhhhhhh." *Flesh conjured from the cracks between fantasy and grammar* Death grinds himself against me and I grind back his hard-on bruising my pubic bone he pushes my face into a pillow I can't breathe can't see, my heart is open to the foam mattress, he fucks me from behind page *701 ... filling in the spongy cracks.*

The villagers avoid the gaze of a dead person for death is reflected there, they cover all containers of water at night because spirits wandering during sleep might fall in and drown, they bury the temptress face down so she can't find her way out of the coffin *holy wafers jammed between her lips.* Quincey opens the doors and windows sweeps the house clean pitches the dirt outside to ensure my soul isn't hiding in a corner somewhere.

Perspective gave us that artificial feeling Ed said he doesn't know what Jono was talking about *you* were the mummy ... under the bandages against your heart you held a flashlight *blink-blink blink-blink blink-blink twirling at our feet.*

Love, too, enters through the eye. KK steals my handkerchief and ties it around his cock "to remember."

In lampblack Italian loafers Death always approaches from behind, I'm munching on a peanut butter cookie when I hear him faintly clicking in the distance *Captain Hook* he snags me with his bony finger fists me nightly reaching his long arm up through my gut and clamping my heart, he crawls in my brain boring straight through from one thought to the next, Death pins my outstretched arms like butterfly wings, starting at the back of my neck he works his way down biting so hard I fear he will chew me alive *the skin on my hands and feet falls away ... and then the nails ... but beneath them new nails appear along with a fresh and vivid skin* he twists my body in so many directions I feel like a length of twine in a Cub Scout knotting class *when he fucks me I'm a sheepshank, afterwards a hangman's noose* Death grabs his shirt from the floor and binds my wrists together his sweat embedding my pores, his hand tightens around my throat he does what he wants my saliva dissolving the black ridged in his fingertips *Sam, I never dreamed that playing dead could make you feel so alive* Death has the biggest cock I've ever seen big and stiff as a stuffed muskrat, I couldn't close my hand around it, couldn't imagine taking that taxidermic *Thing* into me, yet I did, stretching my lips around it taut as a rubber about to burst. "You need a larger mouth," he jokes. When we fuck the Thing scrapes away the wall of my vagina *in that rawness all categories explode.*

SX: He didn't force me to do anything he just created situations in which I wanted what he was going to give me anyway. SX: The truth of the matter is I like to be beaten and then fucked like a dog. I don't just mean on my hands and knees, I mean hard and carelessly. I want someone relentless.

With his left hand Death holds both my hands, keeping them away with my arms at full tension: his right hand grips me by the back of the neck, forcing my face down in his bosom. It's as if I'm just a mouth moving soundlessly in graceful dips and circles and rat-a-tat-tats. The teeth occasionally flash; the tongue coyly uncoils, begging release from between the prison of teeth before retracting into the dull cave of throat; little swirls and sparkles manifest and pop, and all the while dark air funnels out in columns like smoke *I have come to the very end I am at the very brink where I am now is the extreme point* my white night-dress is smeared with blood, and a thin stream trickles down his bare chest.

I lost the photos from my wedding—all that remains is a contact sheet *black and white miniatures of insect people at some sort of ceremony* as I place a lupe against the scratched matt surface Roberto's backyard leaps forward ... wooden stairs ... three-tiered cake crowned with wild flowers ... clusters of "starving artists" orbiting around plates and champagne punch ... potato salad elbows bushes folding chairs life seems so manageable through my convex bubble *nothing but clicks in time* that's me standing in the center of rectangle 14 cotton lace and cheek-length bob bright as infrared, my eyes are closed my smile inward and serene, helium balloons float above my head like wishes that have all been answered *one becomes suddenly picturesque to oneself and one's wavering little individuality stands out with a cameo effect* in shirt and tie and goofy military burr KK leans into the far left of the frame, his right hand is cut off by the horizontal edge, in the other he holds a glass of Scotch and a cigarette, his downward gaze links us *proud husband and blind ecstatic wife* his face is radiant his thin lips parted *muscles strain with the effort of looking, my eye is that close to the moment* I scoot across the page I'm carrying a brightly wrapped present to the bedroom when Death walks through the door trailing our past behind him like tin cans *I haven't seen him for months* he says, "Do you have anything non-alcoholic to drink?" Neither blond nor brown his hair is colorless as if waiting for a mood to strike *incredibly emaciated yet so ordinary—a stick figure* the dissolving flesh has left dark circles around his eyes, his delicate skull and tibia press against his skin as if the skeleton were breaking through to form a solid shield of bone *seal up the seven openings to the soul and a being could live forever* I was carrying a foil package with a magenta bow when Death walked in *the uninvited guest the fairy tale* the first thing he said was "Do you have anything nonalcoholic?" He kissed me on the cheek and I felt frumpy in my gauze dress with lavender flowers my droopy orchid corsage *the slightest flutter of my pulse obscene* all my tenses coagulated. I found myself outside on the sidewalk crying, behind me a tall wooden fence with knot holes KK's arms come through them encircling my shoulders a cloud of Scotch and heat and cigarette smoke, the rest of the guests fade into the background like extras in a party scene smiling and chatting to one another in barely audible murmurs *something more than hanging out but less than participating* do extras have lines or do they ad lib, self-consciously gossiping and joking about the absurdity of their situation? *No matter how hard you try to push the horror back onto the screen it keeps coming at you with its greasepaint smile its cabochon eyes.* Is there an extras union? Are they trained to mouth gibberish like the nonsense copy in advertising layouts, from a distance it reads as text but up close: "glyf ug towims dorh" in justified columns or ragged right.

According to the midget psychic in *Poltergeist* some of us get lost on our way to the Light, hang around spooky and enraged the TV screen gulps down a little girl, a deluxe console, things meant to be stationary begin to move about YOU WANTED TO DIE FAMOUS *holy wafers are hard to come by she sticks potato chips between the corpse's lips* when I was human I didn't play around with (e)motion, I knew only two speeds Stop and Go, and when I went I was *driven* SCREEEEEEECH dead stop. Go. Screech. Now this endless gray drone this in-between—sneak to the toilet bend over poke finger down throat *focus pulling: reversing the relationship of fore and ground* vomiting is an early sign of possession I've seen it in video after video *the language of the body as present is merged with the language of the body as absent—somehow the really bad stuff never comes up* I creep out of the bathroom trying to hide my red face *painted devil* my finger swells beneath my wedding band large and dark as a turd *heating ducts and plumbing pipes slick with blood, three pounds of bacteria churning like my computer* all communications are binary PURGE OR RETAIN *a tube of slippage and fungibility—when I am anaerobic I just don't feel like answering the phone* from the inside the intestines really aren't that bad sometimes even a tunnel of love, Dr. Van Helsing looked inside his own once with a periscope, he described religious awe, lots of pink *a place of breakdown like a VCR with a dirty head* the dead watch the living, their eyes are bugged from all that watching *light dark light dark light dark* night and day flicker across my face like cinema *light dark* Quincey Dion *light dark* Quincey Dion Quincey *light* Dion Quincey *dark* Dion. My soul is monstrously jealous had I been a beautiful woman it could not have endured me. I spend the day in bed *a delicacy a lacy suffering* because I can't decide what to wear *emotive fragments pull me along cold fear burning terror if this were a dream I'd surely have awakened heart shivers cunt throbs mid-sentence I forget what it was I was* ... I lie in KK's arms pondering our minute daily variations I hug him at the front door his leather jacket speckled with rain his sweater crackly cool his dress shirt his T-shirt sticky with sweat, he says my smile is crooked *one corner saying no the other saying yes* and kisses me in the kitchen I squeal just a minute my onions are burning *above the stove hang seven pink potholders crocheted by Grandma, blushing snowflakes* no major event on which everything hinges, my trip to the store is told in the same patterns as the latest episode of *Santa Barbara*—even before the denouement is revealed the quick-witted knows which vegetable was purchased which marriage shattered *beyond the narrative drive of orgasm ... his erection is wrinkled but the charge remains in our arms our feet our flushed faces* people and situations fade in, I taste onions, dream of emaciated men—their arms are bound to crosses forcing them to die in the position of Christ, hunched under the weight of the crosses they totter on thin awkward legs like earthbound birds *in a paragraph that has lost its topic sentence how do I choose the next idea, word, pair of shoes?*

When Death crashed my wedding I transcended consistency *all points collapsing into one site, his.* O Wedding Guest! This soul hath been/ Alone on a wide, wide sea:/ So lonely 'twas, that God Himself/ Scarce seemèd there to be.

Argento: The serial killer tapes a row of needles across the soprano's eyes, a blink will shred her pretty lids—up close the needles look like stakes topping a fortress wall, the soprano is the lookout her vision bleared with tears and blood, as one by one his gloved hand stabs and hacks all those close to her, love acts that turn poetic with the seamstress' throat *impaled with a pair of scissors the point sticks out of her dead gaping mouth* the killer is very handsome as he performs the unthinkable for the soprano's amusement his gloved fingers flinging dark thoughts *darker than her dark pupils a dark opera* when she cries in terror he stares back with a mixture of shyness and pride *a hard look equals a hard penis go ahead and touch it* I throw my legs out of bed, beneath my bare foot a thick cold furry CRUNCH a dead mouse *that goddamned cat I'm gonna strangle her* but all the pet books say to praise *good kitty* the killer's desire is focused on a single point a swinging pendulum that glints in a cosmos of jet black, that pulls him *in* he'll do anything to get closer to it but life jumps forward hideous and gnarled obscuring his view OUT COMES THE HATCHET he tapes open the soprano's eyes so she'll see the glint too *insatiable organ hole* seeing too little (to the point of blindness) seeing too much (to the point of insanity) eyeballs gouged with ice picks hypodermic needles binoculars that snap daggers persons blinded by hot coffee acid insect spray or simply bright light eyes reacting in horror at a poised bloody knife an advancing shape or something off-frame *the indefatigable hoof-taps of Mina's keyboard.*

The cords are ready to break loose, release lions.

You lived sort of in the Sunset sort of in the Haight, I remember hardwood floors acres of gleaming parquet and a smattering of cleverly wrapped birthday presents—dominating the sideboard is a portable TV spray-painted with misty chartreuse and black blobs, a punk sculpture, perhaps the picture tube has been gutted and the empty space filled with an anti-nativity *holocaust faces white as ice* a mound of icons from the Orient have overtaken a built-in bookcase, incense infusing elephants and Buddhas, skulls hanging from Kali's ears *the matrix shifts and we shift with it* in a metallic green suit you move from person to person shouting over the music, your waving fingers remind me of the eyeballs in KK's dream—suddenly everyone has fingers growing out of their eye sockets, and eyeballs dangling from their hands—everyone except KK—a man with pink tentacles fluttering above his cheeks scowls, "You're the freak now." Like yours his beauty is an aberration, a burden, a mystery *so many molecules leaking meaning so many categories to get caught between* my heart is a flashlight that blinks on and off as I twirl at your feet.

I could slip and fall, end up eighteen inches tall in a shopping mall.

On his way out to return last night's videos KK says, "Why don't you order the pizza while I'm gone." "Sure I'll order that pizza." Fat chance. I walk to the armoire and pull out a tight white thrift store slip, cut like a sleeveless sheath with wide non-adjustable straps—as I tug it down over my head tattered lace stretches from my shoulders to tight beneath my breasts *frazzled white buds for nipples, engorged* $1.99 for a white trash wonder *hornets' nest in the outhouse, car up on blocks in the front yard* I crawl in bed and wait for my man perfectly lazy and good for nothin' rubbing that nylon over my hipbone rubbing my eyes to smear my make-up *if I didn't reify myself Mina Harker would never get written* KK walks in, "I remember that slip, remember biting that lace that looks like it's already been bitten." Shock of icy fingers along my clit my breasts are no longer breasts but titties *just the thought of keyboarding the word titties excites me* SAY IT he sucks my flowery titties nylon mesh scratching his tongue *a man has to learn to take the rough with the smooth* I want to push his button eyes to see what he sees not the me of the mirror but this clingy white queen with static enough to fill a room *thick puddle across my belly and into the mattress, seeping, a portal* he collapses, "Where are we?"

When, at the end, she turns the tables, she herself becomes a kind of monstrous hero—hero insofar as she has risen against and defeated the forces of monstrosity, monster insofar as she has herself become excessive, demonic. Her corpse is disinterred and the villagers set about the task of tearing out her heart. The butcher, old and maladroit, begins by opening the belly rather than the chest. He rummages about for a long time in the entrails without finding what he seeks and finally someone informs him that it is necessary to cut into the diaphragm. Her heart is torn out to the admiration of all the bystanders. Their imagination struck by the spectacle fills with visions *from a certain angle any-one can be made to look as if they've lost a limb* an operation is performed to introduce order. The only things left intact on the woman's head are her ears, all the other facial skin is loosened and pulled up tightly under her chin, the butcher cuts off the excess and closes the incision with metal staples, it's something like taking in a dress. The thin red scars on her eyelids are swollen but not very visible. The corners of her mouth turn up in a pleasant and friendly manner making her seem more awake, not so sad *the style and positioning of the elements in the pose become an almost unbelievably glamorous combination* her lips look a bit "stretched" but that's good because she has a small mouth. Her cheeks are numb in places with occasional needles of sensation, and her ears feel as if they belong to someone else.

Machines litter the halls chrome and porcelain they look like a cross between an overhead projector and a Maytag washer, straps and nozzles flailing about like demented prostheses, there are no windows here we don't need any we have these machines to look *inside*. I walk through a room lined with lightboxes *chilly blur of white-white black-black* negatives large as life map hands skulls stomachs *a flat and squishy world where matter has no substance* everywhere I turn bodies are hooked to or duplicated by metallic contraptions *with all these edges the potential for bruising is tremendous* a woman says to a man who is scrubbing his midriff, "If you're going to get slop on you it's better to get gastric slop instead of blood"—another man lies on a gurney, an arched steel band floating above his nose and cheeks like a halo that has slipped—a little boy runs toward me with a long vacuum cleaner–type hose attached to his throat—a bloated gray-haired woman rolls by, her feet peeling in large chalky flakes *repulsive to my first person gaze but a third person might bend over and bathe them with her long faithful hair a third person might do anything* FOCUS ON TARGETED IMAGES ONLY none of the subjects wears socks.

Glass beads are dropped in her mouth a hen's egg is tucked under each armpit and needles are placed in the palms of her hands the woman cannot open her mouth to shriek or wave her arms as wings or open and shut her hands to assist the flight when Death walked into my wedding I stopped believing I was a deep person.

Where are we?

People are in transit here pushed through antiseptic aisles, IVs jingling beside them *appendages of alien lifeforms* plastic bladders drip dayglo green rootbeer brown, ambulatory subjects pull their own IVs, the bags of candy-colored fluid hanging from metal racks set on wheels—a thin man approaches clenching his rack like a cane, his veins are being filled with yellow, his seersucker gown is stretched across a huge belly—he looks nine months pregnant hobbling with his shoulders thrown back as if he needs extra leverage to thrust his bulbous growth through the disinfected troposphere *from the back a slit of naked ass* I have no right to see this.

There's a mortician in my life *a friend of a friend* through Sing she answers my interment questions *why don't the saints rot why did villagers believe exhumed corpses were still alive* Claire likes to talk about her job, says we'd be amazed how many men come through with cigarette burns on their forearms *probably self-inflicted* I imagine men alone behind lit windows frustrated self-pitying angry, forearms flop forward in unison, cigarettes plunge and grind *acrid singe of hair and flesh* recently Claire did a famous Hell's Angel who died of cancer, "Boy was he in great shape, but you wanna talk about scars …" The corpse is a thriller she gives away the ending to, a thing with no secrets—my mind reels against my own transformation *drained then stuffed, lips stitched together* GIVE ME MY ME BACK if I were the psychopathic donor in *Body Parts* I'd retrieve my arms and legs too, rip them right off the recipients' torsos, eely veins squirting fuchsia slime *I am an experiment gone haywire* there are no cigarette burns on the psychopath's forearm.

Moving between two worlds like Persephone … it's that awful season again I collapse inward anti-orgasm condensing heart and lungs to rubber I have to lie on one of those beds that rock you around just to keep you breathing *the wisdom of isolation and bitterness* no more dust and water for me—from now on I dine on bread and beer. A man bursts through the swinging doors still wearing his blue gown his plastic surgical cap, he's holding a folded blue towel out in front of him as if it were fragile, precious, he says, "Do you know where I take the breast biopsies?" *All the softness in the world growing sour in his hands* I answer, "I don't know anything."

The bloodjet is poetry.

Death thrusts himself towards me point blank ... I am fractured and repeated a line of cops at target practice, headphones mute my exploding weapons—across the room paper silhouettes silently grow holes—when the firing stops they glide forward on metal tracks *a line of flat men lacy as snowflakes* BULL'S EYE Maniac Cop barges in, his face gashed his icy grip funnelling the ungraspable, he blasts each of us through the heart—a row of red-splattered uniforms *my bodies* flop like rag dolls to the ground POINT BLANK *there are really only two characters: a mobile being who penetrates closed spaces and an immobile being who is that damp dark space* a bicycle speeds past a woman on the sidewalk grazing her royal blue coat, she turns quickly towards the cyclist *shoulder-length perm trembling* and shouts, "I *need* your lust. I *need* your lust." Her tone is impassioned pleading dignified, Glynis Johns circa 1962, "More than anything else in the world I *need that*—Lust."

Strong medicine in the soothing warmth of a hot liquid.

I take a deep breath, step into the hallway move my eyes from side to side scanning for another body announcing chaos, the walls are beige with a band of orange extending a foot from the ceiling *orange for energy* my mother drew the sun with an orange crayon and that drove me crazy. "The sun is yellow," I'd whine. "No it isn't, listen to your mother!" Hand rails run the length of the corridor I hear a child screaming, when I turn the corner it's a little blonde girl she'd be pretty except the left side of her face is half an inch lower than the right *like a Picasso* her mother is yelling, "Stop it! Stop it!" I turn another corner, a child is jittering in a wheelchair trembling arms stretched out straight like a sleepwalker's, refrigerator-white face bright pink circles on cheeks *the rouge of a rag doll* tense circle of lips wide wide circles of eyes—

she looks remarkably surprised, mother helplessly fluttering about. Terrible tunnels. I turn another corner and—I'm not kidding—Peter Coyote walks by *a giant surrounded by an entourage* posted on a door behind him: CAUTION RADIOACTIVE MATERIALS NO EATING OR DRINKING BIOHAZARD PROTECTED *if you open this door a loud alarm will sound and police will be called* the door is already open I peek: a white rat is sprawled open on its back a white-coated technician bends over it with a scalpel, shimmering pink intestines *does anyone ever walk out of this alive* when I asked my mother about operations she said they throw your extra parts in the trash—I imagined a circular wastepaper basket, gray enamel, with a pair of human legs sticking out of it *how could anybody ever survive* this was around the same time I believed spaghetti grew on trees, massive boughs drooping like weeping willows from the weight of all that pasta. My mother sprinkled bread with vinegar and salt and pepper because she was raised during the Depression. "Glad you could use the aprons," wrote Grandma. "Would you like to have some cute magnetics for your fridge? Hope everything is okay with you and Kevin. Give him my love and a whole bunch for yourself."

Mechanical arms turn into sculptures the body is so difficult to probe, so deep and airless *when the area to be imaged is beyond the acoustic window linear molecules are injected into the brain* why can't the skin be transparent like a glass of water *half empty half full, I begin to feel limited by my singular sex organ* the fluorescent tube is bright as love the ceiling is poked with thousands of holes, beneath this silent galaxy I lie fluffy and white, bleached sheets mounded over me I'm like this huge baked Alaska two pink feet peek out *lines and callouses on the soles map the body's secrets but it takes a Gypsy to read them* the gleaming floor reflects the legs of my gurney as my head floats through the miles of corridors—a homunculus lives in my right ear he says jump off and run *sweetness drips through my exposed plastic veins* I am tired of his nonsense *it's as if I'm some escaped idea that accidentally fell out of someone, someone who has voice has visibility has embodiment* in the blue room they will insert a catheter in my thigh and push it along the "major pathways" until it reaches my brain *this is the halfway point the tunnel of return* if you're smart you always leave room for a sequel the monster may be shot burnt frozen exploded but in the last frame the mad preacher regenerates a shred of its flesh in a Mason jar *I am but a temporary here my flashing green eyes my full set of teeth my hennaed hair I come and I go and only Dodie's poor convulsing body knows the difference* memos concerning "serious cardiopulmonary events" are sent on pale blue paper.

When I resurface Death's standing over me, naked, watching. His skin is drenched in red light, glowing with it. I reach my arms up toward his. We stay in this picture for some moments as he savors the exquisite little gulf between my gesture and his body. When he moves an inch closer, my hand runs slowly down his velvet belly, over the red-liquid skin, and I draw him to me.

Bette Davis learns in *Mr. Skeffington* "a woman is beautiful only when she is loved." An ever-flirtatious belle it takes nothing less than disfigurement by diphtheria for her to see the light. Overnight (ten minutes in movie time) Fanny ages 20 years her hair falls out she puts on white pancake make-up and long clumpy eyelashes, in a girlish voice an octave higher than Davis' own she chimes, "Have I changed?" Her former beau stutters, "Ch-changed?" When the husband she dumped midway through the picture for the fast track *bathtub gin and a thousand marriage proposals* returns penniless from a concentration camp Fanny doesn't want to be seen by him. Eventually she descends the long winding staircase to find him in an easy chair a broken man. Hearing her enter he stands up and clicks his cane across the parquet, stumbles, Fanny rushes to him, "Oh, Darling did the Nazis blind you?" At last a man to whom she will always be a knockout *the language of the body as present is merged with the language of the body as absent* she takes his arm and turns to the maid, "Mr. Skeffington has come home." As they mount the stairs she is finally loved, finally beautiful. THE END. "That was disgusting!" I snort. Rendezvous is crushed, a broken man in an easy chair, he wanted me to like the picture. Outside my building two men live behind a ring of dumpsters like pioneers in a circle of wagons *extra parts* ruddy and smudged they watch me put my key in the door. "And one more thing," I'm thinking, "why didn't they call it *Mrs.* Skeffington?"

Vomiting is its own orgasm *the immaterial realm of the beyond pulsing through my lips* I wipe the acidic smear from my cheek and I look in the mirror: pallor weakness and languor *I am a Victorian consumptive* an image so sexy I put on something high-collared and jerk off the other end *violet-scented urine* IF ART IS NOT TO BE EMBARRASSED BEFORE EXPERIENCE THEN IT MUST BE SOMETHING MORE have subject lie in a decubitus position with affected side up *the Virgin Mary no longer appears to me daily, only on my birthday and in special times of need* I spread my thighs a wide V of spotlight trails to murk beneath the knees, I'm afraid the lightbulb will shatter into a million shards that cut my face to shreds. *SX: We are in space here. Not space-like jargon, I mean space—like Star Trek, black holes, limitlessness. I mean it's just like when Hal the computer cut the rope on that stupid astronaut— things are just drifting away.* For my museum-quality models I sculpt polyurethane bodies over pneumatically-driven skeletons, then I texture and paint the silicone rubber skin with fur animal fat wire and batteries—I arrange them in vitrines containing stuffed hares nests and moldy honeycombs *life as a corpse to be embalmed by the writer* no one knows what color the originals were, but critics surmise a variety as great as that of today's birds I DON'T WANT TO LOSE MY LIFE TO ART, SAM—the only way out of this jam is to emulate Agent 007—perfected in an underground lab his pen is secretly a gun-camera a swizzle stick a bug a laser-bomb a cellular phone a hook to attach to cliffs and dangle from *the name is Harker, Mina Harker* when a beautiful woman forces him at gunpoint to write that she Fatima Blush was his best ever 007 points the pen at her breasts and launches a missile, Fatima explodes, her fiery spasms hurling off the screen *the uncanny return* POW! *of the repressed excess beyond the text* I am bioengineering a clone from ancient DNA from the stomachs of insects preserved in amber, a series of technical breakdowns lets the characters escape to breed in the wild and eventually terrorize the world *a radically uninhabitable position* KK said god made his basic machinery but I flipped the switch, he's at a party in grad school very drunk when a pet monkey gulps his dick like a big banana and sucks him off, the monkey was trained by his friends—that's all I know *did you come how big was the monkey did it seem to enjoy it did it scratch you what do monkey lips feel like* all my pleas are met with an impatient "I don't remember." His cock is under erasure and my cunt is a camera I spread my thighs a wide V of spotlight trails to murk beneath the knees *from the frying pan into the fire* it is undecided whether this is indecent self-display or a rare aesthetic moment.

KK moans in his sleep, "Oh beautiful!" His back is to me and I'm on the other side of the bed curled around the cat, her claws against my naked breasts *retracted* "Oh beautiful!" it could be me *what difference.* I found a letter the other day that KK wrote to Steve: "I've met three or four writers with more glamor (Robin Blaser comes to mind), and three or four with more sex appeal— but Sam's personal beauty was astonishing. At first it formed a screen behind which one could hardly see his work. One day he came over to visit and we watched the John Huston film of *Reflections of a Golden Eye.* Elizabeth Taylor and Marlon Brando. In a just world, I thought, they would be sitting in my living room watching Sam and me on the screen." I roll onto KK's hard-on he awakens. "What were you dreaming of?" "Little plastic toys—you put a quarter in a machine and there's this crane you operate to pick up the toys." "What'd they look like?" "There was a whole series of glittering prizes." "Did you get any?" "No."

I never saw you when you were sick, but after your death, in a dream, I find a video taped during your last days. As soon as you come onscreen I turn my head away, you're talking to me but I'm afraid to look as if you were the creature from *The Fly* and I was nine again—every time a commercial for *The Fly* came on I'd squeeze my eyes shut and run into the bedroom bumping into walls, after a couple of weeks I got pretty banged up—in my dream a voice says *watch, listen it's still Sam in there, your friend.* Okay. When I awaken I pick up the gray envelope from Amagansett DO NOT BEND in it are 2 1/4 contact sheets of your photo session with Robert Giard the month before you died—Giard's never shown these pictures to anyone *SX: I used to imagine people out of my past watching me through a crystal ball or some sort of telepathic power I never knew they had* we're all in space here—in the silent galaxy we have no whirring autopsy blades, only a semi-circular saw, I grasp its cross beam and with a rocking motion crack open your sternum the space doctor reaches in and pulls apart the rib cage we poke around for a bit then stitch you back up with carpet needle and twine, a thick knobby seam bisects your chest like Lee Harvey Oswald's in *Life* magazine *an image so famous it's tossed across a million coffee tables* I rip open the envelope. You're gaunt, yes, but these days I see men on the street who are more so, thin men meeting friends for coffee and pastries thinner men getting out of cars with canes—it's your eyes that shock, Sam, eyes too large for their sockets eyes round as globes and large enough to swallow the world eyes that seem to be pinned open with details rushing in like locomotives. You look exhausted. I pull out your boxcar glamor shot (BEFORE) your face looks chubby, vicious with youth *horizontal bedroom eyes heating*

234

up the frame with a careless sexual nature that slightly threatens and promises nothing I clip Giard's contacts on my copystand (AFTER) so that as I write I can stare back at you, and keep staring until this new Sam no longer startles but IS. You collected dusty vomit-encrusted *things* I could only imagine held at arm's length between the tips of finger and thumb, your lover's scarred face was like a map X's and lines curved around the cheekbones in a constant motion of intersections and near-misses, you pushed him against the wall and licked and probed every little trench and ridge and rent *sucking out the invisible poison* your eyes will remain unreadable to me, will never "reveal"—but that's not the point, is it—the point is to look, not in horror not in pity or even in compassion, but to look as precisely as possible at the ever-wavering presence right in front of one—this is the closest beings as imperfect as we can come to love.

Goodbye/ my dream of me/ goodbye/ my mystery/ goodbye.

Love,
Mina

October 17, 1994

Dear Sing,

So here I am, working on my ending, going crazy with endings *bye-bye book, so-long lover* Dodie's handing me one eviction notice after another, my lease on her body she says is OVER *this letter is "the land's end: the last fingers, knuckled and rheumatic,/ Cramped on nothing."* I try not to be pessimistic as Plath but, Sing … we were at my kitchen table eating ratatouille when suddenly I was on my knees, tugging down his pants licking the crack of his ass—at The End of that crack is a dank smelly hole, that's where Dodie plans to stick me—can you see why this letter's taken months to wrestle to a finish, I'm like the anarchist in *Five Came Back*, being flown home at gunpoint to my execution—when the plane crashes in the rain forest near a tribe of natives who decapitate their victims, fill the heads with hot sand and shrink them, I'm happy. *A few of his cells stick to my tongue like specimens, instead of sending them to a pathologist, I swallow.* I've been fucking my brains out *my brains are all fucked out* you know how it goes, Sing, your writing goes down the tubes like an unfertilized ovum *blood on his cock blood on my thighs blood on the towel beneath my bun* I am a feminist artist I buy lipstick wholesale in five-gallon buckets and cast it into urinals the color of menses, urinals that glisten and gape. You are my opposite number—wired on espresso vibrating in a chair *an artist and a feminist* sticking close to those cigarettes *living alone is scarier than a movie*—the last time I lived by myself was in 1977—the street hustlers next door boomed the lightwell with Donna Summer, they never seemed to sleep these gaunt boys hanging out the front windows luscious as orchids, "Hi, hon, wanna party?" Whenever I switched off the kitchen light cockroaches rustled the garbage, trapped, frantic, huge, like the anxiety attack clawing my chest *Love to Love You Baby* I'd come home feed the cat and dart out the door. The rare times I did sleep there, or sit down, the cat glued herself to my lap and wailed—so I flew her to Nebraska for a couple of months to cool out with Nature. Her name was Molly, a beautiful calico. The night of my wedding she wouldn't eat, then after fifteen years died of kidney failure *nice timing, Molly* unmoving in her tiny cage she felt hollow against my palm, not a purr, a plastic tube sticking out of a shaved spot on her front paw, fluid dripped through it chlorophyll-green as if the vet were transfusing her backwards from animal to plant *then the tube turns umber* mineral *then empty* air.

Fingers undulate over belly shoulder ass, fingers parting thighs, "You're a kite," he says softly, "and I'm a key attached to you— electricity is inevitable, it's in the air." *I want the warm hand the warm hand doesn't call me by name.* "Kite and Key," he muses, "I like the initials: KK, like me. And for you I would say, 'You're the Dog and I'm the Bone.'" "DB is for Dodie—what about MINA?" *I'm the Doppelganger and she's just a Body* chin stubble scratches my cheek, "How about 'You're the Mouse and I'm the Hole'—or 'You're the Mustard and I'm the Hot dog.'" *The warm hand shimmies across my cunt, pauses to sniff then burrows.* "You're a Mountain and I'm a Hiker you're a Mouth and I'm Homeless you're Miserable and I'm Happy you're a Million and I'm a Hundred you're Magic and I'm History." The warm hand twitches *you're the Minutes and I'm an Hour you are the Map and I am the Highway you're the Mud and I'm the Hut …*

KK arranged the evening: pizza (you nibbled one slice, I snarfed down three) and Argento's *The Bird with the Crystal Plumage* (when a painting reawakens her latent psychosis the gallery-owner's wife goes on a stabbing spree *blood slides across bodies, a dress*) I'd remember more details if we hadn't switched off the video and run to the Filipino market for another bottle of red wine, I paid as you poked the packages of brightly-colored rice flour confections, then we walked past the "empty" lot that's scattered with rusting chunks of car frame *beneath the streetlight their shadows jag across gravel, so cold* I told you about the woman who crawled out from behind one, tugging down her miniskirt, and you remarked, "Whenever anything comes up I always ask myself 'what would Drew Barrymore think of that?'" Since then I've become a dedicated student of Drew Barrymore's screen work—Drew chewing her lip as her tiny fists cup a pistol, Drew swinging over a canyon in cowboy boots, Drew in a bad wig (Leslie says the fakey hair is a good touch, reminding us of the artificiality of film—I interrupt, "Do you really think *The Amy Fisher Story* is that sophisticated?"). In *Poison Ivy* Drew's décolletage cut to the heart, in *No Place to Hide* some wardrobe idiot stuck T shirts beneath her rhinestone-studded bustiers, white tee beneath her black bustier, yellow tee beneath white bustier, "I'm five four!" Drew exclaims in *Vogue*, "I'm a pygmy!" In *No Place to Hide* Kris Kristofferson raises his head to the sky and wails like the creature in Dali's *Civil War* STRETCHED TAUT. Drew's ballerina sister rips open her tutu, a man fondles a breast and barks, "I own you." Then he slashes across her chest a triangular symbol that looks like the logo for a hiking gear company. It's very sexy. The female dick from homicide exclaims, "There weren't any defense marks on her arms, she didn't resist!" Cut to Drew, stiff black satin humping her cotton jersey tits, she cocks her hip and drones, "Yeah, it's a bummer." Detective Kristofferson blows up, "Your sister gets murdered and it's 'a bummer'? You're dressed like a 14 year old whore!" Then he decides to become her father and buys her baggy sweatshirts and chinos *a reverse-evolutionary effect*—of her descent into drugs alcohol and obscurity Barrymore says, "Believe me, from being the most famous child in the world to doing an *Afterschool Special* is kind of a bummer." In *The Bird with the Crystal Plumage,* even though the Italian cops have a room full of whizzing computers that look like giant reel to reels turned on their sides, it's the American novelist who cracks the case—midway through our second bottle of wine he climbs up a ladder and through the window of a doorless brick warehouse where an artist who looks like a chubby Rasputin feeds him cooked cat for dinner—you shook your spiked platinum head at the TV and screamed, "What is happening in this movie?"

You're a Monkey and I'm Human.

I stop in Cafe Istanbul for a caffeine and diary-writing fix. Twin banks of shirred cloth drape from the center of the ceiling *a long cerulean canopy beneath a star spackled desert night—beasts peek through spiky leaves, flat eyes glowing* as I squeeze into one of the chairs crammed against the wall I grab a table for balance, but the top comes off in my hands, a large brass tray with a fluted edge like a pie crust. By the front window three young African men sit cross-legged on cushions, relaxed in loose cotton pants and sandals, the green shirted man squeezes a stream of honey into his tea and stirs it with a knobby foot-long twig. He hands the twig to the rose man who does the same—when the waitress approaches the three men stretch out their arms, clasp hands, close their eyes, and the teal man recites something, incense curling above their heads, sharp and sweet—I turn back to my espresso—sip—and continue jotting in my diary *lesbianism still not dealt with in my writing, mainly because* I glance up and Quincey walks through the door, watery as ever. I haven't seen him for months, haven't said a word to him since that awful night three years ago when I screeched, "Get out!" and slammed the door—he floats to the counter, orders and sits down a table away *reclaiming lesbianism would put me firmly into a marginalized group, a membership I could use to bully straight liberals. Got to go.* As I pack up my stuff Quincey looks over—his face muscles tighten but his eyes spiral open like a camera lens, finally my presence clicks and he emits a single syllable: "Hi." I snap back, "Hi. Sorry I'm here." He stutters, "Want to talk?" I shrug, "Okay," and suddenly Quincey's beside me nursing his Turkish coffee, we take in one another's presence for a bit … then he blurts out, "I don't know what to say—I was never happy with the way things ended." Silence. "I must have seen you out of the corner of my eye … last night I dreamed I walked into a room—you and KK were there," he looks down at his coffee, "but you ignored me and I walked out." "Great!" KK breaks in, "Now you have an ending for your book." "Some ending!" I cry through the receiver, "We didn't say anything exciting enough to write about." "No— but you're living a narrative!" Quincey splashes a bit of ice water into his cup, says it makes the grounds sink to the bottom, "shocks them somehow," we talk about movies, Avital Ronell's class on Nietzsche, his in laws, his job, my desire to own a cuddly terry cloth bathrobe like Madonna's in *Truth or Dare* but every time I find one in a thrift store it's rough and scratchy. "Yeah," he laughs, "like an old wash rag." *The intimacy of the ordinary* it feels like it's been three days instead of three years HOW DARE HE NOT BORE ME a couple of times he gives me one of his looks, one of his there's-so-much-that-I'd-like-to-say-but-can't looks—Dodie averts her gaze, but I argue: why not gently pop those eyeballs from their sockets, carry them home, gingerly scoop them up at midnight, jiggly eggs in your palm, soft-boiled so *much to say* I raise them to the full moon, chant SAY IT SAY IT.

KK says, "What does this mean, 'His cock rises to his eyeballs'?" "It means his look was a come on." KK's eyes roll up and back like Kit Cat's do on my wrist watch, "Does every man you write about *have* to have an *erection*?" YES—wherever I go they poke up at me, like picket fences or tombstones *monuments to my percolating oomph* my life has been a field of hard ons, row upon row of them, densely packed, evenly spaced, endless as Arlington Cemetery *leaping from the museological to my sensational* YES. Hard clits too.

Light, yellow, spreads across the wall, red velvet, Quincey's arm rests on the table beside mine, untouchable arm, it might as well be across the room with the chainsmoking young bohemians—one guy with round wire rims and a cherubic smile takes a drag from his Camel filter and exclaims, "I love the idea of subliminal scents. It means that we're like—*animals.*" *Puff, puff, exhale* Quincey holds his coffee cup with both hands and stares at the grounds, as if reading the future, then he looks up quickly and announces he's become a vegetarian—like me, Rendezvous, Dennis C.—*The Letters of Mina Harker* the world's first vegetarian vampire love saga—except for KK with his TV dinners from Canned Foods Outlet CONTENTS AND PORTIONS MAY NOT MATCH THOSE LISTED ON THE BOX Quincey's words are innocent but his gaze locks mine, bent on bending me LOVE JUNKIE he grunts and I'm in the bathroom with my pants off, perched on the edge of the sink, legs spread, waiting … hanging from a wooden dowel a rough-hewn curtain splits the room in two, behind it are stashed a string mop and rusty bucket on wheels, Dodie's soul is back there too caught by her own soapy reflection, she drops into the bucket and drowns. When I tilt my head Dodie's features reappear on the drab cloth, fuzzy and greenish, mildewed, the door swings open and Quincey's cock flops down my cunt like a salmon. As Quincey gets up to leave the cafe he says, "Now when we bump into one another we can say hello." I bump the table and coffee sloshes onto the brass tray *the evocation of an orifice,* "Maybe."

I went home and bawled; KK marveled, "It's just like the end of *The Way We Were!*" He took me in his arms and sang, "If we had it to do all over again, would we, could we?"

Tacked to the opposite wall, maroon fez, pin-striped vest, black drawstring trousers, the vest bulges where it's tucked in so that out of the flat plaster a "belly" protrudes—Cafe Istanbul, where you and I had coffee—this is not a memory but a buddy picture, and you are my sidekick, the kooky psychic Madame Sing—you stub out your cigarette adjust your turban and gaze at the empty table to your right JUMP CUT TO THE FUTURE a tiny cab speeds across the etched brass and stops in front of the tiny hotel on 57th Street, a tiny couple walks towards the curb, Quincey and his wife Lucy. Mina (played by Barbra Streisand) is across the street handing out leaflets, behind her a BAN THE BOMB banner is strung across a gargantuan coffee cup. When she spots Quincey (played by Robert Redford) remembrance rumbles·through her like the earthquake that brought them together—the evening of the big quake the phone rang, I picked up Quincey's thin nervous voice, "I was worried about you" *his first call without an excuse* and I said to myself so this is really going to happen. In *The Way We Were* I run through the traffic waving, Quincey presses money into the concierge's palm, still handsome, still vapid. He's been dissipating his genius writing a TV show, "Oh, there's an experience everything happens so fast you shoot it all in one day live on the air everybody running around." I tell him to look me up, "There's only one Kevin X Killian in the book." "What does the X stand for?" I shrug my shoulders, my wet lippy smirk curling up the side of my face like a slug *behind me Madame Sing shifts in a wooden chair, clairvoyance throbbing her temples, "Mina, do you have any aspirin?"* Lucy (played by some nobody) disappears and Quincey and I hug *forever*—you could get up go to the john pour another glass of wine light up a cigarette pad back to the living room plop down on the sofa "Did I miss anything?" "Uh uh" and we'd still be hugging. I'm gyrating but his groin eludes me. He pulls back and smiles, "You never give up, do you?" "Only when I'm absolutely forced to." Long bleary lips palpitating, I lift my chin, "But I'm a very good loser." "Better than I." I jut my teeth forward lick the beigy ripples that bisect the screen/my face, take a breath shake my head, "I've had more practice." With my brown kidskin glove I brush the hair from his forehead, we embrace again *this is the land's end the last finger* he runs to his cab, yelling back, "See you." My lips move silently in a dozen directions, "Memories may be beautiful, but yet what's too painful to remember …"

The stick turns into a snake the water into blood it rains frogs.

Late Saturday night the door buzzed and I ignored it then it buzzed again and I peeked out the bedroom window *dark hair gleaming beneath the streetlight* Dion stood in the alley gripping my front gate as if he were Superman about to wrench apart the wrought iron bars and leap inside, red cape flapping against his ass (as Drew would say, "I usually groove hard on the type of free spirit he is") I hadn't heard from him since the night I slammed his car door and he disappeared to Louisiana. Now he lands on my step like a lost letter—brown-stained and crumbling it's discovered in a sack in the back of a postal vault *a declaration of love an invitation that would have saved my life* but the sender is dead and I can barely remember what he looked like *messy black hair tossed back into a ponytail* I dropped the curtain and turned to KK, "It's Dion, please get rid of him, please." KK trucked down to the landing, leaving Dion on the pavement, deadbolt between them. "Can I come up?" "No." *Mad Hornet Masculine Hijinx,* "Why are you in town?" "My brother died," he claimed, "in a knife fight." "How awful." "Well, yes, he was the handsomest guy I ever knew. He was lucky—the guy didn't slash up his face." For emphasis Dion leans his head against the gate, rusty bars indent his cheeks, frame his ice blue eyes his broken nose his moving mouth, *maybe* he has a brother. "Is Mina afraid of me?" Three years of empty then BANG Quincey BANG Dion *movie monsters come alive—come out of screen—invade audience—carry girl victims back into picture to become slaves in movie. Never seen alive again! Beware they might get you! Warning!! Monsters run loose! Sit on your lap! Can you take it? NOT 3 D. For the horror thrill of your life see what happens to the pajama party girls when they meet the mad doctor's girl crazed monsters. Girls bring your boyfriend to protect you see if he's man or mouse. Monsters capture beauties. Come alive*—then after two years of fighting it, on June 11 at Land's End, Rendezvous sticks his hand up my skirt, runs it along my black tights, masturbates the taut nylon crotch *beneath it my cunt bleeds mucus, slippery and colorless as dreams*—or a child's runny *nose* clit muscles cramp from too much desire, outside the car a triad of raccoons rise up on hind legs and rummage through a can of garbage, through his chinos Rendezvous' cock leaps into my palm thick and sleek as a seal with a blunt snout—KK says, "Great, you're already working on your sequel!" *Mina Harker II: Is There Ever a Moment When All Four Feet Leave the Ground?*

Poor Jennifer Jason Leigh—strung up between two semis, close-up to wrists bloody from rope cuts then to Rutger Hauer's boot teasing the accelerator then to his blue-eyed fascist grin *Quincey's cheek and jaw squared to a higher power* I sip my chamomile tea and exclaim, "God, is he sexy!" KK shakes his head, "You're terrible." He knows I *love* Jennifer Jason Leigh *tiny firecracker* next to her Drew seems so … lethargic … blue-tinted photo of Drew lying on a chenille bedspread in black lace bra and panties, her right leg is raised as she pulls on a Doc Martens *thin black wedge between her icy thighs* loosely grasping the upside-down boot edge, arms trailing back to her shoulders like ivy, head rolled toward the camera she looks out indifferently, breathing through her mouth—even her name, Drew, sounds like a failed exhalation—Jennifer Jason Leigh's body is stretched taut and pink as Bazooka sticking to your shoe, if Rutger Hauer puts his foot down she'll snap.

The coast so grainy, fog washing out hills, highway, ocean to a nearly monochromatic gray—at Pigeon Point a glowing yellow-white cone bursts from the sky and streams into the gray water.

Quel sunset! Rendezvous pulls off the highway along a gravel road. Approaching a lighthouse I say, "His cock was a lighthouse and my cunt was a circle of farmhouses around its mighty base." Succulents cover the ground, their sappy leaves dense spikes of green cheese. We park the VW and walk along a dirt path, the lighthouse like all lighthouses is grand and ancient, white paint cracking and peeling off in large dull flakes. The buildings turn out to be a youth hostel—arms wrapped around each others' waists we continue past a half dozen identical square huts, more like barracks than cottages, with a motley collection of drapes hanging in square metal-framed windows, bunk beds behind them. A couple of young Germans enter one carrying 6 packs of malt liquor. Out back we find a battered wooden pier, walk to the end of it, wind blowing hair in face, damp chill stinging cheeks, seeping through my cotton jacket, I cling tighter to Rendezvous, his body more a wind block than a source of warmth—hip to hip we lean over the salt-stripped guard railing *wood as gray as the weather* and absorb the churning ocean, the Ascension sunset, flock of pelicans in the foreground, tug boat on either side, a massive wave breaks against the pier, shooting up a wall of lacy white—everywhere I look seals leap in unison, three or four at a time, extravagantly, ecstatically. Rendezvous points, "That's a big fucking seal." On a deserted road in Berkeley a falling star flares towards us and disappears, we lean across the stick shift and make wishes. In Pacifica the horizon bleeds from yellow to pink, at the end of the beach Rendezvous and I huddle on a log. The parking lot's now so far away that the teenagers who drink beer around a bonfire look like upright ants holding cans in their claws. The wet sand reflects the sunset, sleek and pink as a body double, Rendezvous sticks his tongue in my mouth then both his lips, I gulp, he pushes against me *deeper and deeper* as if he's trying to stick his whole face down my throat. Beneath his jacket his back is the warmest thing in the world I pull out an arm and reach for his cock but my hand collides with glass and metal, I drop his wire rims in my purse *the erotic force of night lit modeling* the horizon shrinks to a faint salmon crease between dark rolling ocean and dark unmoving sky, Rendezvous recites Rilke *Ein mal jedes, nur ein mal. Ein mal und nichtmehr.* I go for it in a big way, lick his lips and moan, "Time to pee," then I pull down my panties and squat behind him, spread knees resting on the log *tinkle tinkle* he shakes his head and smiles, "You are *so* male." He sticks his finger up my cunt *ein mal, ein mal.* After a couple of weeks we hardly go outside, barricade ourselves in rooms and fuck fuck fuck. Our next move is to pop bits of food into one another's mouths and sloppy kiss with juice running down our chins. He turns on his computer and tells me to read the screen, "To walk in front of the car. To be in a different spot in night, but always with the night before you, after you. To release yourself back into that night...."

My sequel comes over and fucks me six times in one week, my sequel is keeping Dodie from finishing *this* book. Hooray!

High contrast black and white photo of Drew Barrymore, black copy flush center in a narrow column over a wall, "'It's more about freedom than sexuality,' says the actress of being photographed nude, 'If you're naked in a classy way, there's something totally free about it.'" Drew's nakedness has dissolved to grain, her nipples melting into gray pools of aureola *cross-legged classy in white heels with large bow ties at the ankles* three bobby pins stripe the side of her plastered-down bob, penciled eyebrows arch with mild surprise across her forehead *wide, empty, slick as the paper she's printed on where did her nose go* her fragrance is Guess, "a spirited blend of fruits and florals," Drew leans back in an easy chair her arms flung straight up, gardens blooming from her armpits, hands turned outward, fingers spread as if she's throwing shadow puppets on a wall: rabbit hopping, duck quacking, or a man stooped in a wheelchair—it's Larry Eigner—

facing a packed auditorium, with a large orange flower arching from the back of his chair and over his head, he listens attentively to Charles Bernstein's vigorous delivery *take it/ every atom of me/ belongs to you/ across distances/ one space* beside me Rendezvous sniffs his fingertips, "I can smell you on me." *A toy cart/ up ended, a/ begging dog/ quiet* Drew frolics with seagulls across Coney Island's deserted beach in short shorts (about $105) and combat boots, her Emporio Armani trench (about $615) flaps in the breeze, as do her arms *lines in small detail/ similars large* Drew in lace and feather wrap top and satin pants, cigarette dangling from her full recumbent lips, a dame who's been around the block, once she was a star but now she spends afternoons in the filtered light of her bungalow clinking the ice cubes in her Scotch, smoke curling above her head like a memory, the bell rings, she opens the door cocks her hip, "Yeah, babe, whada ya want?" The camera goes click click click click *post coital but without the wrinkles to savor it, bigger than life like a Jeff Koons figurine* I imagine Drew kitty-corner to Michael Jackson and Bubbles in a stark white gallery, gold trim gleaming, tiny red lightbulb at the tip of her cigarette. Whenever sex is over I feel like a has been.

The guy next door has gone on vacation, leaving me his key *scattered across the nightstand: condoms bright as lollipops, KY, a box of 50 latex gloves* I lie in his bed, knees up, legs spread *mirrors in every direction* my cunt stares back at me, striated like a walnut shell *cock ring, black leather bondage straps, empty bottle of AZT* Rendezvous comes in and lies on top of me, brushes his chest against my nipples *hard on wriggling across belly* he releases his weight and grinds from side to side, brown hair sweeping down his chest and trailing off into a sparse pubis—in my arms Rendezvous *turns* from library science grad student *turns* into this grunting stinking animal, sucking my lower lip until it swells up like a blister *whenever he leaves me he feels like throwing up* he grinds harder flattening me against the mattress *balls of energy pop through the thickness of skin, pulse along his torso* OOMPH (FX: swirls of effervescent stars superimposed over lovers' bodies; close up flash of blue iris, curve of Rendezvous' cheek) he catches a glimpse of us in a mirror: joined but still two, a human and a human, or horse and a horse ... then he closes his eyes and everything dissolves to smoke ... the next day he writes, "Who can call this death, with the body disintegrating more rapidly than your or my own body. How hands evaporate from out of veins and condense where the skin returns. How the body momentarily is incapable of continuing its inner disease." Two months later and Tom is back, I hear his wheezing through the walls.

Disturbed by sensations I seduce myself with objects, seeking the shattering of Mina and a subsequent reestablishment of borders, making repetition possible *an ecosystem an environment of collected pieces* thus do I vampirize the world, endlessly searching out new metaphors upon which to displace the energy of primary repression, the realization of Mina as Other. "Quincey ... Dion ... Rendezvous ..." Scooping up seconds of Burmese potatoes Earl Jackson, Jr. proclaims, "You can't end a book that way." "Why not?" Professor Jackson shakes his head as if to fling some good sense from his brain directly into mine, "You just can't nobody will buy it." I see the woman from *Night of the Living Dead* the blonde woman with the long face maybe it's the woman from *Carnival of Souls*—no matter, I'm in the farmhouse surrounded by boarded up windows and carnage—Quincey, Dion, Rendezvous lumber across the long wooden porch, laughter drooling from their embalmed jowls, they pound the front door with fists as dead as hammers, they're trying to break inside and kill me, or my credibility. I put down my chopsticks and stare at Earl's multi-colored hair, "But it happened!" "It doesn't matter. You CAN'T."

Speak for yourself, Earl—I am a post-punk Milton waging a one-woman war against structure, taste, logic and even words themselves *the visceral insistence of my provocative finish* decades from now geneticists will excavate my bones, scrape off brittle DNA and one of the great mysteries of the 20th century will be solved, that I Mina Harker am the lost princess Anastasia *blue blood, blook block* I stick my thumbs in my armpits, flap my elbows, strut in circles, jut my chin forward and back as I screech *bawk-bawk-bawk bawk-bawk-bawk* what animal do I remind you of?

Quarter to ten Sunday morning, I'm sitting up in bed drinking coffee and eating toast with almond butter. A breeze comes in through the window, fresh, coolish, spring like. Black cat curled on the floor, wind and light through lace curtains blow shifting patterns across his back, a cathedral like texture. KK's beside me sleep breathing, we're in sheer pleasure of existence territory. Then Rendezvous barges in—he stands in my living room in his Gethsemane pose: feet together, back erect, arms stretched out stiffly on either side. I stick my face in his, breasts grazing his T shirt, "Are you Jesus?" "Yes, I died for your sins. Fuck me." His arms collapse around my waist *no madness without meaning*. Rendezvous and I naked on my "Cafe Society" sheets, a riotous cut paper pattern of people drinking coffee in a Paris cafe *orange and salmon faces, no features, green shadows* one of the customers' heads is bigger than the others', shaped like an inverted teardrop, with a mysterious spiral design on the side … huge cranial capacity, disappearing chin … he's one of Whitley Strieber's bug eyed aliens! Sliding across this mosaic of space invasion I imagine Rendezvous is David Bowie in *The Man Who Fell to Earth* and I am Candy Clark, instead of a cock he has a full body erection, soapy slime exuding from his every pore, he wraps me in an alien sex cocoon *pitter patter(n)* he bites my earlobe, "I love you." His tight puffy lips are delivering, but I don't believe it *kiss kiss*. "Whatever that means," I reply. He rolls his head across a cluster of diners *white cups, two-toned lavender shadows,* "'It doesn't *mean* anything. It's a performative." "A performative?" "Yes, like 'I believe' or 'I promise'—it doesn't represent, it performs." Beneath our bodies a crowded room of gaudy blotches crumples, the blotches represent people frozen at tables, hunched figures without eyes or mouths, sad and telepathic, silent as Bob Kaufman.

There's this guy at Mission Grounds every Saturday at the same table, the one in the very back next to the bathroom, I've come to look forward to his determinedly messy hair, short but poking out all over the place *the buzz saw look* his thick black glasses, mismatched thrift store slacks and suit jacket. I don't know his name. He bums a cigarette and declares, "Sometimes spiritual people wear signs across their chests that say 'I don't want to talk.'" The following week I look up from my spinach and salsa crêpe and he's standing in the doorway *changed,* he removes his glasses and stares off, his eyes are too intense, shifted in opacity or reflectivity like contact lenses in werewolf movies just before the eyes glow red. He steps slowly through the cafe cranking his head from side to side, palms together and pointing upwards *yellow and ivory light bounces off sharp delicate cheekbones* suddenly he parts his hands and swipes them quickly back and forth in front of his face, then back to prayer position, lips moving, no sound. Then he settles at his table and continues praying, occasionally he stands up, swipes his face, turns around in a circle and sits back down. I pull aside the waitress, "Is he freaking out on acid?" "Oh, no. He's crazy." I push my cold crêpe across the table *he's my kind of man, I'm a love junkie* as I get up to leave he's yelling at the owner, "Can you tell me why I don't have any money, can you tell me that much?"

Cool World: in a see-through bikini dress Kim Basinger struggles to maintain human form, but her body keeps popping back into cartoon, into a frizzy-headed circus clown, her curves her mobile facial details zapped between dimensions *big-bellied buttoned-eyed bulbed-nose bozo like Pennywhistle* deep down all characters want to be human *if a cartoon kills a person that person is turned into a cartoon too, too bad it doesn't work the other way around* Dodie's murdering me in this letter, Sing, when it's over I'm over—Kim and I scramble up the side of a skyscraper, there's a rod on top that will lock us in the real world we have to find it and grab it—even though this will destroy the balance of everything—a wiseass cop yells, "What do you have, ink for brains?" *All fucked out.*

Rendezvous and I drive to a desert lake in Nevada *five hours in an airless Rabbit, the highway itself the spiky line of fever on a grid* we get a room for $26 a night at an off-season fishing lodge, *very* off-season—we're the only guests. Our first morning, Rendezvous bursts out of the shower driblets of water still clinging to his back, cock poking out like an exclamation point, "I was jerking off and thinking of you, and I said to myself, why not have the real thing!" He knocks the rough draft of this letter to the floor and pushes me onto the bed. Thus it goes with sequels. His *Lyotard Reader* topples off too, falling open to a passage underlined in red ink *the inexpressible does not reside in an over there or another time but in this: in that (something) happens.* Here and now is this sentence, Sing, my legs are clamped around his back. I'm waiting for the next sentence to arise. It's Dusty Springfield: "And the world is like an apple whirling silently in space. Like a tunnel that you follow to a tunnel of its own." Orange polyester drapes above our heads, etchings of giant trout on the wall, his fucking is slow and subtle, followed by a few minutes of intense rhythm, he comes with little suppressed grunts, then he springs off the bed and grabs his Reeboks, "How about a walk!" Other vacationers stay in RVs with American flags planted in the sand (hear Elton John overdubbed with gulls).

Is that the sound of distant drumming or just the fingers of your hand? The shower is efficient, goop rinsed away the moment it's made. And so it is with word processors, I highlight *that line the walls* and hit the Backspace key, type *in*, double-click on *person*, type *him* I haven't seen *him* in two days—fuck this endless editing FUCK HIM NOW. Not writing, *writ(h)ing*.

On the way back from our weekend we stopped at what we'd been assured was the best Sunday brunch in Reno. Rendezvous started to pout and roll his eyes as soon as he spotted the thatched roof, gabled chimneys, diamond-shaped panes of the Alpine super-cottage: Heidi's. "We don't have to stay if you hate it." "No, no, I survived Bard, I can survive Heidi's." We slid into a circular booth and scooted until we met thigh to thigh under a painting of a St. Bernard—a waitress in a dirndl skirt and pinafore took our order, and we amused ourselves with the festive goose motif on the wall *think teal, mauve, cream* the service was quick—within minutes I was scraping cheese from my omelet, about a pound of it, a white mass on the side of my plate sweating orangy fat—Rendezvous valiantly ate his *puffy lower lip shifting from side to side, pooching forward* he swallowed and surveyed the room, which was packed with corpulent, chortling middle Americans—the women wearing either floral dresses or sweatshirts, strawberry lips dragging those ultra long thins, the men in leisure jackets that pull across their backs when they lift their arms—Rendezvous dropped his fork in disgust, "It never ceases to amaze me how this country could be so full of ugly people. They should get off their fat asses and do something besides watch TV." "What's wrong with these people," I retorted, "they look like my parents."

Each of his eyes is studded with different color cones, when he blinks one then the other the world switches from warm to cool and back again, Ektachrome on the left Cibachrome on the right, he says his whole life has been devoted to the gaps between blinks. "My mother's right about me—I'm thirty-three, no job, no prospects, and my girlfriend is moving out." *What's wrong with being a slacker* I think *you can fuck me when KK goes to the movies.* His voice rises to hysteria, "Like at sunset when I look at the trees and they share their green, what does that *mean?*"

The cushion of my rattan chair curves around my back, strips of sunlight edge the drawn red cotton shade, headphones cup my ears, the afternoon filters through tingeing the dimness with crimson, Drew Barrymore's latest release rolls silently across the TV screen, *Doppelganger,* a horror remake of *Breakfast at Tiffany's.* Drew plays "Holly Gooding" in Audrey Hepburn drag: pearls, sheer scarf wrapped about dark hair and then her neck, cinched-waisted coat, full skirts. I sip Orvieto from a bell-shaped glass, Madonna's "Deeper and Deeper" throbbing my skull *falling in love, falling in love* a sudden urge to abuse the plants HER DOPPELGANGER IS COMING Drew's C cups swell to double D, her mouth puckers, her body twists with the virulence of a stop-motion botanical film, the virulence of a new green shoot poking her head through the soil, awkwardly wriggling through the latex tight air, guzzling the sun, her nose bleeds, cobwebs unfurl between her fingers *deeper and deeper and deeper and deeper, sweeter and sweeter and sweeter* the scariest effect is Drew's youth. "I never had a childhood and I sure as hell don't want to grow up." An aging diva at sixteen, Drew exudes an unwavering otherness, her contemporaneity a material force in its own right, an energon sucking the life out of those around her *not gonna let you slip away* advising Drew on legal matters, 60's rebel George Maharis has the charisma of a Disney automaton, woodenly nodding a salt and pepper wig that makes his head too big. It's hard to believe this is the same man I was in love with in the sixth grade. George Maharis was the wildest cat to enter my living room EVER dark, angular, attitude-intensive (I read in a fanzine that once he got evicted from his walk up and to get even with the asshole landlord he painted everything, including the toilet, black)—nothing could make me miss an episode of *Route 66*, I lay on the floor as close to the TV as possible, eyes raised, mouth dropped, as effervescent youth zipped cross-country in a Corvette. Two "pals" named Todd and Buzz enmesh themselves in other peoples' dramas, share motel rooms, eroticize, and move on—I recast every female lead as a child, me, imagined myself sandwiched between their bucket seats, the heat of their manly torsos thrusting my puberty forward, ergo my *thing* for fucking in cars HER DOPPELGANGER IS COMING Drew fucks her evil psychiatrist stabs her greedy mother with a butcher knife *you're gonna bring your love to me I'm gonna get you* the wind whooshes wildly, the shower turns to blood staining her pearls, Drew finds herself in a white T shirt crucified to the wall, glowing cross above her head—all this is intercut with shots of birds. For some reason.

I met Rendezvous three years ago and went after him like a bat out of hell. KK huffed, "It's because he looks like Quincey." Another Waspy blond—a knock off of Quincey's haute couture, Rendezvous' shoulders never hung right, his seams quickly frayed—he said the longest he'd enjoyed sex with a woman was two weeks—I kept him jumping for three months—that makes me the winner, I guess *high school track star* Rendezvous' body is long and athletic but there's a pudgy boyishness to his face. I sigh, remembering Quincey's tragic angularity, his frail perversions *quick, my Gauloise, smoke twirls in columns out of either side of my mouth like horns* Quincey played Chopin to my brassy Judy Davis—as Drew Barrymore explained, "'What's my *motivation* for this scene?' Hel lo! Shoot me if I ever say that!" When I run into Quincey at Cafe Istanbul he's just had his hair cut, a 3/4" crew, he runs his hand across the top of his head and says softly,

"I feel like I'm in the Marines." With his blond burr and the spots of sunlight bouncing off his jaw he looks cute and dramatic at the same time, like a Horst photograph. He's aged these past three years *not yet forty* I want to kiss every line radiating from the corners of his eyes, to suck out the pain like snakebite venom, especially that which I caused. I tell him, "I bet Marines have more fun than most of the people we know."

The intimate horizontality of this page.

I do not *mean* I perform—see my swiveling neck my changing mouth, arms that open wide—a tremendous pile of meat that sings "I love you"—then I explode. My arms fall off, my head rolls to the ground, smoke pours from my body. Now that Rendezvous and I have parted, love itself is a metaphor. KK and I lie in Scott Watson's basement in a comfortable bed fortressed with cinder blocks and a damp pitch black, I imagine us clinging to one another in a bomb shelter, I can't decide if it's war-torn London or the Cuban missile crisis with an alternate ending BOOM BAM ZAP GRRRRRPPP *tufted with scorched down their ribs were fused in a final frantic embrace* Beethoven's 7th blasts through the beamed ceiling—KK sleeps through it, his cock twitching against my thigh *Von Karajan's baton.*

The night Rendezvous and I broke up they added Bravo to our basic cable lineup. The first thing I watched was *Soldier of Orange*, and guess who's in it—Rutger Hauer! KK made fun of his array of cute outfits—Rutger in tennis ensemble, rustic sailor turtleneck, plaid flannel to meet the Dutch queen, RAF uniform, bare-chested coal-shoveling get up, tails. When I arrived at Rendezvous' apartment the scent of Pine Sol assaulted me, his kitchen floor was covered with maggots, not the big ones I remember in a garbage can when I was three and we lived in the projects in Gary—or the ones that drop from the ceiling of the girls' school in *Suspiria*—these were dwarf maggots that skittered across the linoleum. He was bent over, frantic with a paper towel—hear the word "fucking" repeatedly. He washed his hands and we climbed onto the bed *animals strike curious poses* a bed he still shared with the girlfriend he "split up with" last winter but refused to tell about "us" *they feel the heat* we had sex *the heat between me and you* I went into the kitchen to chop vegetables and he made the bed, fluffing and smoothing the comforter, lining the teddy bears in a row across the pillows, forgetting to throw away the condom he'd tossed on the (ex)girlfriend's nightstand *limp, translucent, crinkled, leaky with sperm* he was pouring rose hips tea when she came home from her desktop publishing class ("Like a cup?" "No thanks") she entered the bedroom, flinched, and the three of us leapt clumsily into the scene he had scripted—the (ex) played Mothra, the languorous caterpillar monster; I was tall wingy Rodan; and he lumbered about as Godzilla. The condom starred as Ghidra, the three-headed electricity-breathing space dragon—if Mothra Rodan and Godzilla don't set aside their monstrous egos and work together Ghidra will destroy the world (as Drew would say, "Bummer!") Rodan flies through the air and pecks Godzilla's giant head. Godzilla stomps on his hind legs and kicks rocks at Rodan. Rodan waves her mighty wings and barks, volleys the rocks back with her head. Caterpillar Mothra raises her pinky-brown tube of a body and out of the hole in the tip she sprays white foam on Rodan and Godzilla to calm them down. KK laughs, "Cum shot." Mothra: "All three of us must fight against this new monster to save the earth." Rodan: "It's none of our business if the earth perishes." And Godzilla agrees. Now Rodan says she'll just fly away. Godzilla: "We have no reason to try to save mankind. We've always had trouble with men and men hate us." Rodan: "Yes, he's right." Rodan beats her breasts, which are bumpy as ginger graters. Mothra's eyes glow red. Ghidra demolishes Tokyo. Rendezvous crackles his barnacled spine and stumbles backwards, his mighty tail knocking down a bridge, then he hurls boulders at Ghidra causing a landslide, Ghidra screeches and spits electricity, Rodan squirts juices out of her cavernous cunt causing a tidal wave, Rendezvous wrestles Ghidra's tail as Mothra flies on my back spraying and cocooning Ghidra's three massive heads in white cotton-candy *spun cum* the condom freaks and flees, flapping and writ(h)ing into the horizon. The world is saved. Our relationship is over.

Thus did I understand that Rendezvous and I were involved in a conflict of *form*—he approached me from behind sneaking up on my subconscious like a tracking missile (he calls this letting things pass, I called him a passive-aggressive asshole) I'm the William Tell type, firing at a person point blank (he called me a controlling bitch, I call this getting things out in the open) FACES RED, EYES BULGING *Shakma the killer baboon breaks through the mirror (mistaking it for a victim) breaks through the image's cool surface, leaps straight into the incinerator—blazing orange tongues whoosh and wag as if Hell itself were taunting him, "Ha! Ha! Shakma!" the victim slams the door* Rendezvous got involved with me because I kissed him *with drugged lipstick my lower lip gaped open like a crimson urinal* I got involved with him because he aimed this ray gun from across the room to unzip my clothes, I was wearing a vermilion and hot pink latex top that zipped up the front and a matching miniskirt that zipped on the diagonal, vermilion thigh-high boots—sparkling lime-green dashes sputtered from the end of the ray gun barrel ZIP(UN)ZIP(UN)ZIP I could never resist a man with *remote control* Rendezvous' cock like the rest of him is rosy and well-scrubbed, he thought it was small but it's not *nothing but horses in the shower at the gym* his nipples face outward on either side giving his chest a surreal wall-eyed appearance, his love-making was elusive, Carmelite almost—if he found out something would help you come, he never did it again, but, Sing, denial can be so sexy *endings telescoping inside of endings* I came home, lit a candle, and crawled in the bathtub (slosh of lavender-scented water) hot mascara-stained tears streamed down my cheeks, black and oozy like rotting melting eyeballs—the phone rings, KK picks it up. "Do you want to talk to Sing?" My mouth stretches open spewing snorts and howls *this is what it sounds like when doves cry*. KK stammers into the receiver, "I don't think it's a good time." Braves in warpaint threaten to cut off pieces of Black Robe's body and feed them to him. "You mustn't cry out when you die," warns the wise chieftain, "or the Iroquois will steal your soul." IIEEEEECHHHH! EIEEEEIIIIEECCHHHH!

All these intellectuals marching through my vagina.

KK says I should leave out my break up with Rendezvous because that makes the ending too sad, "Leave some room for hope." HOPE: I cackle in his face, like Barbara Steele, Faye Dunaway, Bette Davis in *Another Man's Poison*, Dorothy Tutin as Anne Boleyn. Catherine Clément, *Opera*: dead women dead so often, those who die disemboweled in a cruddy attic of smoggy London those who die for having embodied too well those who die of nothing, just like that, those who die poisoned, gently, those who are choked those who fold in on themselves, peacefully MON-STERS CRASH THE PAJAMA PARTY a nun lies naked on an examination table in *Bad Lieutenant*, fear and harsh lighting mottling her skin like fat-laced beef *the aggressive palpability of her large breasts and thighs* through the dark sliver of open door my eye shines like an owl's—a doctor picks off male pubic hairs with tweezers and drops them in a plastic bag marked EVIDENCE *cigarette burns on belly, crucifix rammed inside* she forgives. Not me. Don't think I'm going to sit here like a wimp and passively transcribe Dodie's dictation—my fingers grow biceps, attack the keyboard NO MADNESS WITHOUT MEANING. *Carry girl victims back into picture to become slaves in movie.*

At a certain point, Sing, the feminist artist has to start saying NO to life, YES to writing *my sequel was canceled due to lack of studio backing*. Last week I got a letter from my fan in Washington, D.C. He wrote, "Maybe what we most have in common is a love of words, we're hopelessly indentured to clauses and modifiers, gerunds and infinitives, we'd like to screw around with fonts more if we had more time." I answered, "You seemed to be flirting with me in your last letter. Not a good time, David— right now I'm watching movies where women kill men." *Blue Steel, Ms. 45, I Spit on Your Grave*, KK clucks as I shout "yeah!" and clap. Susan Howe signs my copy of *My Emily Dickinson*, "In memory of *The Texas Chain Saw Massacre*."

All these suitors whizzing past, you're probably confused. Let me recap: there's KK, the husband, the highway I've been cruising these past eight years. Quincey is the service road that runs alongside, smaller, separated by a wire fence vined with morning glories, always visible. Dion is a wrong turn off—but as long as you're there you might as well groove on the local scenery, maybe catch a movie, grab a vegiburger and fries, then wind back to course. Rendezvous is a rest stop, you squat down, relieve yourself, and move on. David is a signpost THE END 4 MILES ... THE END 1 1/2 MILES ... I grew up half a block from 80 94 leading into Chicago, a stretch of interstate notorious for accidents—we didn't have block parties in Indiana, accidents brought us together—at dusk on a summer evening dozens of families amble past tract houses, all in the same direction, like pod zombies in a 50's sci fi flick, tummies filled with meatloaf and barbecue, ambling down Oakdale Ave. to 176th: on the other side of a narrow strip of weeds: smashed Corvettes, blood, flames, sirens, flashing lights, "Look, Mom!"

Sometimes when I'm really down I feel like roadkill.

Black puddle of panty hose, navy puddle of nylon dress, KK kneels on the dirty linoleum and licks my clit, the floor buckles beneath us dark and fertile as sludge I grab onto a kitchen chair for balance. KK looks up, lips and chin glistening, "My love for you is kudzu vines grown all out of control." I brush the sweaty hair from his forehead, laugh, "That's a good one." "Forget it, Mina—you keep writing down your compliments, people are gonna think you're vain—like that awful Anais Nin!" *How can I translate his erection—conductor's baton, tube of toothpaste, knobby African flavor twig, rectal thermometer, bird's beak, shark, rampant member ...* I push his face into me, fingernails scratch my ass, those same nails he dreams shoot from the tips of his out-stretched arms, grow all the way around the globe and stab him in the back, his tongue shoots through my cunt *speaking in tongues* my grinning face sways ghostlike across the window, the refrigerator hums like a shower and my mind is water, the tongues say, "Ummmmmm."

"Not *another* sex scene!" KK tosses my manuscript on the coffee table, "It would be nice if the reader could occasionally see me doing something besides coming." He picks it up again, "Here on page twenty-three I've got a hankie tied around my dick, on page thirty you hang your underpants around my neck—people are going to think I'm a hat rack!"

Our first night in Nevada, after a month of stolen fucks we're finally sleeping together, I lie in my nightie my breast aflutter with excitations while Rendezvous bangs around in the bath-room, the toilet flushes the door opens and he appears at the foot of the bed in a T shirt, boxer shorts, and sweatshirt—he looks like the kind of person who'd ask you *where's that Preparation H* he switches off the light and the mattress sinks with his weight—on the other side of the curtain there are so many stars they scare me, this desert blackness—the sheets are cool, Rendezvous' arms tighten around my waist, clamp me to his sweatshirt and boxers, he's silent and thick like a log, if a log could kiss could suck my tongue until it tugs at the root *there's not enough breathing room in any one spot* I roll away, "Why don't you talk to me, why do you always have to act like such an alien." He groans then—nothing. Alone in all this dark I feel as if my safety cord has snapped and I'm floating away from the moon into the endless vacuum of space, "Well?" He says our best moments together are when we're silent. But an experience without words is not quite an experience for me *skin and bones* with Quincey there was no line between our fucking and banter, "I'm going to do this to you!" "Oh, yes, do it! Do it!" *Will this dame ever stop yacking?* IIEEEEECHHHH! EIEEEEIIIIEECCHHHH! A week before filming of *Guncrazy* began Drew Barrymore saw *Twenty One* and was so charmed by Patsy Kensit's look she cut off all her hair. "The producers freaked out," says its director, Tamra Davis, "but I thought it was great, a stroke of genius." So impressed was I with Drew's look in *Guncrazy* my hairdresser razored off all of mine, in the mirror my truncated do pokes out every which way, deep red like a devil's, I bring my palms together in prayer position then swipe them quickly in front of my face *stroke of genius* my dyed hair looks more natural than my (real) blonde hair—maybe it's because I pencil my pale brows—otherwise they'd look like maggots humping across my forehead, I never should have spent the night with Rendezvous FIRST THING IN THE MORNING, NAKED, SQUINTY-EYED, CRINKLED I never should have let him see me that way *he leaps out of the shower brandishing a bottle of Pine Sol, beads of water still clinging to his shoulders* a has been even before I became a has *with our romance we exposed ourselves to a strain of pathology that was almost unendurable, it came up through the vents* figures prone to impossible poses, gestural exaggerations, an arm, overly long, reaches up to squeeze a breast *his particular style of fucking you over, of screaming NO more* true love is seeing all sides of a person, knowing what those other women, those past lovers know, the focused intimacy of his rage, the target beam of his automatic weapon *red ball of light on my forehead red death on my forehead for me alone.*

And it always ends like that, language's lines of escape.

Before the awesome difficulty of this ending my housekeeping has collapsed—in a messy room I sustain myself with tortilla chips, vanilla malt balls from the health food store, coffee, and popsicles—writing's like being abducted by a religious cult, overload the system with sleep-deprivation and carbohydrates, you'll believe anything—I'm sucking a Vampire's Secret ice pop *Black Cherry Water Ice with a Cherry Sauce Center* ARTIFICIALLY FLAVORED, KK found them at Canned Foods Outlet. Mud-colored tube on a stick, the tip melts in your mouth to reveal a tunnel of scarlet gel—I get the gory attributes, but what's the cylinder supposed to *be*? A fat segment of artery? A penis with VD? KK says it's blood in darkness. "Isn't that a bit esoteric," I huff, "for a popsicle?" I go down on it my lips numbing my head spacey with sugar, it tastes exactly like my memory of Smith Brothers' cough drops *throat image* the box is black with three oozing pops stacked in front of a full yellow moon, a green-faced vampire is about to bite, VAMPIRE'S SECRET, the top of VAMPIRE'S is flat white but the bottom half luridly sloshes and drips blood *a word not yet full, not yet satiated* this is by far the grossest frozen treat I've ever encountered *the cryogenic suspension of another great myth* Sing, I'm scared—there's me and there's you and then there's those super orgasms I read about in *New Woman* ART REAWAKENS MY LATENT PSYCHOSIS my first victim is Rendezvous I slash the shape of a popsicle in his bared pubic area *my natural allegory* I lay in an erotic haze day after day with my book, dreaming of the seductive mirage released by his flesh as it evaporates from his bones, of his beautiful teeth unveiling themselves from beneath the thinning tissue of his lips.

Turn to the last page—does my soul get saved?

Steven Shaviro, *The Cinematic Body*: "These ice pops are wildly discontinuous, flamboyantly antinaturalistic, and nonsensically grotesque. Yet the more ridiculously excessive and self-consciously artificial they are, the more literal is their visceral impact. They can't be kept at a distance, for they can't be referred to anything beyond themselves. Their simulations are radically immediate: they no longer pretend to stand in for, or to represent, a previously existing real."

Even though I promised KK I wouldn't, I send Quincey a letter, a card really, of a small featureless figure in a bed with a hot water bottle on his head, to the left of the bed pounces a cross-eyed Godzilla, a cross-eyed alligator peeks out from underneath, a pink and green cross-eyed bird monster lounges to the right *Heard you were feeling rather beastly* open it up: *Get Well Quick* then:

> Dear Quincey—
>
> I bought this card for Sam D'Allesandro when they were still saying he had "the flu." Then I found out he had AIDS and never sent it. Last night I watched *Hiroshima, Mon Amour* on Bravo—I couldn't help but think of you. The woman in the movie's schlocky obsessive longing—her tragic sighs before the inevitable forgetting of her German soldier lover—I think the tragedy lies in the fact that the forgetting is only *conscious*— something remains, in the cells, in the nerves, that keeps you climbing the walls with impossibility. I think you know what I'm talking about.
>
> —Mina

The devil appeared to Dodie on a fireball demanding, "Kill Mina!" I told her to stop listening to heavy metal.

Two thirty a.m., I've been trying to get to sleep for three hours, abandon KK to the damp cotton sheets, lie on the couch, bored, restless, my mind jittery with static, might as well masturbate—I'm too lazy to use my fingers, what's in the living room that I can hump my desire against—the remote control, a curvaceous stretch of plastic marketed as "ergonomic" POWER EJECT REWIND RECALL I wrap it in the hem of my nightgown, lie on my stomach and wedge it against my clit—now for some scenery MEMORY CLEAR RESET Quincey said hello to me at the Susan Howe reception—we meet in the bathroom, I pull down my pantyhose and lean over the claw-footed tub *scouring powder's gritty perfume* Quincey drops his jeans and fucks me from behind *I lunge against the cold rim, belly startled* his hands are tied—with what?—my pantyhose, he'd like that, he always liked it when I "made" him fuck me, I reach back and pinch him until he bruises *the cheeks of my ass are two semis he's hitched between* "harder, harder," umpf umpf Umpf, a bar of soap tumbles out of the metal dish looped over the edge, we look just like the living *chugalug chugalug* avidly claiming our gobbets of skin and entrails *his beard corroding the back of my neck* is this physically possible? Where are my knees? *Like a tunnel that you follow to a tunnel of its own* I press a palm against the bottom of the tub to keep us from toppling over, to keep my head from banging the wall *blood from my temple inching in rivulets down the curved porcelain* STANDBY TRACKING POWER MEMORY my hips thrust with his thrusts, the remote clicks from channel to channel frantically and irrationally as a decapitated chicken—Quincey's wife, Lucy, zips her buttery suede jacket and sighs, "I feel this terrible headache coming on," Susan Howe discusses Melville with a long-haired woman *Bar-tle-by Bar-tle-by Bar-tle-by* friction sparks my clit "*harder, harder*" bars of moonlight steal past the windowshade and spill on the floor, high above in the inky night Dion watches, his face grinning, green cheese *the grounds sink to the bottom, somehow shocked.*

"You can never get away from me," KK murmured, "I'll follow you everywhere like death follows life." But now that THE END is near will he still say so? In a couple of pages Mina is history, but he'll still go to work, put out those quirky novels and plays, make love to Dodie whenever they can agree that that's what's happening *what will it be like in never-never-land* Sing, I feel so tiny, so scared, please write me into a book of your own. Everybody says the vampire thing has peaked—it's time for a little genre-bending, don't you think? You could rescript me as a psychopathic demon possessing a god-fearing parishioner. Or, I could be a *real* woman in your book. Mina Harker, true crime Medea—I'll kill my babies *a feminist has to sacrifice for her art.* We play *Hiroshima, Mon Amour,* KK kisses me and says "I love you, I forget you." I relax my face into a droop of French despair, "You destroy me with your beauty, go away."

A wandering Mina falls into an eerie series of events that culminates *a has been exotic dancer a wacked-out disciple of the Devil* I saw off the hand of the man I have murdered/loved, centuries later when Rendezvous takes the stake from my heart I wreak bloody revenge against the local village *some hilarious shots of me running around naked while KK holds a thumb over the camera lens to block out my vital organs* I get my hands on an ancient amulet that enables me to manipulate an army of monstrous readers *doll dwarfs battle the crushing giant beasties* I absorb evil from the souls of brickhouse sex kittens, make the move on everyone from young studs to old men *the ending is gritty and shocking, a terrific party film—no story line to follow, just sit back and enjoy the nostalgic lineup: alcohol and drug abuse, withdrawal, wild make-out scenes, robbery, and jail; some of the oldest "teenagers" ever seen on screen* a girl without shame I take the violent plunge into adulthood but keep my decapitated readers' heads alive *submit to the master or be frozen in his cold-storage harem FOREVER* I am the mistress and the bride of a gorilla—the rooftop is my lovers lane, the sidewalk my finishing school, the sky my cerulean canopy. *Ocean/ night/ great waves and/ small in/ perspective/ the wind under the stars/ quiet sound.* KK and I glide against one another, long, silky, ebullient, fading with the last dusky rays of sun into the night—cool breeze from the window, rumble of a tow truck on 11th, perfectly-timed frisson of KK's hand against my clit into my vagina *the last fingers* out of the darkness I cry out, vowels funneling across octaves from my throat to the alley below where hookers quarrel with johns and figures hunched in blankets smoke crack, lungs collapse, moist, gurgly *he's Magic and I'm History* KK comes quietly, gulping, as if the air were a mouth bit he desperately needs to grab onto—KK the highwire dancer hanging by his teeth netless—slow pan from his straining jaw-neck-torso-ecstatic-erection-legs-feet-nosediving-toes to the packed bleachers below, a thousand upturned heads, fingers sticky with cotton candy—KK wraps his arms around his chest tightens his bite and spins and spins *alas, and round this center the rose of onlooking blooms and unblossoms* the Big Top grows dizzy—BUT WAIT—this isn't Fellini's ending, it's MINE *Maestro, herd out the elephants!* KK crouches over me on all fours, "I'm your house." His chest is my ceiling, his cock and balls dangle above my belly *light switch? door knocker? skeleton key?* he nibbles my ear, whispers, "This is what you always wanted, isn't it, a house that talks."

Love,
Mina

Acknowledgments

Versions of these letters have previously appeared in *Real: The Letters of Mina Harker and Sam D'Allesandro* (Talisman House, 1994) and *Answer* (Leave Books, 1993). Also in the following anthologies: *The Art of Practice: 45 Contemporary Poets, Exhausted Autumn, High Risk, The New Fuck You: Adventures in Lesbian Reading, Primary Trouble: An Anthology of Contemporary American Poetry*, and *Moving Borders: Three Decades of Innovative Writing by Women*. Also in the following journals: *14 Hills, 6ix, ACTS, American Poetry Archive Newsletter*, Athena *Incognito, Barscheit, Big Allis, Bomb, Boo, Capilano Review, Farm, Gallery Works, Giantess: The Organ of the New Abjectionists, HOW(ever), Inciting Desire, Ink, Lingo, Lipstick Eleven, Mirage, Open 24 Hours, Ottotole, Poetics Journal, Red Wheelbarrow, River City, Russian River Writer's Guild: Eight at Otis, Sodomite Invasion Review, Some Weird Sin, Talisman, Wray, Writing*, and *ZYZZYVA*. My thanks to the editors for their support of my work.

I will be forever grateful to Michael Gizzi of Hard Press for publishing the first edition of *Mina* in 1998. Michael was a brilliant poet, editor, and friend, who I will always hold in my heart. Much gratitude to Eileen Myles and Joan Larkin for their behind the scenes efforts in lobbying for the reprinting of *Mina* by University of Wisconsin Press in 2004—and to Dennis Cooper for his wonderful introduction to that edition. Thanks to Semiotext(e)—and to Benjamin Segal and the rest of the staff at Covington & Burling LLP for negotiating the return to me of the rights to *Mina*. Love and thanks to Chris Kraus and Hedi El Kholti for once more bringing *Mina* back from the grave. Thank you Emily Gould for recontextualizing *Mina* for the present moment in your provocative, spot-on introduction to this edition. And Laure Prouvost—Mina and I love having your boobs on our cover. Thank you for that, and, more broadly, for inviting me into your world.

ABOUT THE AUTHOR

Dodie Bellamy's writing focuses on sexuality, politics and narrative experimentation, challenging the distinctions between fiction, the essay and poetry. In 2018–19 she was the subject of *On Our Mind*, a yearlong series of public events, commissioned essays and reading group meetings organized by CCA Wattis ICA. With Kevin Killian, she coedited *Writers Who Love Too Much: New Narrative 1977–1997*. A compendium of essays on Bellamy's work, *Dodie Bellamy Is on Our Mind*, was published in 2020 by Wattis ICA/Semiotext(e).